SINT SINK TALES
&
OTHER DISTURBING FRICTIONS

Oxbow Lake the 2nd (et alii?)

If you don't laugh at our books,
you're probably dead . . .
or should be!
ShipWreckPublications.com

Unsolicited Praise for Oxbow Lake's
Sint Sink Tales & Other Disturbing Frictions

"My place in literary immortality yet again unthreatened by this dried up lake of a non literary source. It's too dam bad to fear."
-- Mark Twain (You Dead Tube)

"This f**ckin' book is f**kin' terrible and the f**kin' author of this f**kin' book is a f**kin' inarticulate f**kin' idiot!"
-- R. D'Nero (actor, wit, literary critic and political commentator extraordinaire)

"If I weren't already dead, reading this book would kill me yet again. It appears that not only can't you keep a good man down, you can't keep a plagiarizing bastard down either. Ask my good friend Raymond Kennedy. Now William Saroyan, one of my literary companions here in the afterlife, is alive enough to be really pissed off too!"
-- J. D. Salinger (scratched on a bar near Columbia)

"It can still be safely said that Dave Barry is the second funniest writer alive (and quite possibly the third), and that Carl (stuttering a's) Hiaasen remains at 10,001 behind an ethnic German graffiti scribbler named Sanas the Fakir from Jaipur, India, who spray paints the same joke on bathroom walls about a snake charmer who gets bitten between his legs by his pet cobra!"
-- Kramer Killread, Editor (The New Tampa Guide to Sane Auto¬mobile Repair)

"I find Oxbow Lake's latest book to be as vulgar and despicable as his first two. If I were you... and thankfully I am not... I wouldn't waste my time reading any of them. Looking at their covers is disgusting enough!"

-- Charles Dickens (channeled through Hugh Hefner who is also apparently dead)

Other Award Winning Books by Oxbow Lake the 2nd

...and perhaps other authors as well?

The Adventures of the Posse of Little Horses

Spanking Yesterday

See the back pages of this great tome for titillating nibbles and more information about these two award winning novels... both novels having won the prestigious but now defunct Costa Concordia Award for Fictional Excellence

If you already own a copy of these award winning novels, it can never hurt to own a second or even third in the opinion of both the publisher and author(s)

Dedication

I dedicate *Sint Sink Tales & Other Disturbing Frictions* to the newly constituted awards committee at ShipWreckPublications LLC who, on April 1st of 2018 and in their great literary wisdom, awarded my wonderful tome the *Andrea Doria Award for Frictional Excellence.*

WORDS OF EPIGRAMMATIC WISDOM

"Facts and truth really don't have much to do with each other"

-- William Faulkner

Author

"Sometimes you have to lie to tell the truth!"

-- Kramer Killread the 1st, Esquire, Editor-in-Chief of
New Tampa Guide to Sane Automobile Repair

Oxbow Lake: Winner of the 2018 Andrea Doria Award for Frictional Excellence

In the past on April 1st, ShipWreckPublications LLC proudly awarded the prestigious *Costa Concordia Award for Fictional Excellence* to the author who best epitomized extraordinary frictional excellence in all the senses... sight, sound, smell, and touch... upon the recommendation of a carefully selected committee of judges who were appointed to that esteemed committee by the staff at ShipWreckPublications. These judges were chosen for their reputed excellence in the fields of academia, cinema, publishing and literature and for their independence from any external influence that would sway their opinion.

The judges of the *Costa Concordia* willingly agreed to become members of the awards committee and participate in the awards process... after given an offer they could not refuse, so to speak... the power of money and greed being what they are in academia, cinema, publishing, journalism and literature as they are in any profession such as that of politics in our own House of Representatives and Senate. Sadly, like our own K-Street congressional whores, initially all our judges wished to appear to not participate in the process while profiting from that participation and to have their committee memberships remain anonymous.

While Oxbow Lake's second novel *Spanking Yesterday* eventually won the award, the committee vote was one vote for giving this wonderful novel the award and 17 abstentions. The one awarding vote was cast by a judge who wished to keep private certain pictures and video (which they were) and his name anonymous (which it was not). The 17 abstaining judges whose reputations could not be affected by the public release of certain pictures or even video requested that their participation in the vote be anonymous (which

7

it was not).

In the press release announcing the award, we followed the FBI's rhetorical practices and changed the word "abstaining" to "supporting" to describe the participation of these 17 judges in the awards process in order to remain true to the facts as we wished them to be felt, seen, smelled and heard. We remain confident in the integrity of all those who participated in the awards process... just like the FBI!

To wipe the slate clean award-wise, save payoff money, expedite the process and follow already established and accepted awards practices in the publishing industry by such publishing giants as St. Martin's Press, we've established a new award: the *Andrea Doria Award for Frictional Excellence.*

The winner of this award is determined by a committee of all the winners of all previous ShipWreckPublications awards... in this case, all the winners of the now defunct *Costa Concordia Award for Fictional Excellence.* Since the last two (and only) winners of this award are Oxbow Lake the 2nd (author of the award winning *The Adventures of the Posse of Little Horses*) and himself (the author of the award winning *Spanking Yesterday*), Mr. Lake and himself were charged with determining the winner of this new award, the Andrea Doria.

On April 1st of 2019, in a fair, unbiased and unanimous vote, the newly constituted committee awarded this year's first and hopefully annual *Andrea Doria Award for Frictional Excellence* to none other than the author of this tome, *Sint Sink Tales & Other Disturbing Frictions...* and that winner is none other than, **Oxbow Lake the 2nd** his very self... or to put it more directly, me!

-- Oxbow Lake the 2nd

8

A Copyright Notice Still Like No Other and Even More Greatly So

Like Oxbow Lake's two previous tomes, this great tome is most likely a work of both fiction and friction created in the fevered mind of an author (or perhaps two authors… and maybe even three). This situation is not unprecedented in American literature as *Huckleberry Finn* had two although the three authors in today's instance may be somewhat unprecedented. Thus the characters, incidents, and dialogue are not real in that sense of the word. Any resemblance to actual persons, events, real or imagined, or living and/or dead is entirely coincidental in the interpretation of that word most favorable to the author (or authors) of this great tome whether that number is one, two or possibly three.

To prove my point, the author or authors… several of whom might be considered ghost authors in some literary circles if they in fact existed… well, none of them used the purported incident in which three individuals urinated on a portrait of Governor Nelson A. Rockefeller which they'd taped to the side entrance to New York State's Capitol Building at 11:59 pm, Friday March 17, 1961 (which happens to be St. Patrick's Day) after hearing that the boarding house where they lived in the Albany neighborhood known as "the Gut" was to be demolished to make room for the construction of what became the Nelson A. Rockefeller Empire State Plaza. Since DNA testing had not yet been invented, the urinating culprits were never identified and caught although it is rumored that said culprits had walked to the Capitol Building from Swifty's Irish Pub… although I am forced to admit that this incident may not have actually occurred and thus could be included in the various stories in this award winning tome in spite of the restrictions herein documented. However, whatever the case in this instance, the author (or authors) of this great tome have not ruled out using this incident in a future great tome.

Thus the opinions, ideas, notions, emotions and feelings expressed in this great tome may or may not necessarily be those of the author (or authors), the publisher, those who participated in preparing this great tome for publication, those who read this great tome, and/or those who do not.

ShipWreckPublications is probably a trademark of **ShipWreckPublications LLC.**

For information about special discounts for bulk purchases, please contact the **ShipWreckPublications Unique and Little Used Sales Department** at be498ar@earthlink.net or visit our web site at www.shipwreckpublications.com. We highly recommend that *Sint Sink Tales & Other Disturbing Frictions* be made required reading for all social science, linguistic, history, literature, engineering, biology, medical, language, computer science, agriculture, technical communications and religious studies programs in all our colleges and universities. We feel that actually all of Oxbow Lake's novels and tomes should be required in all of the above programs as well as all women's studies, African-American studies, and Hispanic studies programs as well English as a second or third language studies programs. We can arrange sweet deals for Instructors and Professors (and you instructors and professors know what we mean)!

The ShipWreckPublications Speakers Bureau can liven up any meeting of *hoi polloi* that you can muster into a conference room, hall, living room, kitchen or garage... particularly if the projected audience can and has read at least one book in the last decade. Technical tomes of a scientific and mathematical nature do not count in this instance.

We realize that the previous condition might limit the sale of our speaker services, but we thought it appropriate to state since we want you to get your money's worth. For the most part, an audience of ill literates would not enjoy and/or profit from a healthy dose of one of our speaker's lectures as we incorporate very little slap stick in our lectures. However, for an additional fee, this situation can be easily rectified as we are fans and aficionados of the Three Stooges, both past and present.

There is one caveat to the above limitation concerning ill literates. We believe that older dyslexics, particularly if their dyslexia is severe enough to prevent them being able to read a book, can still attend one of our lectures and appear to enjoy and profit from them as these dyslexics have usually developed coping mechanisms so as to appear to be well read and thus will also strive to appear to enjoy the lecture. As an added bonus, older dyslexics will probably rate your efforts at scheduling one of our lectures very highly as they want to appear to fully enjoy and understand the lecture, and any negative comments on their part would require an understanding of what was said in order to state specific reasons for their dissatisfaction… an understanding they are unlikely to have at least concerning specific literary references.

Younger dyslexics tend not to fall into this limitation as they most likely have learned to use audio books and thus in most cases are more literate in an auditory sense than their non-dyslexic peers.

For more information about our audio books, whether or not you're dyslexic, please contact the **ShipWreckPublications Audio Books Department** at be498ar@earthlink.net or visit our web site at www.shipwreckpublications.com. We guarantee that our speakers will be pretty much as advertised and always dress appropriately.

For the terms of our speaker services and to schedule a speaker, please contact the **ShipWreckPublications Speakers Bureau** at be498ar@earthlink.net or visit our web site at www.shipwreckpublications.com.

Speaking of our web site, take a gander at it. You'll enjoy the topics, particularly if you have even a shred of humor in your bones and enjoy someone else's eye getting poked.

www.shipwreckpublications.com

Designed by Karen Mathis
Mathis Web Masters Unincorporated
Manufactured somewhere in the United States of America. Due to the structure of the internet, the exact location is difficult to impossible to determine but we're pretty sure that location is in the US of A.

Disturbing Sint Sink Tales & Other Disturbing Frictions

Copyright © 2019 by Oxbow Lake the 2nd, Ward A. Bobb the 3rd, or Robert A. Ward III, take your pick.
v2.0
ISBN: 978-0-9839766-2-2
This edition is published by ShipWreckPublications LLC
Cover design and illustrations by Karen Mathis
Photos by Lisa Lazzero (alias Lisa Lazzaro)
ShipWreckPublications LLC
9745 Fox Chapel Road
Tampa, FL 33647
Visit our website at www.ShipWreckPublications.com

LIKELY PRINTED IN THE UNITED STATES OF AMERICA

**TO CONTACT THE PUBLISHER OR OXBOW
LAKE TO EXPRESS YOUR ADMIRATION,**

EMAIL TO:

be498ar@ earthlink.net

Contents

Fact, friction, humor and the uncomfortable truth when writing fiction 17

SINT SINK TALES & OTHER DISTURBING FRIC-TIONS...25

In Sint Sink there are walls of many colors 27

Slappin' Ain't Hittin' 64

Robert Marinelli's Italian-American Human Comedy 73

The Blattella Chronicles 169

The Swiftian Nomination of One Legs de Coa Coa 208

Gimpy Sean McGillicuddy's Miraculous Assumption 224

The Tangled Web of Porcine Love, Arboreal Sex and Constitutional Law 244

The Twisted Tale of Killian Sullivan the 3rd's Alleged Platonic Imposed Molar Extraction 284

Envirobortion: an immodest proposal to save the environment and enhance human nutrition 293

The Great Nose-Hair National Crisis....................................308

Who is Oxbow Lake, how in heaven's name did he get this way and what is his fate?...335

A Posse of Little Horses Teaser 346

A *Spanking Yesterday* Teaser 349

How to Order Oxbow Lake's Books...................................353

Fact, friction, humor and the uncomfortable truth when writing fiction

Fact, friction, humor and the uncomfortable truth when writing fiction... strange title for an essay introducing *Sint Sink Tales & Other Disturbing Frictions...* No? And what's with this word "friction" which appears in both titles? What's friction got to do with fiction?

Fiction that's more than just that which eases the pleasant passing of time must create an intellectual and oft unpleasant heat... and it must be entertaining to enable the reader to experience and bear that heat... that heat caused by the intellectual friction created by plot, character, conflict and prose... all of which may conflict with at least some of what the reader accepts as truth, conventional truth that is... which is why the word "friction" which creates that heat appears in both titles. And humor? Nothing helps a reader bear that heat more than a little humor.

And why did I quote Kramer Killread's epigram "Sometimes you have to lie to tell the truth!" in the front matter? Because his words drip with irony, humor, wisdom and yes, friction... a friction that explains much about the relationship of fact and fiction to truth... and more than a dollop of the former and a chunk of the latter while leavened with humor.

With metaphorical tongue in bulging literary cheek, Killread somehow manages to mumble the word *lies*... his *lies* being a *fiction* that reveals more truth than can a list of facts, particularly when those facts are filtered through that vicious handmaiden *political correctness* and her ugly sister, *conventional wisdom*... filtered fact being a means of hiding the truth rather than revealing, understanding and facing it. Killread uses the word "lie" as a foil... turning its perceived meaning on its head to dramatize his point. Brilliant!

As to facts, many readers believe that while fiction is entertaining, it can't really reveal truth because it is not based on fact as is history. This is the belief of the self-proclaimed literate but quite pedestrian reader who lacks both an imagination and an understanding of the nature of both history and fiction. As my own personal foil, I add another epigram, a corollary to Killread's words: "All history is fiction!" I leave it to you to puzzle through these words and those of William Faulkner on the subject: "Facts and truth really don't have much to do with each other."

My concern here is that handmaiden to fact, today's ubiquitous political correctness... that vicious filter, a filter that's much more than just a political filter. It's become a filter for all things cultural as well. Cultural correctness would be a more accurate term as all things today are political.

In this book I write stories and works of satire... frictional fiction if you will. I do not run my writing through our politically correct filter, that vicious handmaiden, for as I've already said, she obfuscates truth and oft prevents it from being expressed... or even hinted at.

And as our self-centered histories have so eloquently documented, we are only too willing to slaughter another culture's herd of infertile politically correct sacred cows... for their sacred cows must be slaughtered in the name of truth, justice and the American way... our own sacred cows being self-righteously exempt of course from even the mildest of criticisms... until, that is, our cultural roof collapses crushing all those sacred cows.

Our historians and cultural grand poobahs have spent many decades slaughtering one of history's largest herds of sacred cows, those bred and so tenderly kept and viciously protected by the Victorians in England... that land where the metaphoric Mrs. Grundy, Victorian England's vicious handmaiden of sexual political correctness, stormed around stamping out all that threatened the most sacred of

18

those sacred cows, Victorian concepts of sex and the sexes. Mrs. Grundy made the very topic of all things sexual verboten in Victorian polite society.

While the Victorians recognized two of them, sexes that is, the manner in which those sexes dressed, comported themselves, talked and wrote about their sexuality... and even conducted their intimacies as those two recognized sexes physically intertwined... all things sexual were carefully defined and that definition being, well, quite Victorian, for while there were two recognized sexes that was pretty much it from a hanky-panky standpoint or even a hanky-spanky standpoint.

However, while mum was the word on all things sexual in Victoria's world, Victorian men banged the sexual drum often... if not loudly... with the populous and popular Victorian prostitutes wandering about... and many of those drum banging men were very prominent in Victorian society... their élites... like Winston Churchill's philandering old man, Lord Randolph, who caught the Frenchman's disease while banging that drum and then slowly and inexorably marched down Syphilis Alley to insanity and death while his fellow Victorians clothed all those salacious piano legs in their homes with pantaloons so as not to expose their families and guests to naked legs of any sort.

For a century our culture has been lampooning and viciously criticizing those Victorians for their philandering ridiculous rules, regulations and actual behaviors involving sex... with a special emphasis on its repression of women's sexuality, mostly if not exclusively by men, and homosexuality, *à la* the trials and tribulations of one Oscar Wilde.

But what of today's vicious filter of political and cultural correctness concerning all things sexual? What conventional sexual proprieties do the élites of our culture wish to protect with their vicious filter by their Mrs. Grundy?

We can start with New York City, our capitol of cultural communications and fortress of political correctness. That fine city now recognizes 31 genders... and those who support these 31 genders have a corollary belief: sexuality itself is not biological but rather a social construct. (Have these denizens of sexual constructs never watched a sexual construct like say the voluptuous Scarlett Johansson or any number of equally voluptuous well-constructed actresses who buttress our Hollywood élites as they construct that construct of theirs against some well-endowed hard-body hunks of the male construct as those two constructs use their obviously different constructs to complement each other and thus compliment each others' constructs... or is it "compliment each others' complement"?)

To put muscle behind the recognition of these 31 genders, we don't have one Mrs. Grundy. We have a whole commission of them, New York City's Human Rights Commission. This commission of financially militant Mrs. Grundy's fines those businesses who dare not to recognize all 31genders... every single one.. six-figures... in dollars. (In the minds of this commission of Mrs. Grundys, these figures are a clear indication that the figures of both women and men are like the numbers of that six-figure fine... that is, slightly different but not enough to make much of a difference except, of course, when there are six of them preceded by a dollar sign and followed by the word "fine".)

While "man" and "woman" are miraculously included in New York City's list of genders, so are such new genders as "gender bender" (which is self-defining, I guess), Hijre (whatever the hell this is), Drag Queen (an old standby), Two Spirit (an American Indian term... it's always good to inoculate a list of controversial things with something American Indian), "gender gifted" (which I thought we all were, regardless of our gender) and the ever popular "pangender" (for those in love with kitchen utensils while working in the food preparation industry?). The list goes on for another 23 genders. I've decided not to enumerate the additional 23 genders fearing that were I to do so, I might inflict the much feared gender dysphoria on you, the poor reader... a sin I could not "bear to bare"... or is it "bare to bear"?

And what if an employer uses the wrong gender pronoun more than once after what was undoubtedly a very stern correction... such as viciously forcing the very offensive pronouns "he" or "she" on some poor unsuspecting self-proclaimed Hijre... well, that commission of muscular Mrs. Grundy's fines that viciously inconsiderate employer another six-figures... none of which are constructs.

Kinda makes pantalooned piano legs look pretty rational.

Who will un-pantaloon our culturally correct sexuality? Who will risk junking the filter and bearing to be ostracized by yelling, "Today's piano legs should be unpantalooned"?

Why someone not far from this very page!

And then there's the other great shibboleth of cultural and political correctness: racism. Today the way to destroy someone is to accuse him or her of racism... the accused almost always being white, for as I have learned, it is impossible for any people of color... any color, that is, except white... to be racist. An exception being that African-American "white supremacist" rapper Kanye West, who wandered off the progressives' African-American plantation to earn that ironic title.... and today's black majority in South Africa also being a little recognized exception that apparently proves the rule... or maybe it was Zimbabwe or Myanmar or Japan or Red China or Harvard University or...).

And foolish me. I thought that 350,000 white Union soldiers... give or take a white Union corpse or two... died in the Civil War to end slavery in all its social, economic and political manifestations. Little did I know that those 350,000 white Union soldiers died because of their support of tariffs causing economic barriers to international trade... those boys from Ohio had all that trade stuff pretty much understood as they died fighting those economic dunces dressed in grey and screaming economic idiocies about those tariffs like economically stupid banshees.

And what does today's vicious filter remove from social discourse regardless of its use... unless of course you're of the color that is most insulted by the word's use... in which case you can use it as often as you like and in any way you like. The word is "nigger". If you're unfamiliar with its present day usage, listen to any rap album... particularly the very popular ones, most of which are purchased by white teenagers, who are unknowingly genetically racist because of their race. Strange.

The word is so offensive, that many high schools have banned Mark Twain's *The Adventures of Huckleberry Finn* because Twain uses the word "N-word", as they call it, 219 times. Just one example of this censorship: a parent of a mixed race junior at Friends' Central School in Philadelphia complained that her son felt uncomfortable when reading Twain's novel because the word was not "inclusive". She opined at a board of education meeting, "This is great literature. But there (are so many) racial slurs in there and offensive wording that you can't get past that."

And so the novel was banned from an 11th grade class in American literature.

Because some snowflake felt uncomfortable? Mark Twain's *Huckleberry Finn* is a moral journey that leads Huck to the understanding that the slave Nigger Jim is a human being and that slavery is just plain wrong and inhumane. Twain's use of the word

22

is historically accurate and heightens Huck's moral dilemma as he works his way through the differences between what he's been taught about slavery and what he experiences as he floats down the Mississippi with Jim.

This novel is not an okay novel... this novel is not a good novel... this is one of the great novels of not just America, but of the entire world... and to think that an 11th grade student is so immature that he cannot read this great novel because it makes him feel *uncomfortable* boggles the mind of any rational person who has not been made captive of our politically correct culture. The novel is supposed to make the reader feel uncomfortable. It's full of friction leavened with understated humor. Feeling uncomfortable about the word "nigger" is the point of the novel!

I suggest that this poor mixed race snowflake of a student in Philadelphia get some backbone before he melts in ignorance and learn about how uncomfortable many innocent black men felt as they were lynched for being niggers.

And to put a exclamation point on my point, the knives of cultural correctness were, and I guess still are, out for another uncomfortable novel, Harper Lee's Pulitzer Prize winning *To Kill a Mockingbird...* which uses the dreadful "N-word" 48 times.

Oh the lack of inclusion! Oh that uncomfortable feeling that overwhelms a student as he or she reads a story about a courageous white Southern lawyer who defends a falsely accused black man of raping a white woman as that white lawyer faces down a white racist lynch mob... that uncomfortable feeling being brought on by reading the historically and accurately used word "nigger".

To deny Dame History is to invite her back for another whack at our civilization and not allowing the use of the word as it was used in accurate historical and literary contexts is an invitation for such.

In the stories and works of satire in this tome, I use the word "nigger" seven times, six times in the first story, "In Sint Sink there are walls of many colors" and once in a second story, "Robert Marinelli's Italian-American Human Comedy".

The first story is actually not a story about race. Rather it's a story about tribes, tribal warfare and class. All four tribes in the story are from the same class, the lower class. One of the tribes is Italian-American, two of the tribes are African-American, and a fourth is French-Canadian. This much feared word is used as it was in that time by the individuals of those tribes... as were the words 'guinea' and 'wop'. In the second story, the word is used by an African-American to self-describe himself, something that is common even today.

While both stories are fiction set many years ago, they are, like all fiction, based on experience and reflect the use of language in those times and in those places. Not using the word would greatly reduce the effectiveness and truthfulness of the stories. Using the word will, perhaps, play a small role in overcoming Dame History's abhorrence of a vacuum, habit of repetition and love of the forbidden... and cause the friction necessary to burn the tips of her amoral fingers... at least this once.

-- Oxbow Lake the 2nd

SINT SINK TALES & OTHER DISTURBING FRICTIONS

THIS PAGE INTENTIONALLY LEFT MOSTLY BLANK

(THE ABOVE VERY LIKELY BEING AN UNNECESSARY EDITORIAL OVERSTATEMENT)

IRRELEVANT NOTE FROM THE AUTHOR:

HAVING RESERVATIONS IS NOT NECESSARILY A GOOD OR A BAD THING... IT ALL DEPENDS ON THE MEANING OF THE WORD AND THE NATURE AND QUALITY OF THE RESERVATION.

In Sint Sink there are walls of many colors

A life of reservations...

William Mead Warden the 3rd loved movies. He had loved them all his life. In search for one to watch, he channel-surfed through the literally hundreds of channels available on Direct TV to find one. Bruce Springsteen's *99 Channels and Nothing to Watch* wafted through his brain as he surfed unsuccessfully. Then serendipity struck his eyeballs and Springsteen's voice went silent, for our insipient hero had come across a scene where a couple of Indian boys... Native American teenagers... were exchanging words that could lead to fisticuffs.

Warden didn't know at the time that they were Yakama Indians, but it was obvious that they were Indians, that they were living on a reservation and that they were throwing insults at each other... insults that could lead to fisticuffs. That was good enough for him, for he loved movies about Indians, particularly Indians living on reservations, and he loved movies where insults were thrown... insults that led to fisticuffs. It looked to him like this movie would have all four. He put the remote down and watched as the scene progressed:

The smaller of two Indian teenagers said "Your dad's on the run... he ain't ever comin' back. You know what he did. He burned down your house and killed your auntie and burned your mom... and he was drunk!"

The larger Indian teenager said "He is so comin' back. I know he is! What you said ain't true..."

The smaller Indian teenager naively replied "Is so true and everybody knows it... that's why he ain't comin' back. He's gone. Just like Willie White Swan's dad. He ran away too and he'll never come back and

27

Oxbow Lake The 2nd

Willie even said so".

The bigger Indian interrupted, "Shut up Michael or I'll beat shit out of you again."

The two Indians were named Donovan Red Corn and Michael Bird Song. They lived, perhaps survived is a better description, on their reservation in Yakima County, Washington. Donovan was the bigger and the more physical of the two. He was direct, angry and intimidating. His almost inadvertent opponent was much smaller and wore glasses. He was Michael Bird Song, a teller of odd tales that were mostly ignored by those he told them to. I say "inadvertent opponent" because the smaller and apparently naive Michael seemed to say things without understanding why what he said so upset the much larger Donovan. He continued to say them as Donovan grew more and more angry.

It was obvious to William Mead Warden the 3rd that Donovan could beat the tar out of Michael when he could no longer bear Michael's words and that he had apparently done so on a number of occasions. The question hiding in William Mead Warden the 3rd's head was *Why would Donovan want **his** father to return?*

William Mead Warden the 3rd was now positive that he'd hit the movie viewing jackpot, but then another panic struck him. The movie was already well under way. He hated not seeing a movie from title to credits... kind of an intellectual thing with him with a generous spicing of OCD hot sauce thrown in for good measure. Not seeing a movie from the very beginning to the very end ruined the movie for him. He grabbed the remote in a panic and pressed the button to view the Direct TV Guide. There was still a chance he could save the movie.

Then there it was on the screen... the movie title *Fire and Water* and after the title, there was one of those little reverse arrows. He still had a chance to save the movie. He pushed the remote control button for the double reverse arrow and prayed. With any luck, Direct TV would reverse to the very beginning of the movie and he'd be able to watch the movie from the title shot to the last credit. He held his breath since sometimes his internet connection was too slow for reasons he did not understand and the rewind would not complete. If that happened, it'd be unbearable for him to watch the rest of the movie. The rewind bar now on the screen slowly moved along towards a complete rewind. This forward moving bar did not comfort William because the bar would often move toward the end with a little smidgen of space left and then it would come to a screeching stop and he'd get a message about a mysterious slow internet connection and the rewind would terminate.

But this time the internet gremlins slept for the reverse had completed and a male voice said, "Looks like arson... one female deceased... another female badly burned but still alive... one male still unaccounted for..."

As the opening scene progressed, William Mead Warden the 3rd saw the smoldering remains of house...

William felt that he had a lot in common with teenage Indians trapped on a reservation such as were the Yakama teenagers in *Fire and Water* for he had felt trapped on a sort of reservation when *he* was a teenager. Back then he didn't analyze his situation on his *reservation* in socio-economic or historical terms, for he had neither the knowledge, experience or sophistication to do so. In his mind it was a feeling... a kind of shared experience, for it was true that his *reservation* didn't conform with the formal definition of that word when that word followed the word *Indian*.

However, it was also true that Italian-Americans like him living in poor neighborhoods alongside poor African-Americans were trapped in a geography that defined and limited them and that was difficult to escape, for although William Mead Warden the 3rd had an Anglo name, the rest

29

of him was Italian-American through his mother's ubiquitous family, the Zerrellis. This entrapment and isolation was his life... a feeling... and subconsciously this feeling drove his love of movies about Indians living on reservations. Unbeknownst to him, he identified with them.

So it was obviously true that he hadn't lived on a *reservation* like the one where the word *Indian* preceded the word *reservation*, but he still had that feeling of entrapment... that feeling of inferiority. Even though he had lived on his reservation many years ago where *his* fellow braves called him Billy Club, the memories of his life on his self-defined and particularly odd *reservation* stayed with him. In fact he had never succeeded in pushing those memories deep below the surface no matter how hard he tried. They always hung around the surface of his consciousness and popped up at the most inopportune times.

His reservation was on the southside of Sint Sink Village in New York State, about 30 miles north of New York City on the majestic Hudson River... more precisely on Colonial Street where his house faced Sint Sink Prison. He was unaware of the great historical irony casting its long centuries-old shadow over *his* reservation, for the prison had been built on the site of the village of a small extinct tribe of Leni Lenape Indians, the Sint Sinks... and the Colonials had named their village Sint Sink and later their prison where his father was a guard or as the guards themselves preferred to be called, a "corrections officer"... although the "corrections" seemed to consist of long sentences, much recidivism and eventually, for a select unlucky few, a hot seat on Old Sparkie as New York State's electric chair was called back then by those in the know.

William Mead Warden the 3rd... Billy Club as his fellow braves called him... was one of those in the know, for his father, William Mead Warden the 2nd, held the unofficial title of "Captain of the Death House" where he had worked five shifts a week for many, many years and where this final correction was occasionally administered. The senior

30

William witnessed and actually participated in all these final corrections. The men incarcerated on Death Row... they were almost always men, with several notable exceptions... spent much time and effort with lots of time-consuming legal wranglings and appeals to prevent their final "dance" with Old Sparkie. Thus the senior William got to know those he helped into Old Sparkie quite well before helping them ride the lightning into the afterlife on New York State's dime.

Billy Club could see Sint Sink Prison's great white wall from the bedroom that he shared with his two brothers. His Zerrelli cousins lived upstairs and in the house across the driveway lived some more Italian-American kids, the Marinellis. They were all Italian-Americans... a kind of tribe, the Guinea Wops as their rivals called them... including Billy Club... what with his mom, Rose Zerrelli-Warden, her ubiquitous Zerrelli brothers and sisters, and her guinea father, Pop Pop, young Billy Club's Italian grandfather... all of whom lived either with them, above them in the second floor apartment or close by. The only thing that wasn't guinea wop about William Mead Warden the 3rd was his name.

Just up the street across from the great Sint Sink Prison water towers and in the shadow of those stark metal prehistoric creatures stood a four story tenement in which poor black families and even poorer broken black families lived... the home of yet another tribe, a rival tribe. It was the kids of these families and broken families that named the tribe of Italian-American kids "the Guinea Wops."

In turn, the Guinea Wops called this other tribe on this neighboring reservation the "Tennie Niggers" or less formally "the Tennies"... a shortened form of the word "tenement." The Tennies reciprocated, calling "the Guinea Wops" just "the Wops." Both tribes shortened the formal tribal names of their rivals not out of any sensitivity to the language but just because it was easier to yell shortened names during their various tense and occasionally violent confrontations... confrontations usually

31

beginning with a series of insulting chants making the shortened tribal names a chanting necessity .

To complicate matters, there was yet another tribe of black kids further down Colonial Street on the far border of the Tennies' reservation... not far from Abraham Brockman's iconic neighborhood store, for this was the time of family-owned neighborhood stores before the corporate conglomerates seven-elevened us to death. In fact there were five, count them, five family owned neighborhood stores... four on the ends of the tribal territories and one sprinkled in the middle.

Tribal neighborhood stores and that other tribal reservation...

Abraham Brockman's was the best of the five neighborhood stores by far as Abe... sometimes called 'the Jew' by his customers, who often surrounded this religious sobriquet with the words "cheap" and "bastard"... but not in his presence... well Abraham Brockman allowed his patrons to run a tab which the families of the Wops made extensive use of. When the tab got too high in old man Brockman's judgment, he cut off the credit and demanded payment of the tab in full. When he did so, the Wop families could not shop there, cursed the "cheap Jew bastard" and as a result of this credit catastrophe created by "the cheap Jew bastard", patronized the other four family owned neighborhood stores on a cash-only basis... that is until they could pay off the tab at Brockman's, for Brockman's was also by far the best stocked of the five tribal stores and his store was the only one that allowed the Wop families to run a tab... provided of course it was a reasonable tab. Once an unreasonable tab was paid off, a reasonable tab was immediately re-established and the financial process began anew. Rarely did the black families, broken or otherwise, shop at Brockman's which was a bit odd given that Brockman's was by far the best stocked of the five family owned tribal stores and was located on the far end of the two black tribal reservations.

That second black tribe was the smallest of the tribes and occupied the smallest reservation. Actually this tribe was made up of the members of a single large black family, the Worthingtons. Momma Worthington ran the family with an iron fist... which was necessary since she supplemented her own children with a large number of foster children. For reasons unknown to all but Momma Worthington herself, most, if not all of her foster children, came from Cleveland. Since many of the members of this smaller tribe were foster children, they had various last names that were not Worthington.

The Tennies called this tribe "the Navaho Niggers." It was obvious that this name was considered a grievous insult by the Tennies, particularly the word "Navaho" but it was unclear as to exactly why. What was clear was that the Tennies did not like this smaller black tribe one bit.

Perhaps the Tennies used the word 'Navaho' because they considered Indians in general and Navahos in particular to be lower on the socio-economic scale than blacks although this was never verified. What was easily verified was that the Tennies considered this name a grievous insult and that was good enough for their rhetorical purposes.

However, it remained unclear to the other tribes as to why this was so. As a result, this supposed insult was taken by the so-called Navaho Niggers as a badge of honor and a reason to ally themselves with the Wops, for as with all tribal rivalries, the enemy of my enemy is my friend... most of the time. In the name of succinctness, the braves of all three tribes, including those of this smaller tribe, called this third smaller tribe "the Nava-hoes" and not "the Navahos" ... this creative rhythmic and elongated linguistic contraction accepted by all including this third tribe even though the slang word 'hoe' had another and more common pejorative meaning. However, this linguistic succinctness was deemed more important for it was easier to chant "Nava-hoes" and it sounded a lot better to the ear... chanting being an important and oft used means of verbal communication between tribes.

All of this swirled about the inside of William Mead Warden the 3rd's head as he watched Victor Joseph and Thomas Builds-the-Fire trade insults... insults that eventually led to Victor Joseph's threat to beat the crap out of Thomas Builds-the Fire again.

The sounds of tribal life...

This trading of insults by Victor and Thomas Builds-the-Fire reminded William Mead Warden the 3rd of the great insulting competitions that broke out between tribal friends and foes alike on *his* reservations... a kind of ritualistic rhetorical fist fight of wit and quickness under great pressure. The tribal braves, all of them, called these verbal battles "soundings". When you attacked your opponent with an insult, you "sounded" him. Sometimes these verbal fistfights broke out because of bad blood and sometimes they just broke out for no apparent reason... occasionally these sounding rhetorical battles turned into actual fisticuffs although this was relatively rare, for there were rules... undocumented and oft argued, but there were rules and fisticuffs during or shortly after a sounding battle was considered impolite by all the braves of all the tribes... unless of course you were the losing sounding combatant in a fistfight during or shortly after a sounding battle.

You sounded your opponent and he quickly sounded you back... until one of you ran out of quick-fire sounding retorts and you lost... much to the delight of all who witnessed this battle of rhetorical fisticuffs. It was a lot like the rapping contests of today without the boring "music" and the overly long and often difficult to understand insults. Sounding was quick fire stuff and not for those faint of heart and slow to the draw.

Billy's younger brother James was a sounding champion... perhaps the sounding champion for all three tribes even though he was a Wop and more particularly, white. To challenge him was to risk a humiliating defeat and when that occurred, the words "you been sounded, bitch!" echoed through the brain of the humiliated and defeated as the other braves celebrated your defeat and added to your humiliation. Most often these vicious soundings took the form of "Yo momma" insults, for one's mother was considered sacred, particularly by the black braves, many of whom did not have a father living at home.

Wop James sat on the front stoop of his house facing Nava-hoe Willie Worthington. They were buddies even though members of two different tribes as the two tribes were most often allies against the much larger Tennies tribe. Willie looked James in the eye and out of nowhere said, "Yo mama's like a toilet... she round, white and smells like shit!" It was the proverbial "sounding ambush" and probably the best way for a challenger to sound Wop James into defeat. Why this ambush at this time? Remains a mystery to this day to all who were there including Nava-hoe Willie Worthington himself. As I said earlier, sometimes these sounding battles just broke out.

However, Wop James was cool which is one of the reasons he was considered the sounding champion... the other being he had an encyclopedic arsenal of insults at the finger tips of his tongue so to speak, many of which he created. He coolly replied, "Yo mama so ugly she scare brown shit outta toilets!" and the contest was on... James' sounding retort being considered by the bystanders to be particularly effective since it was quick and turned the ambusher's white *toilet bowl-shit* metaphor against him. These soundings could be quite linguistically and metaphorically sophisticated.

Nava-hoe Willie stumbled a bit but yelled, "Yo mama so fat she fell outta both sides her bed."

35

Then a smiling Wop James retorted, "Yo mamma so fat she sit on a quarter and boogers shoot out George Washington's nose."

This particular sounding was new to all present and flummoxed poor Nava-hoe Willie. To add to poor Nava-hoe Willie's flummox, the great white sounder had done so with a "Yo momma's so fat" sound that bested poor Nava-hoe Willie's "Yo momma's so fat" sound. Shouts of "You been sounded, bitch!" rang as the vanquished Nava-hoe Willie hung his head in shame. Challenging Wop James to a sounding contest was a dangerous thing to do even if you ambushed him.

This land is my land, that land is your land... from the Water Towers to the Holland Hose Fire House...

With apologies to Woody Guthrie, the three reservations were also the tribal homelands for all three tribes... this land to be used and defended, for the braves of all three tribes, like all indigenous peoples, were very territorial. However, this tribal territorialism included the desire to not only defend agreed upon territorial boundaries but to expand them. Thus there was the constant threat of territorial loss and the constant desire for territorial gain lurking in the collective hearts of all three tribes... although notably less so on the part of the Nava-hoes who had less territory, even less desirable territory, and fewer braves.

As Nava-hoe Willie licked his sounding-inflicted wounds under the thunder of the much dreaded chants of *You been sounded, bitch!*, Wop James smiled, basking in the glory of yet another victory in that battle of rhetorical and metaphorical fisticuffs. Then his smile turned to a grimace of fear and then of anger as he pointed toward the prison grounds on the other side of Colonial Street, and yelled, "Look... the damn Tennies... there... under the water towers."

Sure enough what looked to be a Tennies war party had gathered under the nearest water tower in their territory on the prison grounds. The Tennie braves were screaming and jumping in place. Heads kept bobbing up and down.

Wop Billy Club counted heads as the Tennies' heads bobbed up and down and then he yelled, "Twelve... maybe fourteen."

The Tennies' screaming turned into a chant of some sort which Billy could not understand, partly because of the distance and partly because the chant itself consisted of words intentionally slurred by the chant's rhythm. After several minutes of rhythmic chanting and jumping in place, the war party slowly danced from their territory toward the territory on the prison grounds claimed by the Wops.

To better understand the strategic situation, you have to know the lay of the territorial lands. On Colonial Street itself, the territories were well defined and the boundaries never challenged, for that was where the tribal houses were... that was where the tribal families lived... that was where the parents or parent of the tribal braves lived. This section of the tribal lands for all three tribes was unchallengeable.

However, there were tribal lands on the prison grounds across from Colonial Street and between the Sint Sink prison wall and a chain link fence along Colonial... territories claimed by the Wops and by the Tennies. This is where the Wops and the Tennies fought to protect and expand their territories. These prison grounds were bounded from Colonial Street by that eight-foot chain link fence about ten feet from the far curb. This barrier was no barrier at all for the braves of all three tribes as they easily went under, around and over the fence... depending where they were.

On the prison grounds and across from the home of the Tennies, stood two huge water towers. On the other end of the prison grounds across

37

from the homes of the Wops stood the Holland Hose Fire House... these structures setting the boundaries of the recognized tribal lands on the prison grounds. Along the narrow neck of land between the two tribal lands, the Wops had dug a trench and a low sort of wall consisting of piled rocks. This was intended to be both a boundary and a barrier. The Wop braves could duck behind the wall, hunker down in the trench on their side of stone wall and fire their missile of choice, chestnuts, at the braves of the attacking Tennies tribe using sling shots or just chucking the chestnuts. Rocks were thought to be too dangerous.

Billy Club yelled, "Invasion!" and five Wop braves and two Navahoes ran for the chain link fence across the street, dove single file at the fence's base and slid through a small hole they'd dug under the fence in a series of choreographed moves they'd obviously done many times.

Billy Club ducked below the pile of stones they called "Stone Stop" and again yelled, "Wait... don't fire until I nail the first one!"

The six remaining defenders jumped into the trench and ducked behind the stones of Stone Stop. Billy Club and one other brave had sling shots in their back pockets, the rest were going to deliver the chestnuts the old fashioned way. In preparation for an attack, the Wops had already piled chestnuts along the trench... chestnuts they'd gathered from the Chestnut Lady's front yard... so there was plenty of ammunition readily at hand to fire and throw at the attackers.

The Tennies war party chanted: "Guinea Wop... duty squat! Guinea Wop... duty squat!" as they rhythmically danced toward that pile of stones generously called Stone Stop. The Tennies braves were armed with long sticks... a formidable war party that was well armed and outnumbered the Wops almost two to one. Many of the Tennie braves also carried garbage can lids which they used as shields. As they approached the wall, their leader Chubby Miller yelled from behind his shield, "Shit your pants you duty squat Guineas!"

Wop Billy Club stood, pulled back on his sling shot and yelled "Eat this shit, you Tennies bastard!"... firing a well aimed chestnut at the screaming Chubby Miller... the chestnut sailing just above Chubby's garbage can shield as he peeked over it... nailing him in the forehead.

Chubby dropped his shield, skidded to a halt and went eerily silent. He just stood there without moving a single muscle. Then he screamed bloody murder... a long woeful scream. The Tennies braves came to a screeching halt just in front of the screaming Chubby. Blood poured from Chubby's forehead. He turned and ran like hell for the tenement and got there in what would have been record time had such records been kept. He was followed by twelve other braves who had lost the taste for battle given the bloody retreat of their leader.

For the Wops, Hector himself could not have defended Troy any better. Billy Club shook a fist at the retreating Tennies' war party and yelled, "Stay on your own side of Stone Stop, you bastards!" The other six Wop and Nave-hoe defenders yelled various epithets at the retreating Tennies war party... most of which cannot be repeated without great offense to the reader. As Nava-hoe Willie watched the quickly retreating Chubby Miller, he said, "I didn't know that fat nigger could run so fast."

Billy Club smiled and said, "Neither did he. Think Moe could beat him in a race?"... Moe being *Moe the Frog,* or more formally, Richie Grimaud, a French Canadian refugee adopted by the Wops and who made Chubby Miller look rather svelte. The Wops pronounced Moe's last name *Grr-moe* after being told the "d" was silent and then inadvertently extending this rule of silence to several other letters... thus leading to the nickname of "Moe" to which they gratuitously added "the Frog" in honor of his French-Canadian heritage.

Nava-hoe Willie smiled and said, "Maybe *Moe the Frog* could beat too fat Chubby...provided you nailed that French-Canadian round boy between the eyes with a chestnut too... but given Moe's head, it might

just bounce off"... as *Moe the Frog* was not known for his intellectual prowess.

A Pyrrhic Victory of sorts overwhelms the Wops as they win the battle but lose the war territorially speaking...

The Wop and Nave-hoe defenders retreated to Billy Club's porch across the street from their territory on the prison grounds... all seven of them. The chatter of victory filled the air:

"Billy... you nailed the bastard!"

"Great shot!... over Chubby's shield and right between the eyes!"

"Did you see the blood pour from Chubby's head! He was bleeding like a stuck pig!"

This last comment brought an uncomfortable silence to the seven braves, for it dawned upon the Wop and Nava-hoe braves that the chestnut that Billy Club shot at Chubby Miller may have really hurt Chubby badly. In the heat of battle, things had gotten out of hand. In the past, the battles between the Wops and the Tennies had always been fierce but within certain mutually but unstated agreed upon limits. Victory was gained by forcing the enemy to beat a hasty retreat... suffering great embarrassment... the vanquished fearing fear itself... that second fear caused by the possibility of physical harm... not actual physical harm.

Moe the Frog yelled, "Look!" as he pointed down Colonial in the direction of the tenement. A hefty black woman with a chubby kid in tow was marching towards them... the chubby kid with a towel wrapped around his head. Behind them marched a bunch of other black kids. There was none of the usual chanting of insults. The entire group marched in a grim eerie silence. All that could be heard was the sound of their feet hitting the pavement as they marched.

The group of marchers came to a halt before the stunned seven Wop and Nava-hoe braves on Billy's porch. The hefty black woman yelled, "Look what yo boy did to my son!" Nothing happened and so she yelled again, "Look at my son. He's cut bad and yo son did it!"

Billy's mom, Rose Zerrelli-Warden, opened the front door and stepped onto the porch... at which point Chubby's mom, Pearl Miller, tore the towel from her son Chubby's head revealing a nasty cut right between the eyes just above the bridge of his nose. She stood silent for several minutes to allow the scene to penetrate the brains of all the observers on the porch.

Pearl Miller then pointed at Billy and yelled, "Yo boy did this... with a sling shot!"

Rose turned silently to Billy who shook his head a frightened yes. Without raising her voice, she turned back towards Pearl and said quite calmly, "Take him to the hospital and get him stitched up. I'll pay for it." With that she turned, walked back into the house and closed the door behind her.

An exasperated Pearl stood there looking at the empty space on the porch previously occupied by Rose. She obviously had more to say but now no adult to say it to. She looked down at Chubby's head, grabbed him by the arm and marched him back down the street to the tenement.

"Captain of the Death House" remains so regardless of where the house is...

Old man Warden sat on the couch next to the apartment entrance, a Camels cigarette with a long ash dangling from his lips and a full glass of Piels beer with a full foamy white head poised in his right hand as he gloried yet again in his unofficial title of "Captain of the Death House" and celebrated another fine day of correcting those who had broken at least one of New York State's laws in capital fashion... an empty quart bottle sitting at his feet and an already opened full quart bottle ready for the drinking poised on the end table next to which he sat. Accompanying the full quart bottle of Piels beer on the end table was a half empty pack Camels cigarettes and a dirty ashtray strewn with cigarette butts.

Billy and his brother James sat on the top step of the porch twenty feet away. James stared at the great white Sint Sink Prison wall that stretched beyond the territorial prison grounds on the other side of the chain link fence. He bit his lip and said, "When will it be safe to go in?"

Billy rose, scratched the back of his head and said, "Probably now. Dear old dad's already put away a quart. His reflexes are slow by now... reaction time bad. Let's go. I can't wait any more. I gotta take a leak." He took off full speed down the hallway, flashed through the apartment's entrance passed his father and jumped putting two more hand prints on the living room ceiling.

Dear old dad staggered to his feet and took a swipe at the air previously occupied by the racing Billy. As he did so he spilled his glass of Piels and his momentum carried him back into a seated position. Then James flashed by almost unnoticed... both boys now safely in the kitchen, a room too far given dear old dad's present condition.

Dear old dad yelled, "I toll you stop messing up ceiling. If I get hands on you, I'll... " He stopped mid sentence to refill his beer glass and went silent.

Billy set the kitchen table for dinner. He placed six plates and accompanying silverware evenly spaced on the table... a place setting for his mother, his brother James, his baby brother Andrew, Aunt Carina, Pop

Pop Zerrelli and himself. He never set a place for the old man since he never ate dinner with the family and remained sitting on the couch in the living room drinking his Piels beer and smoking his Camels cigarettes.

Momma Rose put a plate of meat loaf slices on the table, a plate of string beans smothered in tomato sauce and a stack of Italian bread. The boys began their voracious chow down.

As Billy forked a second slice of meat loaf onto his plate, he heard, "That chestnut you shot at that nigger kid yesterday cost me 23 dollars and 17 cents. Money don't grow on trees, ya know."

Billy had learned most painfully not to reply to dear old dad's outbursts.

"Stay the hell off the prison grounds. I'll call the cops myself if I see you, James or any of those idiot asshole friends of yours on the other side of the fence. And after the cops are done with you, I'll tan your hide!"

The following day Billy broke the news to his fellow braves, "We can't play on our territory in the prison grounds any more. My asshole father's going to call the cops if we do and then he's going to whip my ass. He'll whip James too and after the cops get done with you guys, you'll go home and likely get your asses whipped."

The braves sat on the curb on Colonial and stared across the street at their former territory on the other side of the chain link fence. The Tennies were playing some game around the base of the two huge water towers. But for some reason none of them moved towards the unoccupied and now former Wop territory.

James said, "Look, the Tennies got a free pass to take over our territory and instead, they're stayin' at the far end of their territory. Looks to me like they're avoidin' our land. What's up?"

45

Billy thought for a moment and said, "My guess... they don't know we've been banished. Maybe they think we're tryin' to set them up. Who knows... besides the last time they invaded our territory Chubby Miller got nailed between the eyes."

An obviously flabbergasted Moe the Frog yelled, "Where we gonna play?"

The territorial battle continues...

Like all native peoples facing more powerful "competitors", in this case the Sint Sink police department and their not-so-secret informer, the Wops migrated south of the Holland Hose Fire House, their traditional southern territorial boundary, and into the territory claimed by the southsiders, yet another gang... this one French-Canadian with a strong Greek flavor.

The southsiders were older and had outgrown the playing of war games in their territory on the prison grounds, for they had graduated into Sint Sink Village's larger world... a world that for them included burglary and the protection racket. The elder William Mead Warden had often speculated as to which side of Sint Sink Prison's long white walls the southsiders would spend most of their lives finally concluding that the determining factor would be the efficiency of local law enforcement in which he placed little faith in spite of his use of them to punish the Wops who, to both his great satisfaction and consternation, counted two of his own sons in their number.

Seven Wop and Nava-hoe braves sat on Honeysuckle Hill looking down into the valley between them and Little Mountain and beyond into the southsiders long held but now little used territory.

Wop James mused, "Think they'll care if we use their territory?"

Brother Billy Club replied, "My guess... depends on how they feel.

46

They could care less and then one day they care a lot and beat the shit out of us. That's just how they are."

Wop James, after several moments of deep strategic thought, said, "Suppose we stay way towards the prison wall near Little Mountain. The southsiders pretty much stay away from there what with the guards in the towers always watching them." He pointed to his left and said, "Their club house is way over there... under the cliffs... in the valley. You can't even see it from here. They'd never see us unless they came lookin' for us. Little Mountain blocks the guards from seein' us. And dear old dad can't see us down there either. It's ideal."

Bobby Marinelli's eyes lit up at the prospect of occupying southsiders' land and he said with great passion, "Let's do it! The pricks don't deserve the land."

Billy Club, recognized as the final voice in all gang matters involving strategy, said "We got to be careful. The guards don't mind us running around down there as long as we don't look like we're claiming the land. We gotta build a club house what with this territory being so far away from our houses and it can't look like a club house... a kinda fort and it can't look like a fort... and we gotta build it where the guards can't see us building it from the towers. Sometimes the guards send a cleanup up party of cons to keep the valley clear of dead brush... fire hazard stuff... so whatever we build has gotta look natural... like a pile of rocks. They don't do anything about rocks."

The braves cheered Billy Club's strategy and proposed club house. They had rhetorically and metaphorically crossed Sint Sink's proverbial Rubicon and were about to do so physically as well.

A fort well constructed and proven somewhat worthy...

Over the next week the Wops with the help of their allies, the Nave-hoes, placed stone upon stone until they had built their fort complete with a low stone roof supported by a series of thick tree branches. It was a unique design for it looked, as Billy Club had specified, like a pile of rocks from without. There was a narrow opening on the side of the fort facing Little Mountain which was both the entrance and exit. In the walls were firing holes so that the braves could shoot chestnuts with their slingshots at any attacking foes while still protected by the stone walls and roof. On the ground in the middle of the fort's floor, the braves had collected a huge pile of chestnuts... enough to last through a prolonged siege... and three jugs of water... for the braves knew that they lived not on firing chestnuts alone.

Wop and Nave-hoe braves sat in their newly constructed fort marveling at what they'd built. Actually they had no choice but to sit as the stone roof was very low. Wop James said to no one in particular and thus to everyone in general, "We gotta name the fort. Every fort has a name... usually a cool name."

Silence reigned. Lots of names popped into the braves' heads but none of the braves wanted to put forward a name which could be potentially ridiculed as not being "cool".

The fort thus named itself by just being what it was: a fort. And so the braves called their fort rather prosaically "The Fort" ever after.

As they sat in the comfort and safety of The Fort, they were engulfed by the sounds of a familiar chant, "Guinea Wop... duty squat! Guinea Wop... duty squat!" The seven Wop and Nava-hoe braves were stunned. Apparently a Tennies war party had somehow made it through the Wop's previous territory and down into the Southsiders' plain undetected. They must have been spying from Honeysuckle Hill as the Wops and Nava-hoes built The Fort. Thankfully, they couldn't or just didn't bother to mount an attack until after The Fort had been completed.

Bobby Marinelli peered through one of the firing holes and yelled, "It's the damn Tennies and there's a bunch of them... maybe 20 of the bastards."

The Tennies circled The Fort and started pelting it with stones. It was obvious to the encircled Wop and Nava-hoe braves that this was a full-scale revenge attack for the injury to Chubby Miller who was not amongst the attacking Tennie horde. While the encircled braves were safely ensconced in The Fort, they were also trapped.

Billy Club yelled over the chanting, "Fire at the bastards, keep them away from The Fort and a hail of chestnuts shot forth from the firing holes. After the first volley, the Tennie war party, while still encircling The Fort, enlarged the circle so as to be beyond the effective range of the chestnuts shot from the firing holes. It was a Mexican standoff... even though there were a number of racial and ethnic groups involved in the encounter, ironically not a single one of them was Mexican.

Then a series of screams shot forth from the encircling horde. The Tennies war party scattered for what appeared no reason. Bobby Marinelli peered out his firing hole and said in barely a whisper, "Jesus Christ... I don't believe it."

The other two firing holes on that side of The Fort quickly filled with eyes, one set being that of Billy Club, who said in a voice that approached a scream without quite getting there, "It's Big Moe"... Big Moe being Moe the Frog's older brother Charlie Grimaud... I refrain from using the term "big brother" for although Charlie was known as Big Moe, he was considerably smaller or at least thinner than his younger brother Richie Grimaud or Moe the Frog... this situation caused by the tribal conventions for formulating nicknames being linguistically complex and not

49

necessarily logical.

Big Moe appeared from the valley between Little Mountain and Honeysuckle Hill. He was screaming at the top of his lungs, "Death to Tennies! Death to Tennies!" He was balancing a huge stick, more a semitree log, at his waist with both hands as he ran toward The Fort. He was quite the sight, more an apparition... a young man balancing an eight foot semi-tree log in the air as he ran full speed at the Tennies encircling The Fort and yelling "Death to Tennies!" A headless horseman could not have created a greater panic on the part of the Tennies war party.

The scattering Tennies ran for the hills... at least Honeysuckle Hill... and scampered up the slope to the far right of Honeysuckle Hill's cliff and the valley separating it from Little Mountain... the Tennies running for their lives apparently seized by a panic that overwhelmed any rational thought they could have had about what exactly a Big Moe would or could do to harm them as he ran toward them with a huge eight foot semi-tree log balanced at his waist and sticking into the air.

Sometimes there is no rational explanation for irrational behavior. As the Tennies war party retreated in panic, Big Moe, still balancing that eight foot semi-tree log in the air, disappeared down the valley and out of sight... how or why he appeared as he did in the first place a mystery to all who witnessed this "apparition" from both within and without The Fort.

Another Day, another tribe, another self-inflicted problem...

Billy Warden and Anthony Marinelli, Bobby Marinelli's little brother, sat on Billy's porch steps sipping Pepsis and gnawing on Devil Dogs, for their bodies were in desperate need, as interpreted by them, of an injection of massive amounts of sugar. Their not-so-guilty pleasures were unceremoniously interrupted by a distant scream: "They got Bobby... they got both of 'em!"

The two Wop braves looked up and running towards them down the middle of Colonial was none other than Moe the Frog, who at the time was proving that he could have given the wounded Chubby Miller a race for the money.

Moe stopped at the walkway to the Warden house, bent over grabbing his knees and huffed and puffed as never before. Billy and Anthony slowly stood... both hands of our braves dropping to their sides while still holding their Pepsis and Devil Dogs. Finally they trotted towards the huffing and puffing Moe the Frog realizing that anything that could cause the hefty Moe to run as he did had to be investigated further.

Billy bent over towards the heavily breathing Moe and said, "What's up?"

Finally catching his breath, Moe stood and wheezed, "And they got your brother James too! They got both of 'em!"

The effort of wheezing out this last statement caused Moe to grab his knees again and resume his huffing and puffing causing his verbal communications to be temporally halted by his need for oxygen.

Billy yelled, "For Christ sake Moe, what the hell's happened?" Then Billy and Anthony straightened up, drained their Pepsi bottles and bit off a big chunk of Devil Dog... for nothing, not even possible imminent danger, could prevent the two braves from fulfilling their bodily need for sugar.

Finally Moe overcame his oxygen deficit, stood and said, "The Southsiders got Bobby and James... captured both of 'em. I told 'em not to do it, but they did it anyway and now the Southsiders got 'em. I got away."

Anthony, with an expression of great puzzlement, asked, "You told them not to do what? What'd ya tell 'em not to do?" Billy listened as he licked the remains of the Devil Dog from his fingers and then tossed his drained Pepsi bottle into the hedges lining the front lawn. While awaiting Moe's reply, Anthony did the same, licking his fingers of the precious remains of his Devil Dog and tossing his drained Pepsi bottle into the hedges.

Neither was littering. They were merely storing their empty bottles for later retrieval and the two-cent deposit they'd get for returning each bottle to virtually any of the tribal neighborhood stores... their efforts at conservation being economically and not ideologically or racially driven, for while they enjoyed that Indian brave on TV with that tear running down his face as he observed white people littering America, it was the two-cent deposit that inspired them, for that two cents went a ways toward yet another Pepsi bottle, this one filled with that wonderful sweet black liquid.

Finally Moe straightened up, breathing more normally, and said, "They broke into the southsiders clubhouse and got caught stealing a case of beer. They coulda got away if they just dropped the beer but they got greedy and then they got caught. The Greek knocked 'em down and a couple of other southsiders grabbed 'em and dragged 'em back to their clubhouse. I ran like hell and got away."

The southsiders, as already noted, weren't your ordinary neighborhood tribe. They used to be but they grew up and now were players in the Sint Sink village crime underworld. True they were bit players now, but they had plans and they had an ambitious leader, Guy Le Claire, an older French-Canadian kid.

The Greek who knocked the beer-greedy Bobby and James down to earth was none other than Alexis Something-or-Other... nobody could pronounce his last name and thus he was known even by his fellow southsider braves as The Greek Something-or-Other... shortened of course to just The Greek. He was a big muscular kid who made Moe the Frog's intellectual acumen look pretty acumened. Alexis Something-or-Other was the southsiders' muscle. Guy Le Claire pointed and the Greek beat the crap out of whomever Guy pointed. It was a simple formula but a very effective one that enabled Guy to dominate and lead the southsiders... which, in turn, allowed the southsiders to dominate the corner of Holland and Quarry and the parking lot for Schwartz's tribal neighborhood store. At said parking lot underage kids could buy beer and cigarettes... at a premium price, of course, and no one ever haggled over that price.

That cigarette and beer black-market service for the younger braves of the other tribes provided by the southsiders was mostly a daylight and evening affair. At night the southsiders broke into empty houses and closed stores, stealing whatever they found of value. Guy, being a good tactician and shrewd businessman of sorts, had his minions rob houses and stores outside the tribal neighborhoods while selling protection to the tribal stores within the tribal neighborhoods.

He was smart enough to charge a weekly amount that was an annoy-ance to the owners of the tribal neighborhood stores... but not so annoy-ing as to cause the owners of the tribal stores to revolt and contact the police... many of the payments being in product, that is, cigarettes and beer... which the southsiders turned into cash by selling these products to younger braves at greatly inflated prices... and some of which they used for their own satisfaction. Like I said, Guy Le Claire was shrewd beyond his eighteen years.

When Bobby Marinelli and Billy's younger brother James tried to rob a case of beer from the southsiders' clubhouse, they broke a number of tribal laws... all of them accepted by all the neighborhood tribes and thus considered universal and sacred.

Oxbow Lake The 2nd

First law broken: the law of tribal domicility... that is, a tribe's clubhouse was sacred, inviolable ground. Violating this universal and sacred law in and of itself warranted the most severe of punishments. Second, our two Wop violators of first universal and sacred tribal law broke yet a second universal and sacred law: the law of tribal possession, for they not only broke into the southsiders' clubhouse, they took something out... that is, they stole something... the stolen item being a case of beer in this case... which led to the final broken universal and sacred tribal law: the law of tribal living... the braves of one tribe were not allowed to mess with the means of another tribe to make or do whatever was necessary for that tribe to exist and even thrive. In this instance, a southsider living was selling beer to the younger braves of other tribes, including the Wops, and one of the ways in which the southsiders provided for their tribal sustenance. Having broken all three universal and sacred laws meant that Bobby and Billy's younger brother James were to have the very most severe of punishments that one tribe could mete out to the braves of another... and in this case, the "braves" of another being two Wops.

Having said all of this about universal and sacred tribal laws and their violation, I feel compelled to note that the braves of all the tribes would probably not have described these universal and sacred laws and their violation in the words that I have used, but even in their less articulate words, they would have expressed the same meaning... and in such cases as The Greek Something-or-Other or Moe the Frog, those individuals would have understood all of the above without the use of any words at all.

Ironically, in spite of all the legal and cultural universality and sacredness of these tribal laws, and for that matter of all the other universal and sacred tribal laws, all the braves of all the tribes violated all of these universal and sacred tribal laws all of the time, for it was their very nature to do so... which is probably the most universal, if not sacred, of tribal practices and possibly laws.

Billy Club, Anthony and even Moe the Frog knew and understood all of the above... with varying degrees of specificity... as did the two violators of the above described universal and sacred laws. Billy looked toward and beyond the Holland Hose Fire House and said, "We gotta do some scouting... see what's up. Bobby and James are gonna get the crap beat out of them one way or another"... which "one way or another" chosen being both unknown and frightening to them and assuredly even more so to Bobby Marinelli and James Warden.

The southsiders prove themselves Christian but in a rather medieval sort of way...

Billy Club, Anthony Marinelli and Moe the Frog laid on the edge of Honeysuckle Hill watching the events far below as those events unfolded. It was hard on them but they had no choice but to do so.

Moe the Frog whispered, "What you think they gonna do to Bobby and James?"

Billy Club, somewhat annoyed by Moe's unanswerable question, said rather loudly in a reply that could not be classified as an answer to Moe's unanswerable question but could be classified as a statement of the obvious that had obviously escaped Moe, as often happened, "For Christ sakes, Moe, you don't need to whisper. The southsiders would need a telescope to even see us... and even if they could hear us, what could they do? Nothin'! That's what!"

Undeterred by Billy's previous statements, Moe again whispered, "What they gonna do?"

An obviously frustrated Billy Club yelled, "What they goin' do to Bobby and James? Who the hell knows? But you can bet it's gonna hurt like hell!"

As they watched, a trumpet sounded what appeared to be taps and Bobby and James appeared at the far end of the plain arising from the lower valley where the southsiders' club house was located and hidden from their view. The two captives stumbled along as it was difficult for them to keep their balance because their hands were tied behind their backs. Every now and then one of the dozen or so southsiders surrounding them would give one of their captives a shove putting them off their stumbling stagger and the mystery bugler would sound his trumpet.

Billy said, "That's gotta be Tommie T... the prick"... having identified the mystery bugler... "Someone ought to shove that horn up his ass!"

The southsiders marched their bound captives to the edge of Little Mountain and passed The Fort which they did not recognize as anything other than a pile of rocks. They shoved the larger of their two captives, the larger captive being Bobby Marinelli, to the ground. They took the smaller captive, Wop James, to the base of Little Mountain and pushed him down on the ground face up.

Anthony said from his perch on Honeysuckle Hill, "What the hell they gonna do now? It don't look good."

Two southsiders held James down staking his arms and legs to the ground. Two other southsiders worked diligently with hammers pounding stakes into the ground around the spread-eagled James. The Wop observers could hear James screaming but they couldn't tell exactly what it was he screamed other than the fact that the scream was of a very high pitch.

There were two huge truck tires laying on the ground at the base of the long slope down the north side of Little Mountain. The tires had been there for years and had been pretty much ignored by the Wops who knew not: 1) how they got there, or 2) why. Our Wop observers were about to surmise the reason for one and know the reason for two.

Billy Club pointed at his spread-eagled brother and yelled, "Shit! See what they're doin' to James? They're tying him down... spread-eagling him. What the hell for?"

There was no reply. Just a lot of heavy breathing as the three Wop observers watched and waited for events to reveal what exactly the southsiders would do to their two captives. As they watched, southsiders pushed both truck tires up the slope of Little Mountain and above the spread-eagled James Warden.

Billy, realizing what the southsiders were about to do, yelled, "Fuck... fuck... fuck!"... an expletive rarely used by any of the braves and thus a much more expressive word than that same word is today, for today the word has been reduced through overuse to a mere conversational spacer more like a vulgar "ya know" than an expression of great emotion.

Billy stood as the southsiders, having pushed the heavy truck tires to the top of the slope on Little Mountain, yelled something down to the south-siders surrounding the spread-eagled James and they scattered away from their spread-eagled captive. From the top of the slope a southsider pushed a truck tire, rolling it down the slope towards the spread-eagled James. As the tire reached the bottom of the slope, it went airborne as it hit a hump of dirt and bounced over the spread-eagled James.

Another southsider pushed the second truck tire down the slope. The truck tire rolled down the slope and went airborne as had the first. However, unlike the first truck tire, this one landed squarely on Wop James' chest. Billy, Anthony and Moe the Frog could hear James' painful, high-pitch scream. They remained silent.

Two of the southsiders grabbed the seated Bobby Marinelli by the arms and held him upright. Tommie T, the southsider who had accompanied events with his trumpet, walked over to Bobby, placed his trumpet to the side of Bobby's head and over his right ear and blasted a long and loud sour note. Bobby screamed bloody murder.

The southsider war party cut the spread-eagled James loose and released Bobby who slumped to the ground. One of the southsider braves yelled something at the two captives... probably something about as close to Christianity as they would come... which the Wop observers at the crest of Honeysuckle Hill couldn't quite understand. Then the war party wandered back along the plain behind Little Mountain and disappeared into the valley beyond the plain and out of sight.

The three Wop scouts scrambled down the Honeysuckle vines and into the valley between the hill and Little Mountain. Billy ran to his brother lying spread-eagled on the ground even though he was no longer tied down. He yelled to his brother, "You okay?"

James labored to breath and started to cry. He whispered between sobs, "My chest hurts... real bad."

Billy helped his brother to his feet who yelped loudly as he arose.

Anthony ran over to his brother and knelt before him, "You okay?"

Bobby looked up and said with a puzzled look, "What?"

Anthony yelled at the top of his lungs, "You okay?"

With an even more puzzled look on his face, Bobby yelled, "What'd ya say?"

The three Wop scouts helped their tortured fellow braves down the valley between Little Mountain and Honeysuckle Hill to Prison Hill Road and slowly helped them up Prison Hill Road ever so slowly and back to the safety of their territory on Colonial Street.

Billy Club formulates his own rule of war: If the enemy is stronger than you, get someone else to beat the crap out of him...

The senior William Mead Warden sat in the living room as was his post-work habit. True there was a beer in his right hand which the senior Warden raised to his lips... a Piels with a fine white foamy head on it. He took a series of long slow swallows of the golden liquid... his Adam's apple bobbing up and down as he did so. Having drained half the glass, he rested it on his knee.

However, instead of his left hand holding cigarette as was usually the case, it held a piece of paper which he raised above his head and yelled, "Know what this is? I'll tell you what it is! It's another god damn bill from the god damn hospital... that's what it is! When the hell did this come?"

He crumpled the piece of paper in the palm of his huge left hand and threw it on the floor. He mumbled to himself in that *I've already drunk a quart of Piels* sort of way, "What's it for anyway? Did Billy clock another nigger kid again?" He paused and finished off his glass of Piels and mumbled yet again, "I'm gonna tan that boy's hide."

Rose stood before the stove in the kitchen frying huge slices of breaded eggplant. Every now and then she'd dip a cooking fork into the pan of frying eggplant, spear one of the slices and flip it over... flipping quickly and efficiently and so skillfully that she did not splatter the bubbling oil as she did so. Without turning she yelled, "I got it for them treating James. He broke ribs."

The old man picked up the pack of Camels, shook it so that a cigarette peeked out of the pack. He put the pack to his lips and pulled out the peeking cigarette with his teeth. With the Camels cigarette bobbing in his lips, he yelled, "When the hell he break his ribs?"

59

Oxbow Lake The 2nd

Rose yelled, "This afternoon. I think some of those Southsider thugs beat him up. Don't know why... I don't think they need a reason. They blew out Bobby's ear drum too with a trumpet. He's deaf in his right ear now. Doctor says his hearing might come back?"

Billy sat silently at the kitchen table doing his homework but listening very carefully to the conversation. He knew that there was no way the Wops could ever challenge the Southsiders to a rumble. There were a lot of them. They were a lot older and bigger. No way the Wops would stand a prayer of beating the crap out of them. He was a realist. Challenging them directly was suicide.

Then an idea struck him and he yelled, "Those Southsiders took James and Bobby to their club house. That's where they beat them up"... obviously telling a tactical lie to further his strategic goal. He let that statement sink in and then said just loud enough to be heard over the frying slices of eggplant, "They beat James up and he had to go to the hospital and they stuck you with the bill."

"God damn right they did, the pricks. Another god damn hospital bill."

Billy smiled to himself and said, again above the sizzling eggplant, "They should pay for what they did. They cost you beaucoup bucks... and all those bucks don't grow on trees. And ya know where their club house is? It's in that hidden valley across from Little Mountain... on prison grounds, that's where... on prison grounds... they oughta pay!"

"God damn right they oughta pay! Those bastards oughta pay for what they did costing me beaucoup bucks."

Believing that the senior William would eventually reach the conclusion which the younger William wanted, the younger William yelled "On prison grounds... that's where!" and continued doing his homework.

The living room went silent... a silence occasionally broken by the clinking of a quart bottle of Piels against a glass... as the senior William seethed with alcohol driven rage.

Three days later, Billy, Bobby Marinelli and his brother Anthony sat on the Marinelli porch. Billy and Anthony were sipping Pepsis. Bobby sat on the far right reading a paperback. Billy, curious to know what so occupied Bobby that he neglected to drink his Pepsi which sat at his side untouched, asked "What you readin'."

"It's a book we read in Miss Kaminski's... The Human Comedy. I pinched it from her class. It's real interesting... about this kid who delivers telegrams during World War 2... telling people their sons been killed... and other stuff like that. Kinda sad."

Up Colonial again charged Moe the Frog towards them. He was yelling something that they couldn't understand. As he got closer, they heard "...and there's a bunch of cons with a screw"... screws being what cons and most of the braves called corrections officers... but not to their face.

Moe the Frog reached the walkway to the Marinelli house, bent over and huffed and puffed until he regained relatively normal breathing and said, "There's a bunch of cons and a screw walking passed Little Mountain. I was smokin' a cig on Honeysuckle when I saw the bastards."

Billy and Anthony continued sipping their Pepsis. Bobby looked up from his paperback.

Then Moe yelled, "And they got shovels and axes and all kinds of tools."

Billy, now realizing what was happening, jumped up and yelled "The old man did it!"

Anthony took his Pepsi from his lips and said a quizzical, "What?"

while Bobby stared blankly at them.

Billy yelled, "They're tearin' down the Southsiders' club house." He rose, drained his Pepsi and threw the empty Pepsi bottle into the flower bed in front of the Marinelli porch. Then he took off and yelled over his shoulder, "I gotta see this!" as he ran down Colonial toward Honeysuckle Hill.

Bobby said, "What'd he say?"

Anthony drained his Pepsi, jumped to his feet and threw the empty bottle into the flower bed as Billy had done. Bobby jumped up and stuffed his paperback into his back pocket. Then the two of them took off after Billy for Honeysuckle Hill trailed by Moe the Frog... Moe knowing why they were running, Anthony not knowing but suspecting and Bobby having no idea at all. They arrived huffing and puffing at the crest of Honeysuckle Hill where Billy stood looking down at a large cloud of dust arising from the distant valley beyond Little Mountain, pumping his fist in the air and yelling, "Take that you bastards!"

THIS PAGE INTENTIONALLY LEFT MOSTLY BLANK

(THE ABOVE VERY LIKELY BEING A MISREPRESENTA-
TION OF OBVIOUS FACT)

IRRELEVANT NOTE FROM THE AUTHOR:

FOR OVER A CENTURY BASEBALL HAS BEEN AS AMERI-
CAN AS APPLE PIE, INCLUDING THAT APPLE PIE'S RAC-
ISM, CHEWING TOBACCO, ALCOHOL AND ILLEGAL
DRUGS... AND HELPING AMERICA REMOVE THESE SOUR
INGREDIENTS FROM AN OTHERWISE SCRUMPTIOUS
APPLE PIE!

Slappin' Ain't Hittin'

Billy Warden crouched in the left-handed batter's box slowly swinging his bat as he stared down his blood rival on the mound, the formidable right-hander, Butchie Moreno. Twilight descended upon the baseball diamond as the two southsiders played out the bottom of the third and most likely the last inning of their grudge match. Gary Reese, taking the formal title of "Umpire" as required by the game's rules, stood safely behind the backstop ready to call balls and strikes, hits and outs. He would be good buddies with one of the rivals after the game, but not both... the name of that buddy yet to be determined.

There were no fielders, no catcher and no other batters, for the rival southsiders weren't playing what they called "a real baseball game." You needed too many players for a real baseball game, so when southsiders couldn't field even a semblance of enough players for a real game, they played a game they called, with much unintended irony, "Pitch, Hit and Yell" although no one involved in any aspect of this game... even those southsiders yelling from the covered stands... were aware of this irony.

It was a simple game that they played often. A pitcher threw a baseball, a batter attempted to hit it and the umpire called balls and strikes from behind the relative safety of the backstop. The umpire was the final arbiter on whether a struck ball was a single, a double, a triple, a homer or an out. The hitter and pitcher yelled what they thought the call should be when the batter struck the ball and the umpire, using criteria set by tradition and prejudice, pointed at the caller he agreed with or yelled his own call. While all ball and strike calls by the umpire were final and uncontestable by rule, both the pitcher and the batter often loudly expressed their disagreement with a call. All other calls were contestable and the umpire sometimes changed his call after a robust discussion punctuated by an occasional wrestling match which the other southsiders rushed from the covered stands to break up after several entertaining minutes of combat.

To simplify the scoring and eliminate the need to keep track of imaginary base runners and at least one source of the endless argument, the southsiders didn't count runs. Rather they counted bases and only the bases obtained by the batter at the plate. Thus a walk and a single were worth one point... a double, two points... a triple, three points and a homer four points. The combatant with the most points won the game after three innings, or two and a half should the home team be ahead after the lead off half of the third inning.

Billy was down five points or bases. He needed any combinations of hits that gave him the five bases or points necessary to send the contest into extra innings. A sixth point secured him the victory. Failure to gain the five or six points insured an ignominious defeat. He had been ahead by a point, but in the top half of the inning, Butchie had hit a double. Billy dutifully contested the hit with a series of well chosen expletives but was overruled by an adamant Umpire Reese. Then Butchie blasted a very long homer to go ahead 21 to 16. Butchie hit the ball so far over the cinder path in center field that even Billy didn't have the nerve to contest it, for had he done so, the southside would have labeled him that most terrible of epithets, a "god damn chicken shit" and no one on the southside, not even a girl, wanted to be labeled a chicken shit, god damned or otherwise.

Billy adjusted his grip on the bat and choked up, leaving a good two inches between his hands to give him better bat control... taking several more practice swings before going into his batting stance. Butchie went into his wind up and threw a fast ball.

Umpire Reese yelled "Steeerike one!" as he pumped his left hand forward for additional emphasis.

Billy turned and sneered at Umpire Reese, took several more practice swings, and set himself for the next pitch. Butchie delivered another fastball and Billy turned on it, hitting a hard grounder which bounced between Butchie's legs narrowly missing the Moreno family jewels as it bounded into center field. Billy yelled "Single up the middle!" Butchie reflexively covered his crotch with his glove as he turned to watch the ball bounce into center field. Umpire Reese pointed at Billy and yelled "Single! Billy down 4... no outs!" Someone from the stands yelled, "Watch it, Butchie... he's squirrelin' you!" meaning in the parlance of the southside that Butchie was in danger of losing his nuts both physically and metaphorically to Billy's batting prowess.

Butchie picked up another ball from the pile of baseballs behind the pitcher's mound, assumed his pitching position on the rubber, rocked and threw a third fastball. Billy smashed a line drive back at Butchie's belly. Butchie reflexively put up his glove and snared the ball before it snared him. Umpire Reese yelled, "One out!" Another voice from the covered stands yelled, "Watch out, Butchie, the squirrel wants to eat yer nuts!"

Butchie placed his right foot against the pitching rubber, rocked and this time threw a curve ball which fooled Billy causing him to hit a dribbler between third and short. Billy yelled "Single in the five-six hole!"

Since it was the last of the third and the game close, situational disputation came into play and Butchie flashed the middle finger of his pitching hand for all to see as he yelled "Fuck no! Ground out!" Umpire Reese, after several moments of deep contemplation, pointed at Billy and yelled "Single to left! Billy down three... 21... 18! One out!"

Billy choked up another inch on the bat, carefully separated his hands on the bat handle several inches to insure even better bat control, took several practice swings and assumed his batting stance in the batter's box. Butchie swirled and threw a fastball which Billy slapped at, sending a slow dribbling grounder to third. Neither Billy nor Butchie yelled anything. Umpire Reese shouted "Two out! Billy still down 3!" Billy was down to his last out.

A deep male voice yelled from the covered stands, "Don't slap at the fuckin' ball. Swing at it."

Billy stepped back from the batter's box, bent over and grabbed some dirt. He stood up and as he rubbed the dirt between his hands, he peered into the covered stands in the direction of the voice. A man sitting in the first row raised what appeared to be a bottle covered with a paper bag to his lips and took a long slug. Billy looked over to Umpire Reese and asked, "Who the fuck is that?"

Umpire Reese answered, "That's King Clancy."

Billy asked "Who the fuck's King Clancy?"

Umpire Reese put his hand over his mouth and whispered, "He used to be a great ball player… best to come out of this dump. Got to Triple A in the Detroit Tiger organization. My dad says the King played a mean third base… could cream the ball, but the bottle got him. Ruined his career. Now he's just a drunk."

The mysterious King Clancy lowered the bottle from his lips and yelled, "Don't choke the damn bat. Makes you slow to the ball. You're killin' your swing. For Christ's sake, swing! Stop wavin' the god damn thing. That's a god damn baseball bat in your hands… not a twirler's baton."

The King's advice pissed Billy off. He stared into the stands and choked up another couple of inches and waved the bat several times before setting himself in the batter's box. Butchie threw a curve which Billy waved at and fouled off.

Umpire Reese yelled "Steeerike one!"

Billy backed off the batter's box, chocked up another inch as he stared into the stands, took several practice swings and set himself in the batter's box. Butchie swirled on the pitcher's mound and delivered his best fast ball.

Billy took a weak swing and sent another slow dribbler towards third base.

Umpire Reese yelled, "Ground out! Three outs! Game over! Butchie wins 21 18!"

Billy threw his bat against the backstop and kicked the dirt, spraying Umpire Reese with a cloud of dust. Umpire Reese smiled and ran to the covered stands where he high-fived Butchie as they entered. Billy slowly walked toward them. Loud jeers from the southside faithful stopped him in his tracks, for the southside faithful were quick to denigrate and loudly, for in so doing they markedly reduced the chances that they themselves would be the targets of denigration.

Billy lowered his head and put his hands of his hips. When he looked up, there before him was a lanky man. His cheeks were sunken but his eyes were bright. It was none other than King Clancy himself, paper bag covered pint bottle in hand, obviously drunk but still standing pretty steady.

"Look, kid, slappin' at the ball ain't no way to hit. Whether you slap or swing, you still gotta see the damn thing and you still gotta make contact with the damn thing, so why not hit it... increase your chances of scoring runs."

Billy, still stung by his humiliating defeat, was in no mood for criticism, positive or otherwise, "Look, Don Mueller's done OK for the Giants slappin' the ball. They don't call him Mandrake the Magician for nothin'. Last year he hit 342. Finished second for the NL batting crown."

"Who finished first?"

"Willie Mays... 345."

"Right, Willie Mays, a real hitter. He could hit and hit for power making him twice the hitter of that fuckin' slapper. Mueller's an insult to the art of hitting." He took another swig from his bottle and shoved it into his back pocket and walked over to the batter's box. He yelled over his shoulder as he picked up the bat which Billy had so recently thrown in disgust, "Throw me a couple of balls. See how it's done."

What Billy saw was red as he jogged out to the pitcher's mound. He thought to himself *No fuckin' drunk's gonna tell me how to hit.* In the fading light, he picked up a baseball and as the King stood in the batter's box adjusting his grip on the bat, Billy threw at him. The King raised the bat and hit the ball harmlessly away before it hit him... with the butt end of the bat... like he was using a pool cue to hit stationary pool balls. The King yelled, "Nice try, asshole. Throw another one."

The southside chatter in the covered stands quieted as all eyes turned to the new contest being waged on the diamond. Someone yelled, "Did you see that. That drunkin' asshole just hit that ball with the end of the bat." Tribal loyalty kicked in and one of the southside faithful yelled "He's a lucky son-of-a-bitch, Billy! Nail the bastard!"

Billy, not really needing much encouragement, picked up another baseball and threw as hard as he could at the King without winding up, hoping to catch him unprepared and plunk the drunk bastard. The King nonchalantly tapped the ball away with the butt end of the bat again and as the ball harmlessly dribbled toward Billy on the pitcher's mound, the King took a couple of practice swings, set himself in the batter's box and yelled, "I like you kid. You got spunk. Can't hit for shit but you got spunk. Throw me a pitch this time."

Billy picked up a ball, went into his windup and threw his best fastball. The King slammed the pitch over the cinder path and beyond the war memorial monuments in the distance. Billy turned and watched the ball land. Someone yelled, "Did you see that. It's gotta be over 400 feet. Damn!"

The King stood in the batter's box and yelled out to Billy, "Throw me another one" which Billy did. This time the King slammed the ball even farther. The southside faithful became silent, awe struck by the two thunderous hits.

The King put the bat on his shoulder and walked out to the mound. "Look, kid, it took just as much skill to tap your two dribblers for outs as it did for me to hit those two balls out to the monuments. Why not hit it to the monuments? It took your buddy two hits to get six bases. Hell, it was going to take you six singles. Too much chance for something bad to happen. Besides, slappin' at the ball ain't hittin'. It's somethin' else… an inferior skill. Anybody can do it."

Billy's awe of King Clancy's two prodigious blasts drowned his anger. The King rested the bat on the ground, leaning it against his thigh. He pulled out his bottle from his back pocket and took another swig. "Look, kid, when you choke up on the bat and leave a space between your hands, you have to grab the bat hard… causes your swing to slow down, ties you up. Steals your power." He shoved the bottle into his back pocket and grabbed the bat, holding it as he would if he were batting. "See, kid, keep your grip loose. Keeps your hands and wrists flexible." He laughed as he said, "You know, kid, grip the bat like you grip your dick when you're taking a piss." He handed Billy the bat and walked along the third base line. He took the bottle from his back pocket, raised it to his lips, lowered it, shook it a couple of times and threw it at the corner post of the fence alongside the baseball field. The bottle shattered as it hit the post squarely and the King continued walking into the darkness.

THIS PAGE INTENTIONALLY LEFT MOSTLY BLANK

(THE ABOVE VERY LIKELY BEING SO OBVIOUS AS TO BE SELF CONTRADICTORY)

IRRELEVANT NOTE FROM THE AUTHOR:

ITALIAN-AMERICANS ARE LIKE ALL AMERICANS... EXCEPT FOR THE ITALIAN PART!

Robert Marinelli's Italian-American Human Comedy

A life's detritus unboxed...

Agita... agita... agita[1] ! Tomorrow is the big birthday party for my youngest grandson Tommie. Unfortunately the site of this birthday party is to be our lanai. Why unfortunate? I had stored a bunch boxes out there... boxes I'd carried, toted, trundled, and moved with us for the previous 15 years... maybe 20... of our nomadic lives... boxes of what I call the detritus of our lives in general and mine in particular.

Detritus is a funny word... kinda scientific and kinda literary... which appeals to me. In fact, it's one of my favorite words. It means now dead formerly living things... pieces and whole... as well as their accumulated fecal matter, shit... in which other living organisms grow and in doing so decompose those dead bodies... pieces and whole... turning all that dead stuff and its shit, fecal matter, into new organic stuff. Well the stuff in those boxes is kinda like that... the detritus of our lives. It's what happens to all our memories and the physical manifestation of those memories... our past.

On this bright warm Florida morning, I pulled one of those boxes from the pile and gently set it down on our long picnic table which would be the center of tomorrow's birthday celebration. I plopped down in front of that box and stared at it, took a long sip of my handy cup of Italian coffee... leaded... I make it every morning in our Kuerig... you know, with those little cups that you put in the coffee maker. I sipped and stared some more at that damn box. I was

---

1   Agita is Goombah Italian, a kind of Italian-American dialect, and means heartburn or indigestion, usually caused by someone else's demands or behavior.

73

determined to get rid of all but the important stuff and had to start somewhere... this box being that somewhere.

Actually the wife Susie had already provided my determination. She also provided the definition of important: stuff that any normal person would judge to be important information about the family... and... anything that could mean money like an unknown insurance policy... she also being the arbiter of all that's normal as in a "normal" person à la Susie.

I suspected she would be the final judge of what was really important as well after I've completed my mission and made all my determinations. Anyways, I was under orders... strict orders... to sort through all those boxes... there were 13 of them... and to get that number of boxes down to a reasonable number... my prescient wife Susie having pre-determined *that* reasonable number of boxes being two... which we would store on one shelf in the garage to rot in the heat there instead rotting in the heat out here.

Fear can be a wonderful motivator... as Sam Johnson once said, "Nothing sharpens a man's mind like the prospect of hanging". I'd tried to do this several times in the past without the wife's fear factor... well actually many times... before every hop in our hop scotch around the Hudson Valley and then this long leap down here to New Caledonia, Florida, over the last two... no make that six... no, at least eleven... years.

My every attempt ended the same way... inaction, depression and an unchanged number of boxes... and then carrying that burden of 13 boxes on our next hop and then that long leap. Now I faced the prospect of a hanging metaphorically speaking. I'd either get down to two boxes or end up with none. The wife was right, I'd have to get rid of this heavy chain that I've carried around my neck. I was worse off than Jacob Morley in Dickens' *A Christmas Carol.* Ole Jacob had

74

to die first to be condemned to carry around his heavy chain of old bad memories. I'd gotten my chain early in the form of 13 boxes of memories... most of which I suspected were bad... and I was still alive. For some reason... and I'm not exactly sure why... I felt compelled to get my chain down to what seemed an easier to carry number like the predetermined two... and not zero. I was a little flummoxed as to why even two were necessary but something whispered inside my head, "Don't throw the detritus of your life away."

So I took another long swig of that Italian coffee... leaded... thrust my fist into that first box and pulled out as many papers as my fist could grab and threw the pile down on the table before me. I sorted through this pile one sheet at a time. At first, it was easier than I thought.. an old phone bill... on the way to the floor, another old phone bill... on the way to the floor, an old water bill... on the way to the floor... the discard pile growing quickly on the floor next to the picnic table. I actually emptied the box and threw it on the pile. I pulled another box from the pile, put it on the picnic table, reached into this second box of my detritus and pulled out an old paperback. Tucked in that old paperback was this report card from Sint Sink High School where I graduated from in New York. It was the report card for my Sophomore year.

The paperback was William Saroyan's *Human Comedy.* We'd read the novel in Miss Kaminski's class. I loved the novel so much I pinched my copy, read it again and again and obviously kept it with my other "valued" detritus. I enjoyed it even more when I read it out of my choice rather than Miss Kaminski's demand... my Italian-American mind having an Italian-American mind of its own... as always.

I put the novel aside on the picnic table... laboring to push my Sisyphean detritus up my own personal hill. Susie poked her head into the lanai and said she was driving over to that big Italian deli in St. Pete's to buy provisions for tomorrow's birthday party... news I welcomed. It meant she'd be gone most of the afternoon which was the good part. The bad part: the time of suffering my prospects of hanging became that much longer.

I worked my way through those boxes and as hard as I tried, I could not get below four boxes. One's flotsam and jetsam is another's detritus, I guess. What to do? What any self-respecting Italian-American would do. Do what you must and lie through your teeth, so I hid two boxes in the attic, put two on the shelf in the garage and stuffed our huge green trash barrel on those silly wheels so that nine boxes of flotsam and jetsam looked like eleven boxes of the stuff... living to fight the battle of the essential detritus another day, hopefully in the very distant future.

I grabbed another cup of Italian coffee... leaded... and entered one of those caffeine fueled moments of reflection sitting back at the picnic table in my lanai. I pulled the report card out from between the pages of Saroyan's novel and read down the list of classes. I was kinda shocked as I had pretty much forgotten about my Sint Sink High School years. I aced chemistry and physics and advanced algebra... and even history. But I got a mediocre 81 in English Lit... my favorite subject taught by my favorite teacher... and my major in college. And where'd I end up? Writing the great American novel? No, no! I ended up in that new fangled profession called programming working for that international tech giant, KTI. Who'd a thunk!

I spent the rest of the afternoon fingering through Saroyan's novel and contemplating my detritus fueled memories of my sophomore year at Sint High School after a fruitful day of surreptitiousness and anticipated prevarication .

OMG, eight-ball, corner pocket...

The mamaluke[2]! My grandsons were feeling their pasta... both of them... and giving me agita... had been for a long time. Tommie, because it was his eighteenth birthday, strutted around the house like a peacock. He couldn't wait to exercise that God-given and most precious of rights, the right to obtain a motor cycle license so he could finally ride his bike legally.

His yet-to-arrive older brother Vinnie, having already celebrated that birthday right, peeled through his world hell-bent for leather riding his own personal crotch rocket, a brand spanking new Yamaha YZF-R1 as he brags. God only knows how he paid for the damn thing... he has no job as far as I can tell. When forced to foot, he strutted around even more confidently than did Tommie since he had more than 365 days of additional practice... each one of those days apparently adding to his sense of omniscient immortality. There was no other way to describe it: the stunod[3] were, in the mirror of their own eyes, hot-shit... and all-knowing, immortal hot-shit at that... hot-shit that didn't need to wear a God damn helmet!

Sometimes I felt like some aliens had taken possession of those grandsons of mine while they babbled in the maternity ward and turned them into alien spawn... you know, like some extra-terrestrials from outer space... like those body snatchers in the movies... leaving us with these two possessed babies. The older the boys got, the more convinced I became. True, they looked like Marinelli, but that was about it. They certainly didn't act like it. Here we were, eighteen years after Tommie's alien possession, gathered at the house to celebrate his passage into what can loosely be described

2 Agita is Goombah Italian, a kind of Italian-American dialect, and means heartburn or indigestion, usually caused by someone else's demands or behavior.
3 Morons

as his manhood. La Familia Marinelli milled about anticipating the celebration, drinking Bud and Chianti… becoming more boisterous by the minute, for the smell of simmering tomato sauce and sizzling meatballs, sausages and other guinea delectables was slowly driving it to culinary madness. The antipasti had just about run out and cries of "More gabbagul[4]!" bounced off the walls. There was still plenty of Bud and Chianti to fuel its passion.

My sister Annette (the younger alien spawn's God Mother) yelled angrily at her latest boyfriend, one Anthony "Big T" Rossi (the reputed son of a mafia crime boss who's rumored to be keeping Jimmy Hoffa company below ground someplace in New Jersey). My son Johnny (one of the alien spawns' many uncles) stood in the doorway to the wife's kitchen staring at the bubbling tomato sauce with his own "Here's Johnnny!" look. Wife Susie (alien spawn Grandmother and Johnny's sainted mother) stirred the sauce with a huge wooden spoon which she lifted from the giant sauce pot from time to time and shook ominously at our hungrily staring son, yelling "Gabish[5]!" at him as she did so.

A bunch of Marinelli… relatives of varying degrees of familia attachment… and several non-Marinelli… friends of various kinds… frantically jostled about my lanai where the long picnic table was set for the meal as the aromas drifting from the wife Susie's kitchen thickened. The din of angry conversation slowly drowned out a loud stereo blasting Dion and the Belmonts… *now listen people what I'm telling you, aaa keep away from-a Runaround Sue*. However, a hungry Italian-American family is an unstable social group, and this particular Italian-American social group was getting hungrier by the minute and thus more unstable by each of those aromatic minutes…

---

4   Gabbagul is Italian slang for capicola, an Italian dried and cured ham cold cut laced with white fat.

5   Understand

78

even the non-Italians, for acting Italian, particularly before meals, is contagious!

The mother of the alien spawn, daughter-in-law Mary Ann, waved to me from Susie's kitchen. I carefully worked my way through the familia mob to her. She whispered, "Where's Vinnie? The antipasti's almost gone. There's no more gabbagul and the natives are getting very restless. We can't eat without Vinnie. Go ask Tommie to call his brother and find out when he plans to bless us with his presence."

I even more carefully worked my way back through the milling un-stable familia mob to Tommie, who sat at the long table where this younger alien spawn's birthday would also be celebrated. I yelled to him above the din, "Tommie, where's ufratu[6] ?"

The younger alien spawn replied, without looking up, "Oo-fra what? Speak English. Quit the guinea talk." I have to admit that I lay the Goombah Italian on a little thick during family gatherings. Partly habit I guess... partly to annoy the little bastards.

Without thinking, I yelled "Buchalla[7]!" waving my open hand at him as I considered whacking him on the back of the head but held back, it being his birthday and all.

He looked up at me and said almost apologetically, "Oh, it's you."

Instead of the buchalla he deserved, I said very politely, "Call ufra-tu... your idiot brother Vincent. Your mother wants to know when he plans to make his grand entrance at the house."

With his ever-present cell phone in hand, he thumbed a couple of keys and yelled, "S-Bat-D!"

---

6   Your brother
7   Italian slang for a dried cod fish used to threaten to spank unruly chil-dren

Oxbow Lake The 2nd

Puzzled, I asked, "S-Bat-D?"

He replied, "My battery's dead. Give me your cell."

Still puzzled, I said, "I get the 'Bat-D' part. What's the 'S' mean?"

"Shit... it means shit." He shoved an open hand at me rapidly opening, closing and opening his palm with his fingers threateningly, and demanded, "Gimme your cell."

I looked down at him, reconsidering my concern for the sacredness of his birthday. After several seconds, I decided yet again not to violate that sacredness, and said, "Shouldn't you be ASKING me for my cell phone... you know, making a request that includes the word 'please'?"

With a look of annoyance, the younger alien spawn replied, "If you want to know where Vinnie is, give me your cell... *please*"... the tone with which he said 'please' turning that polite word into a grievous insult. I regretted my earlier consideration for the sacredness of his birthday.

I waved to the wife, who was still vigilantly stirring away in the kitchen, and yelled, "You got my cell phone?" She disappeared from her kitchen then appeared before me with my cell phone in hand. She gave the cell phone to Tommie, and disappeared yet again, reappearing seconds later before the sauce pot with that weapon, that huge wooden spoon, in hand.

My cell phone? It was my first... turns out one of those fancy ones that the Verizon tech guy recommended. The stunad[8] said it was, and I quote, "PDN", which he then translated to mean "pretty damn neat" and, by the way, on sale with a $50 instant rebate. He kept babbling on about all the neat stuff it could do and quickly lost me in the

---

8   Someone talking bullshit

technical details. I did not lose the part about the sale and the $50 instant rebate and bought the damn thing before the mook[9] could finish his pitch. Paid a total of fifty bucks after getting that instant $50 rebate. They got me with a hefty 24-month contract but all of them do it that way.

Later I learned that the damn cell phone was the favorite of teen agers, particularly teen age girls, because of all its texting capabilities. I used the damn thing to make phone calls. Lo and behold, the stupid phone had one of those hidden slide-out key boards for texting. Tommie pushed open that keyboard like he'd been born with the damn thing growing from the palm of his hand. He tapped several keys and began texting away. His damn thumbs did a tarantella across that keyboard: "V Y-T?"

A reply popped onto my cell phone's screen: "G-Bob?"

Tommie typed . . . no fingered, "No T", initiating the following… What? Conversation?

"Uzg G-Bob cell?"

"Y, WAY?"

"GF KLE"

 "ETA B-Day Prty?"

"NLT 20"

"Broccoli?"

"No Fuzz"

I wasn't sure but thought that I may have witnessed actual communications of some sort and asked, "What'd he say?"

9   A knucklehead

Tommie flashed that damn all-knowing smile of his and said, "Vinnie's at his girlfriend Kellie's house. He'll be here in 20 minutes."

My response, "Are you sure?"

Tommie, a bit petulantly: "Of course I'm sure. He'll be here in 20 minutes... no later."

"What about that broccoli? What's that all about?"

"He hates broccoli and I tease him about it all the time."

I wasn't sure what was more confusing, the text messages or Tommie's explanation which seemed to resemble English, so I asked, "What about that 'fuzz' message?"

"He has a clear shot to the house. No speed traps."

I asked, "How's he know that?"

The reply, "He just does. He'll be here in 20 minutes . . . no later."

I said... asked, "20 minutes?" and got a very bored reply:

"That's exactly what he said. He's at his girlfriend Kellie's house and will be here in no later than 20 minutes. P-A-D... plain as day!"

There it was... the evidence... they spoke in tongues... alien tongues... they texted in tongues... alien tongues... they were possessed... the alien body snatchers possessed them. They were alien spawn!

I waved to his mother in the kitchen who was desperately slicing loaves of Italian bread with a long serrated knife. I raised my hands above my head and made two fists. Then I opened my fists waving all my fingers and thumbs. I quickly repeated the fist-to-fingers-and-thumbs a second time. His mother nodded 'yes' and continued frantically slicing away, piling up slices of Italian bread on the kitchen counter.

The Marinelli familial mob, seeing the pile of slices, jostled its way to the pile, grabbed two slices, one for each hand, and jostled its way passed the stove where it presented the slices to the wife, who ladled a small amount of the bubbling tomato sauce over each slice with that huge wooden spoon. The mob nibbled away at the sauce and bread as it stumbled back to my lanai, disproving the belief held by my Jew friend, Sydney Schwartz, that Italians could not do two things at the same time... doing either thing well not being one of his criteria. Sydney, by the way, pushed into the jostling line like he was born a Marinelli to get his two slices of bread and sauce. We were safe for another 20 minutes.

I spent the *NLT 20* nervously rolling pool balls about my old pool table at the far end of my lanai, watching them bounce over the warped felt table top, as I awaited the grand entrance of one *V* and his *GF KLE*. There was a buzz from the living room and Momma Mary Ann yelled, "They're here!" as the seas parted and Vinnie and his girl friend appeared... my possessed older grandson attired in enough leather to cause grieving in all the damn cattle herds roaming north Florida... his bright red hair hanging down to his ass hole. His GF KLE, however, was not so covered in leather with the possible exception of her feet, for she was shod in purple, knee-high boots which may have been leather. She wore what I call Swiss cheese jeans... jeans full of holes that she most likely paid a pretty penny for... the holes being very expensive additions through subtraction. Her face was obscured by a dark face shield protruding from a helmet covered with a multi-colored psychedelic design. They were quite the couple for eyes to behold.

Without so much as a "hello", my older alien spawn grandson yells,

"Where's the food! I'm starved!" and lo and behold, large platters of spaghetti, cooked a *dente*, appeared on the long picnic table, followed quickly by bowls of tomato sauce, platters of meatballs, sausages, pork ribs, several huge bowls of salad, several piles of sliced Italian bread and many jugs of Chianti.

Grandma Susie yelled, "Mange[10]!" and the birthday feast was on. The familia mob charged the long table and somehow sat itself relatively peacefully... that is without any major injuries (although my brother Anthony did sprain his ankle as he stumbled to win the chair closest to the platter of meatballs)... seating pretty much determined by unwritten rules of familial relationship. Platters were shuffled about, plates filled and the consumption of large amounts of pasta and meat commenced. In one of those puzzling mysteries of Italian-American society, the enthusiastic consumption of food did not reduce the din of the talk, for not only could la familia Marinelli eat and walk... it could also eat and talk, proving to even skeptics like Sydney Schwartz that it could eat and do just about anything.

After finishing off the spaghetti, sauce, meatballs, sausages and pork ribs, the salad bowls were passed around, for good Italian meals always end with bread and salad... Italian bread, of course.

Tommie, having finished his spaghetti and meatballs, stood and yelled, "Where's my birthday cake!"

His Uncle Anthony, the sprained ankle not affecting his appetite, yelled back, "Sit down. Madonn[11]! We're still eating. Let the dust settle." The rest of the family shouted support forcing Tommie to slouch back into his chair with a frown that reached down to his boots, mumbling "K-M-R-A-A[12]" ... whatever the hell that means...

---

10   Eat
11   Holy Mary
12   Kiss my royal American ass

as he did so. A goodly number went back for a second or in some cases a fifth helping, for the salad seemed to fuel their appetite for more. Finally, after another hour of eating, drinking and yelling, the Marinelli familia and friends sat about the table "letting the dust settle" once and for all with only the yelling continuing, for in la familia Marinelli, the dust did not go gently into that good night. Nothing did.

Eventually the platters, plates and other eating utensils of various kinds disappeared from the table. Tommie's storm clouds dissipated, the prospect of cake and gifts spreading a shit-eating grin across that alien spawn face of his. La familia was also in high spirits, high spirits fueled by a meal featuring the wife's tomato sauce, the world's best, and gallons of Bud and Chianti. And now... the cake and coffee!

Momma Mary Ann and Grandma Susie appeared at the entrance to my lanai with a huge birthday cake between them, the mother of the alien spawn holding one end and the grandmother of the alien spawn holding the other. Nineteen candles glowed above a colorful design of an Italian flag on one side of the cake and an American flag on the other... above the flags... the name "Tommie" and below, the words "Happy Birthday". The mob burst into "Happy Birthday", some in English and some in Italian, as the cake was placed before Tommie.

My blowhard grandson blew out the candles with ease as the familial mob ended the birthday song with a crescendo "happy birthday to you!", mostly in English.

Tommie cut himself a huge chunk of cake and started chomping away. Momma Mary Ann gave Tommie a gentle scaffoombaggia[13] and said, "What's wrong with you anyway?" as she picked up the knife and took over the cutting duties making quick work of the job.

---

13   Goombah Italian for a slap at the back of an unruly head

Oxbow Lake The 2nd

There was plenty to go around and lots leftover.

My younger alien spawn of a grandson, having already devoured enough cake to drive a first-grade class into a raucous sugar high, sat before the remnants of his destroyed birthday cake surveying his pile of gifts, which were mostly envelopes. With great ceremony, his alien spawn brother placed a large box before him. Tommie tore open the box and pulled out a black leather motorcycle jacket. It was a very strange jacket as it had no arms. He held it up and shouted "G-D[14]" ... followed by a whole series of additional G-Ds.

His brother shouted above the continuing din, "Look at the back!" and Tommie turned the jacket over and there spelled across the back of the jacket was the phrase "LIVE FREE OR DIE" spelled in white letters above a coiled rattlesnake. In spite of Florida's August heat, Tommie donned the jacket as another huge smile spread across his face. He made quick work of the envelopes and had a substantial pile of cash before him when he finished. My guess... he now had enough saved for a down payment on a new crotch rocket. Having eaten birthday cake, the rest of the familial mob settled in for more coffee, this time spiced with shots of anisette, and some fresh made, crispy pizzelle, courtesy of the wife.

Tommie, however, was in no mood to settle in. He bounced around the table... couldn't sit still... as his restless youth, now fueled by that sugar high, put him into overdrive. He needed action, movement... and so he pointed at me and yelled, "Bob, how's about Vinnie and me against you and Johnny in a little game of eight-ball!"

A challenge had been thrown at me in front of la familia and in a most insulting manner! Imagine... my alien spawn grandson calling me Bob like I was some mook he hung out with. As to my son, their Uncle Johnny... he was reduced to just Johnny... a mere Johnny!

14   God damn

What someone calls you means a lot. When Tommie threw that eight-ball challenge at me and Johnny, he threw it at someone he called "Bob"... that Bob being me, his grandfather and someone named Johnny... that someone being his Uncle Johnny. He must have thought that he and Vincent were our equals and he undoubtedly thought that after handing us a humiliating defeat at eight-ball, both he and his alien spawn brother would be our superiors. They needed to be taught a lesson and real bad.

It was time for a little alien exorcism. Those two mook of mine had to be yanked back to Earth, but first things first. My reply: "Tommie, I am not Bob to you and Vinnie. I am Grandpa Bob... 'G-Bob' if you like. As to your Uncle Johnny, he is your Uncle Johnny. That word 'UNCLE' is very important. Got it?"

Unfazed, Tommie corrected himself without missing a beat, "G-Bob, you and Uncle Johnny against me and Vinnie... a little game of eight-ball."

The field of battle: my old, weathered pool table that took up the back half of my lanai. I knew that table like the back of my hand. The surface along the far rail was a washboard. It was hard to see, but any ball struck with authority along that rail for the far corner pocket, jumped off the table like it was shot from a cannon. I could easily roll a ball into this wash-board zone, but once it was there, there was no way to pocket the shot. Minnesota Fats himself couldn't make that shot.

The boys could shoot pool. I knew that. Vinnie hung out at Corkies, a local sports bar featuring bad food, cheap beer, a bunch of pool tables and a clientele to match. Tommie spent a lot of time there too, undoubtedly giving his counterfeit ID a good workout each night. I suspected that both my dear grandsons were well practiced in the art of eight-ball, so they wouldn't be pushovers. However, they weren't practiced on my table.

I knew son Johnny played sometime for he often went to sports bars to watch the New York Giants since he rarely got them on TV out in Portland. He was pretty good but not on my table. Only I was good on my table.

I glanced over at Johnny, who smiled and said, "OK by me. Let 'er rip!". I don't think he realized the gravity of the challenge. I replied to Tommie, "Your UNCLE Johnny and me would be flattered." I placed special emphasis on the word 'uncle' to drive home the point that son Johnny also held a position above them in the Marinelli familial pecking order of life, which they obviously didn't acknowledge.

Son Johnny and I watched Vinnie as he grabbed the one cue stick still intact from the wall rack. Two others remained racked: one broken about two-thirds from the handle, the sharp end making what was left of the cue stick look like a stabbing spear. The other one had lost its tip when my brother Anthony threw it at the wall after losing a bet to me... last year. I don't think he's played since and over a $20 bet. Go figure. There wasn't a fourth.

Vinnie pointed the only whole cue stick at me as he stared down its length. He yelled over to me, "Don't you have any better sticks than this. There's only one and its warped."

I smiled, "No. We'll have to share that one." It was the same cue stick I'd used to take that 20 bucks from my brother Anthony.

I whispered to Johnny, "You any good at this?"

He whispered back, "I'm OK. I ain't no Minnesota Fats. Not that it matters much. I use a strategy that almost always works."

"Strategy? What's your strategy?"

"I wait until after the football game and my potential opponents have downed a couple of gallons of beer. My strategy: only play drunk opponents, the drunker the opponent, the more successful the strategy. I only shoot against what I call 'wobblers', guys who have trouble standing steady."

"Well that wobbler strategy won't work today. These kids ain't wobbling at the present time."

"True, my wobbler strategy won't work with those two bozo nephews of mine… at least for this game, but we got to get an edge… an insurance policy. They're probably pretty good… cockier than hell. Tommie wouldn't challenge us, particularly the way he did, if he didn't think he and his brother could beat the livin' crap out of us."

"Pride cometh before the fall! Their pride, their fall… not to worry." As the boys high-fived on the far side of the table in celebration of their expected victory, I whispered "Get the eight-ball on the far rail between the side pocket and the far pocket and keep it there. That's our insurance policy."

Johnny looked at the table and then back at me and then back at the table and smiled.

Vinnie, still upset about the cue stick, pointed it at us, stared down its warped length and yelled to me, "G-Bob, this cue stick sucks."

I yelled back, "What, you need perfect conditions to beat your old grandpa and uncle? You two turned chicken shit on me?"

Tommie grabbed the cue stick from Vinnie and said, "We can beat you with broom sticks. We'll take the solids. You get the striped."

As I racked the balls, I asked Tommie, "So you think you can beat us?"

Tommie smiled, "You bet. You ain't got a chance in hell."

"You're pretty confident. Exactly how confident? Maybe twenty bucks worth of confident?"

Vinnie grabbed Tommie and whispered in his ear, smiling like he'd belled the cat.

Tommie smiled back as he listened and said, "Make it a hundred old man and you're on? We'll even let you break."

I hesitated and said, "A hundred? That's a lot of money?"

Vinnie chimed in, "Look, Bob... err G-Bob, are you in or out? You're the one who suggested a bet."

I took the cue stick from Tommie and said, "Well, OK, but it's a lot of money to bet". I quickly pulled two fifties from my wallet and slammed them down on the rail.

Tommie took his birthday stash from his back pocket and covered my two fifties with five twenties. The battle was joined as the Marinelli mob and friends surrounded the table.

I slammed the cue ball into the rack and sprayed balls all over the table, pocketing one solid, the two-ball. On my next shot, I hit the three-ball and banked it into the eight so that the eight-ball came to rest in the washboard about a foot and a half from the far corner pocket. The rest of the balls were scattered all over the table. I had my insurance policy.

Tommie laughed out loud, "Hey G-Bob, that was the dumbest shot I've ever seen. You missed an easy shot... the seven-ball. I'm up!" He methodically pocketed three solids and a striped as well, scratching on his third shot. He smiled and said, "You're up… Johnny" an intentional and obvious 'mistake' followed by a slow correction, "I mean Uncle… Johnny."

Johnny studied the table. There wasn't much there for him to shoot. His best move was to tap a solid and not disturb the eight-ball, which he did. His most successful shot: an expertly stroked non-shot.

Vinnie could hardly contain himself as he surveyed the table. He had an open table and several easy shots before him. He quickly pocketed three stripes. The last striped was a nice bank shot. He banked his next shot, pocketed that last striped ball and did so in such a way that the cue-ball gave him a clear shot at the eight-ball. He could hardly contain himself. He was already spending his half of my 100 bucks.

Tommie yelled in alien tongues, "G-F-I… U-R-T-M!"[15] and Vinnie slammed that cue-ball into the eight. The eight hit the lump in the felt before the far corner pocket, and flew off the table.

Tommie screeched, "O-M-G!"[16]

Vinnie ran over to the far corner of the table and rubbed his hand along the felt, "The game was rigged! You scammed us…"

I interrupted him, "Did I hide the table? No! We didn't scam you. You were scammed by your own self-centered arrogance… both of you. Who beat you? Uncle Johnny and G-Bob did, that's who! That's G-B-O-B to you!"

The Marinelli mob and friends howled with laughter as I picked up the two fifties and five twenties, folded the wad and pushed it into my shirt pocket. I raised my hands in victory and yelled, "Mannag-

---

15   Go for it, you're the man
16   Oh my God

gia alien spawn!"[17]

Louie Zerrelli versus the world...

Louie Zerrelli, my father-in-law, is a lot tougher than he looks. At first glance, he appears to be a pushover, but he's a guinea to the depths of that guinea soul of his. Little things like reality rarely get in his way. I sat at his kitchen table waiting for him to finish his Thursday chore... taking out the trash... so that I could drive him to his doctor's appointment. The chore was apparently very complex... complex beyond explanation to someone such as yours truly, namely me... what with blue bins and green bins and trash barrels and all sorts of recycling procedures that had to be done just so. I figured 'screw it', let the old man take out the trash if it makes him happy... well maybe 'happy' isn't the right word. At least it'll give him a purpose, the old mook.

As he puttered about the apartment gathering up his complex trash in a single, small trash bag, he kept mumbling to himself. It was like I wasn't there... hell, sometimes it was like he wasn't there either, at least all there: "Some fuckin' life! Work for 50 years and end up in this rat hole... living with a bunch of wet backs, god damn spics... stunod... who don't even speak English. I gotta get the hell outta here." He complained about the 'god damn spics', as he so poetically put it, all the time now.

He'd been living in the 'rat hole', his federally-subsidized, low-income apartment, for seven years. Actually, the place wasn't all that bad... small kitchenette, living room and bedroom with a bathroom, all set up for the elderly with all those hand rails and other stuff for old people. It even had a safety pull chain to get help should he fall

---

17   Curse alien spawn!

in the bath tub. The damn place was designed for the elderly which he most certainly was… and getting more so every year. He'd be 85 in January.

At first, he seemed satisfied with his little apartment when we moved him down here. Well maybe 'satisfied' is too strong a word. Maybe 'not pissed off' would be a better description. Anyway, he was not far from his two sons Louie 2 and Tony 2 and their families. And his "obedient" daughter, my darling wife Susie and me only an hour's drive away. It was Florida… Port Good Hope, Florida (as it turns out, a wonderful place for people not named Louie to spend their golden years). There would be no more freezing cold, no more snow, no more ice, no more of that spring slush, and no more state income tax. Good riddance to Albany, New York, dirty slush capital of the world. Like I said, things seemed OK for a while… until it became apparent to him that his evil daughter and her mook husband had stuck him in this rat hole to live with a bunch of God damn spics who couldn't even speak English!

His anger-driven dissatisfaction didn't happen all at once, but rather grew one death at a time. As the older residents, many of whom had become his friends, slowly died off, they were replaced by much younger residents who for some reason now qualified for the federally-subsidized, low-income housing for the elderly even though they weren't very elderly, at least compared to him. Most were Hispanics… many of them speaking broken English with a thick accent. Ironically, even if they spoke the King's English, Louie wouldn't understand them since his hearing was so bad. As the years of attrition passed, Louie got more and more pissed off.

When he had arrived those seven very long years ago, the first order of business… actually the second, the first being moving him into the rat hole… was getting him his primary care physician, which

93

turned out to be one Dr. Anil Ishwari. It took some doing since Louie, like me, was on Medicare... a lot of the doctors weren't taking new patients, particularly Medicare patients. Louie was a Korean War vet and thus qualified for veterans medical benefits, which he also used. But he needed that primary care physician and he wanted an Italian. Susie and I sat with him for hours reading through the yellow pages, going down the list of physicians. We called every damn doctor with an Italian-sounding name in Port Good Hope and then several of the neighboring towns... and there were a bunch of them... but none were taking on new patients. None!

We broadened our search to the Indian sub-continent and finally found Dr. Ishwari. It was pretty clear that he wasn't Italian. Unfortunately, he was listed as 'Ishwari, Anil' in the yellow pages which Louie read without his glasses as Dr. Ishwari Anil, skipping that nasty little comma in the middle, going directly to the Anil and misinterpreting the name Anil, which he'd never seen before, into the word 'anal', which he had. Thus, in that sound-deprived, addled, guinea mind of his, that new primary care physician of his became Dr. Ishwari Anal... which he shortened into Dr. Anal and so it was ever after. He referred to his new primary care physician as Dr. Anal, he wrote Dr. Anal on his calendar, he called him Dr. Anal when he spoke about him and he even called him Dr. Anal when he addressed the good doctor in person... much to that good doctor's consternation. After Louie completed his Thursday chore, we were off to Dr. Anal!

With the first part of this intellectually challenging, trash-collection chore completed... that of gathering his complex trash... Louie grabbed his cane and, with his precious single and very small trash bag in one hand and his cane in the other, he shuffled to his front door... scuffle-thump, scuffle-thump, scuffle-thump... to complete the second and final phase of the task... depositing the single and very small bag of trash in the collection bin behind the elevator on the first floor. I jumped up and opened the door for him. He stared at the outside of his door for a minute and then yelled, "What the fuck's this!" for there, taped to his door, below his red and green 'Merry Christmas' sign, was an official looking notice of some sort with a large red 'IMPORTANT' plastered across the top. He looked at the notice and mumbled yet again, "What the fuck's this?"

He dropped the trash bag and tore the notice from the door. He read it aloud to himself, "To All Residents... Please remove all decorations from your door by no later than noon tomorrow. Door decorations violate Federal Housing Regulation..." His voice trailed off as his face reddened with anger. "On Christmas fuckin' eve, I have to remove my Christmas decorations... on Christmas fuckin' eve?" He crumbled up the notice and threw it into the hallway. "Now I can't celebrate Christmas? Who the fuck wrote this regulation?" He wacked the crumbled federal order with his cane, sending it skidding down the hall's tiled floor.

I watched him as he picked up his trash bag and limped down the hall... scuffle- thump, scuffle-thump, scuffle-thump... to the elevator, shuffling along with his cane rhythmically tapping on the hard tile floor. When he reached the elevator, he pushed the down button, waited for all of 30 seconds, threw his trash bag against the elevator's door and scuffle-thumped back toward me, chugging like the little engine who could. When he reached the crumbled federal order on the floor, he gave it another whack with his cane sending it skidding up the hallway passed me as I stood at his door. To hear him tell it, most days were 'not his day', but today had the makings of being particularly 'not his day'. As he pushed by me back into his apartment, he mumbled, "Some fuckin' golden years!"

He scuffle-thumped over to his phone, plopped into his favorite chair… had to be his favorite since it was his only chair in the living room… and dialed what I later learned was the apartment building's office on the first floor. He mumbled to himself, "I gotta get a haircut tomorrow for Christmas."

The phone he was calling must have only rung once, and before anyone could answer, he quickly hung up. Then he dialed the same number again and waited for someone to answer. He always dialed twice, hanging up the first time, that first time being his test to make sure that the phone system was working. He didn't want to waste any time on the phone if the system wasn't working. To ole Louie, phones were mysterious and expensive. Once he was sure that the system was working, he dialed again, this time in earnest.

He didn't trust technology, even old established technology like telephones of the land-line variety. He often told me of the old times when his family didn't have a phone… almost no one had a phone back then. In guinea gulch, where Louie's family lived, the Gregorios did… that is, they had a phone. They lived two houses down and you could use their phone for a nickel. Old man Gregorio would even take messages for you if someone called you, again for a nickel a message.

Hell, Louie often spoke of life before television, a time when there was only radio. A lot of technology had happened since… none of which he understood or trusted. Susie had given him a cell phone last Christmas… one of those cell phones designed for old people… you know, with extra big buttons and pre-programmed to make calling someone easy. The entire cell phone thing blew his mind. How could you make phone calls with such a device? There were no wires. I understood his reluctance to use cell phones. I had one and it was always mysteriously dropping calls. To prevent losing his cell phone, he kept it stored in his kitchen closet. To preserve the batteries and reduce the electricity he had to use to charge the batteries… and thus pay for, he kept it turned off… pretty much eliminating his receiving any calls on that mysterious device.

Susie had protested both these practices vehemently. One day she "dialed" him on his cell phone three times and got no answer, so she dialed him on his land-line and still got no answer. She was worried sick about him. She called brothers Louie 2 and Tony 2 and got their voice mails. Fearing the worst, we drove down to his apartment, arriving in record time, ran up three flights of stairs (the elevator was out of order), and pounded on his door. We could hear his television blasting away. She pounded again and yelled, "Dad, you OK!" She got no response and hurriedly opened the door with her spare key. There he was, sitting in his favorite and only living room chair, watching television.

We ran into his apartment unnoticed. He finally looked up and yelled, "What the hell are you doing here?"

Susie ran over to him, "You okay?"

He waved at her and yelled, "Get out of the way. A-Rod's up. Yanks down by one… Gardner stole second… two outs… three-two count… bottom of the ninth." The old bastard managed to keep everything about the Yankees straight although the rest of his life seemed to pretty much escape him.

The Yankee announcer yelled, "It's long… it's far… see yah!" Louie swung his fist into the air and yelled, "Fuck the Red Sox…. Fuck the Red Sox!"

Susie grabbed the remote from the end table and turned off the TV. She yelled at him, "Dad, where's your cell phone?"

He yelled "Why'd you turn the game off?"

Oxbow Lake The 2nd

This time, Susie screamed at him, "Where's your damn cell phone?"

He yelled back, "How the hell should I know? In the kitchen cabinet over the ice box, I think. Why?"

I retrieved it and gave it to Susie who waved it at him. "You've got to keep it with you at all times and keep it turned on." She turned it on and handed it to him. He turned it off.

She calmed down and merely yelled, "If you keep the cell phone turned off, no one can call you." His retort, "I'm saving on electricity. You know, electricity ain't cheap. I don't have to keep it on all the time. I'll turn it on when I need it. Then it doesn't have to be plugged into my electricity and charged. If I need to make a call, I can use my real phone." He always referred to his land-line as his real phone. Unassailable logic in Louie World! As a result of Susie's demand, he religiously carried his cell phone with him no matter where he went... always turned off.

Someone answered the phone he'd dialed a second time and he yelled, "Chantelle... that you?" followed quickly by, "Why the hell do I have to take my Christmas decoration down from my door? First you raise my rent and now you tell me I can't celebrate Christmas!" Apparently he was talking to one of the building's administrators. Another pause, "Federal regulations my ass?" Another pause, "Fire hazard? When's the last time you had a door fire in this rat hole from a 'Merry Christmas' sign? And I'm protesting your raising my rent again... this time officially!" Then he slammed down the phone. He mumbled to himself, "Someone's always tryin' to tell me what to do."

It was off to Dr. Ishwari's. At the elevator door, I picked up Louie's single and small bag of complex trash and when we got to the first floor, threw it into the trash bin behind the elevator. Louie paid no attention for he remained preoccupied with the indignity of having the people who raised his rent now demand that he take down his 'Merry Christmas' sign, which, by the way, was his only holiday decoration.

Dr. Ishwari's office was only four or five blocks away so we were there in no time. Louie scuffle-thumped into the good doctor's office straight to the receptionist's window and said, "Angela, where's Dr. Anal?"

The receptionist smiled and said, "Louis, it's so good to see you. Dr. Anal will be with you in several minutes. Please have a seat." The receptionist, one Angela Garcia, had given up correcting Louie when he referred to Dr. Ishwari as Dr. Anal and must have decided it was easier to just go along with it, for not going along with it led to a long, loud and confusing conversation which only made Louie angry. While everybody else went to Dr. Ishwari, Louie went to Dr. Anal and that was that!

Louie took a seat, mumbling the whole time about having to re-move his Christmas decorations from his door and how he planned to officially protest the raise in his rent. I interrupted his mumbling and asked, "Why the appointment?" Louie doesn't realize it but he actually reads lips, so sometimes when he's close to you and can see your lips as you speak, you don't have to yell.

However, even though you don't have to yell at him in these cir-cumstances, he still feels compelled to yell at you, which he did, "It hurts when I piss and I feel like I have to piss all the time. My dick hurts! Sometimes my balls hurt too!" The lady in the chair next to him moved several chairs away.

Finally, we get called into one of Dr. Ishwari's examination rooms.

Dr. Ishwari is already there and greets Louie with a "Mr. Zerrelli, how are you being today?" in that Indian accent of his.

Louie yells, "What'd you say?" He turns to me and says, "I never understand what Dr. Anal says to me. He doesn't speak English very good." He turns back to the good doctor and yells, "What'd you say, Dr. Anal?"

Dr. Ishwari yells, "Hello, Mr. Zerrelli. How are you being today!"

Louie yells back, "Look Dr. Anal, if I were being okay today, I wouldn't be here!"

The good doctor replies, "Mr. Zerrelli, I am not being a proctologist. I am being a GP doctor." Dr. Ishwari apparently did not follow his receptionist's strategy regarding his name. Maybe it was more difficult for him since it was he who Louie called Dr. Anal… it was his anal in question so to speak.

Louie turns back to me and yells, "Did he call himself a protectionist?"

I wave at Louie and yell back, "No. He said 'proctologist'… not 'protectionist'. He said he's not a proctologist. He's a general practitioner!"

A puzzled look appeared on Louie's face, quickly replaced with an angry one, "I don't want him to practice on me. I want him to know what the fuck he's doing. Let him practice on the god damn spics."

Further explanation would obviously only make things worse, so I sat Louie down on the examination table and said to Dr. Ishwari that Louie had difficulty urinating and that when he did so, it was painful.

Dr. Ishwari's very loud difficulty communicating with Louie… perhaps miscommunicating is a better word... wasn't new. Two years ago, the good doctor just got tired of yelling at Louie. Seems that every year he had to yell louder to get Louie to misunderstand him until the good doctor was literally screaming, so he attempted preventative action and sent Louie to an audiologist to get his hearing evaluated... an effort that had obviously failed.

 Anyway, it was me who took Louie to the audiologist at Dr. Ishwari's request. The audiologist tested Louie and found that he had lost 50% of his hearing in his left ear and 30% in his right. Louie was, as they say, deaf in one ear and couldn't hear in the other, and that was two years ago. It's a good bet his hearing hadn't improved with age. The audiologist recommended that Louie get a set of hearing aids.

Then we ran head on into another of Louie's technological fears: his fear of hearing aids, for Louie was convinced that the government used hearing aids to brainwash people and control them! No way was he going to allow big brother to whisper sweet nothings in either of his ears. I sympathized with Louie's fear of big brother but less irrationally.

The good doctor yelled to Louie, "I must be checking your prostate."

Louie yelled back, "Damn right I'm protesting. They're raising my rent. Why are you checking my protest?"

The good doctor yelled, "You must be lowering your pants and bend over the examination table."

Louie, who didn't trust anyone, particularly a doctor, yelled back, "Why the hell do I have to lower my pants because I'm protesting my rent? Are you going to whack my ass to punish me because I'm protesting? Conspiring with the Federal Housing Authority? Did that government Mafioso bitch get you to do this?"... that govern-

101

ment Mafioso bitch being Chantelle, the administrator for his apartment building who he'd called earlier. He slid to his feet, grabbed his cane, shook it threateningly at the good doctor and yelled, "You stay the hell away from my ass. Chantelle and the Federal Housing Authority can go fuck themselves and you can too."

The receptionist Angela Garcia must have heard Louie threaten the doctor, for she burst into the room with a pad on which she'd written in large block letters "DR ANAL WANTS TO CHECK YOUR PROSTATE."

Louie read the note and said, "Well why the hell didn't he just say so?" as he turned, dropped his pants and shorts and bent over the examination table.

I gently removed his cane from his grasp and leaned it against the wall beyond his reach. Then Angela and I demurely excused ourselves... she to her desk and me to a chair in the reception room. It was now up to our two protagonists to work out the particulars of the prostate exam in the privacy of the examination room. I sat there listening to them yell at each other for the better part of an hour wondering what was in store for me. Here I was, a seventy-year old man taking care of an eighty-four year old man. Was I living a nightmare and witnessing my Christmas future like some god damn Italian-American Scrooge?

My turn in the medical barrel...

How ironic... two weeks after taking my father-in-law Louie Zerrelli to his appointment with Dr. Anal, it was now my turn to be subjected to the much vaunted medical care system of the U-S of A. Nothing teaches you what it's like to be in the barrel than... well..

being in the barrel. Apologies to Louie!

I sat in the waiting room of the clinic… doing what the fuck you do in a waiting room… namely wait. Waiting always pisses me off and waiting after some twinkie gives you a verbal going over for being a mysterious 50 minutes late really pisses me off:

"Mr. Marinelli, you are late for your appointment. Your appointment was for 9:00 and it's 9:20. "

"What, a lousy 20 minutes?"

"Well, actually, you're 50 minutes late and that's almost an hour. We request that you arrive 30 minutes before your appointment."

"Then why didn't you make the appointment for 8:30 instead of using this mysterious 30-minute late rule to gig me."

"Sir, it's our process. We request that all patients arrive 30-minutes before their scheduled appointment."

"Look, I'd a even beat that mysterious 30-minute rule but for all the construction and all the detours in this so-called medical complex. It's complex all right… so complex it'd a made Christopher Columbus break out in a sweat! I found a cancer clinic, a heart clinic… hell, I even found a maternity clinic. Unfortunately I don't have cancer, I don't have heart problems and I'm not pregnant. If I had a cancerous heart caused by pregnancy, I'd a had my choice of clinics and been on time… even with that mysterious god damn 30-minute gig rule. All those temporary signs you guys put up pointed to a 'clinic' but they didn't say what kind of clinic. They all had names of people not names of kind."

"I'm sorry that you had difficulty finding us. Next time, please allow for sufficient travel time to arrive 30-minutes before your scheduled appointment."

"Why? Is there some kind of minimum wait requirement in order to see a doctor… a minimum of say 30 minutes. This is my third physical here and the other two times I had to wait almost an hour. If I got here 30 minutes before my appointment, I'd have waited an hour and a half. I don't remember this mysterious 30-minute rule."

"Mr. Marinelli, we instituted the rule earlier this year and we have the rule for a reason."

"What's the reason?"

"Efficiency."

"Hold it! Who's efficiency?"

"Why the clinic's, sir."

"So it's for your efficiency. Are you paying me?"

"No sir, you must pay us."

"So I must pay you so that I can wait so that you can have a more efficient operation and make more money."

"Sir, that's not how we view the process."

"Apparently."

"Please take a seat. When your name is called, proceed to Station 2 to fill out an appointment registration form and pick up your medical folder." That medical folder business confused me since I had my folder with me. Dr. Shelton gave it to me after my physical last year. I thought I was to keep the damn thing.

Anyway, I felt like I was about to blow a gasket. If I did, I'd probably be at the wrong clinic for blown gaskets and if I ever found the right one, there'd be that mysterious 30-minute wait rule before my blown gasket could be treated. I thought to myself 'Thank God I have lots of life insurance.'

My friendly repartee continued: "Lady, why can't I fill out that registration form now. Isn't that what that mysterious 30-minute rule is for?"

"Mr. Marinelli, please have a seat. Others are waiting to be signed in." Sure enough, there were… a whole bunch just waiting in line behind me… waiting to be told to sit down and wait after their punctuality had been thoroughly vetted by little Miss Twinkie, medical gatekeeper extraordinaire.

First, they make it almost impossible to find the god damn place. Then when you wander across the damn place, you get yelled at for being late and then you find out you're actually an extra 30 minutes late. Then you wait for some more abuse. You never know what to do to end the waiting… or better yet, not wait at all. It's like a prison sentence that lasts a mysterious amount of time, set by some person you don't know who never tells you. You sign a sheet of paper and then someone who doesn't know you from Adam says "Please take a seat and we'll call you" and you take a seat and wait some more after they lay into you and piss you off for being late, and after you've suffered through their torturous process, you pay them for the privilege.

The place not only pissed me off, it gave me the creeps. I think that it is somehow affiliated with the University of West Coastal Florida, Jihad University to those in the know… a fact that I do not find comforting. They don't call it Jihad University for no reason. The place is full of A-rabs, a number of whom support terrorism in one way or another. There was that one professor Allie something-or-other that finally got nailed by the Feds for running a charity that collected money to kill people they didn't like. Fortunately, Allie's buddies didn't like Israelis more than they didn't like us, so for the moment, we were safe from Allie's terrorist buddies. I did not find this comforting. This was the outfit that was going to give me a physical, their third whack at my body since we moved to Caledonia... well not really Caledonia, more north of Caledonia... New Caledonia.

Gatekeeper Twinkie yelled "Mr. Marinelli, please proceed to Checkpoint 2. Just follow the yellow footprints."

Being an old hand at their so-called process and in spite of my lack of knowledge concerning that mysterious 30 minutes, I did not follow the yellow footprints on the floor, which took you the long way around. I went directly to Station 2 where another receptionist said to me, "Please take a seat. I'll be with you in a minute."

I asked, "Did I just spend 45 minutes waiting in the 'waiting room' at what I presume is Station 1 to come here to wait again? What was that other 'wait'? Practice? I don't need the practice. I've been practicing waiting for 70 years."

This gal was not a pretty young thing like the other one. I was sure this babe could beat the snot out of me with one arm while drinking a mug of beer with the other. She looked at me with that stern Nurse Ratchette stare and said, "I'm sorry that you feel that way. We are very proud of our excellent customer service. Every year our patients give us excellent ratings."

I thought to myself, *If you do those customer sat interviews, I don't wonder. One of those death stares of yours would freeze Superman faster than a chunk of kryptonite.* She continued, "We are having difficulty locating your medical folder."

I still had my folder from last year tucked under my arm. Thankfully, Nurse Ratchette did not notice as she was preoccupied with the pile of folders on her desk. Her biceps bulged rippling a tattoo of a fire-spitting dragon as she angrily filed through the pile making me very reluctant to bring this fact to her attention. She said, "I'm sorry Mr. Marinelli but you'll have to wait until we locate your folder." Talk about the horns of a dilemma! The very thought made my hemorrhoids ache!

I was in for an infinite wait unless I turned over that folder. And if I turned the damn thing over to Nurse Ratchette, I'd probably get beaten severely about the head and shoulders. The only positive: I was already at a medical center and had waited more than the proscribed 30 minutes necessary to be subjected to their process.

As I contemplated my next move very carefully, a miracle occurred. Nurse Ratchette excused herself and I was left alone at her desk. I quickly placed my folder in the pile of folders on her desk and meekly took a seat in the Tier 2 waiting area, having already served my time in the Tier 1 waiting room.

Nurse Ratchette returned to her desk shaking her head in obvious frustration and disgust. She mumbled to herself, "The process is designed to prevent this from occurring"... the ambiguous 'this' apparently being my lost medical folder. She plopped down into her desk chair and mumbled again "one more pass through..." and her voice faded as she carefully picked up each folder, read the name on the folder and placed it off to the side of her desk. She then mouthed the words, "Marinelli comma Robert.... here's the sucker... how could I have missed it?"

She opened the folder, read from a checklist on the back of the front cover and said, "That's odd... no check for Checkpoint 4." She looked up at me with her death stare and said in the voice of the grand inquisitor, "Mr. Marinelli did you complete the process last year and return your folder to Station 4 after your physical?"

107

I about shit my pants. I thought to myself *You shoulda wore your mouth piece to protect what's left of those pearly whites from ole Nurse Ratchette here when she goes to the head after working the body.*

I said rather meekly, "Well as far as I can remember…" (one of the advantages of being old is that you can play the 'I don't remember' card and people will cut you some slack). Unfortunately, the Ratchette wasn't one of them. She said to me quite sternly, "Did you process through Station 4 after your physical last year? Did you or didn't you? Yes or no!"

Now I'm not one for lying… unless, of course, it's absolutely necessary. The present situation involved my physical well being and thus fell well within this category, so I replied, "Yes, I remember now, I handed that folder to someone else." I had to be ambiguous since I had no idea about that mysterious Station 4. All I remember was that Dr. Shelton gave me the folder and left. I thought the damn thing was for me.

I liked Dr. Shelton. He was in his sixties and suffered many of the same ailments that plagued me. My elbow and shoulder and even my back were arthritic and hurt all the time. He had a tennis elbow which bothered him. He took that joint stuff with glucosamine and chondroitin too. My doctor up in New York, Dr. Hernandez, had said there was no evidence that the stuff worked and that I was wasting my money, but I creatively misunderstood him and persisted.

One of the reasons I chose Dr. Hernandez was because he was a Philipino and spoke with a strong accent. Thus by creatively interpreting his recommendations, I could choose which to follow… which to ignore. And when necessary, I could reinterpret what he said so that I could do pretty much what I liked. Beer, beef and a good cigar... here I come!

Anyways, taking the glucosamine and chondroitin pills lessened the pain and my joints moved more freely although they still bothered me. Dr. Shelton said, and I quote, "If taking that stuff makes you feel better, screw the research and keep taking it. In fact, double the dosage!" I did as instructed and got full range of motion of my right shoulder pretty much back... and with less pain. I did not want to get such a brilliant clinician in trouble with the formidable Nurse Ratchette for his lack of directions regarding Station 4 and so I fled to ambiguity for his sake... and, given the circumstances, mine.

Nurse Ratchette mumbled, "Hmmmph!" to herself, gave me the folder and said fill out the first sheet in the folder and proceed to Station 3, Examination Room 4" both of which I did, but this time following a bunch of stupid yellow footprints to Station 3 and then with a little luck, I bumped into Examination Room 4... the fourth examination room in Station 3... which I entered. Who says I can't follow instructions!

After yet another wait, a young woman entered the examination room. She was a knockout... athletic body with an ass that wouldn't quit. I gave her the folder which she opened and perused. She bit her lip, handed me a medical gown and said, "Please remove your clothes and put on this gown... the open end in the back". Then she turned and left. As I changed into the medical gown, I thought to myself, *Miss Nubile Nurse could arouse the dead and she just might work her magic on me!* for while I wasn't quite dead, I evidenced at least several of the symptoms of those who were if you catch my meaning.

Miss Nubile Nurse returned and asked me to step on the scales. She measured my height and weight and recorded the results in my folder. I modestly held the back of the gown closed as I went through the process.

She said, "Please have a seat. I need to take your temperature, heart rate and blood pressure." I complied and she did her thing, again recording the results in my medical folder.

I asked, "When will Dr. Shelton show up? How is he, anyway?"

Miss Nubile Nurse continued writing in my folder and without looking up said, "Oh, Dr. Shelton? He left us last year. He's in private practice now."

The conversation continued: "Who will give me my physical?"

Miss Nubile Nurse replied, "Why I will. I apologize. I'm Dr. Andrews. I'll be your doctor at least for this exam."

Then it dawned on me. Hit me like a ton of bricks. I knew what was next. I had written in that stupid folder that I had difficulty pissing… probably caught it from hanging around my father-in-law, ole 'some piss and lots of vinegar' Louie Zerrelli. I was about to get a prostate exam. And that Nubile Nurse wasn't a nurse at all. She was nubile all right but a nubile doctor and she was about to shove a couple of fingers up my ass. No woman had shoved fingers up my ass in years and the last one to do so was a member of a Las Vegas profession all right, but not a medical one in the strictest meaning of the word 'medical'.

Miss Nubile Doctor said, "Please bend over the examination table. I need to check your prostate."

There it was! I panicked, "Maim… rather Doctor… no offense but I'm 70 years old and I've only taken my clothes off… you know… gotten naked before a woman for one reason and this ain't the reason. Could I have my prostate checked by a male doctor?"

She smiled at me and said, "I understand. Many of our older male

110

patients have never been examined by a female doctor and request a male doctor. Dr. Humperdinck will be in shortly to continue your physical."

I was relieved but not completely, "Doctor, when this Doctor Humperdinck gives me that prostate exam, could you excuse yourself from the room? No offense, but… "

Before I could finish my statement, she interrupted me, "Mr. Marinelli, I understand. Like I said, many of our older patients feel this way. The medical profession has changed over the years and some of our older patients have not adjusted to those changes."

I thought to myself, 'Shit, if I were 25, the situation would be a lot worse. Hell, I'd a had a steel hard-on the second she appeared in the examination room. That'd a made things interesting.' She smiled that comely smile of hers, offered me her hand, which I shook, and she turned to leave the room. When she did so, I had second thoughts about her not giving me that prostate exam. That's the last time I saw her. I wondered what she'd write in that folder of mine... probably in giant red letters 'MODEST DIRTY OLD MAN!'

I sat my bare ass down on that cold plastic examination room chair and awaited the arrival of one Dr. Humperdinck. There I was waiting again, this time with a cold ass.

Finally Dr. Humperdinck stormed into the room. I immediately noticed three things about him: one, he had an appropriate last name; two, he packed a lot of pounds on a very short frame, and three, he was very pissed off. I thought *My request for a male doctor must have interrupted his third lunch.*

Without an introduction of any sort, he got right to the crux of the matter, "Bend over the examination table" which I did and as I did so, my gown parted exposing my now very cold ass to the bastard.

111

I watched him over my shoulder as he put on a pair of latex gloves. He took a tube of lubricant and squished some onto my asshole. Then he shoved what felt like his entire fist up my ass.

I yelled, "Whoa, Doc. Two fingers. That's a two finger asshole... at most."

He paid no attention to me and pushed what felt like his fist around the inside of my ass. I thought that I'd piss. Fortunately, I did not.

He said in a flat unemotional tone, "You have hemorrhoids."

I yelled, "Do tell!"

He smiled the smile of a fuckin' SS sadist, withdrew his fist from my ass and handed me a paper towel to wipe myself clean of all that lubricant. I kept mumbling to myself over and over, "Thank God for petroleum jelly!" Whoever invented the stuff ought to be made a Saint!"

Dr. Fist-First Humperdinck opened my folder, wrote some stuff and read. Without looking up he said, "Sit! On the examination table!" like he was commanding his pet dachshund... which I obediently did.

He said to me, "You're overweight. In fact, you are obese, bordering on morbidly obese. According to the latest NIH charts, you should weigh 170 pounds."

I was taken aback. I weighed in at 241. Since I was over six feet, I figured I was maybe twenty pounds overweight. Certainly not obese and no where's near morbidly so. I weighed the same for the last two physicals and I wasn't obese then, so I objected, "Doc, how can I be obese now? I weighed 241 pounds two years ago and I wasn't obese... I weighed 241 pounds last year and I wasn't obese. I weigh

241 pounds this year and suddenly I am? The last time I weighed 170 pounds... this was years ago... when I was training for the New York City Marathon... I looked like a survivor of Auschwitz. Felt terrible."

He pointed to a chart on the back of the door and sure enough, according to the new NIH weight chart, I was obese. I said to the bastard, "What? I weigh the same and suddenly, because of some god damn chart, I'm obese. Obesity by chart! Who the fuck is the NIH anyway? ... the poundage police of America! Where do you fit on that god damn chart!"

He said in a tone that reminded me of Hannibal Lector, "It is none of your damn business!", threw the folder down on the chair and left in a very hefty huff.

As he left, I yelled, "Have an extra donut on me, Dr. Fatso!" I dressed, picked up my precious medical folder, said to myself, "Fuck the bastards" and stomped out. I followed the magic yellow footprints and snuck passed Station 4, keeping my precious folder securely tucked under my arm and never went back. Never got a bill from the bastards either. They're probably still looking for that god damn folder of mine. Serves them right! I hope Nurse Ratchette has a fuckin' breakdown flexing those biceps through thousands of folders."

As I left the building, I thought, "Maybe Louie ain't all that crazy."

A man unconcealed gives an anatomy lesson...

We'd lived in Florida for... what... seven years and I still didn't have a concealed carry permit. I had a carry permit in New York... no easy thing to get... thanks to an old-time Dutchess County Sheriff who, unlike most of the law enforcement brotherhood in that state of victims, actually promoted gun ownership. I was used to carrying my Sig Sauer 225 nine millimeter semi-automatic and continued to do so even after we moved to Florida, for Florida was a lot like the wild west... kind of a swampy version of Texas. Hell, like Texas, Florida had no income tax (one of the reasons I found the state so attractive), was loaded with cattle ranches and Hispanics and had a civilian population armed to the teeth both legally and illegally, so in many ways, Florida was a lot like Texas but with a lot of alligators and no Alamo. Driving on I4 was our Alamo what with all the unlicensed illegal alien Hispanics driving broken down unregistered uninsured pickups without brakes at 120 miles an hour after a couple of pops of tequila!

Anyways, I got to thinking about my carrying around my Sig 9 without a concealed carry permit. It occurred to me that if I were to shoot someone when not on my property (thank God for Florida's castle law), there could be complications, particularly if my aim was good. The way I figured it, the better my aim, the worse trouble I'd be in with the law without that permit, and kind of conversely the worse my aim, the more trouble I'd be in for another reason. One of those 'choose-your-poison-can't-win' situations that seem to have plagued my life. Still I procrastinated for some time as I hate bureaucracies, particularly government bureaucracies, just like I'd hate large painful warts on the end of my dick. Thus I do my best to avoid both if at all possible. As a result, I had never gotten one... that is a concealed carry permit... not large painful warts on the end of my dick, which I also never got.

Then late one July 4th night, an incident occurred driving home the precarious position I had placed myself by not having a concealed carry permit. I was standing in my driveway smoking a Padrone 4000 cigar... a natural leaf Churchill, my favorite smoke, admiring all the fireworks my neighbors were sending skyward. Those rockets were going off all around me filling the night with thundering floral displays. Inspired me to hum the Star Spangled Banner. Every year the damn fireworks got louder and more professional looking.

For those of you from New York and the pussy states up north, the 4th can get pretty boisterous in Florida as firecrackers, rockets… just about any kind of fireworks you could want… are readily available unlike in New York where selling even lady fingers is considered a capital offense. A couple of weeks before the 4th, these fireworks tents start popping up throughout Florida… in parking lots and empty fields all around the place like mushrooms during the rainy season. You can go into one of these tents and buy as many fireworks as your little bang-bang heart desires and even charge them on your Visa card. This year, the 'box of rockets' seemed to be the fireworks of choice. Put the box in the middle of the road, light the fuse and run like hell. Rockets… I don't know, maybe six or eight… go off one at a time maybe 30 seconds apart. Awesome…

These fireworks tents are manned 24-7, are hooked up to a temporary phone line for processing credit card purchases, and sport a port-a-potty for the convenience of the sales help and desperate customers. It's a glorious example of how swiftly capitalism can react to meet a seasonal market demand. This demand occurs twice a year, around the 4th and around New Years Eve. There's only one catch: you have to sign a paper stating that the fireworks you've purchased are for agricultural purposes only. Never did figure out this 'buy, sign and light' policy, but whatever the reason, I'm all for it.

I was into humming the second verse of our national anthem when I noticed a small fire in the recreational area at the end of our street. The fire got bigger and between bursts of fireworks thunder, I could hear some kids whooping it up. This was definitely not a good situation. We had had several fires up there earlier in the year… my guess, started by delinquent teenage thugs who were up there getting high smoking pot from home-made plastic soda bottle pipes. I'd find the soda bottle pipes littering the park when I walked the dogs during the day.

Since school was out, they'd already burned a wooden swing set and two trees. Fortunately those fires were self-contained and burned themselves out, but one of these times, these asshole teenagers were going to start a major fire that would set the conservation area aflame and destroy a bunch of houses in the process... one of those houses being mine.

It hadn't rained in a month as we were suffering through another dry spell so the chances of fire spreading to the conservation area were great. The fireworks were scary enough. The threat from an out-of-control bonfire was a lot scarier. I grabbed my garage fire extinguisher and walked down the road to the recreation area with my trusty Sig 9 strapped to my belt. When I was on my property, I didn't bother to conceal the weapon and now didn't have time to do so.

I walked between a row of trees into the field swinging a fire extinguisher as I strode along and when I rounded the bend, sure enough, there were five teenagers standing before the bonfire passing around one of those soda bottle pipes toking away and laughing like a bunch of hyenas. I stood there in the shadows beyond the fire for a minute or two observing them. They were a rough looking bunch... definitely not locals... two blacks and three whites. Every now and then one of the assholes would throw some brush or an old limb on the fire stirring up the ashes and sending a cloud of sparks into the sky.

I walked into the light of the fire and one of the assholes noticed me: "Hey old man, what you want up here. This ain't yer property. Get the hell outta here."

The others laughed and another one of the assholes said, "You lookin' for trouble? Get yer ass outta here before you get it." The other assholes laughed. Like I said, they were a tough lookin' bunch.

I set the fire extinguisher down and put my left hand on my still holstered Sig 9 and said, "You get the fuck outta here, assholes…"

One of the assholes… a black kid with those stupid dread locks covering his head… stepped forward… my guess the leader… and said "Or what? What you gonna do? Call the cops? Yell at us? Get your sorry old ass outta here old man before something real bad happens to you."

I pulled the Sig 9 and kept it pointed toward the ground, my arm hanging relaxed at my side. "You boys ever hear of chest, chest, head, chest?"

Mr. Dread Locks said, "Look old man, we don't need no an-at-toe-mee lesson, especially from a old cracker like you. I'm only gonna say this one more time… get yer ass outta here before something bad happens to you." His asshole buddies laughed.

I held the Sig 9 up and pointed toward the fire and said, "This here's my teacher friend. He gives an-at-to-mee lessons to assholes like you. He's kind of the ultimate teacher. He's gonna teach you where your chest is and then he's gonna repeat that lesson to be sure you got it and then he's gonna teach you where your head is and then, being an excellent teacher, he's gonna review where your chest is just to make sure you haven't forgot. He's very thorough and no one ever forgets the lesson he teaches."

The leader laughed and said, "What you gonna do? Shoot all of us?"

I leveled the Sig 9 at his chest and said, "Yup! I'm gonna give you a quick an-at-to-mee lesson as you put it, and then I'm gonna teach the rest of this class of assholes some more biology. You know, stuff about the circulatory system and what happens when it gets full of new holes."

I pointed the Sig 9 at his feet and fired... BANG! The assholes all jumped back and Mr. Dread Locks yelled, "What? You fuckin' crazy or somethin'?"

I fired a second time at his feet and yelled, "I think I'll start with your feets, boy! Dance, you asshole... Dance!"

All five turned and ran like hell across the field to the road on the far side of the park. I yelled "If I ever see you assholes again, my teacher friend here is going to give you a lesson or two that you'll never forget."

Fireworks were exploding all around, so no one noticed the couple of pistol shots. I holstered my Sig 9, put out the fire with my fire extinguisher and walked back to my house thinking that it'd be a pretty good idea to get a concealed carry permit.

A man still functional...

With memories of using my Sig 9 to teach an anatomy lesson to a bunch of hoods still rattling around my brain, I determined that I'd best learn my own lesson from the incident and get that concealed carry permit. The question: how do I do it so as to have as little as possible to do with the State of Florida's bureaucracy and as cheaply as possible so as to have as little impact as possible on the family budget, which Susie monitored with the enthusiasm and discipline of an unreformed Ebenezer Scrooge... at least as far as *my* spending went. I made several calls to local gun shops and ranges. Most of them offered concealed carry classes that ended up getting you a permit. Cost: 100 bucks… cheap at half the price!

One of the gun shops that didn't give the class suggested that I take the one offered at the Florida Gun Show. Well guess what? That class did everything and for close to half the price: 60 bucks. The gun show was held every other month at the Florida State Fair Grounds in Caledonia and guess what?… there'd be a show this coming weekend. Hot damn!

I'd always wanted to go to the gun show but every time there was one, I had some other commitment. Somehow my retired weekends weren't so retiring. Anyways, I was determined to go this coming Saturday and get that damn permit.

Saturday rolled around like it always did and I drove down 310 to the fairgrounds, paid my five bucks to park, my eight bucks to enter the show and was off to the races. As I walked into the large auditorium, a lady handed me a handbill advertising the concealed carry permit classes. The next class was at 2:00, so I had a couple of hours to kill… probably the wrong word to use given where I was.

The place was packed. There were men walking around the crowded aisles, many of them with rifles or shotguns slung over their shoulders. There were a lot of women wandering the aisles as well and many of them had rifles or shotguns slung over their shoulders. Camouflage was the dress of the day, both feminine and masculine. There were booths and counters all over the place loaded with just about any kind of rifle or pistol or knife you could want. And you could purchase anything even remotely related to rifles and pistols from bullets to holsters and beyond. Some outfit was even selling RVs fitted out for hunting. I wondered if the sides of the damn things were bullet proof.

The crowd was very polite as impolite could lead to severe chastisement given that the crowd was literally armed to the teeth. As someone bumper-stickered once "An armed society is a polite society." This society was very polite. I wandered about the aisles saying 'excuse me' a lot and taking in the crowd. I felt at home. Lots of crackers... most overdressed in their "Sunday best" even though it was Saturday... that is, lots of extra large camouflage outfits, including the women. However, I kept my opinion as to size and style of dress to myself. I thought I could hear the faint sounds of dueling banjos playing *Deliverance* in the background.

There were an inordinate number of very military looking arms for sale. Apparently the crowd hunted, and what did they hunt? My guess, homo sapiens... at least that's what they appeared to be armed to hunt. Like I said, the crowd and me were very polite, but if the government became too impolite, these guys and gals were equipped to chastise said government most forcefully. God, I love Americans... politely of course.

Well the loud speaker announced that the concealed carry permit class would begin in fifteen minutes. The class was held on the second floor balcony so I made my way up a darkened stairwell at the end of the hall to the balcony. As I walked into the light at the head of the stairway, I found myself in a long line that slowly moved toward a table. Beyond the table were maybe 50 wooden folding chairs and at the head of the chairs, a podium.

There was a woman sitting behind the table collecting money. Apparently this was a cash only operation. Nowhere was this noted, not in the handbill I'd been given, not in any of the posters plastered around the hall, not anyplace. Thankfully I had brought a hundred bucks to buy some nine millimeter hollow points and hadn't purchased them yet so I had the cash. When I reached the woman behind the counter, she looked up and barked at me, "Forty dollars for the class and fifteen bucks for finger prints, five bucks for the photo. The whole package... sixty bucks cash." This was a tough bitch that was used to ordering people around and now one of those people was yours truly.

She looked Hispanic. Had a dark complexion, jet black very short hair and piercing dark brown eyes. She was a little heavy set in a very sexy way with heavy breasts... maybe she was an off-duty cop. At least she looked it... and she had a very commanding way about her. If I ever had to be frisked, she was the cop for the job in my book. Why I bothered to notice the details of her appearance is beyond me. At seventy, actually 69, these details of feminine appearance had pretty much become irrelevant... even in my world of male fantasy. Maybe it was just habit. If so, it was a habit I enjoyed... indications, I guess, that I was not quite dead yet.

Anyways, I said, "I'd like the whole package." Without looking up, she took the cash, counted it, handed me a receipt and barked, "Take a seat, class begins in fifteen minutes" and then she barked "Next!" Gave me the chills... hope still sprang eternal... A young woman who looked like a younger model of the woman who took my cash and yelled at me, handed me a folder of papers and smiled. The apple had apparently not fallen far from the tree.

I wandered up the aisle between the two rows of chairs and chose a seat about halfway from the front... which was also halfway from the back. I was not one for sitting in the front of class... a 65 year-old habit developed and reinforced during 13 years of New York State mandated public education, followed by four more at an unexpectedly expensive state university... a habit that was dying very slowly, in fact, apparently more slowly than I was.

Sitting up front was for brown nosers... people who did their homework... which was not me. You know, those assholes who always shot their hands up to answer the stupid asshole questions the teacher asked to be sure you were awake... the ones who always got those stupid gold stars at the top of their homework... the ones that the teacher always smiled at when she handed them their corrected homework. Most of these assholes... the ones who sat in the first row... were the last ones chosen when we played kickball during recreation... one of my two favorite periods... the other being lunch. Anyways, when we played kickball, I always went for the head when a first-rower kicked the ball to me. Felt good to nail the likes of Neddy Mueller in the face and make him cry and then go over and say how sorry I was as he balled away.

Sitting in back, which was my first strategy, was for trouble makers. Took me a couple of years, but sometime around the fifth grade, in Miss Bateman's class, I learned that sitting in the back row could bring you more attention and agita than sitting in the front row. When I sat in the back row in Miss Bateman's class, Flip Johnson parked himself on one side of me and Georgie Green on the other. Flip always fell asleep and Georgie picked his nose and threw his buggers at the kids in front of him. Both of these behaviors brought us... meaning me... under constant surveillance, defeating the advantage of being in the back row. After a semester of back benching and being in Miss Bateman's constant field of vision and the object of her correction, I modified my seating strategy and became a middle bencher which is where I was today.

A young woman sat at the far end of the row. Hell, now everyone seems young. I asked her, "This seat taken?" She smiled and said, "No, it's all yours." She was thin and jittery... a little hyperactive. She looked down into this huge purse and said, "I hate waiting."

I thought she was talking to me and replied, "I hate waiting too. I've done almost 70 years of it and it's starting to get to me." She laughed and looked up a bit surprised that I had replied and said, "Oh, there I go again talking to my purse. Sorry about that. I didn't mean to disturb you with a silly statement about my impatience. You'd think that after all those years teaching high school English, I'd learn the virtue of patience. I guess I'm as slow a learner as you are."

I smiled, "So you teach English?"

She smiled back and said, "Yes, for eleven years."

"And you're getting a concealed carry permit? To carry while you're teaching?"

"I can't really talk about it, but we've had two shootings across the street from the school and one teacher was beaten up pretty badly in the parking lot."

"Which high school?"

"I'd rather not say. You understand why, don't you?"

I knew why and replied, "Understood. Topic ended."

She smiled, put her arm into her purse up to the elbow, pulled out two ball-point pens and said, "You'll need a pen" as she handed me one of them. "You can keep it."

This other lady took the podium and started yelling something about the mic not working and we'd have to listen carefully. She was a dirty blonde and older than the other lady at the counter, but she too had that slightly heavy set, tougher than nails look. She was wearing one of those sleeveless shirts and her biceps had defini-tion. She yelled, "There's plenty of seats up front. Move up front, please." She pointed at a skinny dude, looked to be about 15, sitting in the back and he sheepishly moved to the front row. Nobody else budged. Made sense. People who are applying for concealed carry permits tend to be people who don't want to be pushed around and told what to do.

Miss Dirty Blonde with biceps muscle definition walked us through all those forms one field at a time. A god damn mongoloid idiot could follow the instructions... except for that skinny dude in the first row. That good lookin' gal, the young one who handed me the folder, hustled up the aisle to help the skinny dude. She bent over to point at a field on one of the forms and that nice round behind of hers came into full view and distracted me causing me to get a field or two behind... because of her behind. Not dead yet!

After we got done with all the forms, this other guy took the podium. He looked almost as tough as the dirty blonde. He told us about gun safety ("treat the gun like it's always loaded"), where we could carry ("don't carry in a school, a government building, a bank, an airport or a bar") and when we could shoot someone ("when you are threatened with violence and feel your life is in danger").

I noticed that the thin hyperactive lady English teacher got even jumpier when Mr. Law and Order said that you couldn't carry in a school. From my perspective, I thought that not being able to carry in a bar was pretty stupid. Hell, chances are that's when you're most likely to need the damn thing. Mr. Law and Order ended his talk with "it's better to be judged by 12 than carried by six" which I liked a lot.

Along the way, we were called one at a time to get our photos taken... by that young woman. When my turn came, she pointed to a white screen taped to the wall. I walked over to the screen and she commanded, "Glasses off!" I complied quickly and as I looked up, she snapped my picture. She gave me the photos (she wielded one of those Polaroid-like cameras... only digital). I was shocked for I looked like an elder Charles Manson. This was not good. I had to send the photo to the State of Florida along with a bunch of other documents including a set of my finger prints, which were taken next. I feared that when state officials saw my photo, they'd deny me the permit on the grounds that anyone who looked like I looked in that picture was obviously insane, probably a sociopath prone to violence and thus someone who should be denied the right to own a firearm no less carry it around in public, concealed or otherwise, and then they'd use my finger prints to hunt me down and incarcerate me in some snake pit of a loony bin.

Next we took a test on all the stuff Mr. Law and Order told us. The test was a snap since Mr. Law and Order told us what the questions were and what the answers were, first, one question at a time during the lecture and then at the end, all at once just before we took the test. To make things even easier, it was either true/false or multiple choice, I can't remember which.

After I finished the test, I took it up to the counter where the young woman, the one who took my Charles Manson photo, corrected it. I got a 100. Like I said, a mongoloid idiot could have passed that test. To my surprise, two people, one man and one woman, did not pass that stupid test. Whatever category's below mongoloid idiot, that's where they belonged… you know, the loafers and diaper crew. It's a good thing they were denied… for their own good… as they'd probably have killed themselves loading their weapons. Although from the standpoint of thinning the herd, maybe not so much. At least they did not appear to be together, genetically speaking.

After that test is corrected, you have to sign a document saying you told the truth and weren't a felon or a crazy person and the document had to be notarized. Back to that lady with the wonderful heavy breasts and dark brown eyes. I signed the document in front of her, showed her my Florida driver's license and she notarized my state-

125

ment that I was pure as the driven snow criminally and psychologically speaking. She handed my license back to me with a beaming smile and said, "Mr. Marinelli, you're the oldest person to take this class in a month of Sundays. It's so good to see someone your age that's still functional. Gives us all hope." That's the word she used "functional". I was about to say "And it's so wonderful to be processed by someone with such sexually functional breasts," but I did not since there was a very good chance she was armed. However, the sentiment remained with me to this day as you can tell.

Now we had to drive to a shooting gallery at the end of Philips just off 75… you know, a firing range… to get certified that we could safely handle a firearm. That was part of the requirement to get that concealed carry permit. We were given a certificate which we had to sign and get in a long line that went out the door of the range. I noticed that the two genetically challenged students were not in line so I guess the test worked in a very lowest common denominator kind of way.

As someone exited the actual range, he or she handed you a pair of ear muffs and eventually you pushed open the sound proof door to the actual range where Mr. Law and Order stood. An older kinda fat lady with gray hair pulled back in a bun was standing next to him. She looked a lot like my third grade teacher Miss Searles. She held a pistol aimed at a target maybe ten feet down range. She yelled, "But suppose I don't hit the target? Will I fail the test?"

Mr. Law and Order yelled, "Lady, it doesn't matter. Just fire the weapon!"

She turned to reply moving her arms towards Mr. Law and Order and yelled back, "The gun is very heavy. I'm afraid I'll miss."

Mr. Law and Order, with the reflexes of a striking rattlesnake,

126

grabbed her arm to keep the weapon pointed down range, and yelled "Keep the firearm pointed at the target. Listen lady, the only way you'll fail this test is if you shoot me and that ain't gonna happen. You are here to demonstrate that you can handle a firearm safely. The State of Florida doesn't give a damn if you can't hit what you aim at. It only cares if you hit something you're not aiming at. Fire one round, I'll sign your certificate and you're outta here without killing me."

The lady yelled, "Round? What's a round. I thought I was firing bullets? I've seen pictures of them. They're long and cylindrical."

Mr. Law and Order was losing it. He had a gazillion would-be students of pistology to process, one of them the next asshole in line… that asshole being me… and this lady was a cork in his bottle of progress towards his next class or lunch or his next drink… probably served at an establishment where he wasn't supposed to carry but I'd bet my bottom dollar he did. Anyways, he yelled in a voice loud enough to scare the crap out of the little children hundreds of miles away waiting in line in Disney World's Magic Kingdom, "A round is a bullet, you idiot. If you don't fire that god damn round… errr bullet… at the target, I'm going to flunk your ass."

She looked at him with her steely blues and yelled in a voice that would scare the parents of those little kids in Disney World's Magic Kingdom, "Young man, there's no need to be insulting, vulgar and profane." Her arm steadied, she looked down range and in a show of skill that would put Dirty Harry to shame, nailed the target, an image of the upper torso and head of a man, right between the eyes.

Mr. Law and Order grabbed the pistol, put in on the counter, signed her certificate, let out a loud sigh and yelled "Next!" Next being me.

I fired my cylindrical round without killing Mr. Law and Order, grabbed my signed certificate, and got the hell out of there with my envelop of all the papers necessary to mail to Florida's Department of Agriculture for that precious concealed carry permit. The next Monday, I wrote a check for $117, slipped it into that envelop and mailed it to Florida's Department of Agriculture... registered mail to confirm that that precious package arrived where I sent it. Hot damn, three months later, my concealed carry permit arrived at my door with my Charlie Manson picture plastered across the permit.

Contentment destroyed by its ubiquitous enemy, necessity and necessity's second cousin...

I sat in my lanai sucking on the stub of a Padrone 4000 cigar... a natural leaf Churchill, my favorite smoke... drawing out one last good puff. In a moment of great contentment, I lifted my head slightly and blew smoke gently into the air... watching the smoke dance out through my lanai's screen and into the back yard... savoring the moment... that is, until my contentment was destroyed by the jarring words: "Why do you smoke those stupid things? They stink."

I looked up from my now destroyed contentment and there was Susie yelling at me through the barely opened patio sliding glass door.

"Didn't you hear the phone!"

"Phone? How could I? I was out here with the lanai door shut tight."

"Well you shouldn't 'a been out there smoking. You smoked yesterday."

I was allowed the privilege of smoking one cigar every other day by the powers that be... those powers residing in the ever gentle breast of my dear wife.

128

I returned fire, "No I didn't. Yesterday the Yankees lost in 15 innings and I watched the whole game in my office." I have a room I call an office to avoid the inevitable argument that would ensue should I call it what it really was: an old man's 'man cave'. I continued my defense, "I didn't smoke one damn puff yesterday."

Susie dropped her ritualistic accusation of outlawed cigar smoking which was occasionally correct but always worth a try on her part even when it wasn't. I, of course, always countered with an unassailable argument that I did not smoke the previous day even though I occasionally had. This accusation dropped, Susie went on to her next accusation and since there was no rule banning repetitive accusations, she did so, this time dressing her previous accusation in the clothes of a question: "Didn't you hear the phone?"

"No. I was out here with the lanai door shut tight so none of that dreadful cigar stink, as you call it, would foul up the living room... on your orders by the way." I found it best to defend myself using Susie's own words against her because doing so made it more difficult for her to refute my counter arguments. However, as experience had shown innumerable times, my doing so did not stop her... it only slowed her down a bit.

I strategically moved on, "Who was that on the phone?"

"Mary Ann. Her car overheated. She wants someone to pick her up. She's parked just off 275 at the Wolfss exit. She needs you to pick her up." The lanai door closed and Susie disappeared.

I carefully laid the cigar butt on the edge of my favorite cigar ashtray, being careful not to crush the end the cigar butt. By allowing the cigar butt to extinguish itself reduced the stale cigar odor... which even I found unpleasant although I'd never admit it to Susie.

I stared down at that ashtray. It was one of my prize possessions.

I'd purchased it at the Columbia Restaurant's gift shop many years ago during our first visit to Ybor City right after we'd moved down here. The ashtray was white with indentations at each corner for a cigar. The border and the indentations were streaked with ocher yellow over which a green and brown leaf design appeared... obviously stylized tobacco leaves. The design had a distinct Caribbean look. Across the white center of the ashtray in big blue letters appeared:

COLUMBIA
SINCE 1905
CIGAR BAR
RESTAURANT

Unlike most stuff you buy today, it was not made in China, making it even more valuable in my eyes. Apparently someone named "Talavera" made it... "Talavera" being a distinctly not-Chinese name.

Anyways, reality destroyed this second moment of contentment as my thoughts turned to rescuing my daughter-in-law Mary Ann off of 275 at the Wolfss exit and how to do it without actually driving down that ever-treacherous highway.

That spelling of "Wolfss" always bothered me. I couldn't understand why the good people of Caledonia would spell it that way with those silly double s's at the end. It was obviously intentional. If it wasn't, they'd made the same mistake hundreds, if not thousands, of times. Given the public education system in Florida, I suppose it's possible, but still quite unlikely. I figured if it were wrong, it wouldn't be the only wrong way they'd misspell the stupid name.

Anyways again! Back to daughter-in-law Mary Ann. Her husband Vincent, our oldest son, was killed in a stupid helicopter accident during training for deployment to Iraq leaving poor Mary Ann with two boys to raise. Doing so became a La Familia Marinelli affair.

Susie and I and the rest of the Marinelli clan did what we could but with obvious limited success as those two alien spawn grew pretty much on their own and became who they were in spite of us.

Just last week, when the central air conditioning over at Mary Ann's house conked out as the temperature outside soared into the very high 90s, I went over there and found my two grandsons frying in the living room and playing their 107th consecutive Xbox game which consisted of killing a bunch of things. They did manage to soldier through the lack of air conditioning but were quite disappointed in their kill scores. They demanded relief... that is, a working air conditioner which someone else had to make work.

The situation was critical. I called one of the gazillion air conditioning companies in the phone book that made "emergency" calls. Some guy in a gray uniform showed up in less than an hour, did his hokum pokum magic and cool air again blew through the vents of the house... much to the relief primarily of my two alien spawn grandsons who were overjoyed at the prospect of their gaming kill ratios returning to their very high norms.

Much of my pain at paying the outrageous repair bill was dulled by the joy of knowing that the kill ratios of Vinnie and Tommie would return to their norm and the imaginary world in which they lived so much of the time would again be safe for democracy or whatever those imaginary worlds were safe from after my two alien spawn grandsons had killed a large number of various kinds of creatures at least some of which appeared to be human.

As I gazed at that Padrone 4000 in its final death throes after giving its life for my pleasure and contentment, I formulated a strategy that would enable me to get Mary Ann's car repaired without my driving down the ever-dangerous 275. I called AAA from my ever trusty land line and arranged for them to fix Mary Ann's car or tow it to a repair shop. I then called Mary Ann on her cell phone to let her know that AAA was on the way and told her that if AAA had to tow her car to a repair shop to call me back and I'd pick her up there and take her home. Another drive down the ever dangerous 275 averted... another crisis creatively averted!

The bagging of Albert literally and Vinnie metaphorically...

It was somewhere around three o'clock in the A-M and the phone, the land line... as Louie would say, the real phone... rang and rang and rang. When it became obvious that the ringing would never stop, my darling Susie gave me a gentle knee to the butt and mumbled, "Answer that, my love."

I rolled out of bed, stumbled to the kitchen where the ever-reliable landline phone lived, hugging the wall. I stared at it as it rang and then finally picked up the receiver. I didn't need to put it to my ear as a voice blasted into the silence: "They've got Vinnie! They've got Vinnie!"

It took my brain a couple of seconds to click into gear and realize that the person screaming was my daughter-in-law Mary Ann and the name she was screaming was that of her son, the eldest half of my two mamaluke grandsons, that being Vinnie.

I tried to calm her down: "Take a breath... and then tell me who's got Vinnie?"

The voice audibly gasped for air and then blurted out, "The sheriff... the sheriff got him... and they took Albert, too!"

That "Albert" name flummoxed me. "Who the hell is Albert?"

"They made Vinnie put him in a burlap bag and they took him away too!"

"A burlap bag? Vinnie had to put his friend into a burlap bag... before the police would take him?" Things were getting weirder and weirder.

"Yes... they made Vinnie put Albert into a burlap bag."

"Why?"

"So he wouldn't bite them, I guess."

Not knowing what question to ask next and fearing that should I actually formulate one, Mary Ann's answer would make me doubt my sanity and not just hers, I said quite forcibly, "Just wait there. I'll be right over. Don't do anything."

I heard a muffled "yes" and then a click as the phone buzzed that *I don't have a call for you. Would you like to make one?* sound. I gently placed the receiver in its cradle and stood there for a moment trying to figure out where the bedroom was.

I found myself dressing after apparently relying on muscle memory to find my way back to the bedroom. As I sat on the edge of the bed to put on my sandals, I yelled over my shoulder to my still sleeping darling wife: "Susie!"

I got no reply. Then she stirred, rolled towards me and mumbled a sleepy "What?"

"I'm going over to Mary Ann's. The sheriff took Vinnie and his friend Albert. They made Vinnie put Albert in a burlap bag before they took the two of them away. They were afraid Albert would bite them. I guess they didn't think Vinnie would."

Susie rolled away from me and mumbled even less distinctly... given the urgency of the situation: "Okay dear. Lock the door on your way out."... ending our rather 'tense' exchange.

I arrived at Mary Ann's after a shaky drive down 75. The traffic wasn't bad but the texting drunks and pot heads were out in full force weaving from lane to lane. Luckily they were all driving in the right direction, south, as was I and thus making it much easier to avoid them than had they been driving in the other direction. As the news would blast out every couple of weeks, driving in the right direction, no matter how shakily, was not always the case.

I jumped out of my pickup and ran to the door to Mary Ann's house... which was no longer there. Shards of wood covered the doormat across which appeared in all caps the word 'WELCOME', a word which took on a certain irony given that the last individuals to pass over that doormat did so in a somewhat less than gentle and welcomed manner. What was left of the door was leaning against the wall just inside of where it had been, at least part of which had been outside before the welcoming ceremony previously mentioned.

There before me sat Mary Ann on the couch in the living room silently sobbing in what I'd call a state of shock. Tommie sat at the breakfast bar facing her and drinking a coke. The place was a mess with papers strewn about the floor, two toppled dining table chairs blocking the way into the dining room and all kinds of possessions... shirts, books, pants and so on... blazing a trail to Vinnie's bedroom.

Tommie took a sip from his coke and said, "I told him not to beat the crap outta that kid even though he deserved it."

"What kid?"

"That thievin' little bastard Willie Williamson. His backyard's right behind ours... on the other side of the fence. Grabbed him tryin' to escape over the fence... beat the livin' crap outta him."

"Why? Why beat the crap out of this kid Willie Williamson?"

"I toll you. Because Willie's a thievin' little bastard. He was easy to catch because of Albert."

"You beat the crap outta him? I thought you said not to be the crap outta him?"

"I didn't. Vinnie did. Vinnie caught him tryin' to escape and beat the livin' crap outta him."

"And beat the crap outta him? For what?"

"He was stealin' Vinnie's stuff and Albert stopped him. That thievin' little bastard was scared shitless of Albert. That's why Vinnie caught him."

"How'd Albert scare this Willie kid?"

"Just by bein' his self."

The more Tommie clarified the situation, the more confused I became. Quite unexpectedly, the more I learned, the less I knew: "What was this thievin' little bastard Willie, as you put it, tryin' to steal?"

"Vinnie's cash and his stash... that's when Albert did his thing."

"What thing?"

"That's when he bit the little creep... and bit him good. Albert bit him and Vinnie beat the livin' crap outta him. That's why the police broke down the front door... because of that little creep."

Things appeared to start to make sense... foolish me: "So that's why the sheriff had Vinnie put a burlap bag over Albert's head?"

"Hell, Vinnie put that burlap bag over all of him. Had to. Albert was pissed."

Back to informed confusion: "Okay, I get that this Willie Williamson was... well... a thievin' little snot. But who the hell is Albert? Is he some kind midget? Had to be if Vinnie could slip a burlap bag over his entire body. No?"

"No. He's actually pretty big for a blue-eyed leucistic... he's like an albino only he's not. Can't be. He's got baby-blue eyes. He's actually pretty valuable."

"So Albert, even though all of him fits into a burlap bag is a what... a large blue-eyed leucistic... and that's like an albino only he's na..na.. not." I was beginning to stutter... the confusion was overwhelming.

"Right. You look confused." ...*and what an understatement that was...* "Look, get into Vinnie's bedroom and that'll explain the whole thing."

I followed the trail of detritus blazing its way to or possibly from Vinnie's bedroom, depending on your point of view, with Tommie in hot pursuit. I'd never seen the inside of Vinnie's bedroom as he always kept the door locked and locked with a pad lock. Sometimes the padlock was on the outside of the door... I guess when he was out... and sometimes on the inside... I guess when he was in. This door wasn't pulverized for it remained on its hinges but it had been smashed open. A padlock still locked hung hopelessly on the inside of the smashed in door.

There inside Vinnie's sanctum sanctorum was a bed, a chest of drawers, a desk, a table and on that table a huge tropical fish tank without any water. All the drawers of the chest of drawers were pulled open and all kinds of Vinnie's personal stuff was scattered on the bedroom floor.

The fish tank was no different in that its floor was also a mess too. Oddly it had no water and thus no fish. Instead there was a huge pile of sand in one corner and a water dish and what looked like a fake cave in the other.

I asked, "What's the fish tank for? There's no water and no fish."

Tommie smiled and said, "That's not a fish tank. It's a terrarium. It's where Albert lives. Albert's not a fish. He's a morph ball python and a beauty... a baby blue-eyed leucistic... very rare... very valuable."

I stood there for a long minute staring at the 'fish tank' and then said, "Albert's a god damn snake?"

"Yup! A blue-eyed leucistic ball python. Vinnie named him Albert Einstein. We call him just Albert... by his first name. For a ball python, he's pretty smart... that's why Vinnie named him Albert Einstein. He's Vinnie's security system."

Instead of the situation becoming clarified, one mystery had merely been replaced with another... my moment of clarity lasting mere seconds before being replaced by yet another imponderable as confusion again reigned in the brain of yours truly. All I could say was a confused, "Security system? What the hell was Albert securing?"

"Vinnie's stash of weed... and his cash. Vinnie kept his cash there too. See where the latch to the window above Albert's house is? It's broken. That's where that snotty little thievin' bastard Willie Williamson tried to steal Vinnie's stash and his cash. The idiot reached into Albert's house and Albert bit him. Pet stores and reptile handlers call python's like Albert unmannerly. Vinnie calls him a one python security system."

Finally my brain caught up to the situation. Vinnie was selling weed... that's how he could afford that crotch rocket of his. He left his 'stash and cash' in the loving hands... coils?... of Mr. Albert Einstein. This little thievin' bastard, as Tommie so poetically characterized him, one Willie Williamson, broke the window latch, opened the window, reached into Albert's house to steal Vinnie's stash and cash and Albert 'the genius python' bit him and then Vinnie beat the little thievin' bastard up. My guess... and it wasn't much of a guess... the little thievin' bastard squealed to the sheriff and the sheriff's posse was only too eager to go all-swat on their newly identified danger to western civilization, break down several doors in the domicile of yet another relatively innocent citizen and frighten that relatively innocent citizen out of her freakin' mind with tactical 12-gage shot guns and several Glocks... and then frog-march her son off to the county jail. Who'd a thunk?

That left 'only' one question: "Tommie, why'd the sheriff's posse take Albert? They arrested not only Vinnie, but his damn python."

In a reply that seemed both very weird and strangely appropriate, "I dunno? Maybe they thought Albert's a co-conspirator or something."

Vinnie buys a get-out-of-jail card by undercovering himself...

Recovering what was left of my sanity, I staggered back to the living room followed by a strolling and unperturbed Tommie. We both took a seat at the breakfast bar facing Mary Ann. I asked her, "How'd it go down?"

By now Mary Ann had pretty much recovered what was left of her sanity: "I heard someone yell outside... outside the house in the front yard... and then there was this loud bang and a bunch of men armed to the teeth ran into my bedroom. I had no idea who they were. At first I thought it was a home invasion. Then the only one who wasn't armed to the teeth yelled at me, 'Sheriff's department. We have a search warrant' as he waived a piece of paper in my face."

Then Tommie, who remained remarkably cool now and most likely then, said in about as calm a voice as was possible and still be awake, said, "They busted Vinnie's door open... he pad locks it from the inside when he's in there... musta pulled him outta bed... and then there was a bunch of shouting. Vinnie yelled at them and they yelled at him. Then there was this long silence and then the whole bunch of them, including Vinnie, marched outta his room... all the deputies had holstered their pistols and shouldered their shot guns... looked like tactical 870s... probably 12-guage. One of the deputies carried a burlap bag and two plain brown paper bags. Vinnie was handcuffed behind his back. And then someone in Vinnie's room yelled 'Rifle!' All the deputies quick drew their pistols... probably Glocks... and unshouldered their 870s. I dove for the floor. Mom did too. I thought for sure those idiots were about to unload their damn weapons on us. Looking down the barrels of a bunch Glocks and 870s in the hands of wanna be gun fighters ain't a lot of fun. Then the deputy in the Vinnie's bedroom yelled 'All clear!' and the swatters again holstered and shouldered their weapons... with what looked like great disappointment spread across their ugly faces. Then the sheriff's deputy who wasn't armed to the teeth said, 'We're taking Vinnie in. He'll get his phone call." They frog marched Vinnie outta the house and it was pretty much over."

About three hours and four cups of coffee later, the phone rang and Mary Ann answered it. It was Vinnie calling from the Indian Road jail. She looked up and said, "Vinnie wants to know what to do?"

I grabbed the phone and yelled, "For God's sake tell them the truth.

Tell them whatever the hell they want to know. You're at their mercy. They got you dead to rights. I'll call a lawyer and get you bail." Vinnie agreed and hung up.

Before I could get a lawyer, only about two hours later, Vinnie emerges from a sheriff's patrol car in front of the house. He leans into the open patrol car window apparently talking with the officer in the patrol car. He then calmly saunters in through the now always open front door... a burlap bag hanging from his left shoulder and a smile on his face.

Mary Ann yells at him, "What happened! How'd you get out?"

Vinnie smiles the smile of the mouse who just sold the cat some weed at great profit, and says, "They released me and Albert... no charges... provided I go undercover. The sheriff says he doesn't give a damn about me... or Albert. He called us 'small weed' as opposed to 'big weed'. They want 'big weed'... you know, the suppliers. Two, maybe three up the supply chain from us"... the 'us' being Vinnie and Albert, I guess.

I could guess at what Vinnie meant generally speaking with the term 'small weed' but the particulars both intrigued and worried me: "How small is...was... that 'small weed' business of yours?"

Vinnie, again smiling the smile of that very successful mouse weed dealing dealer, says, "Small but very profitable. I never dealt *dreg*. Always dealt *reg* and rarely *pon*."

I had no idea what the hell he was talking about: "What the hell's all this dreg, reg, pon business?"

"That's the right word for it, business. I run...make that ran... a very profitable business. I always met my customers' needs... good product fairly priced. Never sold dreg, sold mostly reg and sometimes pon. Dreg's weed mixed with twigs, dirt and other crap... you know, the dregs. It's really cheap bottom of the barrel stuff. Never dealt it. *Reg's* regular, medium grade weed. It's good stuff, pretty pure. It's my main product. Then there's *pon*, hydroponic, top of the line stuff... very expensive. I sold reg all the time and pon on special order... usually to teachers."

"Teachers?"

"Yeah, teachers... my best customers. Always paid, never complained... given their position and all. Most of my customers were kids I know. Unlike the other dealers, I always gave advertised weight. If a customer complained, I'd re-weigh the bag and if it was short, I'd make up the difference and throw in a little extra. I kept my customers very happy... before and after the sale."

Vinnie was obviously a very good business man. I asked him, "Why sell weed? Couldn't you sell cars or houses or anything else?"

"I fell into dealing. Remember when I worked at the Children's Museum last summer. Well there were a bunch of these guys working there as part of their sentence... a bunch of convicted criminals... doing their community service. Most of them had been convicted of possession... weed. Well one day I'm cuttin' grass... how ironic... and there's a bunch of these community service cons smokin' out by the equipment shed. I go over to get a gas can and I smell the weed. They get all hot and bothered but I say, 'No worry, man, could I have a toke?' and this guy they called 'Double Time' gave me the joint they'd been sharin' and I took a good toke."

"Double Time?"

"Yeah. Double Time was a nervous son-of-a-bitch. Always twitchin' and jumpin' around. The next day they were out by the shed tokin' away and I said, 'Anyone got a bag for sale?' and Double Time

141

says, "Yes... yes... yes..." and I says okay D-T... that's what the other convicted criminals called him... you're on. And he sold me a dime bag... a bag of reg. pretty good stuff."

So you were already smokin' weed?"

"Oh yeah... for years. Couldn't drink booze... makes me sick."

"So how'd you fall into the business of dealing weed?"

"Well I share a joint with my buddy Monty and he asks me if I can get him a bag. The next day I buy another bag from D-T. Then a friend of Monty's asks me to get him a bag. Before a knew it, I had a bunch of customers. I was adding a small charge for the service. Finally D-T says, 'You gettin' too big for this nigger. You gotta start dealin' with Benny. I'll get you a contact. Nobody deals with Benny direct. My advice... stick with the weed. Don't get into H or the other shit he deals. Cops don't care too much about weed but they sure as hell will drive up yer ass if you deal H.' That's my success story."

Vinnie's great undercovering...

Months go by and no one contacts Vinnie. At the Sheriff's demand, Vinnie keeps dealin' and makin' good money. My guess, they want Vinnie to keep all his contacts live. Then one day Vinnie gets a call and he meets with the Sheriff's undercover narcos. They give him some clothes to wear and a confiscated Mercedes to drive and tell him to set up a meeting with this guy Benny, the kingpin dealer... and a gym bag with twenty thousand bucks inside... in small used bills. They want him to look like he's got the money to swing the deal which he already had thanks to them.

As Vinnie tells it:

"I told those idiots that if I wore that monkey suit and drove that stupid Mercedes, I'd never get to meet Benny. His lieutenant would give me the once over, know I was workin' the law just by lookin' at me dressed in this monkey suit and drivin' this stupid Mercedes. There'd be no meeting. It's got to be leather jackets and motorcycles. They know who I am. Besides, I did have the money. You gave it to me!"

And so it was.

Vinnie sets up this 20k weed buy as he tells it... has told it many times... with the kicker that this was supposed to be just the beginning:

"I drive to the Shanks down in the projects on my cyckle dressed like always... ripped jeans, leather jacket, no sleeves... my Yankees hat sittin' backwards on my head... no damn helmet. I know the narcs ain't after Benny for dealin' weed. He's dealin' hard drugs too. If there's a market, Benny sells it and there's a big market for the hard stuff and his customers ain't all in the projects. Lots of lawyers and other big shots are into that white powder. Some are into the hard stuff. Benny's customer base is a slice across our fine city's entire population. You got the money, Benny's got the product. He ain't prejudiced."

Just as I thought. This undercover work is dangerous. Vinnie wasn't dealing with some yuppie wanna be's. He was dealin' with a hard-nosed bunch. There'd been several murders down in the Shanks. All 'drug related' as reported by the news. I felt that maybe Vinnie should have served his six months and been done with it. Better to live with a record than be dead without one, but it was too late for that.

"I drive down to the Shanks and wait. I'm backed up by this undercover narc slumped over some garbage cans. I'm wired and there's a van down the street full of swat guys armed to the teeth. I'm not sure who I should fear most."

Obviously Vinnie was starting to have second thoughts about this whole operation... losing that feeling of immortality that has infected his thinking for years. He waits for almost an hour. No one shows up and he's told by the undercover narc to take off... which he does. While the narc is walking back to the van, he's confronted by a bunch of hoods who tell him to give them his wallet. The narc pulls a Glock instead of a wallet... the swat guys storm out of the van itchin' for a fight... and they get one. None of the swat guys gets nailed but two of hoods do... all seven them are arrested, handcuffed and driven away... two in an ambulance. Turns out to be the notorious Black Sharks and so the operation accomplished a lot but none of it involved Vinnie. The upside, Benny and his crew knew it was a set up and Vinnie is now out of the game and probably safe.

Planning for the great matrimonial lobster bake...

Our youngest daughter, Susie 2, may be getting married. Certain electronic events have occurred indicating that this may be the case, for we have learned that there are, or may be, certain documents on the internet which contain information indicating that such an event is, in fact, in the planning stages.

What proof do I have to support this belief? An email... I got an email from Susie 2... came last night... a very personal email... came addressed to both me and Susie 1, my dear wife and Susie 2's mom. I know it was very personal since the word 'PERSONAL' appeared across the top of the email and in all-caps... the all-caps apparently used to indicate that the email was and is VERY personal.

The email stated something to the effect that she and Leonard were planning a wedding and that if we wanted to invite someone, we could access a spread sheet over the internet on Google and add the names and addresses of those we'd like to invite. There was no statement in the email indicating that if we added names to that Google spread sheet, those added names would in fact be invited. There was, in my mind, the distinct possibility that this was a nomination process and not an invitation process... at least through implication. As the head of the Marinelli La Familia, it was my problem and my problem alone to solve... much to the wife's great and vehemently expressed consternation. But being the head of an Italian family, even in America, was what it was and the was... was me!

There was also no indication in the email as to the date, time and place of this potential matrimonial event in that all-caps very 'PERSONAL' email. Perhaps I'd find this information in the mysterious Google document referenced in the very personal email if I could ever find and access it. It occurred to me that perhaps we'd have to add our names to that Google spread sheet to be sure that we'd be invited or at least be nominated for the honor.

If you think it's confusing for you, think of my confusion as a man who spent his early youth listening to the radio for evening entertainment as television was yet to be invented or at least commercially available. And now there were cell phones and Google and a bunch of other stuff... all of which were other worldly to me. My sympathies for Louie Zerrelli grew as I contemplated my own potential technological Waterloo.

To keep communications straight, now even more important to me on this day, I... we, the "we" being the Marinelli family... had nominally differentiated the two Susies numerically. Thus the "Susie 1" and "Susie 2" previously expressed. It wasn't always this way.

Oxbow Lake The 2nd

When Susie 2 was a kid, we called her Little Susie. Susie 1 thus, quite naturally, was Big Susie. The differentiation became somewhat meaningless and very confusing as Little Susie grew up to be a lot taller than Big Susie... like a foot taller. To clarify this potential confusion, we changed the names using the numbers 1 and 2... "1" meaning "the first" implying age rather than size with age being pretty much less mutable, comparatively speaking, than physical size, like with Kings and Queens, particularly when one of the individual's sizes changes considerably. As with all social change, this social change was not totally successful as many older members of our guinea tribe, being human and older and Italian, still used the "Big" and "Little" designations which threw confusion into the ranks of the younger members of our beloved guinea tribe. *Mox nix*... generationally confusing forever!

As to my previously noted first matrimonial invitational conundrum? Perhaps I had to nominate me and Susie 1 for an invitation by adding our names and address to that list on that Google spread sheet if we wanted to attend... assuming that we would also pass mustard and actually be invited if our names were added to that mysterious Google spread sheet. The name and password to access said matrimonial spread sheet were included in the email. I felt socially and electronically molested... physically googled if you will... in broad daylight... and take it from someone who has recently experienced such a humiliation, being googled is not a very pleasant experience. I feel emotionally dirty from my guinea cerebellum to my guinea medulla oblongata and back.

As is obvious, I'm not much of a google person... in fact, given my recent humiliation, my circumstances and my age, you could say I'm actually an anti-google person, but I'm getting ahead of myself.

I could call Susan ...Susie 2 that is... on my cell phone, but it was still early morning here in south Florida and she and Leonard lived in that bastion of political correctness known as San Francisco. It was even earlier out there… very much so. If Susan kept her cell phone on all the time, I'd a called just to piss her off, but I knew that she turned the damn device off when she went to bed. I learned this through direct experience and may, in fact, have been inadvertently responsible for the establishment of this practice, so I knew that calling her at this time would be a fruitless attempt at a small act of revenge and basically a waste of effort and cell phone minutes.

So I had no choice but to face the source of my being googled, namely the Google itself, in search of more information concerning my daughter's potential wedding… information that may be contained on that Google spread sheet. Talk about romance! Besides, I thought that it might be a good idea to familiarize myself with the details of this potential matrimonial event before speaking with Susan. It was, after all, the proper thing to do.

I entered the stuff as indicated in Susan's email and got a message back from the dreaded Google asking me for my g-mail name and password. G-mail? I thought to myself 'What the fuck is g-mail? Is that better than say… email since 'g' bites farther into the alphabet than 'e'? And what happened to f-mail? …which just might be a better name given my present circumstances. Had the technological satyrs that lurk in the forests of Silicon Valley googled my mind yet-again and invented another way to violate me? Am I jousting with a frightful mythological beast come to life?'

Having failed to crack the secret code and get any information from the dastardly Google, my technological and thus emotional molester, I thought that a more personal touch was in order on my part and so decided to wait until mid-morning to call Susie and speak *manu a femanu* regarding her potential wedding ceremony at some future date, at some future time and at some future place. Like I said, she lives with Leonard out in San Francisco and we live in Florida... Caledonia (actually New Caledonia), so I'd have to wait before I could call her in hopes she'd turned on her cell phone. It was also the inadvertently polite thing to do. At 11:30 AM, 8:30 AM San Francisco time, I called Susie. What follows is a fairly accurate record of our conversation:

"Susie, you there?"

"Who's this?"

"Susie, it's your Dad."

"Dad? That you? Speak up!"

"You getting married?"

"What'd you say?"

"Susie, are you getting married?"

She said something muffled by static and then "Check the Google document. It has all the details!"

"Susie, I can't... "

Then the call was dropped and my cell phone went dead. From what I could tell she did not say she was getting married but then again she didn't deny it either. So much for the personal touch *à la* the cell phone. For reasons only an electrical engineer can understand, I could not get any bars to redial Susie and thus could not continue the exchange of irrelevant and confusing misinformation. Back to the drawing boards!

My darling Susie (Susie 1) is so anal retentive that she even keeps track of keeping track. She documents everything. Can be a real pain in the ass with all this keeping track of things, particularly my things, but occasionally the pain pays off, so I asked my super anal retentive wife for help. She accessed her long and apparently complete master keeping-track document and sure enough turns out, according to her cross-indexed master Word tracking document, I do have a g-mail account unbeknownst to me and with a password which Susie had cross-referenced twice.

For the life of me, I can't remember ever getting one of these but I apparently did at some previous point in time in my previous life. There was the possibility that the wife got a g-mail thingy for me and had neglected to tell me. She often 'helps' me in this way. For the sake of my mental health, I just hope that if this wasn't the case and I got my own, I didn't do so last week.

Ole Susie didn't stop there. She got on the dreaded Google and using my mysterious g-mail address and password, got at this matrimonial spread sheet stuff and printed it out along with another document which had the date, time and place as well as a schedule of events for this apparently great family matrimonial event. The document even included a very detailed menu for a Lobster Bake at said great matrimonial event. The spread sheet was a long list of all the invitees almost all of whom were relatives of Leonard's family. I counted them. There were 52. Susie and I were on the list as well as 11 others from Susie 2's side of the family. If my math was right, that's approximately a 4 to 1 ratio.

Sure enough, there was a plan in place for what appeared to be a Lobster Bake on Labor Day weekend of this year… an event to take place at Leonard's parent's house in Connecticut. The menu was very detailed. Looked to be a terrific Lobster Bake.

However, there was scant information about a wedding ceremony. In fact, there was none. This was quite puzzling. Leonard had invited 52 people... most of whom had Canadian addresses but with a bunch from Connecticut. Susie had invited 11 people. I was relieved to find that her brothers and sister-in-law and Susie and me were included in the 11. Six other names appeared on her list, none of whom I recognize... all from San Francisco... probably friends. I thought to myself, 'That's some crowd!'... noting that more people outside the family were invited than from within and a bunch from San Francisco to boot!

Look, I'm a pretty tolerant guy. I don't give a shit what you do as long as you leave me the hell alone and don't threaten my family. That's a very Italian-American point of view. If you want to know more about it, watch *Godfather 1*. Aside from those who attempt to physically harm my family, two kinds of people really piss me off: 1) Those who consider themselves morally superior to me, most of whom are eating a free lunch gratis my money and who have the gall to lecture me on what a greedy uncaring asshole I am and 2) those who consider themselves even more morally superior to me and feel obligated to make me do what they think is the right thing usually at my expense so that they can feel better about themselves. Guess who falls into one and possibly both of these categories. Fuckin' Canadians, assholes from Connecticut and those god damn San Francisco Twinkies.

Why Canadians? Those assholes are always lecturing Americans on what militaristic trogs we are for having the death penalty and for spending so much money on our military and for how our health care system sucks. Well my Canadian friends, you leaches have lived under our military umbrella for years and underfunded your military to pay for that healthcare system of yours that doesn't work. How do I know your stupid socialistic healthcare system doesn't work? Check the American hospitals along our Canadian border. They're full of Canadians.

And those lefties who populate Connecticut? They gave that race baiting idiot Jesse Jackson his only presidential primary victory back when, and they haven't changed. They're the richest state in the union and rate dead last in charitable giving. For them charity begins at home… someone else's home… like my home!

San Francisco? Hell, San Francisco isn't even an American city, and they wouldn't consider becoming Canadian because Canada is too damn conservative. Know how caring they are for the homeless down trodden? Why they care so much about it that the city gave those poor homeless men and women, no doubt victims of greedy assholes like me, free shopping carts. Now that's caring for the downtrodden. Free fuckin' shopping carts!

Looks to me like this Labor Day Lobster Bake was actually a family reunion for Leonard's family with a couple of strangers thrown in to show how tolerant people from Connecticut can be… me and Susie, Susie 2's brothers and sister-in-law being those tolerated. The rest of the family wasn't even invited. My blood was boiling!

I drove over to the Wal-Mart parking lot down the street so that I could get some bars on my cell phone and called Susie again. I dialed and she answered. Here's another fairly accurate record of our conversation:

"Susie, you there?"

"Who's this?"

"Susie, it's your Dad."

"Dad? That you? Speak up!"

"What's that siren? You in trouble?"

"No, I'm on a bus. Going to work."

Then the call got dropped. I quickly redialed to no avail. I thought, *Thank God for modern communication. In the past I'd of had to wait until the evening, called Susie on a real phone, as father-in-law Louie Zerrelli would put it, when she was at home and talked with her. There would have been no instant communication as we have today. Ain't modern communication great!*

At least I lived to communicate another day with my outrage intact. Maybe my 84-year old father-in-law wasn't that far off base with his distrust of cell phones and all this new technology in general. There was an oft-ignored definite and significant down-side to the land of tomorrow!

The great matrimonial lobster bake debate...

For the next week I was seeing purple whenever I thought about that matrimonial lobster bake debate I had with Susie... or kinda had. The damn thing looked more and more like a family reunion for Leonard's family. I could invite whomever I liked, I guess, provided I added their names and addresses to that Google spread sheet. Add fuckin' names to a Google spread sheet? This Google process may have represented modern life but it sure seemed to me that it wasn't much of an enhancement. Rather, these new electronic means of communication seemed to take the humanity out of human com-munication... electronic touchy feely without the touchy feely. As if cute little icons, I think they're called emojis, and those abbreviated little abbreviations like "LOL" gave that personal human touch to all those 'fuck you' emails and text messages. Damn!

Hell, why not hold the wedding electronically on Face book too. Send everyone a gift card for the local Red Lobster, have everyone sign on to the Great Matrimonial Lobster Bake Face Book page on their smart phones right from their Red Lobster dining room after ordering a lobster and bingo! Lobster Bake, followed or preceded by a wedding ceremony of some sort. Mission accomplished with none of that messy having to meet people *manu a manu*, face to face!

It took me several days to cool off, but I finally did and I called Susie back on my trusty cell phone:

"Susie? That you?"

"Dad? Speak up!"

"I am."

"You are what?"

"Speaking up! What's all the noise?"

"I'm on a bus going to work."

"Why are you having your wedding at Leonard's parents' house?"

"We want to get married where we met."

"But you didn't meet at Leonard's parents house in Connecticut. You met in Oak Woods at that stupid restaurant… What was it? The Stooling Mountain Inn?"

"No Dad, it was Spooling... the Spooling Mountain Inn."

"Whatever… it was in New York hundreds of miles from Leonard's parent's house. How many times have you been to Leonard's parents' house? "

"Once. It's close enough. Besides we couldn't afford it anyplace else."

"Why not? No matter where you go, it'll cost what it will cost. Plan accordingly. Maybe I can contribute."

"Well Leonard's parents are already contributing… $10,000… toward the cost of the wedding. They want to invite lots of family and most of them live in Canada and can't afford to fly out to the coast."

"Right! Just as I thought. It's not a wedding. It's a god damn family reunion… their family… all 52 of the bastards."

"No it's not. It's where we want to get married."

"You mean it's where you want to have a lobster bake and host a fuckin' family reunion for Leonard's parents."

If I were calling from a real phone, I'd have slammed down the receiver in high dudgeon at this point… the manly thing to do, but alas, I was on one of those dainty foo-foo cell phones and so I had to resort to viciously pushing a button to end the call… hardly an emotionally satisfying act of anger… more like an act of low dudgeon.

The picture was clear as day. Susie was accepting blood money to make it easy for Leonard's family to attend the Lobster Bake… which was really a family reunion for all those fuckin' Canadians while her family would have to fly from all over the god damn country to attend… all five of us. Fuck that! And if we wanted to invite someone… like other members of our family… we could add names and addresses to a god damn Google spread sheet. What's wrong with this picture? Everything. If this were a real wedding, wouldn't there be some mention of a wedding ceremony in the schedule of events?

After more days of anger and cooling off, I called Susie yet again on my trusty cell phone:

"Susie? That you?"

"Dad? Speak up!"

"I am."

"You are what?"

"Speaking up!"

"Look, our wedding isn't a family reunion for Leonard's family. It's our wedding." I could barely hear her over the sound of honking horns and screeching tires… apparently the noises of San Francisco traffic.

"Where are you? I can barely hear you."

"I'm walking to class."

"Class? What class?"

"A class on writing a thesis."

"What are you thesis-izing, anyway? Web design? Online wedding planning?"

"No, Dad, I'm getting a PhD in philosophy. I'm writing a thesis on the ontological implications of pragmatism."

"Oh."

All this PhD philosophizing and thesis-izing confused me. I thought she'd given up all that pragmatism crap for a more practical plan for her future. The last time she spoke to me about pragmatism, and this was years ago, the only thing I got out of the conversation was a headache.

My darling daughter had majored in opera at some place I never heard of out on the coast and when her prospects of employment appeared rather dim as her dedication and determination to spend 8

155

hours a day screeching foreign words, at least some of which would be in our other mother tongue, Italian, her dedication to screeching flagged and she took on a double major, the double part being philosophy. Now there's an employment winner. Apparently this additional major eminently qualified her to be a waitress. Not a waitress at any ole res-tau-rant. Rather at a fancy, schmancy one and all because of her major in philosophy and pragmatic philosophy, etc., etc. It was probably that pragmatism crap that nailed that high-class waitress position for her.

Her whole view of life confused me. I should think that anyone with the slightest tilt toward pragmatism wouldn't study pragmatism as it's a very un-pragmatic thing to do. How the hell could you make a living as a pragmatic philosopher? Teach other pragmatic philosophers? Seemed like a very small market requiring a very large investment with little hope of a decent return.

Being rather pragmatic myself, I decided to get back to basics and deal with the wedding before another headache struck me between the eyes, "Look, you didn't invite any of the other Marinellis or Zerrellis or Wardens to the wedding? Why not?"

"I don't know which Marinellis or Zerrellis to invite. I don't know them. Besides, there's so many of them. Who are the Wardens? "

Those other Marinellis and Zerrellis were... are my brothers, sisters, cousins, uncles and aunts. Next door, the Zerrellis lived upstairs and the Wardens lived downstairs. We all grew up together on Colonial Street. We were the last white families in the neighborhood as the blacks slowly took over. The other guinea families moved to better neighborhoods, family by family, until we were the only guineas left... then even the Wardens and the Zerrellis left leaving just us.

The Zerrellis and Wardens were also guineas to their very pasta loving hearts like us. Uncle Louie, he lived next store upstairs with Auntie Yo. Our house was next to theirs. Uncle Johnny and Auntie Yo matched Mom and Dad bambino for bambino until there were 10 of us... five kids upstairs and five next door... in what appeared after the birth of all those "masculine children", as the *Godfather's* Luca Brasi would have put it, a contest to see who could finally have the first girl baby since the first five for both families were masculine children à la Luca Brasi. Finally both Mom and Auntie Yo had girls ending the female procreation competition... which by the way Mom won by three weeks and two days... the competition coming down to the maternity ward wire, so to speak.

There were and still are a lot of Marinellis and Zerrellis and Wardens. We're a pretty motley crew, but there's still one thing that we share... that still unites us... at least the masculine children... who were now adults: we're world class beer drinkers... and my cousin Louie 2 is in a class all by himself. He's the Babe Ruth of beer drinkers backed by a very strong bench!

I knew I had Susie 2 on that 'I don't know all those Marinellis' contention of hers: "Well does Leonard know all those god damn Canadians that are his uncles and aunts and whatever? I'll bet he hasn't seen most of those god damn Canadian relatives of his in years. Hell, I'll double down that there's a bunch of them he's never seen at all. I doubt he'd be able to call them by name if they don't wear large name tags."

She got indignant: "Well, if you feel that way, add their names to spread sheet and we'll invite them."

"Look, I'm not adding any names to that god damn Google spread sheet. It's degrading."

"Well, send the names and addresses to me, and I'll add them."

"Okay. I'll send you an email tonight. About the actual wedding ceremony, am I supposed to walk you down the aisle or something? What'll my official wedding duties be?"

"I don't know. We haven't worked that out yet."

"For Christ's sake, you have a detailed menu for the lobster bake and you haven't planned the actual wedding ceremony? Whose wedding is it anyway?"

"It's my wedding, but most of the planning is being done by Leonard. I'm working and going to school. I don't have the time."

"You don't have the time to even participate in the planning of your own wedding? Not very pragmatic of you, my dear."

"Look, I'm taking classes to get a PhD like I said and I'm working too."

"Susie, you're not involved in your own life. Weddings are usually considered significant events in a person's life… particularly for the bride. Why are you bothering to get married?"

"I think it's time."

"Time for what… classes for some stupid PhD? What the hell…"

Then she hung up…. rather pushed a button and ended the call… probably in vicious low dudgeon. Her non-involvement explained a lot. The planning was turned over to Leonard who worked out the details with his parents, probably his mother and BINGO!... a fine lobster bake of a family reunion for a bunch of Canadians. Who'd a guessed?

Anyways, using my trusty pencil, I wrote out a list of Marinellis, Zerrellis and Wardens on a sheet of actual paper... threw in a couple of close family friends like the Jew... and handed the list to Susie manu a femanu, Susie 1 that is. Ole Susie 1, being steeped in computer literacy and liking it, created our own g-mail listy thingy document of invitees out of whole electronic cloth... or is it hole electronic cloth... and sent the damn thing to Leonard who added our entire listy thingy document of invitees to his official g-mail listy thingy document of invitees, apparently making the invitees we nominated in our listy thingy document official invitees on his listy thingy document. Who'd a thunk?

The invitees on both sides of Leonard's official listy thingy official invitational document showed up on the right day at the right time at the right house and in Connecticut as far as I could tell. This in itself was a matrimonial miracle of sorts although not necessarily a harbinger of things to come.

Anglo-Canadian Molson Muscle vs. Italian-American Budweiser Beef resulting in a matrimonial misadventure of semi-great consequence...

All invitees present gathered for the first official matrimonial event, the matrimonial rehearsal dinner held in the large outdoor patio behind the groom's parent's house. There was a certain irony in using the term 'rehearsal' to describe the dinner as it still remained unclear as to what we were rehearsing since the rehearsal consisted of going directly to the dinner... which was overly well attended as everyone who was invited to the wedding attended the rehearsal dinner. We were apparently all in this together although the exact meaning of the word 'this' remained somewhat ambiguous.

At one table sat a bunch of those Anglo-Canadians, at least seven and all of them fine examples of what I'd call rough and ready

Oxbow Lake The 2nd

Anglo-Canadianism. Most were burly fellows possessing certain physical indications that they enjoyed a brew or three.

At a table facing the Canadians sat three of Marinellis... one of whom was me... two Zerrellis and two Wardens... and all of whom, in my estimate, fine examples of rough and ready Italian-Americanism. Some of us, I must admit, were also burly fellows possessing certain physical indications that they... we... enjoyed a pasta dish with red sauce... and perhaps more than one... and of course an occasional Bud.

From the standpoint of the Anglo-Canadians gourmet-wise, the rehearsal dinner lacked a certain completeness as there was no 'real' meat and a fine white wine was served with the meal instead of Molsons. From the standpoint of the Italian-Americans gourmet-wise, the rehearsal dinner lacked a certain completeness as a delicate three-bean salad was served instead of a pasta with red sauce... and, of course, there was that fine white wine instead of Budweiser. However, there was a lot of other exotic kinds of stuff that tasted real good and pretty much covered up the deficiencies noted by both groups with the possible exception of the alcoholic drink accompanying the matrimonial rehearsal feast.

After eating, the two groups of international rivals stared across the patio at each other for many long and tense minutes. Then one of the Canucks named Cam... seemed like all of them were named either Cam or Dougie... yelled in our general direction, "You I-talians like drinkin' beer, eh?"

Our point man Louie Zerrelli... Louie 2 that is... yelled, "Right, eh! Same for you Canucks, eh?"

This Cam...maybe it was a Dougie... yelled, "Enough to drink you

160

I-talian gorbies[18] into a beg."

Louie turned to me and asked, "What the hell's a gorbie?"

I said, "Got no idea but it don't sound like a compliment"... which immediately turned the word into a profound insult.

Louie yelled back, "Gorbie or not, eh. We ain't beggin' you for nothing, *eh, eh!* You mamaluke, *eh, eh, eh!*" This repetition of 'eh' did not go unnoticed by the Anglo-Canadians and they did not take kindly to it.

This Cam, or maybe it was a Dougie, mishearing and thus definitely misunderstanding Louie's retort, and quite possibly not understanding it if he had correctly heard it, yelled, "You got no right to insult our mammas as you put it. You're mammas' not worth a pinch of coon shit either, eh!" This last 'eh' shouted as an emphatic rejoinder to the previous misuse of this expletive and furthermore implying that the Italian-Americans would agree with the somewhat confusing insult that their mammas were also worth less than coon shit.

While not knowing the specific meaning of the previous Anglo-Canadian insult to their mammas, its general meaning was well understood by all the Italian-Americans. They were fighting mad. The Anglo-Canadians, still suffering from the misunderstood Italian-American insult to their mammas, were also fighting mad. However, still being Canadians who were not presently playing hockey, they wanted to avoid unnecessary fisticuffs while still desiring revenge, and so one of the Cams or Dougies yelled "Molsons challenge?"

The Italian-Americans, playing the percentages as they saw them,

---

18   Gorbies is plural for gorby. Gorby is an Anglo-Canadian slang term for an ignorant tourist. The use of this term by an Anglo-Canadian to describe Americans while that Anglo-Canadian is visiting the United States is somewhat ironic on several levels.

believed that fisticuffs were unnecessary given the nature of the Anglo-Canadian challenge. On the behalf of all the Italian-Americans, Louie Zerrelli yelled "Budweiser challenge!"

After much haggling, the two rival groups agreed to call the contest "the Great Beer Can Challenge" with the definition of "beer" from the Anglo-Canadian viewpoint being *Molsons* while that definition from an Italian-American challenge being *Budweiser*... both sides believing that the two beers, while not being equal, were equivalent.

One of the Dougies yelled "Double two-fours. First done has won!"

I yelled, "Two-fours? What the hell's a two-four?"

Another Dougie yelled, "Spoken like a dart![19] It's a case of beer, 24 cans."

---

19   The word dart is a Canadian slang term. It has two meanings. Most commonly it means cigarette. However, it can also mean a chubby gaseous person (an overweight flatulent individual who is usually Canadian but not always).

Some linguists believe that this second meaning developed at a bar in the city of Hamilton, Ontario, in the 1960s. Apparently an inebriated Canadian named Dougie used the word when asking another inebriated Canadian named Cam for a cigarette. The inebriated Cam, mishearing the word, thought that the inebriated Dougie had called him a fart and took the request for a cigarette to be a grievous and gaseous insult.

The other Canadians at the bar, all of whom were also inebriated but only several of whom were named either Dougie or Cam, heard the word correctly but took it to be an insult when observing Cam nail the unsuspecting Dougie in his Molsons muscle. Dougie got his revenge by horking all over Cam's Molsons muscle and confirming the opinion of the other inebriated Canadians at the bar that the word dart was meant as an insult. The nature of the insult was misdetermined when Dougie yelled "I don't smell like a fart!" before nailing Cam and then Cam confirming this misinterpretation by horking on Dougie's Molsons muscle. Thus the word dart came to mean a fat gaseous Canadian at least in Ontario.

I turned to the guys "What'd he call me? A dart?"

Louie whispered to me, "Could be a compliment. Darts have sharp points. Maybe he means you asked a sharp question. Let it slide."

So I yelled "Okay, Two double two-fours... Molsons for you, Budweiser for us. But there's gotta be rules. One, no spilling beer... you spill, you lose; two, no up-chucking... you up-chuck, you lose; three, every can must be emptied before thrown down... if you throw down a can still containing a significant amount of beer, you lose, and four, no piss breaks... you piss, you lose even if you piss in your pants while still drinking."

The number and kind of the two-fours were quickly obtained from the supplies purchased for the matrimonial event as Leonard knew the beer drinking preferences of both sides of the two families which would eventually be united by law through the proposed matrimonial event.

Two chairs were set between the two rival tables, the two-fours were set down next to the appropriate chairs and the chairs occupied by the champions for each tribe. An observer for each tribe was placed next to the chair of the opposing tribal champion to insure that the four sacred rules of the contest were not broken. I represented our side. One of the Cams represented theirs. Then the two chairs were occupied: one by one of the Anglo-Canadians named Dougie, and one by our own Italian-American, Louie... that is, Louie 2.

The two all but royal champions of their tribes charged forward chugging-wise in spite of having already eaten heartily of the exotic faire and drunk much white wine to wash down said exotic faire earlier in the evening. The Anglo-Canadian named Dougie chugged his first Molson and threw it down to the ground. Louie 2 did the same with his first Bud... both cans clunking on the patio pavers all but simultaneously. As both champions drew second cans, the words "empty" echoed across the patio verifying the emptiness of both of the first chugged cans.

And so it went as each tribe cheered its regal champion. The Dougie would pull ahead by half a can and then the Louie would pull ahead by half a can. The contest was well contested so to speak.

However, as the two champions progressed through the first two-four, a careful observer could observe perspiration collecting on the foreheads of both champions... large and many droplets of sweat running down those regal foreheads. An even more careful observer would have also noted that a certain pallor... a whiter shade of pale if you will... had spread beneath the perspiration and across the facial features of both champions.

Around the 31st can of beer, both seated champions wobbled a bit on their competitive thrones. They turned and in the heat of the contest threw their 31st cans down... each grabbing a 32nd. As they began to chug those 32nd cans, two distinct yells pierced the air: "Half full!"

Both champions staggered to their feet, pulled the 32nd cans from their lips and spilled the contents of both cans down their chests and onto their laps. Both champions stood rather shakily, looked down and watched as the stain of their spilled beer ran down their chests, mysteriously spreading down their pants and collected around the flies of both pants. Then the stain spread even more profusely down the inside seams of both legs of both pants.

The two champions wobbled a bit, faced each other, gulped huge breaths of air and then projectile vomited huge chunks of what appeared to be undigested octopus marinating in a greenish substance onto their rivals, covering the Molson muscle and the pasta paunch of the two royal champions respectfully speaking. Then both competitors became less so by slumping back onto their royal thrones as their heads slowly sunk forward and into deep unconsciousness.

All hell broke loose. After much yelling and screaming both rival tribes agreed that their individual champions had broken Rule 1 by spilling beer, Rule 2 by upchucking and Rule 3 by throwing down a can still containing a significant amount of beer... but not necessarily in that order. The Great Beer Can Challenge would now turn on Rule 4, taking a piss break which included pissing in one's pants while still drinking. The question was who pissed their pants and if both champions did so, which one did so first. Upon these determinations the winner of the Great Beer Can Challenge would be determined!

I, with great perspicacity, proposed the 'yellow stain' method which involved the inspection of the underwear of the two now uncon-scious champions to determine which champion had actually pissed his pants... a yellow stain being an indication of the presence of urine. With great delicacy the underwear of both champions was inspected and lo and behold, both had pissed their pants as we all had thought possible.

Now what to do? One of the Dougies foolishly proposed the 'warm-er urine test' which involved touching the yellow area of the un-derwear in question and determining which of the yellow-stained underwear was warmer... the warmer the underwear, the more recent the pissing indicating that the other champion whose yellow-stained underwear was cooler had pissed his pants first and thus was the loser. And we foolishly agreed to it.

Exactly what happened next is unclear. As inspectors for the rival tribes began the very delicate process of gauging urine stain warmth, someone, and no one is sure exactly who, yelled "Molestation!" and a wine bottle, a white wine bottle, flew into gathered inspectors, bouncing off inspectors of both tribes. Each of the rival tribes believed that a member of the other tribe was responsible for the flying bottle because that tribe now realized that they were about to lose the challenge. Both tribes took what they considered to be a defensive posture and offense being the most effective defensive posture, began throwing punches at members of the other tribe's offensively defensive posture.

While it remains unclear who actually threw the first punch, I believe that it was probably the Anglo-Canadians what with their national past time being hockey. After the melee and after the police intervened, one of the Cams claimed that Canadians, particularly Anglo-Canadians, were a peaceful bunch and would only throw punches in self-defense which they thought proved that the Italian-Americans had thrown the first punch and which I thought proved that we had not because of the Canadians' love of hockey, the only sport that recognizes fisticuffs as an integral part of the sport and the only sport that does so and that is held outside a squared ring... like boxing! Enough said.

Matrimonial misadventures, consequentially speaking, and the unexpected appearance of an Elvii...

As it turns out, while it appeared that many punches may have been thrown during the attempt to determine who actually won the Great Beer Can Challenge, there was no verifiable evidence that such had actually happened as few if any of those punches had apparently landed... neither theirs nor ours. Thus the police decided that since they could not verify that anyone had actually been punched during the melee, they could arrest no one for assault. I considered us lucky and kept my mouth shut as did most of the invitees and principals.

However, the police did end up arresting two Dougies, one Cam, two Louies and an Anthony for public intoxication. The three members of each tribal group followed the police out to the road... each tribal group arguing that the other tribal group should be arrested for assault. Once the feet of the six obviously very inebriated individuals hit the town road, the police in high dudgeon arrested all six and took them to the drunk tank where they spent the night and most of the following day. As the night progressed into the following day, the inebriated six suffered more and more... the effects of their hangover coming to a painful climax later the next morning. Had they been challenge champions, they would have forfeited the contest for violating Rule 2 and quite possibly Rule 4.

Lost in all the confusion was the matrimonial event itself, i.e. the wedding ceremony. After bailing out the intoxicated six, all the invitees, including both the Anglo-Canadians and the Italian-Americans involved in the unsuccessful Great Beer Can Challenge, scoured the house and surrounding area for the bridal couple, but none was found.

Two days later the bridal couple sent a series of texts and pictures to us on our infernal cell phones. They had flown to Las Vegas and gotten married at Billy Bob's Used Car Dealers and Elvis Marriage Chapel. There was Elvis himself performing the ceremony before a bright red and apparently used Prius and standing next to our own Susie 2 and Leonard stood an official witness... someone who Susie 2 claimed was the bastard son of someone famous who was dead... someone named Colonel Parker. Since the happy couple had purchased that used Prius at Billy Bob's Used Car Dealers, they were not charged for the marriage ceremony at his Elvis Marriage Chapel. The happy couple's last text read, and I quote, "off to sf details later hope all enjoyed the gathering lol s&l"

And so goes my human comedy for yet another chapter... lol... laugh out loud!

THIS PAGE INTENTIONALLY LEFT MOSTLY BLANK

(THE ABOVE VERY LIKELY BEING AN OXIMORONIC EDITORIAL OVERSTATEMENT)

IRRELEVANT NOTE FROM THE AUTHOR:

ONE BOY'S COCKROACH IS ANOTHER BOY'S PALMETTO BUG... AND SOMETIMES IT'S THE SAME BOY AND THE SAME COCKROACH!

The Blattella Chronicles

The tumid surfaces of ancient bodies...

Sean Murphy Warden lay quietly on his bed watching the far corner of his room. His mind drifted as he mumbled to himself, "Being a teenager is no big deal." The early morning sun rose slowly and peeked through his window but much of his room remained in darkness, particularly the corner where he directed his eyes. Soon the temperature would rise as it did every day and his room would become uncomfortably hot, but for now his room was relatively cool. He was satisfied to lie on his bed and to watch and to wait as an early morning breeze floated in his open window and glanced off his naked body.

His mother had insisted that he always wear pajamas regardless of the weather. She believed that there was a right way for Sean to do things and a wrong way and since wearing the proper clothing promoted modesty and clean living in young men, it was one of the right ways, pajamas being one of those right way garments.

His mom was what is termed in common parlance "a doting single mother"... the "single" resulting from a separation and eventual divorce from Sean's father, Dr. James Mead Warden, two years ago when the good Doctor ran away with Mrs. Jacobs to Albany, New York, where he now taught at the state university there and where Sean had been born.

Sean had learned why his father was no longer around when he overheard Monsignor Donnelly and Gail's mom comforting his mom as she sat at the kitchen table crying her heart out over some note she'd read. Monsignor had said, "It is not you who are living in sin. It is he who is living in sin with a married woman" and Gail's mom had then yelled, "That Jacobs bitch would spread her legs for the mail man! You'd think a man with a doctorate in sociology or whatever the hell he studied would have learned how to keep his fly zipped... Dr. James Warden is a philandering asshole!" Sean's mind got stuck on what Gail's mom first said... the part about spreading legs for the mailman. It confused him and he wondered to himself *Why would anyone spread their legs for anything, particularly a mail man?*

To make things even more confusing, his mom dropped Warden from her name and now used the name Murphy... her maiden name... Fiona Murphy... while Sean kept his father's last name... Warden... and left the name Murphy in the middle... Sean Murphy Warden. Life for Sean Murphy Warden was becoming curiouser and curiouser.

As to his mom's insistence that he wear pajamas during the summer, Sean recently and quite secretly stopped doing so. In late June, when his mother ended his home schooling for the summer, a heat wave descended upon them. In order to save on electricity his mom didn't crank up the air conditioning until later in the day and so his pajamas tops became soaked in perspiration and felt uncomfortable. Not only did his pajama tops feel uncomfortable, they smelled, so he removed them. The heat wave persisted and Sean removed his pajama tops every night, but he still sweated and his pajamas bottoms collected perspiration below the small of his back and so two days later, he removed them as well. Truth was, not only was sleeping naked cooler, it made him feel good. He wasn't sure exactly why but he liked it… a lot.

He feared that his mother would unexpectedly open his bedroom door, find him without his pajamas and throw one of her hissy fits. But for reasons he did not understand, this fear was different than other fears he felt. This fear felt good. And now he always slept naked.

This morning, as he lay there, he felt uncomfortable in spite of the cool breeze from his open window. His bladder was full and cried to be emptied but he did not move. Other mornings when first awakening, he would quickly don his pajamas, walk down the hall to the bathroom and relieve himself, but today was different. He didn't want to chance missing it.

Suddenly, it appeared as it had the previous two mornings. It fluttered down from the shadows and landed with a thud on its brown armored legs in the corner where Sean had so intently directed his attention. The creature was gigantic, at least three feet in length, and took up most of the corner. Its long antennae gracefully waved back and forth before its head as if it were directing an orchestra playing a Strauss waltz. It pulled its two sets of wings back along its segmented body and lowered its plated thorax to the floor raising its head slightly in Sean's direction. It was to Sean a grotesque yet strangely beautiful creature.

Where it came from Sean knew not. All he knew was that for the third straight morning it had appeared, with a thud in that corner. The first morning, Sean had gotten up, quickly dressed in his pajamas and trotted off to the bathroom to relieve himself as was his habit. Upon returning, he had flopped back into his bed and lay there looking wistfully at the ceiling. A thud had awakened him from his reverie. He turned his head in the direction of the thud… the darkened corner off to his left… and there it was, the creature, apparently staring in his direction. For some reason, the creature had not frightened him. Rather, it had intrigued him. Its big compound eyes had looked toward him, its antennae rhythmically cutting through the air. He squinted his eyes closed. When he reopened them, the creature was gone. It had disappeared into the shadows without a sound as quickly and mysteriously as it had appeared.

Oxbow Lake The 2nd

That first morning Sean wasn't sure the creature could even see him. Now, on the second morning, the creature spoke to him in a hollow, reedy voice. Sean could barely understand it.

"My name is Siegfried Blattella Germanicus."

Sean replied "My name's Sean." Then the creature disappeared into the shadows as it had the previous morning.

Today, the creature addressed him directly, "Sean, you have to pee, don't you?"

"Yes, but I waited for you. I didn't want to miss you."

"I'm flattered. I see you're naked. Feels good doesn't it?"

"Yes."

"And having to hold your pee in feels good too… even thrilling doesn't it. Is that why you so looked forward to seeing me so you would have an excuse to hold your legs together to keep from peeing?"

Sean moved his legs together and slowly pressured his penis between his thighs. The pressure felt good. "No, that's not why. I'm interested in you and what you might say. I've never seen a… creature like you. You're quite large and you speak English too. Am I day dreaming like in a story? Are you real?"

Sean detected a sort of smile on what Sean perceived as the creature's face. It answered, "Are you asking if I'm real? Well here's something that's real. Slowly and rhythmically tighten and relax you thigh muscles. Follow the rhythm of my antennae… Feels good, doesn't it? Very good."

Sean did as instructed and tightened and relaxed his thigh muscles slowly and rhythmically, becoming a musician of sorts in conductor Siegfried Blattella Germanicus' imaginary orchestra. As his thigh muscles tightened and relaxed, his penis grew and hardened. He still felt the pressure of his bladder, but now he couldn't pee if he wanted to for some reason. He looked down between his thighs and his penis was longer and harder, its head peeking out from his closed thighs.

Sean closed his eyes and replied in a soft and frightened voice to the creature's last question, "Yes. It feels good."

He heard a faint "It's supposed to." He slowly opened his eyes glancing toward the corner and the creature was gone. He closed them again and continued to rhythmically tighten and loosen his thigh muscles around his hardened penis. It felt good and then better, and he quickened the pace as he tightened and relaxed his thigh muscles. His breathing quickened and then a most marvelous thing happened. His hardened penis began to pulsate and on its own. It only lasted for several seconds but it was a wonderful several seconds. He had never felt such intense pleasure in his life. He lay there with his eyes closed for some time as his breathing slowly returned to normal. When he opened them and looked down at his thighs, the head of his penis no longer peeked out at him. Instead, a thick milky substance pooled across his thighs. He leaned forward on his right elbow and reached forward with his left hand, gently touching the substance with his forefinger. He moved his hand toward his face and touched his forefinger with his thumb. The substance was sticky. As he moved his arms, he felt the substance on his thigh slide down the side of his leg. He watched the substance drip onto the sheet beneath him.

A day and a night passed. Sean lay upon his bed drifting into and out of sleep as he again awaited the arrival of one Mr. Siegfried Blattella Germanicus yet again. He was glad his home schooling year had ended for the summer and his mind wandered. He thought about the daily routine that had ended as well.

His neighbor Gail popped into his head. She lived next door. Her mom home schooled her too and Sean's mom and Gail's mom often coordinated their home schooling lessons. Thus Sean and Gail had spent much time together. She was pretty smart and paid attention during their lessons. She was a good student.

He noticed that when she was reading or concentrating she played with her hair. She'd twirl strands of her long brown hair around the forefinger of her right hand as she concentrated. Sean did not know why, but he found himself often staring at Gail when she did this. He found the movement of her fingers as it wound and unwound those strands of hair to be hypnotic.

As he lay there, he wondered about something that had happened the week before the home schooling lessons had ended. Gail went home after the first lesson and studied alone at her home and by herself. He heard his mom say to Gail's mom, "Sean doesn't need to know about this." And yet she had spent the rest of the week studying the same lesson that he had, a lesson on Greek mythology. At the end of the week, they were reunited for the exam. He had done very well on the exam and Gail had done uncharacteristically poorly. As he lay on his bed, he wondered about the separate lessons. He didn't understand why he and Gail had studied separately since they studied the same subject.

A sudden thud broke his revelry. Sean quickly turned his head and looked into the darkened corner. Sure enough, the thud announced the morning arrival of Mr. Siegfried Blattella Germanicus.

"Enjoy your little lesson in rhythm yesterday."

The reedy voice startled Sean and left him momentarily speechless.

Then he uttered, "Yes, it felt very good. What happened?"

"You masturbated and had an orgasm."

"I did what?"

"That feeling that you had, that was an orgasm. You masturbated, albeit very inefficiently?"

"What was that stuff that came out of me?"

"Let me tell you a little story to help explain it. When the time is right, I can smell this wonderful perfume. See these waving antennae? That's how I smell things. I'm never sure when I'll smell that wonderful smell, but I know it when I smell it. My policy is to keep those antennae waving just in case."

A puzzled look crossed Sean's face as he interrupted, "But I don't have antennae and yesterday I didn't smell anything?"

Siegfried fell silent for a moment and then said aloud but obviously to himself, "This is going to be more difficult than I thought. These humans are so unaware. They apparently have no instincts. They know almost nothing without being told." He sighed the word "evolution" as if questioning its effectiveness.

Siegfried stared at Sean for what seemed like hours to Sean. The creature's antennae gracefully and slowly waved through the air, conducting yet another imaginary waltz. An observer other than Sean might have described Siegfried as "pensive" if such a word could be attached to a three-foot cockroach.

Siegfried mumbled to himself as he puzzled through his dilemma of how best to explain life to Sean. "Hmmm... Not the biblical approach. Too much baggage, too distant from nature. He has studied Greek mythology recently. That's good. I can use that. The anthropomorphic approach would be more effective anyway."

Siegfried raised himself slightly so that he more directly faced Sean and spoke to him, "Remember when you studied Greek mythology with Gail?"

"Yes." It never occurred to Sean to question how Siegfried knew about his study of Greek mythology or the fact that he had not done so with Gail or that the creature even knew about Gail.

"Did you wonder why Gail got upset in the middle of that first class and her mother took her home... and she didn't come back for the rest of the week?"

Sean furrowed his brow in puzzlement, "Yes. We usually study stuff like that together."

Siegfried shot another question at Sean, "Why do you think she was studying Greek mythology by herself?"

"I don't know."

"She was, how should I put this… indisposed for the first time."

Sean's brow furrowed even deeper, "Indisposed?"

"Something was happening to her and her mom wanted to teach a special lesson to explain it to her. Your mom thought it best that you not hear the explanation."

"Was she sick? Did she have something that I could catch?"

"Well, not exactly, but what she had could cause you grief. And if she didn't have it, it could cause someone, perhaps you, even more grief."

A look of total bewilderment came across Sean's face, "Grief? More grief? I don't understand."

"You recently studied Greek mythology, right? Remember the story of Prometheus?"

Sean answered the question as he would have had he been asked to recite the answer by his mom during a home schooling lesson: "Yes. He's the one who stole fire from Zeus and gave it to man. Zeus punished him by chaining him to a rock and an eagle came and ate his stomach every day. No his liver… and it'd grow back at night so that he could get it eaten again the next day."

"Right. But you were only taught half of the story."

Now Siegfried had aroused Sean's intellectual curiosity, "What's the other half?"

"Well Prometheus was a Titan and Zeus had defeated the Titans to become numero uno in the god department. Prometheus didn't much like playing second fiddle to Zeus and wanted to conquer Zeus and get out from underneath his thumb. So Prometheus made a plan, a long range plan. Do you remember what the name Prometheus means?"

Sean followed every word intently and responded as the good student that he was, "Yes, it means 'forethought'. His brother was Epimetheus and his name meant 'afterthought'."

"Good, very good. But let's not get ahead of the story. Well Prometheus creates men from clay. He figures that without worshippers, the gods are rather pointless, and worshippers can be very useful. He plans to cultivate and develop men so that eventually men will become powerful servants and help him overthrow Zeus. Prometheus knows that cunning is more important than strength and that the men he created can learn and develop into the very cunning creatures that

177

he needs to conquer Zeus."

Siegfried stopped his divine narrative for a moment, "Follow me so far, Sean?"

"Kind of. Why doesn't Prometheus just create cunning creatures in the first place? Why wait?"

"A good question. You're on top of your game this morning. Prometheus isn't omnipotent. You know what 'omnipotent' means?"

"Yeah, all powerful."

"Right. Even though he's a god, he has limitations. He can't create experience and men need experience amongst other things to develop into the cunning creatures that Prometheus needs. And here's the really clever part, he thinks Zeus will be flattered by the idea of worshippers and won't interfere with the development of men and by the time he catches on, it'll be too late. It'll be he who gets chained to a rock and have his liver eternally eaten or some other diabolically clever punishment. Got it so far?"

"Yes. I think so. But what about the part where Prometheus tries to fool Zeus to eat the fat and bones of sacrificed animals instead of the meat. That's when his problems with Zeus began. Right?"

"Right again! This little lesson on life just might work out after all. Well, men in order to grow and live need sustenance and fat and bones just won't do it, so Prometheus tries to get Zeus to choose the fat and bones so that the men have the meat. He knows that once a precedent is set in the universe, it's pretty hard to change."

"Why did Zeus choose the fat and bones anyway? He's supposed to be smart and all."

"Zeus was no dummy. He was setting Prometheus up. Yes, he liked the idea of worshippers so he wanted that part of Prometheus' plan to go forward. He realized that for men to survive, they'd need meat, so he chose the fat and bones. It really didn't matter much anyway since the gods ate ambrosia for food. On the other hand, he didn't want men to become too clever, for he too realized the danger that such cleverness could cause him in the future, so he had to handicap them so to speak."

"That's when he took fire from them?"

"Right. And hid the necessities of life from them as well so that they'd have to struggle so hard to survive that they wouldn't have enough time and energy to become overly clever. Zeus had them on the hook for they would always be dependent on him for help, which he could grant or withhold. He was assuring himself a large group of dependent worshippers and wonderful entertainment."

"Siegfried, how does this explain Gail's being... what you called it? ... indisposed... that I'm not supposed to know about."

"In good time, Sean, in good time. What does ole Prometheus think of Zeus' actions? Well he sees his plan falling apart and knows that desperate action is required on his part."

"And that's when he steals fire for the men he's created. Why is fire so important?"

"Because without fire men can't progress and build civilizations and gain the experience they need to become overly clever. Now that men had fire, they'd be on the road to being overly clever. And that's when Zeus went to plan B to counter Prometheus' theft of fire."

"What'd he do next?"

"He created Pandora and her lovely little box."

179

"Pandora was a woman, right? Was she the first one?"

"You got it. She's the first one in a long line."

"Why'd Zeus do it?"

"Remember the story of Pandora?"

"Yup. Zeus arranged for her to marry that Epimetheus guy and she got this box, which the gods filled with all sorts of bad stuff like pestilence and disease. And she was curious and opened the box and all the bad stuff got out."

"Right. First, Pandora was built to be alluring to men, with curves and softness and beautiful breasts. Just the shape to attract men. And she smelled real good too."

"Pandora was like women today? Like Gail?"

"Now you're getting there. So do you find Gail attractive? She's different than she used to be. She's changed. Have you noticed?"

"I think so. She's not so skinny anymore."

"That's not the half of it, my boy. Not by a long shot or even a short one."

Sean thought of Gail and realized that she had changed. Her shape had changed. It wasn't just her twirling of her hair that he had found hypnotizing. As he thought of her, he felt a tingle between his legs and his penis began to grow. His thighs began to rhythmically contract and relax.

Sean closed his eyes as his breath quickened. He heard Siegfried sigh. When Sean slowly, almost absent mindedly, opened his eyes, Siegfried was gone...

The next morning, Siegfried did not appear, much to Sean's disappointment. He had waited for some time, lying naked upon his bed, his bladder full until he heard his mother walk down the hallway outside his room. He quickly jumped out of bed and pulled on his pajamas bottoms.

His mother tapped on his bedroom door and whispered, "Sean, you up?"

"Yup, mom. Out in a minute."

"I'm going to shower, so if you need to use the bathroom, you better go now."

As he pulled his pajama tops over his head, he yelled, "OK, mom." And he heard his mother pad her way back to her bedroom. He ran to the bathroom, relieved himself and retreated to his bedroom. He plopped down on his bed and thought of Siegfried and wondered if he'd ever see him again. Hunger pangs awakened him from his thoughts. He jumped up and headed for the kitchen. As he entered the hall, he noticed that the door to the bathroom had swung partially open. Sometimes the door latch didn't catch. Even though his mother was standing behind the door, he could see her reflection in the full length bathroom mirror.

She stood naked and with her hands felt her one breast, slowly pressuring it with her fingers. Sean was mesmerized. The nipple on her breast hardened as she ran her fingers across it and became erect. Then she moved her left hand to her other breast and supported it as she slowly felt around the breast with the fingers of her other hand and the nipple on this breast also became erect. Sean's eyes were drawn to the place where his mother's legs met. There was a triangle of curly black hair covering the area. He felt his penis begin to harden. His pajama bottoms tented in front of him. His mom turned

181

and looked over her shoulder at her back. Sean watched carefully as she turned. Her buttocks gently jiggled as she moved. His breath quickened and he felt his penis begin to rhythmically pulsate. He quickly grabbed the base of his now hardened penis in an effort to stop it, but he couldn't. He watched as a wet spot appeared on the front of his tented pajamas and slowly spread.

He panicked and still holding his penis with his left hand he hop-scotched to his bed where he flopped down. His chest throbbed. He did not know why, but he began to sob. He pulled himself into a fetal position and fell asleep.

Pandora and her box...

Sean lay in bed trying to fall asleep and not to think about what was happening to him. The more he tried not to think, the more he thought; the more he thought, the more he tried not to think. His life was getting curiouser and curiouser as they say and in most disturbing ways which he did not understand.

He knew things just weren't the way they used to be not all that long ago, but he wasn't exactly sure how or why or even exactly what was happening... but he knew things weren't the same... and it kinda snuck up on him... ambushed him. Things used to be simple... somehow now they weren't... they were complicated... very complicated and in mysterious ways.

Take last week. That huge cockroach... that Mr. Siegfried Blattella Germanicus... had thudded into his life early one morning and spun a tail about Pandora to explain why Gail didn't study Greek mythology with him because of some condition she had... was she sick? What was that all about, anyway?

182

And if all that Pandora business wasn't confusing enough, there was that business of massaging his penis as that huge cockroach had encouraged… taught?... him to do and the wonderful feeling that resulted and the stuff that squirted out and messed up his PJs… which he hid from his mom in the bottom drawer under his sweats. He planned to wash off that stain… that evidence of his sin and perversion… himself when his mom wasn't home… something he had to do before she noticed a pair of PJs missing from the laundry.

He didn't want her to see that stain. It puzzled and embarrassed him… it was evidence of… well he just didn't want to put it into words for to do so would make it even more real and terrible… make him feel even worse than he already did. Better off leaving well enough alone and not put words around what he felt.

Emotionally exhausted from all this not thinking, Sean finally dozed off. It was a fitful, tossing and turning kind of sleep. Images kept swirling in his head like a kaleidoscope of pictures. The images spun so quickly that at first he couldn't recognize them. Then they slowed. There was Gail sitting at her desk studying and twirling her hair. Her ankles were crossed and her legs were squeezed tightly together. He didn't know how he could tell, but he could. Then the image of that huge cockroach thumping down into his nightmare of a dream… staring at him and pointing one of those ugly arms… legs?... at him… laughing with that squeaky high pitched voice of his.

And then there was this image of his mom. At first, he couldn't quite make it out… then he caught her face in a mirror… it was the bathroom mirror. The image slowed and came into focus. There she was standing naked with that triangle of curly black hair between her legs. She was massaging her breasts. At least it looked like she was massaging them… perhaps because it felt good for the nipples on

183

each breast became erect and hardened into wrinkled knobs… wonderful wrinkled knobs. She turned and her buttocks came into full view and jiggled slightly as she continued massaging her breasts.

Suddenly, Sean felt something wonderful happening between his legs. It startled him and woke him up. A warm wet feeling spread. He pulled himself up and looked down the bed. The sheet was tented. A wet spot appeared at the tent's peak. The wetness spread down the tent as he felt rhythmic contractions intensify between his legs. The stain at the peak of the tent slowly spread down the tent until it covered a huge area between his legs. He raised his head toward the ceiling and moaned… one of those low guttural moans as the rhythmic contractions slowed and finally stopped.

Sean plopped back down into his pillow and stared at the ceiling. He was exhausted and his thoughts were disturbing but hazy. Then it struck him… he had wet his bed… but not like years ago. Like the rest of his life, this was different too. He didn't feel relief as he had in the past. True back then there would be some embarrassment but everyone knew that it happened from time to time… especially to boys his mother had told him… so it wasn't a big deal… just some embarrassment… that was all it was.

But this time he felt pleasure… pure pleasure… and that pleasure was in some way brought on by seeing his mother's naked… her alluring breasts… that mysterious patch of hair between her legs… that wonderful jiggling buttocks, and it had all happened in his head… HIS head!

Guilt overwhelmed him… a voice within yelled that he shouldn't feel this way about his mother. It was sinful… even perverted. He didn't know much about perversion. His religious instruction on Wednesdays at Saint Augustine's had hinted at it without actually describing it in words, but he was pretty sure this is what Monsignor

Donnelly was hinting at. And he was piling sin upon sin now. How could this happen? He didn't even try to make it happen. It just did, but it was his fault, for it was his dream… nightmare… and it was he who felt the pleasure… and he couldn't even confess, for to put words around what had happened terrified him. He lie there confused, overcome with guilt… embarrassed beyond the words he feared.

A knock at his bedroom door followed by a voice broke his concentration, "Up and at 'em, honey bun! Breakfast in 10." He froze at the sound of that voice and didn't reply. Then the same voice came again but this time tinged with concern, "Sean, you up!"

He could feel a wetness which was becoming more and more uncomfortable as it cooled. He pushed himself up on his elbows and there it was… still there… a large wet circle on the sheet.

"Yes, mom, just…" as his voice trailed off.

"OK, honey bun. It's your favorite this morning… Mr. Pancakes with strawberries."

He heard footsteps pad off down the hallway. He thought, *At least I wasn't wearing my PJs*. He jumped out of bed and into his dry pajamas. Then he froze staring down at the huge wet spot. The thought that at least he didn't have to deal with disappearing wet pajama bottoms but now he faced an even bigger problem. He couldn't hide this stain. Sheets were too big. He asked himself out loud, "What am I to do? What am I to do? What am…" as his voice trailed off into silence.

Unable to decide on a course of action and fearing that if he delayed his morning appearance for breakfast, his mom would show up at his bedroom door and demand to come into his room. Once she got in, she'd notice that wet spot immediately and then what was he

185

to say... how could he explain it? So he carefully folded the sheet over itself to cover up that sinful, perverted stain and moped off to the kitchen where Mr. Pancakes... and his ever inquisitive mom... awaited him.

Sure enough, there at table smiling up at him was Mr. Pancakes with two strawberry eyes, a strawberry nose and a smiling raisin mouth. And across the table was his mom, dressed in her robe concentrating on her cross-word puzzle. He poured syrup on Mr. Pancakes and quickly cut him up into bite size pieces with a vengeance.

His mom looked up and said, "My, my... my little honey bun... we must be famished the way we're cutting up Mr. Pancakes."

He said nothing in reply and pushed the destroyed Mr. Pancakes around his plate. He bit into a strawberry and a couple of pieces of Mr. Pancake's face, but instead of his usual breakfast hunger, he was preoccupied with the problem of that huge wet spot on his bed sheet and what he should tell his mom about it.

His mom noticed his lack of appetite immediately, leaned forward and looked down at his plate. Sean, not wanting to take a chance that her bathrobe might open even a bit as she leaned forward, stared down at the destroyed face of Mr. Pancakes.

That dreaded look of concern appeared and she asked, "Sean, are you feeling OK? You attacked Mr. Pancakes like you were starving but now you're just pushing pieces of him around your plate? What's wrong?"

He knew he couldn't hide his wet bed sheet from his mother and if he tried, the truth would eventually tumble out of him. It always did. What was he to do? And he couldn't just start talking. If he did that, he was sure she'd figure out what happened... how he saw her naked... how he apparently made an effort to see her naked by dreaming of her and had... well he just couldn't even put the rest into words. After some more agonizing, he decided that a straight confession to 'having an accident' would be by far the lesser of the two evils... that last evil being impossible for him to explain... especially to his mother so he said, "I had an accident last night... I wet the bed."

At first his mom sat up straight and asked, "My little man, are you OK?" and then she smiled and said, "Not to worry. I'll wash the sheets today. Did you put your PJs from last week in the wash?" She smiled again... that knowing smile.

Sean pushed the pieces of Mr. Pancakes around his plate with his fork and said, "I'll check. Can I be excused?"

He looked into her face and she smiled again and said, "Of course, honey bun. These accidents happen sometimes to teenagers. It's nothing to worry about."

Sean was sure she knew, but instead of getting angry, she smiled. The question, *Why did she smile?* haunted him.

Froggy come a' courtin'...

Sean opened his eyes and cuffed his hands behind his neck as he stared up at the ceiling. Summer was over and he had a full day ahead. Today was a biggy... the first day of high school... a real high school... Saint Augustine High School. Home schooling was over. And after school, he'd have his first cross country practice with the freshman team. He'd heard all about how the brothers would be out on the course with their stop watches monitoring the team's workout. And Gail was going to come over to his house and the two of them were to walk to the school bus stop together.

187

He smiled to himself and looked down toward his feet. He casually pulled the sheet up toward his chin exposing his toes. Usually he'd wiggle his toes, scratch his balls… which he enjoyed more and more as he got older… and jump out of bed ready to meet the day's challenges. But this morning was different. How could this be? He couldn't see his wiggling toes. Where were those wiggling toes? He was pretty sure he was wiggling them... but where were they? He could not see them, for a huge and strange belly obstructed his line of sight. A huge belly? Whose huge belly was that? How strange!

This confused him no end for he had always been able to see his wiggling toes. He saw them every morning wiggling away when he woke up. It was how he greeted each day, but for some strange reason, today he could not. He raised himself on his elbows with great difficulty and lo and behold, there they were. He saw those little piggies, all ten of them, as they wiggled away giving him the feeling that things were returning to normal.

Sean felt better now, and proceeded to turn his body onto his right side so that he could free his left hand and lovingly scratch his balls. He loved scratching his balls in the morning when he first woke up. However, this morning his body seemed reluctant to obey his commands, for he couldn't just tumble over onto his right side as he usually did. Instead, it took a couple of tries. The first time, his body almost rolled over but just as it reached the apex of the move, it rolled backwards so that he was again staring at the ceiling. The second time he was successful in getting his body to roll onto its right side but only after awkwardly wedging his left elbow against the mattress and pushing with all his might. He could never remember it being so difficult to turn over for one of his wakening pleasures. What in heaven's name was happening?

He remained still for a moment to catch his breath for the effort of turning onto his right side had been much more physically taxing than usual. After several minutes of puffing away, his breathing returned to normal and he regained his strength. He reached beneath the sheet, over his belly and between his legs with his left hand to scratch his balls. He reached down but couldn't feel his balls. He reached further and still couldn't feel his balls. Where had they gone?

He stopped for a moment staring into space in disbelief and then, in a great panic, ripped off the sheet. He spread his legs, bent forward and to one side, looked down and sure enough, there was a nut sack, and there they were encased in that nut sack… two huge testicles, far larger than he had remembered them being, hanging much lower and drooping from that huge sack of wrinkled skin. He panicked for the first time as worry and dismay turned to fear. Could those two huge balls be his?

He kicked his legs out, pushed himself into a seated position and stuck his feet over the edge of his bed. He let them dangle for a moment and then gently placed them on the cold floor. While seated there on his bed, he looked over at the mirror above his chest of drawers and stared at the image before him. He did not recognize the person in that image which he had assumed was him… but clearly it was not, for the creature in that image was balding and had a chubby jowled face decorated with a long banana nose. Sean raised his left hand to his face and with his forefinger, pushed the nose to the right and then to the left. Sure enough, the creature in the mirror did the same.

He pushed himself up off the bed with his hands and stood. He looked at the now standing body in the mirror before him… and his eyes slowly moved down that foreign image before him. Sure enough, below that huge belly was a huge nut sack hanging there beneath that distended belly… and between two skinny hairy legs. It hung there like a very wrinkled and partially inflated balloon floating upside-down defying the pull of gravity. Could that be his penis dangling down and bisecting that huge ball sack? Couldn't be, for this penis was thicker than his… seemed much longer and fatter… and with a huge purplish upside down helmet pointing toward the floor. A huge purplish helmet at the end of his penis? Couldn't be his penis.

He reached around a fat belly and had to bend forward to reach his penis which he gently fondled. He could see his fingers as they gently massaged the image before him and he could feel his penis being massaged. Usually his penis would jump to attention when he gently massaged it in the morning, but this morning it just hung there, an inert sausage-like tube of meat. He collapsed back onto the bed and sat there staring at the image before him… an image which he did not recognize. He was sure it was in fact not him. It couldn't possibly be him.

He sat there collecting his thoughts and wondering what had happened to him on this very important morning… if in fact something had happened to him. Perhaps he was still dreaming. No "dreaming" wasn't the right word. This was a full-fledged Halloween nightmare. His disturbing thoughts were interrupted by a gentle knock at his bedroom door. It was his mom. She had stopped entering his bedroom in the morning after several rather embarrassing incidents arising from his developing adolescence and his resulting demand for privacy. And to be sure that she wouldn't violate that privacy and invade his sanctuary under any circumstances, Sean had screwed a latch on his side of the door, for a man needed his privacy.

"Sean, up and at 'em, honeybunch. Breakfast in ten." There was no reply and his mom whispered a bit louder, "Sean, are you up?"

Again there was no reply and this time she yelled in that strained whisper of a concerned mother, "Sean, are you OK? You've got to get up. Gail will be over in half an hour. You don't want to be late for the first day of high school!"

Sean snapped out of his disturbing thoughts, looked up at the image before him and realized that if it were in fact his image in that mirror, he couldn't allow his mother to see him... not until this rather frightening incident had passed and he were back to his old self.

He started to answer but as he pushed air through his vocal chords, he had difficulty controlling them. His voice seemed foreign to him... high-pitched and nasal. He didn't recognize it. "Mommm..." His voice trailed off. His mom yelled a second time in that strained concerned whisper, only deeper, "Sean... your voice..." Sean gathered himself and whispered back, "It's my throat... it's a little sore." His mom, obviously relieved that Sean's problem was no more than a "little sore throat," said rather matter-of-factly, "Come to the bathroom. I'll get a glass of hot salt water and you can gargle."

A strange impulse came over Sean. He blurted out in that rather loud, high-pitched and nasal voice that he did not recognize: "You and dad are a fastidious couple. You're fast... but not fast enough... making him hideous!" The words shot forth like machine gun bullets.

He rarely if ever spoke of his dad, not since that shameful separation. It had been a year since he'd seen him. Then thoughts about his mom rushed to the forefront of his consciousness uncontrollably. He pictured his mom on that day he peeked into the bathroom and saw her naked for the first time. Something he did not understand imposed itself on this memory: the words "not fast enough". Not fast enough? Not fast enough for what? He was embarrassed and confused ... and mortified by how his body had reacted at the time.

191

Oxbow Lake The 2nd

There was a long silence on the other side of the door and then his mom said "Fast what?" and then after another long pause asked, "What did you say? I don't understand. Are you sure you're OK?" The worry had returned to her voice.

Sean regained control of his thoughts if not his vocal cords and mumbled to disguise his voice, intentionally speaking in short choppy sentences, "Mom, I'm... OK. Just clearing my throat. Don't need to gargle." He didn't know what to do but knew he needed some time, "Need to stretch. Get into my cross country routine."

There was another long pause on the other side of the door and then an "OK" said more like a question than a statement followed by footsteps retreating down the hallway toward the kitchen. Sean sat before the image that he was sure was not him wondering what had happened.

A sudden thud broke his worried contemplation. Sean quickly turned his head toward the darkened corner of his room where the thud had come from. Sure enough, the thud had announced another morning arrival of Mr. Siegfried Blattella Germanicus. The first in quite a while.

Siegfried smiled, if a Blattella Germanicus three-foot cockroach could be said to smile, and whispered in that rather reedy, high-pitched voice of his, "You have a ready wit, young man. Tell me when it's ready."

Unconsciously and without realizing it, Sean retorted, "You look like a talent scout for a cemetery."

Siegfried smiled, at least it was probably a smile considering the rather different structure of his... face?... and said, "Was that birthday suit made to order? Where were you at the time?"

Sean replied, "I was right here. What's happened to me? I look like a fat old man who says strange things."

Siegfried replied, "It's a metamorphosis of sorts. You're morphing into a re-incarnated Henny Youngman."

"Henny Who? Who in heavens name is Henny Youngman?"

"Who was Henny Youngman? He was the king of one-liners... a fast draw, one-line comic genius for the ages. Don't you remember? You saw him on that show your mother liked... one of those summer re-runs... the Milton Berle show... ole Henny sitting up in a balcony shouting those one-liners down at Uncle Miltie... made Berle look like a fool... remember... you laughed your ass off... wished you could be that funny. Remember? Well you're going to get your chance, for nature, in its infinite wisdom, has decided that humanity needs another Henny Youngman and guess what, my metamorphosizing young tadpole, you've been chosen to become the new frog. If Henny Youngman were here, he'd say something like, 'You'll have a nice personality, but not for a human being.' "

"I don't want to be another Henny Youngman. I want to be me."

"You don't seem to understand. You ARE being you. We can't choose who we want to be. It's better to want to be what's been chosen for us. There's this thing called biology and that evolution stuff that determines who we are. A tadpole can't decide it wants to morph into a beaver. It's going to be a frog and that's all there is to it. It is what it is and it will be what it's going to be."

"But Henny Youngman? Why can't I morph into one of those great runners. Someone like Steve Prefontaine or better yet, Jim Ryan... and win an Olympic event or somethin'. I'm not Henny Youngman! I'm Sean Murphy Warden!"

193

Oxbow Lake The 2nd

"What's in a name? A rose by any other name is still a rose… and as you know, roses have thorns. It ain't all pretty blooms."

"Pretty blooms? Thorns? I don't like being Henny Youngman and I don't like what this Henny Youngman makes me think."

"Think about what?"

"Like about my mom. I don't want to think about her that way."

"What way?"

"You know… THAT way!"

"It ain't all Henny Youngman, my boy. There's still that tadpole thing crawling around inside you."

Sean looked into the mirror and… surprise, surprise, miraculously his image was back to being Sean's image, the image he knew and loved… much to his great relief. He quickly turned to that dark corner of his room where Siegfried had been standing, but the three-foot, obnoxious German cockroach had disappeared again.

Sean looked up at the image yet again, lifted his forefinger to his face and pushed his nose gently to the left and then to the right. Sure enough, the image before him did the same. He looked down at his balls and there they were, two in a cluster… and he no longer had that huge purplish helmet hanging there. Sure enough, he had returned to his old self… his nose was his nose and his nut sack was his nut sack… and his penis had returned to being his penis. It was now standing at attention, hard as a rock. He rolled back onto the bed. He heard his mom pad down the hallway. There was a gentle knock at the door and a soft "Honeybunch, eggs almost ready."

He said in his old voice, "OK, mom, give me another minute." He reached down to his penis which had metamorphosed into a phallus and began to gently massage the beast as he quietly moaned.

O'edipussy...

Sean lay in bed crying… not that hard breath-grabbing kind of cry but rather that soft, sobbing kind of cry. He could feel a tear as it ran down his cheek cupping at his fuzzy upper lip where it met many of its brothers in arms. Reflexively, Sean ran his tongue over the fuzzy meeting place tasting its salty sweetness. He was not naked, for he had already been up and eaten his breakfast… Wheaties, the Breakfast of Champions… so he was dressed in his pajamas as common decency demanded.

He raised his head from his pillow and stared down at his pajama bottoms. There was a tent sticking up into the air… a huge tent that pulled at his waist band, a tent created by an erection… an erection that was so hard, it was painful. He turned onto his right side and felt the pain and without thinking pushed his hands between legs and clasped them so that his tented erection was cradled by his wrists.

It just wasn't right and he knew it, but there it was. He whispered to himself, "Go away… go away…" but it didn't go away. He had felt this metamorphosis occur earlier as his penis had arisen and hardened into a phallus. He didn't think of what happened in those terms, but he knew what was happening even if he didn't know the terminology… and what's more, he just knew it wasn't right.

A sudden thud startled him. He looked toward the still darkened corner of his bedroom where the thud had come from and sure enough, there stood Mr. Siegfried Blattella Germanicus. The thud had announced yet another morning arrival, but unlike all his previous visits, this time the thud occurred after breakfast rather than before

195

as had been the case when Mr. Siegfried Blattella Germanicus had chosen to visit in the past.

Without moving a muscle and thus still cradling his tented phallus, Sean whispered, "Mr. Siegfried Blattella Germanicus? You came late today."

The giant cockroach... perhaps we should use another term... like "palmetto bug" as most Floridians termed his kind and as Mr. Siegfried Blattella Germanicus himself preferred to be addressed since both he and his fellow Floridians knew that the word "cockroach" carried much negative baggage and in fact could be considered a pejorative term. The very sound of the word with its harsh double 'k' sound grated the ear and just plain sounded downright offensive what with that first syllable. However, the word "palmetto" rolled off the tongue... particularly when pronounced with that slight southern accent common to native Floridians... for in spite of Shakespeare's famous "a rose by any other name is still a rose," both Floridians and Mr. Siegfried Blattella Germanicus knew that it'd be hard to sell a dozen of the things if they were called stink weed.

The giant palmetto bug... see what I mean... stood there in the corner with his compound eyes staring in Sean's direction as his antenna waved rhythmically in the air. In that reedy high pitched voice of his, Mr. Siegfried Blattella Germanicus whispered, "Sean, I think that you can address me less formally. Call me 'Siggie'. After all, our conversations have been... how shall I put it... rather personal. Formality, given the circumstances, seems unnecessary and perhaps even inappropriate. What has your panties in a wad this morning?"

Sean gasped and whispered, "Please don't say that... please don't use the word 'panties'. Please... please... please..."

If you had had a series of person-to-person intimate conversations with a palmetto bug, particularly a giant one, as had Sean, perhaps you'd be able to discern what could be termed a slight smile on the… face?… of Mr. Siegfried Blattella Germanicus, or Siggie as he now preferred to be addressed.

He whispered in that reedy voice of his, almost apologetically, "Sean, why are you so upset about the phrase 'don't get your panties in a wad'? It's just a metaphor… a common phrase and a fairly innocuous one at that. And the word 'panties'? Come on, now. What's up?" Then Siggie chuckled… albeit a rather wispy high-pitched chuckle and said, "Oh, I see what's up… and this time after breakfast! How satyric."

Sean shot back, "Satiric? I don't see anything satiric about my condition. It's not something to make fun of even by you."

The palmetto bug, who now preferred to be called Siggie, said in that high pitched reedy voice of his, "I don't mean the 'make fun of' kind of satiric like you read in your English lit book. I mean the kind spelled s-a-t-y-r-i-c… it has a 'y' instead of an 'i'… as in those man-beasts of Ancient Greece… kind of an ancient version of Mr. Henny Youngman only with horns and a tail. He… err you… was hung like a horse… No?… Mr. Youngman being an older less capable version. You're a younger version now that you're back to your old new self. Thus that huge tent."

There was a long silence and then Sean heard the echo of water splattering in the shower and his mother humming some unrecognizable tune. He cringed and rolled onto his back, pulling his hands from between his legs and covering his eyes with them.

Siggie… now with an even better view of Sean's… how should I say this… condition?… shouted… at least what for a three-foot palmetto bug would be a shout… shouted "Whoa there big boy. That's some hard-on. Bigger than I thought possible for someone your age. If it gets any bigger, it'll tear a hole in your PJs and you won't need to unbutton your fly to take a leak although my guess... right now... this very minute... you couldn't take a leak if your life depended on it. That's a real beauty you're sporting there!"

Sean's mom's voice grew louder for she was well into her shower now and the splashing water seemed to encourage her to actually sing... sounded like a Beatles' tune... "love... love.... love..." Sean put his hands over his ears and then in desperation grasped the ends of his pillow and pulled the ends over his ears. Finally, his mom's voice faded and the sound of splashing water stopped.

Sean released his grip on the pillow and put his hands behind his head. He pulled his head up leaning forward and sure enough, his erection was still there... but he knew that without looking, for the discomfort between his legs remained. He pleaded, "Mr. Siegfried... Mr. Siggie... why has this happened to me again? What's wrong with me?"

The giant palmetto bug did not immediately reply but rather stood there waving his antennae about as if in thought. Then he whispered in that raspy voice of his, "You have an erection. You have them often. There's nothing wrong with you. It's all quite natural."

"But this one is different. It's not like that first one... that accident."

"When you saw your mom in the bathroom naked? That was a while ago. You still remember that... incident?"

"Yes, but that was an accident and it's happened other times since, but they were all accidents. I didn't mean them to happen. They just happened. This time was different."

Again the palmetto bug paused as if in thought, then asked, "How different? You saw a naked woman and it excited you. Just happened to be your mother… she's quite shapely for her age and that's some bush she sports. Erections like yours… happens all the time."

Sean pulled himself up on his left elbow and whispered, "No, this time was different."

The palmetto bug… Siggie… became impatient, "Out with it, Sean. What the hell's ricocheting off the inside of that teenage skull of yours? So you have a huge erection. You should be proud of that beauty. Fifty years from now such things will be a distant memory… if you're lucky to live that long."

"Well Mom called me for breakfast like always so I jumped into my pajamas and ran into the bathroom, took a quick leak and headed for the kitchen. I'm sitting there eating my Wheaties and reading the cereal box. They have this old-time story on the back about Olympic Champion the Reverend Bob Richards. I had the box balanced on my knees. I reach over to take a spoonful of cereal and the box falls on the floor so I jump out of my chair and kneel to scoop the spilled Wheaties back into the box. Mom's sitting on the other side of the table doing the cross-word puzzle like she does every morning at breakfast. She's stuck on one of the clues and she's just sitting there doing that twirl-your-hair thing thinking like Gail does. Seems something that girls and even women do. While I'm scooping the spilled Wheaties into the box, I turn and look and there's mom with her legs spread… her robe has opened up… and she's not wearing any… panties. I can see that hair between her legs and I jump up real quick. I don't want her to know… and I don't want to get… you know… but I start to."

Siggie interrupts Sean and wisps, "But that sounds like the previous incident where you saw that naked reflection of your mother in the mirror. Why so upset now?"

Sean turned on his side, slid his hands between his legs and again cradled his erection with his wrists. He closed his eyes and then opened them quickly as if he saw something while his eyes were closed that he did not want to see.

Siggie said in what could be described as all but a yell for him, "Well... out with it! What's different?"

Sean whispered, "A little later, Mom finally gives up on her cross-word puzzle... she raise her arms up, closes her eyes and yawns and stretches with all her might. She pushes forward on her chair and stretches her legs. Quick like, without thinking, I duck down and look under the table and there's it is. She's spread her legs to stretch pushing forward on her chair like I said. And there it was... I could see her you-know-what. I jumped up real quick before she opened her eyes and headed for my bedroom... and I got this huge erection that I can't get rid of. I shouldn't feel this way about my mother. No one should. I've sinned... I'm a pervert and I don't dare confess this to Monsignor Donnelly today... or any day. It's too embarrassing." He looked up in great despair and moaned, "I'm going to hell."

Siggie made something like a giggling sound and said, "Well big fella, I doubt it. It's not exactly what you think. Technically, you could call it incestuous voyeurism, I guess, but like I said, it happens all the time.

"A while back this guy in Vienna... his friends called him Siggie too... gave it a name. He called it a complex... named the damn complex after a character in Greek mythology like they always do... a guy named Oedipus... he named it an Oedipus complex. The word starts with an 'o' but the o's silent.

"Anyway, this Oedipus guy got into a lot worse situation than you. For starters, he kills his old man... not knowing it was his old man

200

that he killed, but still he killed him. Then he marries his mother and apparently screws her a lot since he has a bunch of kids by her. Ends badly for all concerned. When the plot unravels and the secret is revealed, Oedipus's mom-turned-wife commits suicide, this son-turned-husband… this Oedipus character… pokes his eyes out and then punishes himself even more by blindly wandering around Greece so that the rest of humanity can shun him… and his kids suffer for just getting born to the wrong parents… typical Greek tragedy stuff. Hell, all you did was see your mom's hootchie-cootchie and get this huge hard-on. Hardly requiring a blinding experience! "

"I didn't kill my dad, but he's not here. It's only me and Mom."

"There is that, but like I said, something like this happens to all boys as they sexually mature and you're maturing pretty good judging by the fuzz over your upper lip and the size of that erection."

The explanation did not ease Sean's concerns, "What should I do?"

"Masturbate, my horny young friend. Choke that chicken! It's the only way to get rid of that painful stiffy between your legs, my boy. Massage that baby fast and hard!"

"Isn't that another sin?"

"Listen kid, in for a penny in for a pound. Pound away!"

Sean rolled over on his back and looked down at the huge tent between his legs. He looked for ole Siggie in the corner but poof… the huge palmetto bug had already disappeared. Sean looked down at his tented pajamas, slipped them down below his knees and…

Dreadful reality, the words of confession and their absence...

Sean stood in line before the confessional overcome with pure, unadulterated fear. He was now one confession away from his own. He had been second to last in a long line of his cross country team mates, but the line had kept moving... moving much too fast. His hopes of a collapsed roof or some other catastrophe to end his torture faded most painfully as Billy Giordino exited the confessional. Billy was the best runner on the team and he was only a junior. Coach said that he had a shot at winning the regional.

Unlike Sean's other team mates who exited the confessional with head bowed and hands reverently clasped before them as they slowly walked to the back of the church to kneel to do their penance, Billy Giordino exited the confessional with head held high and a big smile plastered across his face as Sean moved closer to what he feared most in life: the words... the words of confession... words he'd have to speak. He was now second in line with only Johnny Fitzpatrick standing before him.

He had wanted to avoid confession in the worst way quite literally but could not this time. The entire cross country team was herded to the church every Friday afternoon after practice by Father McCabe... including the freshman team for the first time this season. Johnny Fitzpatrick, a sophomore, told Sean that coach Father McCabe wanted to clear the decks of sin before Saturdays since their most important meets were on Saturdays and he wanted his runners to run with a clear conscience.

Today's confession was particularly important for St. Augustine's cross country team if Father McCabe's contention were true that his runners ran best when they did so with a clear conscience. To-

202

morrow the team ran in the regional, a real biggie. How the team finished would make or break their season. Sean would not run on the varsity team but he would run on the freshman team in one of the preliminary competitions.

As Sean stood in line, Johnny Fitzpatrick turned and said to no one in particular, "I hate this Friday confession bull shit... oops, something else to confess... we always get that prick Monsignor Donnelly and he's like a god damn DA in there... add two more... squeezes the sins out of you like you're a tube of toothpaste full of them... and then piles on the Hail Mary's and Our Father's like they're going out of style... another sin, damn it! When he gets done with me, I'll be praying till my knees ache!"

Sean stood silently shifting his feet back and forth looking down at the floor... more thoughts bouncing off the interior of his skull bruising his brain as Siegfried Blattella Germanicus would have put it.

Billy panicked as more thoughts bounced off the inside of his teenage skull striking his brain: *Oh no, Monsignor Donnelly. Monsignor helped Mom when Dad took off with Mrs. Jacobs. God, he was at our house every day for a week. He knows Mom and he knows me and he... I can't tell him about...* Billy stopped not wanting to put the images in his head into those terrible things called words... his last great defense.

Before entering the confessional, Johnny Fitzpatrick had looked at Sean as Sean nervously shuffled his feet and said, "Sean my man, you look like you're going to piss your pants. What'd you do? Screw the pooch this week?"

Fortunately for Sean, Johnny Fitzpatrick had quickly turned to enter the confessional armed with at least three more sins to confess before Sean could reply. As Johnny passed Billy Giordino, he turned and said, "And I get to follow a god damn saint."

Sean now stood next to enter the confessional. Thoughts again ricocheted off the interior of his teenage skull and back, smashing into his brain. A bruising confusion reigned.

Did all that stuff really happen? Maybe I dreamed about it like that three foot cockroach. There's no such thing as a three foot cockroach. Siegfried Blattella Germanicus? The only person... thing... that knew about it was that stupid cockroach and I never really told him and he wasn't real and he already knew so maybe it never happened. Maybe he made it up. If I don't say it... maybe it was a bad dream. I don't think I have to confess bad dreams. You only have to confess things you do... well do on purpose. There is that impure thoughts stuff but I didn't do it on purpose. It was a dream made up by that cockroach. He should confess... not me!

A crest fallen Johnny Fitzpatrick exited the confessional and mumbled, "I'm goin' to be here all damn... all night" as he passed Sean who was entering the confessional. Sean knelt and said nervously, "Bless me, Monsignor, for I have sinned. I accuse myself of the following sins."

Sean froze and could not speak. Words were his greatest enemy. Without them he thought he might avoid, no nullify those terrible sins into non-existence.

Monsignor Donnelly, after several very long minutes, said "Yes, my son?"

Sean said again, "Bless me, Monsignor, for I have sinned."

After another silence, Monsignor Donnelly, growing impatient, said, "My son, what are the sins you wish to confess?"

Sean panicked and thought *What should I do?* and started to cry softly.

Knowing that young men who had difficulty confessing usually were dealing with the guilt of having committed sins of impure thoughts and acts, Monsignor Donnelly asked, "Did you look at impure pictures? Did you have impure thoughts?"

Sean answered reflexively, "Yes, Monsignor. I had impure thoughts..."

"And acts? Did your impure thoughts lead to impure acts?"

Sean could not help himself, "It was Gail... I had impure thoughts about her."

Monsignor Donnelly reacted, "Gail Williams? Did your impure thoughts lead to impure acts? Did you touch her impurely?"

"No Monsignor."

"Did you touch yourself impurely?"

"Yes, Monsignor. I did..."

Monsignor Donnelly, driven by both fatigue and the belief that he'd squeezed Sean's most feared confession from him, ended Sean's confession, "Say 10 Hail Marys and 10 Our Fathers for your penance."

Sean continued to cry softly and said rotely, "O my God, I am heartily sorry for having offended Thee and I detest all my sins because of Thy just punishments..." as Monsignor Donnelly droned "Dominus noster Jesus Christus te absolvat... "

After a long silence, Sean leapt from the confessional and ran past a kneeling Johnny Fitzpatrick, whose head was bowed in obvious painful penance. He continued out into the early evening shadows and ran to the dark activity bus, jumped up the bus's three steps and ran to the back shrinking into a seat where no one sat unless all the other seats were taken, particularly on Fridays after confession... *a lead us not into temptation* kind of thought having permeated the young skulls of the recently confessed and absolved.

Not so for Sean who continued to cry softly in the back of the still empty and dark school bus... a bus empty of a driver... and all of the confessed and absolved except for a sobbing and mute Sean who was neither... so very confused, alone and haunted by unabsolved guilt.

THIS PAGE INTENTIONALLY LEFT MOSTLY BLANK

(THE ABOVE VERY LIKELY BEING AN EXAMPLE OF OVERKILLING
RHETORICAL SUICIDE)

IRRELEVANT NOTE FROM THE AUTHOR:

LUNGE THE LUMMIN WITH THIS RECONNOITERIZATION OF A
FLAMMIN' FOOTSIE!

The Swiftian Nomination of One Legs de Coa Coa

As best I can *reconoiterate*, I was dancing the line and stooling at the long bar stretching across the entire width of Swifty's Irish Pub... a well populated bar I might add... breakin' from six... maybe it was seven... *whiskey boiler poppers... lungin' the lummin* for a good rosetta stoning of that rare dialect of English now academically recognized as Swifty's Buzz... believed to be a rare and old dialect of English gone weirdly local and spoken with a Brooklynish twang... all for my doctoral thesis. My left hand ached from all the *scribulation* and my head *oculized weird* as I *scribulated* while *dancing the line.*

Then one Ears Shamus stated to no one in particular, "Hey! Funny what happened." And then he asked, "How the hell did ole Legs get legged in the first place?"... placing particular emphasis on the words "Legs" and "legged" just prior to popping his head back as he downed a shot of whiskey and then chugged a mug of Fitzgeralds beer to complete his most recent "boiler pop" as the Swiftians called it... using the word "legged" in the sense of that peculiar dialect that Swifty's ever-faithful denizens there spoke. Sounded almost like I was sitting at a mystical Irish bar somewhere close to Brooklyn but beyond it... which I definitely was not. Twilight Zone anyone?

Ears wasn't asking anyone in particular and he certainly wasn't asking an outsider like me. He more or less broadcast the question up and down the bar to his fellow Swiftians as if thinking out loud. I had no idea what he was talking about but believed that the conversation showed signs of revealing that Swiftian Rosetta Stone... that key to understanding Swifty's Buzz... that original material that I desperately needed for my doctoral thesis.

However, the question did not seem to befuddle or surprise Shamus's fellow whiskey poppers, but they did take notice. Heads turned toward ole Ears Shamus and shook wisely up and down as lower lips were nibbled and eyes stared thoughtfully into that distant infinity beyond the environs known as Swifty's Irish Pub. Then suddenly a head would flip back as another of Ears Shamus's fellow drinkers initiated his boiler pop... or just "pop" as they often referred to it. More heads bobbed up and down the line in a kind of asynchronous head bobbing dance as Swiftians boiler popped away in silent, profound and deep contemplation.

Like I said, the question did not seem to surprise them. It was as if they'd pondered it often but had never bothered to ask it out loud, not actually caring enough to find the "solution" to the question. Then fate grabbed them and popped the question to the forefront of their boiler popped brains... inhabiting those boiler popped skulls... inhabiting those boiler popped bodies... inhabiting that great and ancient institution known as Swifty's Irish Pub... as few other questions apparently had before. Swifty's people now wanted to have "knowing" of that solution... as they'd say... as far as I could tell not really caring if they actually possessed "knowing" of what had actually happened as long as their "knowing" fit their rather strange world view of what they already knew! Isn't that a universal truth vis-à-vis humanity in general and even more to the point, individual humans in particular... for in the end, isn't all understanding particular and unique to both the individual and the group? Even at Swifty's? Idiosyncrasity... local, universal and forever!

Ah yes, Swifty's Irish Pub. In its more than century's long "heyday"... which continues to today... Swifty's was, and still is, the center of the universe for a singular population and the ancestors of that singular population and the ancestors of those ancestors and all their progeny who eventually became or would become ancestors.

Oxbow Lake The 2nd

In its way it was like one of those tiny Indian tribes that some lucky cultural anthropologist wanders across in the backwaters of the Amazon River that's never been polluted by modern society and pretty much lives as it always had for thousands of years... only Swifty's existed and still exists right here in the middle of our fine city. We'd changed, but Swifty's and Swifty's people hadn't, at least not very much. Swifty's was a backwater cultural island right here in the middle of civilization's mainstream... and thus a cultural anthropologist's surprise and delight...in this case the surprise and delight of Dr. Pasquady Turnstile Murphy the 3rd and eventually yours truly, James Mead Warden the 1st, a student of his before his tragic academic and personal downfall.

For 113 years of living history and still counting... and at least another hundred of oral history before that... or should it be aural... one of Swifty's people could dance the line as they called it... that is, a Swiftian could bang the Old Saint James Street hole in the wall, stool himself, handy a swill, guzzle to completion what they call a boiler pop, shuffle-step stooling right, handy another swill, guzzle it to completion and stool himself down the line until somewhere around 17 swills later, he reached the end of the bar full of happiness... and only one stub lighter at 75 coppers a swill in today's grub. Having stooled out after a very long day of popping and possibly pub grubbing, that line-dancing Swiftian could then leap that great institution, bang a hole in the wall onto Pearl Street, happy walk to the corner of Pearl and State and capture domesticular transportation... sometime way back then a horse drawn trolley... now a bus... for a good-feeling ride home... which was probably in the old camp grounds district... somewhere around Elysian Fields Park domesticularly speaking... in the area of our fine city known at the time as "The Gut".

Now, following Ears Shamus's lead, the fully occupied line of Swif-

210

tian drinkers faced Ears Shamus buzzing that same question or a variant of it concerning one Legs de Coa Coa. True, this rabble of Swiftians asked the question in many different ways... some of those ways being indecipherable to all but those who were conversant in that rare dialect of American English known as Swiftian Buzz... some of those ways were just plain indecipherable even by those fluent in the aforementioned dialect, and in at least some of those indecipherable cases, the indecipherability could be attributed to the liquid sustenance which the conversants "popped" before, during and after speaking... a liquid sustenance served by that long line of Swiftys... the present Swifty standing at 4 feet 9 and 1/2 inches... this most recent version of Swifty being a dwarf.

Actually the current Swifty was more a midget than a dwarf. He qualified height-wise as a dwarf from a medical definition standpoint by slipping just under the medical bar of 4 feet 10 inches. However, with a skeleton and limbs of more normal proportions, he was actually more a midget... that is, from a purely medical standpoint.

However, Swifty's fellow Swiftians took a more cultural and spiritual viewpoint, for they thought Swifty to be genetically descended, at least in part, from a long line of Leprechauns. Their proof: he was "a degenerated fairy" to the very depths of his soiled soul. In spite of his diminutive stature, he was extremely well endowed both physically and psychologically. Being well endowed physically, he serviced such denizens of Swifty's deep as Handy Mary and her tribe of "adventurist" female cousins... to both their and his great pleasure. Being well endowed psychologically, he played impish practical jokes on fellow Swiftians which were considered hilarious by all Swiftians including himself... with the possible exception of the Swiftian bearing the brunt of the aforementioned impish practical joke.

211

Oxbow Lake The 2nd

Cementing this Leprechaunian impression of his fellow Swiftians, Swifty often dressed like the mascot for the Boston Celtics although the Swiftians thought that the mascot for the Boston Celtics dressed like Swifty... Swifty being the original and the mascot being the counterfeit.

Regardless of the era, the Swifty's Irish Pub in existence at this time also served cheap pub grub as it had done for over that more than 113 years... and at least some of those Swiftians now present had devoured the pub grub for a goodly portion of those more than 113 years. And if they hadn't, their fathers and grandfathers had, and in a case or three, even many of their mothers, wives, girlfriends... and even their grandmothers!

When one of Swifty's people... as in this case Ears Shamus... yelled, muttered, moaned, cried, giggled or just plain made a statement in Swifty's Buzz... or as in the present case, asked a question... and that statement or question was indeed decipherable by someone conversant in Swiftian Buzz... as in this case by me, one could still not understand the full import of that statement... or in this case, the full import of the question... unless that someone, namely me, was knowledgeable of the associated cultural history of Swifty's, particularly those cultural events involving those making the statement... or in this case, posing a question... for it was particularly important to be knowledgeable in those cultural events involving not only the speaker... or as in this case, the questioner... but also the ancestors and progeny of the questioner who undoubtedly lived, had lived or would live and participate in the long cultural history of that great institution... which I distinctly had not, was not and did not! Thus while understanding Swiftian Buzz I was unable to understand the question posed by one Ears Shamus concerning the legging of one Legs de Coa Coa.

For as a graduate student of cultural anthropology, I faced an ironical and uncutable Gordian knot in this process of understanding a statement made in Swifty's Buzz... or in this case, a question posed, in that rare dialect of English pronounced with a somewhat Brooklynish twang. As I came to realize, even when one is conversant in Swifty's Buzz and thinks he's knowledgeable of the cultural history of Swifty's, he's dead wrong, for Swiftian cultural history changes as Swiftians themselves speak. Because of what they speak and because of what they spoke as they buzz about cultural events, they change Swifty's Buzz and their understanding of the cultural events that have occurred, are occurring and possibly will occur... thus making a cultural and linguistic hash of understanding. In a rather oxymoronic and ironical way, Swiftian culture and Swifty's Buzz continued to evolve pretty much uninfluenced by mainstream America while remaining pretty much unchanged at its foundation. Confusing?

For purposes of clarification, let's say a fictitious and omnipresent Methuselah, conversant in Swifty's Buzz and all that implied, has actually witnessed all of the momentous cultural events that unfolded and are unfolding in the society of that great institution. His task of understanding is not done, for now he still has to question and to understand the progeny of those "door-nailed" culture-creating ancestors who had participated in that cultural event in order to understand what that progeny understood to have happened... in other words, even our fictitious, omnipresent Methuselah has to speak and understand Swifty's Buzz... which he thought he did. Here's the rub, Swifty's Buzz keeps changing and evolving subtly as a result of all those cultural events that our fictitious, omnipresent linguistically conversant Methuselah is attempting to understand and Swifty's Buzz, the repository of all those cultural events, changes the knowledge of those cultural events as that rare dialect of American English changes as a result of the very cultural events it describes while remaining remarkably unchanged at its foundations. Talk about an ironical and uncutable Gordian knot! As a semi-literate Swiftian… and there were a bunch… would put it, "It'd give even Alexander the Great the *flamin' footsies!*"

And then to make things just a little more complicated for this cultural and linguistic hash, new cultural events are occurring all the time, being influenced by previous cultural events which change Swifty's Buzz as new progeny participate in the new cultural events, speaking a Swifty's Buzz that changes as a result of the new cultural events and thus changing their knowledge of the old cultural events.

I guess, in the long run, understanding the full import and meaning of a statement… or in this case, a question… posed in Swifty's Buzz was impossible even when someone like our ageless Methuselah actually witnesses those events with his very own eyes. Such is life, and just not at Swifty's. As it turns out, understanding is a fragile, amorphous and ever-changing thing, but seeking understanding is necessary for life to be lived even if that understanding is incomplete or, as is often the case, possibly dead wrong… making it quite understandable that a Swiftian would want a solution to this question of *How did Legs de Coa Coa get 'legged'?* as they termed it, without caring if they actually knew what had happened as long as what they knew was generally agreed upon and fit their rather strange world view like that one missing piece of a puzzle! You wouldn't throw out a puzzle because of one odd ill-fitting piece. No, you'd shape that puzzle piece to fit the existing puzzle. It's only human. I had my work "butting my brains" as a good Swiftian would say, for I sought that elusive understanding. Talk about rectal encephalitic behavior on a grand cultural and linguistic scale! Hello rectal encephalitic insertion.

I popped my shot of whiskey and asked Ears, "What exactly do you mean by legged?"

Ears took a drag on his cigarette, blew a thick cloud of smoke out through his nose and said, "Look Prof... *all the Swiftians called me Prof even though I had not yet attained that title*... Legs de Coa Coa had this peculiar nomination of 'Legs'. In other words, he got 'legged' as we say. How'd he get that particular nomination? Nominations like that don't fall off trees. Legs is who he is... or at least was before he got door nailed... and it's important to know how he got so nominated before his unfortunate door nailing."

I sensed that I could use this particular question as a way to organize and present what I had learned about Swifty's Buzz for the thesis I was writing... for the exigencies of my academic calendar were again at my doorstep. I asked ole Ears, "Well what's the consensus as to how Legs de Coa Coa got 'legged' as you say?"

Ears pushed his "newsboy" cap to the side with his left hand and scratched just above his very large and hairy left ear, pulled the cap down again and said, "That's the problem. There ain't no consensus. Seems there's at least three stories. And the boys are pretty much split evenly on what the real deal is knowing-wise."

Louie the Guinea, sitting on my left, yelled to Shamus, "Hey Ears, the reason Legs de Coa Coa got the nomination of 'Legs' is because he was the fastest guy in the seventh grade. He won the dash at the grag-e-ation picnic up at the Elysian Field. I was there... and he won by a lot more than a pigeon's puckered ass, too. He ran like the wind. Funny though, I don't think he ever grag-e-ated."

Shamus took another long drag on his cigarette, squinted his eyes as he stared into the infinity before him and said to no one in particular... pretty much ignoring Louie the Guinea... and said as if to himself, "As I hear it, he was announced as 'Legs' before the race, so he had the nomination before the race. Not sayin' he didn't get the nomination because he could run like the wind. All I'm sayin' is that he had the nomination before he ran like the wind in that particular race up at the Elysian."

Louie the Guinea would not be deterred, "Says who besides you? Were you there?" Apparently truth in Swifty's world could be decided on democratic principles... a kind of settled cultural history and linguistics. Now that I think about it, maybe that's how 'truth' is determined in all of our worlds. After all, it was only several centuries ago that the world was flat and the Earth the center of the universe... the settled science of the astronomy of those times.

Ears Shamus took another long drag on his cigarette and blew the smoke out through his nose again before speaking. Then he said, to no one in particular, as if answering the question without recognizing the questioner, "Cousin Willie were there... says he, 'That's when Legs got legged... nominationally speaking.'"

Louie the Guinea, again undeterred... this time by this latest claim, asked, "Yer Cousin Willie, he grag-e-ated?" Now academic qualifications were being brought into question as a method of determining "truth"... a not unfamiliar ploy even in the culture of our larger world today.

Again Ears Shamus took a long drag on his cigarette, which was now a stub, blew smoke out through his nose and popped another whiskey. Then he stared into the infinity before him and said not to Louie the Guinea but to that entire universe, "No, not then. Willie grag-e-ated the following year... so he was still academically sharp learning wise" and several heads along the line slowly bobbed up and down in quiet agreement.

Louie the Guinea guzzled his Fitzgerald's beer quickly and to completion... if for no other reason than to minimize the opportunity that liquid had to affect his taste buds... said, with a certain finality, "But yer cousin's door nailed. Got hit by a truck right outside the Pearl Street hole in the wall during his happy walk to the domesticular trolley... seven years ago. Right?"

Ears Shamus smashed his cigarette stub into a huge clam shell on the bar, continued to stare into the infinity before him and said, "Tole me before he got door nailed... not after!" The 'not after' said with an emphasis that Ears Shamus thought would end Louie the Guinea's contention and thus end all contention.

It did not, for before Louie the Guinea could respond, and it was obvious that he was about to, another voice at the far end of the line yelled, "Both you duds is blowin' farts through yer moufs academically speaking. Legs didn't get the nomination for his runnin' abilities although he was very swift on his feet, physically speaking. His mum gave 'im. When she was carryin' him, she saw Legs Diamond get door-nailed right up the street. Made quite an impression in her head. That's where the 'Legs' nomination come from... Legs Diamond... and no one's sure about where Mr. Diamond got his nomination either. If it were fer runnin' fast, he was mis-nominated for he weren't quite fast enough." A silence fell upon the bar as the Swiftians marinated themselves in thoughts of Legs de Coa Coa's place in Swiftian cultural history.

I sat there steeped in my own marination. This was the second attempt to academically and scientifically study Swifty's Buzz... me being the second individual attempting to do so. Two years ago, Dr. Pasquady Turnstile Murphy came down to Swifty's from the state university and spent a month recording conversations here. He was intrigued by that dialect now known in academic circles as "Swifty's

217

Buzz"... a nomination due in great part to the good doctor's academic publishing before his Swiftian nomination... that's him at the end of the line... Talky Turnstile. Wave to him.

"Hey Talkie, how's the swill?" Talkie raised his left hand above his head and shot his thumb into the air indicating his approval of the swill he was obviously popping in great quantities. Besides a few academically popular but short monograms, nothing of substance ever came of his Swiftian studies academically speaking as the good professor is rumored to have been clappined during this academic effort and was forced to abandon the effort by his wife who apparently caught a touch of the residue of the professor's academic efforts eventually causing the door nailing of their marriage. In his aloneness, the professor heard the siren song of Swifty's, eventually causing him to lose his academic standing as he went native, so to speak, and chose an academically perishment of boiler popping rather than an academic publishing survivalment.

Southside Willie had warned the professor in Swifty's Buzz about Handy Mary (for as previously stated, not all of Swifty's poppers were men)... Willie saying to the good professor, "Prof, you don't need no Handy Mary's applause! She'll soil you handily!"... Mary having been leprechauned by Swifty his very self... today's modern and midget version of all the descendants of that fine personage... into her *below waisting* behavior... or is it *below wasting* behavior.

However, the professor had not yet fully mastered the dialect and thus was unable to profit from Southside Willie's warning. On a boiler popping slide down the bar as he danced the line, the good doctor of cultural anthropology took Handy Mary's applause line to the privacy of the men's room where the clappin was thunderous... shattering to his metaphorical ears... marking yet another significant event in the cultural history about which I have previously referred.

And this Swiftian cultural event had prompted in an inevitable sort of way yet another cultural event, for as previously stated, at the end of the bar sat a certain Talkie Turnstile Murphy, formerly known as Dr. Pasquady Turnstile Murphy the 3rd, the formerly and internationally renowned cultural anthropologist and my former doctoral advisor.

The good doctor had been my academic advisor before he *patria eo-ed* himself... that is, *went native*, as previously mentioned... as cultural anthropologists call the transformation that led Dr. Pasquady Turnstile Murphy the 3rd to become the boiler popper at end of Swifty's long bar now with the nomination of 'Talkie', a Swiftian nomination dripping with what seemed a certain ironical touch that may not have been intentional, for as it turns out, this Swiftian nomination, which was intentional, had a certain cultural and linguistic metaphorical irony to it.

As the good doctor became more and more fluent in Swifty's Buzz, he talked less and less. He's now about as fluent in Swifty's Buzz as is possible for an outsider to be and he's pretty much reduced himself to a series of grunts, shrugs and gesticulations... his enhanced fluency in Swifty's Buzz apparently causing a certain increased verbal inarticulateness.

How did he end up at the end of Swifty's bar desperately gesticulating for another boiler popper you ask? Well, one day... actually it was late evening, I believe... the good professor Dr. Pasquady Turnstile Murphy the 3rd, while still a Swiftian neophyte, decided to gain the respect of the Swiftians he wanted to record by dancing the line. He broke the hole on Old Saint James and announced his intention. The Swiftians broke out in articulation of various Swiftian Buzz synonym-matic expletive-like huzzahs: "Cup de grace!" "Cour de lemone"... and so on.

219

Oxbow Lake The 2nd

Cruel irony butted itself to make things even more complicated, for the cultural history of that great institution, being both oral and aural in nature, could only be truly known by experiencing... witnessing it as it happened... and thus experiencing the cultural and historical knowledge of the event as it occurred... or hearing about it as it was retold in Swifty's Buzz by those who witnessed said events recounting them in Swifty's Buzz and thus making them unknowable by those who were not conversant in that esoteric and subtle dialect... Swifty's Buzz making an audible Gordian knot of this problem of knowing what had happened of note that required passing on.

As best I can piece together the events involving Dr. Pasquady Turnstile Murphy the 3rd's dancing of the line, the good professor bangs the hole on Old Saint James and declares, "Swiftians, tonight I dance the line!"... this declaration followed by the previously mentioned Swift Buzzian huzzahs.

The good professor implants himself on the first stool and slams a twenty dollar bill down on the bar. Swifty acknowledges the twenty green ones then slides a shot of whiskey and a mug of well-chilled Fitzgerald's beer before him... in fact so well chilled as to become close to tasteless. The good professor pops the shot of whiskey and drains the mug of Fitzgerald's. He quickly stools right and repeats the entire process. After stooling right five times...maybe it was six... each time popping a whiskey and chugging a mug of Fitzgerald's in goodly boiler popping fashion, the good professor realizes that he'd better slow down as there are 17 stools meaning he's got 12... maybe 11... to go. He says to himself, "Do-able but..." He never finishes the statement. However, given the context, the statement self-finishes unspoken.

Randy Handy Mary now enters the picture, all 300 pounds of her. Rumor has it that the handy one is actually part rotund she-wolf and her behavior during the various phases of the moon would indicate that there is some truth to the rumor... her rotundness being constant throughout the entire lunar cycle. Virtually all Swiftians believe this rumor to be fact and that her behavior *is* regulated to a great extent by the phases of the moon... and guess what? Tonight the moon is full and thus most Swiftians believe that Handy Mary wants to become so also, so they act accordingly. That is, during the full moon, all Swiftians give Handy Mary a wide berth which is saying something.

Knowing all this cultural history, Swifty, feeling the lunar pull a tad himself, says to Handy Mary, "Fine lookin' piece of sizzlin' sausage that Professor Turnstile Murphy be. Looks ripe for the consumin' consumation!"

As an "unacculate" and slightly hard of hearing outsider, Professor Pasquady Turnstile Murphy the 3rd knows not this cultural history and hears little and understands less the words of that a degenerate fairy, Swifty his very self... and being left of tipsy, the professor also hears not any words of that she-wolf in female Swiftian dress but he does feel the need to relieve himself in order to prepare for the final 12 or possibly 11 stoolings he must complete... all this lunar lunacy then leading to the aforementioned demise of the now Talkie Turnstile Murphy, née Dr. Pasquady Turnstile Murphy the 3rd, previously a happily married, internationally renowned, cultural anthropologist with a prestigious title and position at the local university up the street and the learn-ed title "Doctor"...

Sal the Other Guinea yelled his two coppers worth toward Southside Willie concerning Legs de Coa Coa's nomination, "He kickin' that reporter bitch in the ass in '92 the reason? That where that Legs nomination of his name come from?"

Southside Willie stared into the mirror behind the great mahogany bar as if he could actually peer into the past and said, without turning to face Sal the Other Guinea, "Naw, we yelled 'Kick her ass, Legs!' Remember it well, so he musta already been tagged... nominationed... unless I misremembered unknowingly."

All this time I was furiously *notating the gimm* as a good Swiftian would say, hoping beyond hope of *lungin' the lummin*... again as a good Swiftian would say... and finally rosette stoning those Swiftian Buzzing bastards by riding the linguistic coat tales of one *door-nailed* Legs de Coa Coa as I *danced the line* to gain *internalship* of those boiler popping Swiftians as I stooled along the bar at Swifty's Irish Pub.

The last thing I remember was Handy Mary saying something about my need for a good waisting, as she put it, to *clear the goo*... whatever the hell that meant.

THIS PAGE INTENTIONALLY LEFT MOSTLY BLANK

(THE ABOVE STATEMENT, WHILE RELIEVING A READER'S FEARS OF
MISSING TEXT, DOES SO AT THE RISK OF BEATING THE OBVIOUS)

IRRELEVANT NOTE FROM THE AUTHOR:

JUST BECAUSE YOU CAN'T UNDERSTAND SOMEBODY DOESN'T
MEAN THEY'RE UNDERSTANDABLE!

Gimpy Sean McGillicuddy's Miraculous Assumption

Swifty, that leprechaunic eponymously named owner and bar tender unique... sitting behind his iconic bar attempting to reconoiterate the aurality originating behind him from the Pearl Street hole in the wall or "hollow" as I had learned they called it in Swifty's Buzz... a rear entry to the establishment from without and a rear exit from within for all gentlemen... stooling at the bar that he lovingly owned and mischievously abused... that bothersome aurality wafting most unpleasantly into that all but sacred institution known as Swifty's Irish Pub... Swifty stooling there, his face doused in puzzlement as an articulate Swiftian would enunciate the sit-she-a-shon in that Brooklynish twang characteristic of their unique dialect of English known academically as Swifty's Buzz.

Being only 4 feet 9 and 1/2 inches but more midget that dwarf... since his arms, legs and head were of pretty normal proportions given his height and the standards of his world... Swifty's legs only reaching the ground when he was standing directly on the floor or some other surface. In virtually all other circumstances, his legs did not... this being one of those sit-she-a-shons since he was stooling himself behind his bar... his legs thus being well above floor level. Using his mostly well proportioned muscular left leg, he forcefully pushed against the lip of his bar to swivel his stooling so that he now faced what he thought to be the origin of the aurality penetrating his ears and those of his fellow Swiftians stooled on the other side of his bar and before him... that is, he now stooled facing the Pearl Street gentlemen's hollow... a rear exit from within and a rear entry from without... to better hear that orality.

The aurality was obviously a feminine orality in nature and definitely not Swifty's Buzz. Swifty thought he heard a chant: "Girls' rear entry not for us. Knock it off or ..." and here Swifty lost the aurality of the orality. He looked over to Handy Mary... that rotund Swiftian adventurist who had just entered the bar from Pearl Street after a long night of walking that street for profit... and asked her, "What's the last part what them flammin' femmies screamin' over at the Pearl Street gentlemen's rear entry?"

Handy Mary plopped her more than ample behind down on a stool, effectively hiding the stool's seat from sight at virtually all angles, and said, "They ain't at the gentlemen's rear entry. They're at the la-dies' rear entry. That's why it's hard to hear what they're screamin'. It's "or get real fooked." They're screamin' "Girls rear entry not for us, knock it off or get real fooked."

For those who have never had the privilege of entering Swifty's Irish Pub from Pearl Street, there are actually two hollows on that street: a main hollow above which there's a sign declaring "Gentlemen's Rear Entry Only" and, up the street a ways, a second hollow above which there's a sign declaring "Ladies Rear Entry Only".

Swifty pulled a snot catcher from his back pocket, blew his nose with a honk worthy of an outraged goose, and asked his fellow Swif-tians stooled on the other side of the bar, "Them flammin' femmies from up top at that high learnin' place?"... that high learnin' place being the state university.

Upon Handy Mary's stooling, Swiftians now occupied 14 of the 17 available stools on the other side of the bar... that long venerable mahogany altar to Swiftian culture that ran from Old Saint James to Pearl and was the heart of Swifty's Irish Pub, which had been at this site for more than a hundred years and some believed that it was the site of the original Swifty's Irish Pub closer to two hundred years ago... those so believing also believing that the term "hole in the wall", meaning doorway or "hollow" in Swifty's Buzz, had its origin from that earlier time when the entries and exits to the original Swifty's Irish Pub were, quite literally, holes in the wall.

Ears Shamus, one of the 14 Swiftian stoolers, popped a shot of whiskey and boilerized it by chugging a mug of the politically required Fitzgeralds swill which camouflaged itself as beer. Swifty, in his great consideration for his fellow Swiftians, kept this swill so chilled that it was virtually tasteless. Ears, having chugged the tasteless swill, then gently set his empty mug on the bar, picked up his lit cigarette, his zigfag in Swifty's Buzz, from the large clam shell before him and took a long draw. He slowly blew a white cloud of smoke over the bar with that thousand mile stare in his eyes as he contemplated aurally the orality piercing those huge hairy elephantine appendages ornamenting both sides of his head and jutting out from below what some called a newsboy hat which those of Irish heritage living in "the Gut" favored even though they rarely if ever delivered newspapers and even more rarely read them.

He stubbed his zigfag in the huge clam shell before him and said, "Talkie, what them femmies flammin' bout?"... Talkie, occupying his usual third stool from the Old Saint James hollow... the front entry to Swifty's Irish Pub which also doubled as the front exit... well, Talkie popped a whiskey and shrugged his shoulders twice indicating that the mysterious femmie flammins interrupting his quiet contemplation of the universe were flammins unworthy of a more articulate response... his shrugging twice implying that there was possibly more than one reason why he found it unworthy of one of his rare oral responses.

Ears, without turning toward Talkie but somehow knowing that Talkie had shrugged twice, said to no one in general but still to Talkie in particular, "Talkie, you been havin' knowin' of them outsider flammin' femmies... had a livin' up there a long time in that high learnin' place... must have some knowin' of the nature of them femmies... no?"

Talkie... formerly of the outsider nomination of Dr. Pasquady Turnstile Murphy the 3rd in his past life and now promoted to the Swiftian nomination of Talkie in his present life... a Swiftian nomination containing more than a touch of irony I might add... well the now nominated Talkie had been a professor of anthropology of some sort at the state university... that high learnin' place. As an outsider, he had spent a considerable amount of time stooling at the bar with the Swiftian natives to study the intricacies of that strange English dialect now known academically as Swifty's Buzz... thanks in part to the then good doctor's own academic publishings.

Things turned sour on the good doctor after he was inadvertently served a bit of *brellock sa-leed*, as the Swiftians called it... meaning clam salad... by the previously mentioned rotund Swiftian adventurist nominated Handy Mary who lived up to her Swiftian nomination temporally speaking by being very handy... at least in this instance. Her rotundness belied a surprising quickness and agility that allowed her to relieve the tension beguiling the good doctor in the haloed confines of Swifty's ladies' room... but... there's always a Swiftian *but* in the world of Swifty's Irish Pub... but, as it turns out, that relief turned out to be very temporary physically, socially, professionally and eventually, legally speaking, for Handy Mary not only gave the good doctor relief, she also gave him a bonus gift: his own tribe of crabs... a gift he inadvertently shared with his dear wife, much to her embarrassing crotch scratching hysteria... causing his domesticular life to suffer a femmie induced medical catastrophe of sorts which, in turn, led to a physical, social, professional, and eventually, legal collapse of his former outsider life... which in yet another unexpected turn caused the good professor to go native... that is, to become a

Swiftian heart and soul... all these turns having a dizzying effect on virtually all of the outsiders and none of the insiders familiar with the tragedy. Talkie was, in fact, one of the few outsiders... which he was no longer considered... who became articulate in Swifty's Buzz and thus earning the Swiftian nomination of "Talkie" indicating that he was now an insider... an insider nomination shrouded in a certain unstated irony.

Swiftian lore has it that the only other outsider in both living and dead memory to become a true Swiftian insider was none other than the recently departed Sean McGillicuddy who lost some of his right leg... the part below the knee... when he was inadvertently run over by the ceremonial horse-drawn trolley on its celebratory run down Pearl Street immortalizing the hundredth anniversary of the city's trolley service... a tragic event occurring after Sean McGillicuddy's first outsider visit to Swifty's Irish Pub... unlucky that... many years ago and before his recent departure from his now mostly one-leg-ed Swiftian sprung mortal coil. After the accident, Sean McGillicuddy gimped about on a wooden leg and became "Gimpy" when he went from Swiftian outsider to Swiftian insider... his wooden leg obviously remaining after his Swiftian conversion.

Swifty, still mystified by the flammin' femmies' chant "Girls' rear entry not for us. Knock it off or get real fooked!" thought out loud, "Maybe them ain't femmies from that high learnin' place. Maybe them's incognified adventurists from up Washington Park way around Elberon. Lots of Johnnie-Joes like their adventurists to look smarty pants. Why they protestin' rear entry and why here?"

Handy Mary became irate, "Them femmies... they're a disgrace to the profession. It's up to them to set the terms of an adventure... and before the adventure starts up. If they ain't rear entry adventurists, just say so and adventure's on or off according to the Johnnie-Joe's clivities adventure-wise. It's their own damn doin'... their own pre-dick-ta-mint rear entry wise. Besides, what they doin' demonstratin' and adventurin' down here on Pearl?"

Swifty took in Handy Mary's words of adventurist wisdom and then continued his private thinking publically, "Maybe they're protestin' because of Talkie. I heard his legally mortified misses is leadin' a purification drive up around there after her unrealized crabbin' by Talkie. I think that gift that Handy gave to Talkie ended up really aggravatin' Talkie's mortified former misses... makin' her publically and pube-i-cally angry."

Ears Shamus added, "Well them femmies know that adventurists are welcome down here on Pearl... I'll admit that they ain't real welcome on Old Saint James... but that's a street with some re-lidge-e-os-ity attached to it. Ain't nobody gonna officially protest their protest on Pearl... what with Swifty's rear entry for ladies right here as a sign of acceptance... their adventurist competition aside." He paused and pointed to his shot glass, "One for the road, Swifty... I gotta hump the hollow what with tomorrow being a big day what with Gimpy's wake and all."

Upon his passing last Wednesday from some unknown affliction related to alcohol consumption, Gimpy Sean McGillicuddy's life was to be celebrated with a wake and funeral... a kind of funereal double header... these celebrations to be held today in the parlor of the boarding house in that section of the city known as "the Gut" where Gimpy had lived and recently expired.

The corpse of the dearly departed had already been carefully laid out there in a hurriedly constructed wooden coffin by Ears Shamus's younger brother, Stuffer Shamus, who, although not a licensed mortician, was an amateur taxidermist of some reputed skill. The remains of the dearly departed appeared pretty good except for his rather bloated belly which looked out of place for those who knew Gimpy before his departure from this life since he was skinny as a rail at the time just prior to that recent departure.

The Swiftians had crowded around Gimpy Sean's coffin in the parlor of his former boarding house. The good reverend Monsignor Easy Monahan, unofficial chaplain to Swifty's Irish Pub, stood before the coffin, which was leaning against the far wall of the parlor. A casual observer would think that the dearly departed had not yet departed and stood... albeit at a slight backward leaning angle and sporting an unfamiliar paunch... gazing out the large bay window opposite and into the street beyond as he awaited the Monsignor to open some semi-religious festivity with a prayer... a festivity that would involve Gimpy's active participation and not his inactive objectification.

As the Monsignor prayed aloud, holding forth a shot of whiskey at arm's length... a shot which he planned to pop signaling the climactic ending of his prayer and the official beginning of the wake...well, Pincher Kowalski, the land lady of the boarding house, abruptly interrupted the prayer and halted the proceedings by yelling, "Pay or leave... and take that God damn stinking corpse with you!"

Pincher Kowalski was known for pinching her boarders when upset with them. She would pinch offending noses... and offending buttocks when the offenders were not facing her at the time of their offense... which apparently occurred often. Pincher was big, Pincher was strong, Pincher was mean and Pincher was Polish... and thus not Irish... and as was now quite obvious, Pincher pinched U.S. coppers as well as human boarding house flesh. She was much feared throughout "the Gut".

Her words having halted Monsignor Easy Monahan mid-prayer... his shot of whiskey still dangling before him from his extended left hand for all to see. With no prayer punch line to warrant his popping of that extended shot of whiskey, his left hand began to shake. He had already spent several minutes praising the high moral standards by which Gimpy had lived as the good Monsignor expected of all Swiftians, for the good Monsignor Easy Monahan was the religious leader to whom all the Swiftians looked for spiritual guidance and to whom they confessed every Friday in a hastily constructed confessional opposite Swifty's ladies' room and where the confessing Swiftians were rewarded with a "forgiving" penance, particularly after ten o'clock in the evening... thus the good Monsignor's well deserved moniker, "Easy", for the good Monsignor believed not in Godly revenge but rather saintly "forgiveness"... particularly after ten o'clock in the evening at Swifty's Irish Pub.

The good Monsignor's extended left hand, in which he held the shot of whiskey, began to shake from fatigue and with the threat of the spilling of the whiskey overtaking the good Monsignor, he popped the shot in a desperate move to prevent his feared loss of even a single drop of that "good" whiskey.

Pincher, mistaking the Monsignor's emergency whiskey popping for a challenge to her challenge, gave the Monsignor's nose a terrible pinch. Monsignor screamed bloody murder as the terrible pinch was both totally unanticipated and extremely painful, fortunately from the standpoint of propriety, the Monsignor was facing Pincher Kowalski at the time of the pinching... and as he dropped to his knees, all hell broke loose.

The Pincher then yelled, "That stinking corpse owes me a week's room and board... six greens and fifty coppers! Somebody pays or Gimpy's stinking corpse gets evicted!"

Swifty pulled a dining room chair into the parlor and hopped onto it. He was now face-to-face with the Pincher, "You can't evict a dead person. Gimpy has already departed from this life of woe and worry."

The Pincher would have none of it, "Oh yeah, well I haven't departed... just watch me... the next place that asshole departs from is going to be this boarding house if he doesn't pay this week's room and board. Being dead ain't no excuse. If he's too damn departed to pay, someone else has to. It's six greens and fifty coppers or the street!"

Swifty replied, "Well Gimpy Sean's fully dearly departed and the fully dearly departed don't sleep in no bed and don't eat no vittles. He's only taking up a little space in the parlor and after the funeral, he's outta here domesticularly speaking. Six greens and fifty coppers for the use of the parlor is outrageous."

"Well them vittles is already bought and paid for... and that room's got to be fumigated since its where the inconsiderate bastard departed from last Wednesday... and he's been ripening pretty fast ever since... it bein' June and a bad time for departin' stench wise. I might even have to wash the bed sheets and fumigate the parlor too. It'll take a week for the rummies around here to forget that and one of them rent the room. If Gimpy can't pay, someone else's got to pay for his lack of consideration departure-wise."

Swifty, a skilled negotiator having honed that skill dealing with recalcitrant Swiftian patrons at his iconic bar after which he was eponymously nominated, started to negotiate without the Pincher realizing it, "Look, Gimpy ain't sleepin' in no room and in no bed and he ain't eatin' no vittles. Granted, he's taking up space in the parlor for 24 hours or until the booze runs out... whichever comes first... but it ain't no week... and we'll keep the parlor windows open fumagtin' wise. I propose we pay you two greens as compensation for your domesticular inconveniences to settle the question."

The Pincher did not expect an offer that required negotiation, for she expected to be paid six greens and fifty coppers or she'd kick the God damn stinking corpse of the now dearly departed Gimpy Sean McGillicuddy into the street. After several very long moments of weak thought, she concluded that a partial payment was better than no payment at all even when that no payment had some personal satisfaction attached to it for she never really liked Gimpy what with him banging around the boarding house all hours of the day and night on that stupid wooden leg of his.

She approached Swifty and as she did so Swifty pulled back and covered his nose with his left hand. Unconcerned with Swifty's possibly insulting defensive action, she said, "Three greens and twenty-five coppers and it's a deal."

Swifty, having expected to pay half of the room and board when he made his first offer, readily accepted: "It's a deal!" and he took off his hat and passed it into the crowd of the Swiftians about him to collect the three greens and twenty-five coppers.

Swifty's hat returned to him with soiled greens and rusted coppers tossed about its interior. He counted the money into the outstretched hand of the Pincher. The count came up 17 coppers short. The Pincher was furious, "Seventeen coppers or he's outta here and I'm keepin' the three greens and eight coppers for today's inconvenience and the fumagatin' and potential sheet washin' and them already purchased vittles."

Ears Shamus saved the day... apparently: "Look, Gimpy's wearing his pocket watch. It still works. Suppose we give you the pocket watch as Gimpy's contribution to his own wake and funeral."

The Pincher thought yet again... a tiring experience given its rarity... and said, "Okay... provided the watch works." She walked over to Gimpy, yanked his pocket watch from his vest watch pocket and put it to her ear. After several more long moments, she yelled, "It don't tick. Deal off." She pointed to two constables in the crowd who were there anticipating free whiskey and yelled, "You know your God damn duties. Now duty that god damn stinking corpse outta here. Consider him evicted."

The two constables, one of whom boarded there, did as requested and very unceremoniously removed Gimpy and his coffin from the parlor and into the street... dropping Gimpy and his coffin rather unceremoniously into the gutter... much to the shock and outrage of the other, more faithful mourners.

Overcome with that shock and outrage and the need for a whiskey popper or three to assuage said shock and outrage, the Swiftians exited the boarding house and surrounded the dearly departed Gimpy Sean as he stared that thousand mile stare up from his coffin in the gutter and into the heavenly darkening clouds above... included in the crowd of mourners, four burly Swiftians who had grabbed the keg of Fitzgerald's swill and the three cases of whiskey that had been set aside to celebrate the living and the fairly recent departing of one Gimpy Sean McGillicuddy.

Thunder boomed and lightning struck nearby... and then a torrential downpour reigned down upon them. As the June thunder storm with its torrential rains struck, the entire group of mourners hot-footed it up Pearl toward the sanctuary of Swifty's Irish Pub, including the four burly men transporting the keg of Fitzgerald's swill and three cases of whiskey.

As the hot-footing Swiftians approached State Street, the traffic light turned red and the entire group halted. Swifty looked back and yelled "Where's Gimpy? Somebody's left Gimpy." With these words as inspiration, Handy Mary and Ears and Stuffer Shamus reverse hot-footed it back to the gutter in front of Gimpy's former

234

boarding house, shouldered Gimpy who still resided there in his coffin and hot-footed it back to the corner of Pearl and State arriving just as the notoriously long light turned green... and then onward all the living Swiftians hot-footed.

As the mourning hot-footers approached the Pearl Street gentlemen's rear entry to Swifty's... with the now shouldered coffin of Gimpy Sean McGillicuddy still in tow and still containing the corpse of the not-so-recently dearly departed, the Swiftian mourners were confronted by an equally large group of those flammin' femmies with placards held high and still in full throat, "Girls' rear entry not for us. Knock it off or get real fucked!"

The lightning, the thunder and the torrential rain ceased. The chanting and hot-footing stopped as the two groups now faced each other in silence. Then one of the older chanters who appeared to look an awful lot like the former Missus Dr. Pasquady Turnstile Murphy the 3rd... mistaken but sure in her mistakeness... broke the silence and yelled, "There's the traitor!" as she pointed at the crowd of Swiftians arrayed before her... probably meaning she'd sighted the actually absent Talkie Turnstile who had already used the Pearl Street gentlemen's rear entry and was enjoying a self-served whiskey popper while simultaneously being misidentified outside before the gentleman's rear entry that he'd already passed through.

The band of flammin' femmies lowered the poles sporting their various signs of protest... signs silently screaming "End Ladies Forced Rear Entry" and "Same Rear Entry for All"... thus converting those poles into lances. They charged the Swiftians as a phalanx worthy of a gaggle of unarmored horseless medieval knights of the feminine persuasion. The Swiftians, in reaction, turtled about the coffin of Gimpy Sean McGillicuddy... a turtling worthy of a maneuver of a somewhat disorganized gaggle of alcoholic Roman legionnaires...

235

the phalanx of flammin' femmies misbelieving that the traitor identified by the somewhat older flammin' femmie's knight was none other than the dearly departed his very self even though that individual was now in the form of a corpse.

Just as the two warring groups were about to clash, a blinding light flashed and then deafening thunder struck. The wooden light pole in front of Swifty's ladies' only rear entry started to burn. The smell of creosote permeated the area. Then a torrential downpour re-commenced. The chargin' flammin' femmies dropped their "lances" and halted inches before the Swiftians.

The lightning and thunder also startled Handy and the Shamus brothers carrying the coffin of the dearly departed Gimpy Sean. Handy Mary flopped onto the sidewalk like a beached whale. The Shamus brothers joined her and as they did so, the now unsupported coffin of Gimpy Sean McGillicuddy, in which the dearly departed still resided, hit the street with a thud and shattered, dumping the corpse of said dearly departed rather unceremoniously into the Pearl Street gutter before Swifty's men's only rear entry.

The two warring parties faced each other in terrible silence, terror in all eyes... and then lightning struck the already burning light pole yet again and thunder reigned down upon them as did the re-commenced torrential rain. In pure terror and ignoring Swifty's Pearl Street rear entry protocol, both groups charged away from the twice struck burning light pole before the ladies only rear entry and through the men's rear entry to escape God's apparent wrath of destruction, jostling into the bar room... all, that is, except for one Gimpy Sean McGillicuddy, who still stared that thousand mile stare... now from the gutter in which he lay on Pearl Street... into Heaven's dark clouds above as those clouds poured torrential rain upon him to the savage accompaniment of the lightning and thunder which he alone of all formerly present feared not!

Gimpy's thousand mile stare along with the rest of him started to float down the gutter on the rain's heavy runoff and back to his former boarding house on lower Pearl... much to the ignorance of the Swiftians who had sought and successfully obtained sanctuary from the conditions which the corpse of Gimpy Sean McGillicuddy now endured.

Inside Swifty's Irish Pub the two warring tribes had successfully found safety and sanctuary... the ire and vituperation melting away from the warriors of both tribes with whiskey poppers all around! Turns out that the socially liberated flammin' femmies knew a thing or two about boilermakers to the surprise and delight of the Swiftians and the Swiftians, with their generous provision of boiler poppers and enthusiastic verbal communication, surprised and delighted the flammin' femmies with their hospitality.

However, it must be admitted that the verbal communication between the two tribes was not fully clear to the tribal communicants of either tribe as they were separated by a somewhat common language on this side of the Atlantic. However, this lack of crisp verbal clarity did not dim the enthusiasm of either group to continue to verbally communicate both orally and aurally, the two means of communication being inextricably and interchangeably related.

Stuffer Shamus stood proudly before the bar, his fifth whiskey pop held high and yelled, "Bein' here to Gimpy Sean McGillicuddy..." He turned toward the back wall thinking to see his wonderful funereal work on display, but to his surprise, there was no wonderful funereal work there to admire and then to toast. He yelled even louder in a voice tinged with great disappointment and surprise, "Where the hell..." He stopped mid-yell to carefully pop his whiskey making sure not to spill a single drop of the precious liquid. Then after several moments of contemplation, he remembered the last place he had seen his wonderful funereal work and took off through the gentlemen's only rear exit to Pearl Street.

Right on Stuffer's tail were brother Ears and the unexpectedly swift-a-foot Handy Mary... all three reaching Pearl Street and observing in the distance the corpse of Gimpy Sean floating down the Pearl Street gutter toward State Street. The three ran pell-mell into the fury of the storm to rescue the now poorly departed who no longer lived up to his Swiftian nomination of Gimpy... death having improved his mobility in the present situation.

It was now obvious to the three rescuers that while the undeceased Swiftians, including Stuffer Shamus, his brother Ears and Handy Mary, joined by the equally undeceased flammin' femmies, had re-treated into the safety of Swifty's Irish Pub, Gimpy Sean, in the form of his corpse, had not. Instead Gimpy undertook an unplanned voyage down Pearl Street's gutter on the runoff of the continuing torrential down pour... as if seeking to return to the boarding house on lower Pearl where he'd lived for over a decade and pay his now other worldly and most likely final respects to his former land lady, Pincher Kowalski.

When he floated to the juncture of Pearl and State, the traffic light at the meeting of these two great thoroughfares turned red and as if by divine order, the corpse anchored itself to the curb in obedience to Caesar's earthly traffic laws... awaiting the turning of the traffic light to green to continue his watery journey down Pearl on his last trip home.

As Gimpy Sean's corpse awaited the traffic light to turn green, the three rescuers tore down Pearl through the fierce storm. They arrived at the corner of Pearl and State just as the traffic light blinked green. Before Gimpy could continue his last watery journey home, they grabbed him and hot-footed their now shouldered prize back through the raging storm and to his own wake and possibly funeral. They stumbled over the pile of wooden shards that had been Gimpy's coffin, through Swifty's gentlemen's only rear entry and back into the safety of Swifty's Irish Pub where they stooled Gimpy at the end of the bar... slumping him forward against the bar's edge. In deference to the niceties of the bar aroma-wise, Handy Mary chocked open the men's only rear exit to Pearl even as the storm continued to roar without.

As the Swiftians and flammin' femmies recommence their semi-wakeful celebration, the two constables, who had evicted poor Gimpy from the boarding house, storm into the bar room from the Pearl Street men's rear entry and exit, followed by none other then... drum roll... Pincher Kowalski her very self... the Pincher apparently having been specifically non-invited to the wake and possible funeral at some point during the commotion caused by the Pincher's post-life eviction of Gimpy Sean from her boarding house... a non-invitation she had taken to be both personal and quite unfriendly.

The lead constable, the one who also boarded at Pincher Kowalski's, points at the slumping Gimpy stooled at the bar and yells, "You got a death certificate for that corpse?"

Stuffer Shamus yells, "Fooken thou... we don't need no fooken death certificate. You know Gimpy lived in the Gut. No one who departs in the Gut needs permission from some crown asshole. He just departs and that's it!"

The lead constable yells back, "Until he gets certified as dead, he ain't officially departed. Gimpy's got to reside at the coroner's until he's certified dead. We're taking him there right now." And with that, the two constables grab Gimpy by the arms and shoulders and pull him off his stool. Stuffer Shamus dives and grabs Gimpy's right leg. His brother Ears and hefty Handy Mary dive and grab Gimpy's left leg. As the two constables yank Gimpy to the floor, the cause of Gimpy's gimpiness comes loose and Ears and Handy Mary are left holding onto Gimpy's now unattached wooden leg. Gimpy flies through the air and lands with a thud on the bar room floor. His unfamiliar paunch busts open and formaldehyde soaked cotton balls spill out onto the floor along with several other unidentifiable flesh-like objects. The two constables let go of Gimpy and back away in obvious horror and disgust.

Then thunderous lightning strikes and the lights go out leaving the bar room in darkness. It takes several minutes for Swifty to corral a bunch of candles and light them. As the candles are lit and light spreads over the bar room floor, it becomes obvious to all that Gimpy Sean McGillicuddy's corpse is not lying on that bar room floor where it should be... surrounded by a pile of formaldehyde soaked cotton balls and several unidentifiable flesh-like objects. A thorough candle-lit search of every nook and cranny of the premises known as Swifty's Irish Bar is made by representatives of all tribes present... but to no avail. Nowhere is Gimpy's corpse to be found.

Many believe that an apparently saintly Gimpy Sean McGillicuddy was called to heaven directly although no one present, including the spiritual leader of those who frequented Swifty's Irish Pub, Monsignor Easy Monahan, could identify the corporal and earthly evidence of this saintliness... concluding that the Lord works and speaks in mysterious ways even in Swifty's Irish Pub... and just maybe in Swifty's Buzz.

With no corpse to certify as dead thus cancelling the need to claim that such certification is an unnecessary intrusion of governmental authority into Swiftian lives, the Swiftians, the constables and the concerned but neutral flammin' femmies belly up to the bar and whiskey pop away.

Without Gimpy's corpse, the celebration at Swifty's Irish Pub is no longer a wake and possible funeral... and his missing corpse also renders his post-departing eviction irrelevant... so under these circumstances Swifty, in an act of charity, generously invites Pincher Kowalski to join them... which she enthusiastically does... although legend has it that she never returned Gimpy's pocket watch... claiming that with Gimpy's apparent "assumption" into heaven as she put it, there's no one to return the pocket watch to on Mother Earth... besides, she is said to have contended, that even if she could, what use would Gimpy Sean McGillicuddy have for his pocket watch since he now resides in eternity where time is all but irrelevant and it didn't work anyways... or so Swiftian legend would have it.

I, James Mead Warden the 3rd, have carefully and faithfully doc-umented the above events which the Swiftians believe to be very important in their religious and cultural history... and from my per-spective, the history of their unique English dialect as well. Unfor-tunately, I still do not have that Rosetta Stone for Swifty's Buzz to include in my thesis. However, I did see something very strange occur that night. From a linguistic standpoint, that event has already changed Swifty's Buzz, for Swiftians now use the terms *assumption* and *ascension* interchangeably, including the good Monsignor Easy Monahan.

I leave you with the following question: Is Gimpy Sean McGillicuddy's so-called "assumption" into heaven a Swiftian legend? Or is it real? I was there and witnessed something occur on that stormy night... something which I cannot explain. One man's... and one woman's... tall story full of burlesque and humor is another's miraculous event! Laugh at this account but at your own eternal peril!

THIS PAGE INTENTIONALLY LEFT MOSTLY BLANK

(IF THIS PAGE DID NOT EXIST, WOULD A STATEMENT TO THIS EFFECT BE NECESSARY?)

IRRELEVANT NOTE FROM THE AUTHOR:

BEWARE: THE MASSAGING FINGERS OF CAPITALISM'S INVISIBLE HAND CAN BE USED FOR ECONOMIC AND ETHICAL SELF-ABUSE!

The Tangled Web of Porcine Love, Arboreal Sex and Constitutional Law

It being Friday, Delton P. Meriwether sat at his desk checking time cards on an all too common dreary and chilly Spring morning in his beloved Hudson Valley. He suffered a splitting headache because of a sinus condition, but as always, he soldiered on. Others suffering a similar medical condition blamed their painful plight on the geographic region referring to this region as "sinus valley". Delton P. Meriwether did not, for to do so in his mind would be an indication of a certain lack of regional patriotism. It started to rain again... as it had all day, on and off... the rain drops pounding on the steel roof above his head adding to his discomfort... but Delton P. Meriwether remained regionally patriotic.

He was a manager in a software develop lab of a famous corporation in the Valley. He managed a technical writing department there. To avoid potential legal entanglements, I will not name the corporation although it is an international corporation with a famous and easily recognized block-letter logo... the logo appearing an awful lot like the crayon drawing of a five year old kindergarten student with absolutely no artistic talent or hand-eye coordination, but as often happens, great financial success brought the wide acceptance of this bad design as a form idiosyncratic genius.

Back in the day, this block-letter crayon drawing of the logo was considered sacred by the corporation and its "integrity" jealously guarded... right down to every single poorly outlined block letter. Much to Mr. Delton P. Meriwether's dismay, he had noticed that recently the logo had appeared in advertising in several other forms... something that would have caused corporate torture and a public hanging for the miscreant who so soiled the sacred logo... back in the day.

244

As an employee and then a manager, Mr. Delton P. Meriwether had been subject to the culture, beliefs and practices that dominated his beloved corporation when the logo was sacred... and he had remained faithful to that culture and its beliefs and practices. In his private life, what there was of it (for most of his life revolved around his career at the aforementioned corporation with the "idiosyncratic" three letter logo), Mr. Delton P. Meriwether lived a quiet and quite conventional life. There was even a rumor that he was a devout Episcopalian.

Personally soiling the sacred logo was beyond his comprehension and had remained so. Should someone in his department act in a manner that was beyond his comprehension and soil that sacred logo even today, he would gladly volunteer to become torturer in chief and enthusiastic executioner. With great conviction he would have half-hung the miscreant, disemboweled him, castrated him, chopped off his arms and legs and then decapitated him... metaphorically speaking. As fate would have it, he had never needed to do so to any employee, all of whom he anticipated would be male should that event beyond his comprehension occur. He could not conceive of a female employee soiling the logo. Besides, how do you castrate a female?

Again back in the day, aside from desecrating the sacred logo, almost everything else was tolerated within the community standards as perceived by corporate management as long as sex was not involved. All employees were considered members of the great corporate family and managers were to act as compassionate and loving foster parents... a kind of corporate *in loco parentis.*

However, the community standards had changed over the years, and as a result, the meaning of *in loco parentis* as perceived by corporate management had also changed with the times. There was less concern about all things sexual and a lot more tough love in all other aspects of corporate life including its modern day interpretation of corporate *in loco parentis*... particularly regarding the concept of life-time employment. However, for Mr. Delton P. Meriwether nothing had changed. Even "old schoolers" still working at the unnamed corporation considered him "old school", for he was the "old schooler" against whom all other "old schoolers" were measured.

As Meriwether flipped through the time cards, he noticed that the time card for one of his employees was unsigned. This breach of procedure upset him as did any breach of procedure. He thought to himself *I'll bet Mr. Raymond Raske forgot to sign his card again.* The phone rang interrupting his thoughts and uncharacteristically he grabbed the phone and yelled into it, "Hello! Delton P. Meriwether, Technical Writing Department" as was required by corporate practice although yelling was not a part of this recommended practice.

"It's me"

"Who?"

"Me. Raymond."

"Raymond?"

"Yes, Raymond Raske."

"Mr. Raske... you neglected to sign your time card this morning."

"I know. I'm not there. I'm somewhere else."

"Somewhere else? Where somewhere else? Are you calling in sick?"

"No, I'm not sick and I'm not home." There was a long pause and then "I need a favor... some help" and another long pause, "Could you pick me up and give me a ride to work?"

"Of course. Where are you?"

"I'm in a phone booth."

"What... a phone booth? Where's the phone booth?"

"I don't know."

There was another long pause as Delton P. Meriwether processed what he had just heard. Then he said, "Look out of the phone booth. Do you see anything you recognize?"

"Yes. I see a school... Lincoln School."

"I know where you are. You don't live anywhere near there. How did you get there?"

"I don't remember."

"Well do not move. I will be there shortly."

As Delton P. Meriwether was about to hang up, Raymond Raske yelled, "Wait. I need another favor" and after a longer pause... "Could you bring a pair of pants and a shirt and some antibiotic cream?"

A stunned Meriwether mumbled a confused "Yes" more as a question than an answer to one and was about to ask several other questions that immediately came to mind but Mr. Raymond Raske had already hung up.

As often happened, Mr. Delton P. Meriwether's mind went into problem solving mode for he was not a big picture kind of manager... not only by training and necessity but by nature... and so the immediate problem before him was that one of his employees, one Raymond Raske in this case, needed a wardrobe of sorts and a ride to work. He thought to himself *Mr. Raske is about my size* and on his way to his mysterious rendezvous with his employee, he stopped at his house and picked up a wardrobe of sorts, including a pair of sandals and a pair of socks just in case, and that tube of antibiotic cream... the sandals because they could be adjusted to fit almost any size foot. He had no idea why Mr. Raymond Raske would need a tube of antibiotic cream but it was on the list and so he brought one with him.

He then drove to the phone booth across the street from Lincoln School. There in a brightly lit phone booth, one of the few remaining in the city, he saw his employee, Mr. Raymond Raske, scrunched over against the cold, a very necessary move on his part given that he was dressed in only a white tee shirt, boxer shorts covered with a colorful floral design... and no shoes or socks. His goose bumps had goose bumps.

Meriwether walked over to the phone booth with a bag containing the emergency wardrobe in one hand and a tube of antibiotic cream in the other. As he approached, Raske slid the door to the phone booth open and the light went out. He held out his left hand and said, "Did you bring the antibiotic cream?"

A stunned Meriwether slowly shook his head yes and handed Raske the tube of antibiotic cream. Raske grabbed the tube with his left hand, jumped back into the phone booth and slammed the door shut with an emphatic bang. Under a bright light, he unscrewed the cap to the tube with his right thumb and forefinger and squished a huge dap of the cream onto the palm of that hand while still holding the cap. With great dexterity he screwed the cap back onto the tube, slid open the phone booth door and slammed the tube of anti-biotic cream into the still open palm of a very confused Delton P. Meriwether.

To his further surprise, Meriwether observed his employee slide the door to the phone booth closed yet again. The light went on illuminating a certain Raymond Raske as he turned away, pulled open his boxer shorts with the colorful floral design with his left hand, stuff his right hand down those boxer shorts and apparently rubbed vigorously as he loudly groaned "Ohhhh!"

He then pulled his right hand from his boxer shorts and rubbed the palm on the seat of those boxer shorts smearing the colorful floral design. He turned, slid open the phone booth's door and snatched the bag containing the emergency wardrobe. He slammed the door closed and again with more great dexterity got fully dressed in the ghostly glow of the light from the lit phone booth... which included placing socks and sandals on his previously unshod feet.

A man of detail, Meriwether asked, "Where'd you get the change to make the call? You obviously had no pockets."

"I sort of hot-wired the phone. Learned how to do it in college. Still works on the old phones."

Being a "solve the immediate problem" kind of manager, Meriwether then asked, "Should I take you home first so that you can change into your own clothes?" as he drove Raske away from the phone booth.

Raske replied, "No. I can't go home. Eloise has locked me out. I think she's divorcing me."

At this point Meriwether's mind short circuited. The events of the morning... an unsigned time card... an employee in a phone booth wearing only a tee shirt and boxer shorts with a colorful floral design... a request for an emergency wardrobe... a mysterious need for and use of antibiotic cream... the same employee not only locked out of his house but about to be divorced. In Meriwether's mind, because of all these events, he was now a corporate *in loco parentis* on steroids.

Having completed the drive back *to the ole bomber factoree* as "old schoolers" like Meriwether called the lab, he shepherded Raske back to that now overwhelmed manager's office.

As they sat across from each other separated by a desk, Meriwether said, "First things first"... a statement which gave him great comfort... "Please sign your time card." He looked down at his wrist watch and said, "Code the first three hours of today as *Code 17B Personal business, unauthorized absence.*"

As Raske was about to put pen to time card, Meriwether's phone rang. He promptly put phone to ear and yelled, ""Hello! Delton P. Meriwether, Technical Writing Department" as was required by corporate practice although yelling was not a part of this recommended practice. Tension had grown within Meriwether because he was still unable to complete his usual "first things first" of every Friday morning... that being approving all of his employees time cards after they had signed them and thus officially verifying their attendance for the week.

Raske put down his pen and listened to half of Meriwether's phone conversation.

"Now?"

"Personnel lobby?"

"Bring Raske?"

The aforenamed Raske watched as a very confused and frustrated expression spread across Meriwether's face and worked its way down his body.

Meriwether slammed the phone down... for his inability to get first-things-first done on this dreary rainy Spring day in sinus valley gnawed at his managerial intestines, a gnawing that got worse by the minute because of his raging sinus headache. He jumped to his feet and yelled, "Please follow me!"

Off the two marched in single file to the opposite end of the lab... one marcher with great purpose and one with great confusion. Just outside the personnel lobby, the two marchers were met by Mr. William Whitcomb, the personnel rep for their area. Mr. Whitcomb put his arm up preventing the two marchers from entering the personnel lobby. He said to our now halted marchers, "Sheriff Lionel Vander Meer is in the lobby. He's already informed me that he's here to serve papers to Mr. Raske. He has served papers here many times in the past and we are very familiar with the legal procedure. You, Meriwether, are to officially observe the proceedings as the manager of Mr. Raske. I am here to observe the proceedings for the corporation. Neither of you are to say anything. Got it!"

Both men shook their heads yes indicating that they understood and had already begun not saying anything. The trio entered the personnel lobby and a very stern Sheriff Vander Meer asked, "Mr. Raske... Mr. Raymond Raske?"

Raske stepped forward and said nothing as ordered. The sheriff handed Raske a bunch of papers and said, "You have been served with an order of protection. You are not allowed to communicate personally with Mrs. Eloise Raske. You must not come within 500 yards of her at any time. You are not to interfere with her when she walks Precious. You are not to communicate in any way with Precious. You are not allowed to enter the house at 105 Lonely Pine Grove. You are not allowed to enter the stand of virgin pine trees on the property at 105 Lonely Pine Grove. You may retrieve your personal property at 105 Lonely Pine Grove under the arranged supervision of the sheriff's office. All property removal must be negotiated through the lawyer for Mrs. Eloise Raske, Mr. Desmond Dirwinkle, Esquire. Do you, Raymond Raske, understand these terms?"

A quite bewildered Raymond Raske shook his head yes and the very stern Sheriff Lionel Vander Meer turned and marched out of the person-

251

nel lobby.

Delton Meriwether and Raymond Raske faced each other across Meriwether's desk. Meriwether said nothing as he pushed a time card and pen across the desk to Raske. He then pointed at the time card. Raske signed the card on which Meriwether had already written 17B for the unauthorized missed three hours.

A much relieved Meriwether, having finally finished Friday's first-things-first, re-assumed his perceived role as a caring corporate *in loco parentis* and said, "I am sorry to hear that you will not be able to communicate with your daughter Precious. I'm sure that you can work out some visitation schedule in the near future. I know it was touch and go when you first brought her home."

A quite dejected Raymond Raske looked down and said, "Precious isn't my daughter. She's our pot bellied pig. She was the runt of the litter. Eloise and I hand fed her. I took two weeks emergency leave... remember... to care for our poor Precious around the clock. Eloise and I provided 24-hour care... in shifts... and Precious pulled through." Tears welled in his eyes and he whispered a barely audible, "And now I can't see her. I can't even communicate with her from afar."

A stunned Meriwether said, "Pot bellied pig? Precious is a pot bellied pig. I thought she was your daughter. I even entered her name as a family member... a daughter... on your personnel record."

Now a stunned Raymond Raske replied, "I never said Precious was my daughter, my human daughter. I said Eloise and I were so happy that Precious had pulled through and we welcomed her into our family like a daughter. I said *like* a daughter. I didn't say she *was* our new daughter"... placing great emphasis on the words "like" and "was".

Meriwether realized that his role as corporate *in loco parentis* was becoming incredibly complicated and that he was entering uncharted territory in that role. He was unclear as to what that role should be now that it involved an employee with a family that included a pot bellied pig named Precious, but he was also sure that as a corporate *in loco parentis*, he had one.

Raske hired a lawyer, Mr. William Perch. Raske's friends had advised him not to hire a lawyer known in local legal circles as Billy "the Fish" Perch, for in those same local legal circles, Mr. Perch was famous, perhaps infamous would be a better word, for three things: 1) he could drink prodigious amounts of alcoholic beverages and thus could "drink like a fish"... the Fish being a particularly appropriate sobriquet given both his capacity to drink prodigious amounts of alcohol and his surname; 2) in spite of having a very lucrative practice, he had never appeared in court in his entire legal career having settled every one of his cases out of court before trial; and 3) he had almost been disbarred for alleged sexual encounters with four of his female clients. Rumor had it that to avoid disbarment, Billy the Fish had nearly bankrupted himself by paying a small fortune to three of the women to drop their charges. He had the fourth accuser declared legally insane causing the Bar's ethical committee to drop this last charge against him.

However, Raymond Raske had graduated from the local high school with William Perch. They had been acquaintances and occasionally friends over the years. In fact while in high school, Raske and his future wife Eloise had double-dated with Mr. William Perch and his girl friend of the moment... usually a very good looking and very young teenager who was rumored to have "round heels".

There was a method in Raske's madness as he hoped that since Eloise knew Billy the Fish, said Fish might be able to negotiate a decent agreement with Eloise even if he had to do so through Desmond Dirwinkle,

Eloise's lawyer... and Billy might even be able to bypass the diminutive Dirwinkle and deal surreptitiously with Eloise directly, something Raske was sure Billy the Fish was capable of.

After weeks of meetings and negotiations with Eloise's lawyer and one ethically questionable and very intimate meeting with Eloise herself... without the presence of anyone including her lawyer... Billy the Fish met with Raymond to give him the bad news, "Ray, I've tried every trick in the book... I even had a long, private and very intimate communication with Eloise without that midget lawyer Dirwinkle present... and it's no dice. No way are you getting visitation rights with Precious. She's a pet and we can negotiate visitation as a part of the divorce but the law cannot be used to force that agreement. The law protects a father's right to have visitations with his children but not with pets. Pets aren't human."

Raymond sat facing the Fish, put his head in his hands and started to weep. The Fish pushed a box of tissues across the desk and said, "Have you told me everything? Eloise told me in our very intimate and private meeting that after what you did, you'll never see Precious again. She screamed at me that you are a perverted unfaithful prick unworthy of Precious."

Raymond's shoulders shook as he wept even more uncontrollably. The Fish stood, reached across his desk, grabbed Raymond by his shaking shoulders with both hands, shook him even more and yelled, "Be a man, for Christ's sake. Pull it together. There's got to be a way. The law is full of holes. All we've got to do is find one of them and slither through, but if you keep balling in self pity, we're dead meat!" As the Fish sank back into his chair, he said, "Take me through everything that happened chronologically from the very beginning ."

Raymond began his tale of woe while still weeping. Between sorrowful sighs, he said, "When we got Precious, she was in tough shape, the poor baby. She was the runt of the litter... her mother refused to nurse her... we took her home and nursed her to health. We paid to get the pick of the litter but we felt so sorry for poor Precious that we picked her."

Talking about Precious calmed Raymond down and he stopped weeping. "Eloise and I worked in shifts twenty four hours a day for almost two weeks. I even had to take two weeks of emergency leave from work. I lost half of my vacation that year since my manager refused to grant me the emergency family leave time... something about corporate rules. He was a real prick about it. He's so stupid he thought Precious was my daughter... my human daughter... which makes his refusal to grant me family leave time even more inhumane... and he stupidly added Precious to my corporate family profile. He's listed her as my daughter, my human daughter. I think she's actually qualified for corporate medical benefits. What an idiot!"

With this last sentence, the Fish jumped back to his feet and yelled "Say again... that part about your stupid manager listing Precious as your daughter" and Raymond did so.

The Fish smiled like a lawyerly Cheshire cat, to mix a metaphor or two, and said, "I'm dating this girl... Eula something or other... Rumba, yes, Eula Rumba... she's a damn knockout... body that won't quit... saw her at one of those animal rights demonstrations last Fall... she and three other girls stripped naked in front of city hall and smeared themselves with what they called pig blood. Got on all the networks. It was actually tomato soup but you get the idea... protesting that pig farm off 32. Four sets of swollen nipples looked about to burst on that frigid day... and ole Eula, swollen nips and all, displayed a bush I'd had wet dreams about for years..."

Raymond looked up at the Fish and said, "What's this naked Eula Rumba with swollen nipples and a great bush smeared with tomato soup demonstrating against a pig farm off 32 got to do with me and poor

255

Precious?"

"Personhood, my man, personhood."

"Personhood?"

"Yea. Ole Eula, between rug munchings, keeps whining to me about the need to establish animal personhood as a judicial precedent. You know, get all animals declared persons and then those animal rights assholes can hammer anyone they want with all those laws that today only apply to humans. She said they could shove the law up the ass of those pig farmers on 32 and make them pray for Vaseline when they appeal the judge's ruling. It's the only thing she talks about between orgasms. Personhood... personhood... personhood... Won't shut up."

"Personhood?"

"Yea, personhood! Wake up you asshole! If we can get Precious declared a person, than all those laws regarding parental rights apply to you visiting Precious. Get it?"

"Kinda. But what's that got to do with my manager and him claiming that Precious is... *then cognitive lightning struck our beleaguered hero between his dull eyes...* I get it. He's listed Precious as my daughter, my human daughter, my real daughter!"

"Right! If we can squeeze that management bastard of yours in court and get the court to accept the fact that through the actions of a legal representative, a major American corporation has granted personhood to an animal and given that animal medical benefits, we're home free. Hell, after the ruling, you can apply to be reimbursed for all the expenses you incurred caring for Precious. She was a god damn personhooded porcine preemie!"

After a long minute as our beleaguered hero contemplated his legal situation and the reputation and competence of his lawyer, William "the Fish" Perch, he asked, "No offence Billy, but are you qualified to make this personhood argument in court. Sounds like a pretty tall legal hill to climb... and in court... perhaps under the watchful eyes of millions. A trial like this could be covered by every major news outlet in the world."

That lawyerly Cheshire cat smile reappeared on the face of Billy "the Fish" Perch, to again mix a metaphor or two or even three, and the Fish yelled, "That's what we want! Millions! I'll get ole Eula and her demonstrating female buddies to flash the burning bush before the trial. That will insure the coverage!"

"After we get all this national... hell international... news coverage, are you going to make that personhood argument in court?"

"Hell no, good buddy. I'd get a new asshole ripped open in court. I ain't no Clarence Darrow or even Spencer Tracy. That animal rights group PEATA or whatever they call themselves now has millions of dollars up the animal rights kaziggie. According to Eula, they're looking for the right case to set the precedent establishing porcine personhood. Once they get that, they'll set another precedent using the first precedent and shut down that pig farm on 32. Their legal team is world class. They'd do the heavy lifting for us... and for free. And this is the case they've been drooling for. It's a natural set up.

"How so? Wouldn't they be better of getting chimpanzees or some other monkey declared a person? They're closer to humans. No?"

"No! The problem with monkeys, particularly chimpanzees, is that it's an easier stretch to get them declared persons but the leap from monkeys to other species is a tougher sell. Eula says they've done a lot of focus group research and pigs give them the best chance to establish a sort of universal personhood for all animals."

Raske smiled, "And there's been all those pig movies... Charlotte's Web

257

has a pig... a human pig and there's those Babe the Pig movies... at least two of them... and Babe's a wonderful human."

"Right. And Eula claims that pigs are very close to humans, physiologically speaking, enabling their lawyers to make a bunch of technical physiological arguments."

The Fish smiled and then continued, "But if you look at it from the pig's point of view, being declared a person ain't all that charming. Humans are really a bunch of pigs... human pigs... even at the upper echelons of society. There's the Kardashions and Harvey Weinstein and all those Hollywood assholes and all those senators and congressmen pussy hounds resigning. What are they? Just a bunch of human pigs. Hell, they give pigs a bad name. If I were a pig, a real pig, I'd find personhood an insult! Even in our dear city, our local society is full of human pigs and I've got the pictures and video to prove it. When all's said and done, what's your poor Precious?"

"A potbellied pig! A real pig!"

"Right. When that PEATA legal team gets through with our local legal yahoos, Precious will be a person and the god damn bottom will drop out of all those pork belly futures! They'll turn eating bacon into a form of cannibalism!"

And so it was. After a series clandestine meetings with the *Protect Every Animal That's Alive -- Forever United*, better known to the world as PEATA-FU, Billy the Fish negotiated an agreement for the PEATA-FU high powered legal team to represent Raymond Raske in court in order to get him his visitation rights by having Precious declared his person-hooded porcine daughter. As a part of this agreement, the Fish became the local legal consultant for the PEATA-FU legal team for a healthy six figure fee, for as he pointed out, he knew the dirt on every judge, DA, court officer, administrator and law enforcement officer in the city. Hell, he even had pictures and video... which also explained why a lawyer who never appeared in court managed to negotiate his way to a lucrative law practice without all those messy and chancy court appearances.

Of course the PEATA-FU legal team wasn't all altruistic peaches and cream in volunteering to help poor Raymond Raske secure visitation rights with his precious Precious. As you know, they had other personhooded reasons.

The team was led by the renown lawyer Estes Philips Williamson the 3rd, Esquire, perhaps it was the 4th. The various articles printed by the mainstream press were not uniform in their description of Mr. Williamson. Some said he was the 3rd. Others, the 4th. Whatever the number, it was this Estes Philips Williamson who had established the legal precedent that there were actually 57 different sexual identities... referred to as the *Heinz 57 Varieties Decision* (nit caps, italics) by the press. Mr. Williamson the 3rd or 4th is credited with overturning three thousand years of sexual prejudice on the part of virtually every previous civilization in human history.

The mainstream culture applauded the decision. Mr. Stephen Colbert, on his popular late-night TV show, dressed in a different sexual identity for 57 consecutive shows popularizing the Supreme Court's decision. As a result of his creativity and daring he was awarded seven Golden Globes, three of those awards for categories that did not exist before the Supreme Court decision.

In Mr. Colbert's wildly celebrated and cheered seven acceptance speeches, he gave full credit to the five Supreme Court justices who ruled in favor of the 57 varieties of sexual identity decision and credited those five Supreme Court Justices with giving him the idea to dress in a different sexual identity for 57 consecutive shows.

Oxbow Lake The 2nd

As you may remember, when the Sexual Freedom League vs. the United States decision was announced, the five justices who voted in favor of the Sexual Freedom League wore masks depicting their favorite sexual identity in order to demonstrate their support for the decision. Justice Ruth Bader Ginsberg, wearing a wonderfully cute mask of Babe the Pig, read a two sentence decision 57 times changing the subject of the first sentence each time. After each reading, the gallery went wild with applause.

This was the historic and cultural background of the previous year and the most recent item on the resume of Mr. Estes Philips Williamson the 3rd, Esquire (perhaps it was the 4th). The *Protect Every Animal That's Alive -- Forever United* in general and Mr. Estes Philips Williamson the 3rd, Esquire (perhaps it was the 4th), in particular, were ecstatic when Justice Ginsberg wore that mask of Babe the Pig. Not only did Justice Ginsberg's reading of the *Heinz 57 Varieties Decision* (nit caps, italics) decision open the back door to total sexual freedom, she also introduced other species into the decision and on an equal plain with humans by wearing a mask of Babe the Pig when doing so! Although the personal and metaphorical reasons for why Justice Ginsberg chose to wear a Babe the Pig mask remain unclear to this day, the very fact that she did so sent thrills up both legs of every member of the *Protect Every Animal That's Alive -- Forever United* legal team. When announcing the decision, Chris Mathews, the MSNBC journalist and anchor, also got a thrill... up both his legs this time... a thrill so strong that he actually fainted on the air in an orgy of delight. (As a result of Mr. Mathews' reporting on the decision, he was awarded the Nobel Prizes for both Peace and Literature later that year.)

To reinforce the Supreme Court decision, NFL Commissioner Roger Goodell ruled that any state government that did not recognize all 57 sexual identities... not 54, not 55 or even 56 but all 57 varieties... would not be allowed to host a Super Bowl game and those states that were never considered to host the Super Bowl would be blacked out from all televised NFL games until their state governments recognized all 57 as well. In a further ruling, Goodell required the players, coaches, staff and even ownership for all 30 NFL teams to pass an extensive test of their ability to recognize all 57 sexual identities in a clinical setting. Those who did not pass the test would be suspended from participation in all team activities, including games, until they had successfully done so.

The owners for both the Seattle Seahawks and San Francisco 49ers immediately petitioned the NFL compensation committee to have Goodell's contract modified so that any member of his extended family, including Goodell himself, would be fully covered for sexual reassignment surgery in perpetuity. NFL team owners voted 29 to 1 to amend Goodell's contract... the Dallas Cowboys being the only team to vote against the contract modification.

The Representatives and Senators of the Democratic party announced that they will wear underwear with 57 distinct colors until all 50 states and the district of Columbia follow the NFL guidelines... that is, the same pair of undies! Billionaire George Soros pledged to pay for the design and manufacturing of the multi-colored underwear and has plans to market the underwear to the public at large through Amazon.com for $52.17 a pair.

Hollywood announced 57 new Oscars, one for each sexual identity. The Academy will award an Oscar for the movies which best depict each of the 57 sexual identities in a favorable light. George Soros has committed to back at least one movie in each of the 57 categories. He has also "volunteered" to star in one of those 57 movies. Which one remains a mystery and speculation has run ramp-ed throughout the industry. Some believe it will be sexual identity 23. Others, 54. The smart money is on sexual identity 23 since it only involves bi-peds.

William "the Fish" Perch primed the main stream media pump with a press release announcing that at the onset of the trial to get Precious the pot bellied pig legally imbued with "personhood", the four "Precious Porcine Pretties" (as he called them), led by the incomparable Eula Rumba, would demonstrate on behalf of the *Protect Every Animal That's Alive -- Forever United* in support of porcine Precious's personhood and Raymond Raske's right to have visitation rights with his precious Precious. In his press release, the Fish did not state that the four Pretties would perform naked but he did include a video in the press release of the Pretties demonstrating against the pig farm off Route 32.

The video was 32 minutes long and covered, perhaps I should say "uncovered", the entire demonstration from practice to performance with the four quite naked swollen-nippled Pretties splashing tomato soup over their bodies... their demonstration climaxing in a carefully choreographed dance of many bending and squatting positions accompanied by the rhythmic chant "Pigs are people just like you... if you don't like it you can go screw!"

On the day of the onset of the trial, 117 news organizations with all their cameras, equipment and satellite trucks crowded the courthouse square and much of the city's downtown. News organizations and their prime time anchors from the world over were present. Even MSNBC's Chris Mathews was there as he had apparently fully recovered from his incapacitating two-legged thrill attack brought on by Supreme Court Justice Ruth Bader Ginsberg's apparent reading of the 114 sentences of the *Heinz 57 Varieties Decision* (nit caps, italics) through her wonderfully cute mask of Babe the Pig.

At 9:00 o'clock sharp, a black limousine pulled up to the courthouse steps and three of the Precious Porcine Pretties, led by the comely Eula Rumba, jumped out... the fourth Pretty not present as she was succumbing to menstrual cramps at the time of the demonstration. The three Pretties present were clothed only in a narrow over-the-shoulder purple sash that read "Personhood for Precious". The Pretties present danced to the courthouse steps with wonderfully choreographed movements and chanted "Precious, Precious she's a like us... give her personhood that's a must!"

Chris Mathews yelled from the crowd of anchors, "Do it again but drive in from the other side so that the limousine doesn't block our view as we're taping." Huzzahs in many languages went up from the crowd of international news anchors crammed into the courthouse square.

The three present Precious Porcine Pretties jumped back into the limousine and the limousine drove off, circled the square with some difficulty and entered the square from the opposite side. An official 117 cameras (and many unofficial ones) with red recording lights blinking away then captured every unobstructed moment of the reprised wonderful *au natural-ly* choreographed dance and rhythmic chant.

For three days the trial proceeded in what even a lazy snail would describe as a pedestrian pace and all without so much as a mention of the word "personhood". After the *Protect Every Animal That's Alive -- Forever United* legal team had called several more witnesses including a research physiologist from Cornell University who made the word "monotone" seem exciting, a somewhat frustrated Family Court Judge Anderson Vander Meer said, "Mr. Estes Philips Williamson the 3rd or 4th, Esquire, do you have any additional witnesses to call?"

The lead council for the *Protect Every Animal That's Alive -- Forever United* smiled like he'd belled the cat and said in his stentorian voice, "Yes your honor. The legal counsel for Mr. Raymond Raske calls Mr. Delton P. Meriwether!"

The legal counsel for Eloise Raske, one Desmond Dirwinkle, immediately and apparently jumped to his feet and yelled, "We object! Whoever this man is, he wasn't on the witness list. No predicate to this witness has been presented to the court."

Family Court Judge Anderson Vander Meer looked down at the diminutive Desmond Dirwinkle and said quite derisively, "Dirwinkle, this isn't about grammar... and stand when you address the court!"

The diminutive Desmond Dirwinkle said rather sheepishly, "But your honor, I am standing."

"You are?"

The Judge, now feeling the growing need for a morning pick-me-up and also the appearance of a careful and sober consideration of the issues at hand, then said, "I am calling for an hour's recess in order to carefully consider the call for the witness and the objection to this request. I would like to see the counsel for Mr. Raske in my chambers forthwith." And with that he quickly left the bench for his chambers.

As the Judge left the bench, that lawyerly Cheshire cat smile now spread across the face of one Estes Philips Williamson the 3rd, Esquire (perhaps it was actually the 4th) while a confused grimace spread across that of the diminutive Desmond Dirwinkle.

Judge Anderson Vander Meer sat at his huge mahogany desk. Before him was a tall water glass containing nothing. There was a knock at the door to his chambers and the honorable Judge yelled rather shakily, "Enter damn it!" and the legal counsel for both Raymond Raske and *PEATA-FU* entered with brief case in hand.

Smiling wryly, the lead counsel carefully set his brief case on the desk.

The honorable Judge looked at the lead counsel and said rather sharply and somewhat shakily, "Well? You know the deal."

The lead counsel opened the briefcase and pulled out a bottle of Macallan M - 1824 Series Single Malt Scotch, which he even more carefully set before the his Honor. His Honor grabbed the bottle, twisted open the cap and filled the water glass before him with the light brown liquid, put the glass to his lips and swilled half its contents with one gulp. He slammed the glass down on his desk and said, rather less shakily, "The recording?"

The lead counsel reached back into the brief case and pulled out a DVD, placed it down on the desk and pushed it toward the good Judge who at that moment was finishing off the rest of the light brown liquid in the water glass. The good Judge looked down at the DVD. As he read the label, his lips moved silently mouthing each word, "Legal Lovers of the Equine World".

The good Judge turned to a laptop on the credenza behind his desk, took the DVD and placed it in the laptop's disc reader. The laptop buzzed away and a video began rolling on the laptop's screen. Both the Judge and the lead legal counsel watched as the video played.

There on the screen stood an obviously pot-bellied man standing on a stool behind a beautiful mare. His head was turned away and thus obscured from the camera. Both the man and the beautiful mare were in their birthday suits... one of those birthday suits not requiring an unsuiting to be birthday suited.

Standing next to the pot-bellied man on the stool and also in his birthday suit was none other than an honorable William "the Fish" Perch, Esquire, who was obviously very excited to be there. The pot-bellied man on the stool turned toward the camera and smiled from ear to ear. It was none other than Family Court Judge Anderson Vander Meer his very self. The expression on the mare's face is unknown as she was facing in the opposite direction although given her body language, she was at least indifferent.

Turning to the lead legal counsel, the Judge smirked and said with a voice strained of great emotion, "Tell that asshole Fish that if he tries to take me down releasing an edited version of this video or using any other video, I'll take him down with me."

The lead counsel smiled, "Clever to demand this particular video. Kinda takes the wind out of... I think the Fish said... 17 other videos whether or not they're edited. But think of it, Judge. In the future this entire scandal might become non-scandalized when all 57 sexual identities have been accepted by the citizenry at large. I think this situation falls under Sexual Identity 38 although there will have to be a series of court challenges to clarify the legal ramifications of each of the 57 sexual identities."

As the Judge poured more Macallan M - 1824 Series Single Malt Scotch into the water glass before him, splashing some of the very expensive light brown liquid on his desk top, he yelled at the lead legal counsel, "Get the fuck out of here" as a series of high pitched human groans emanated from the laptop behind him. As the lead counsel exited, the human groans were punctuated with "Go Judge. Nail ole Daisy May! She's all yours!" The Judge turned facing the laptop and smiled as pleasant memories assuaged his anger.

Glaring down from his bench at the mere mortals before him, the good Judge proclaimed, "I rule in favor of the request for witness Delton P. Meriwether... and sit down Desmond. My ruling is final."

Desmond Dirwinkle replied rather sheepishly, "But your honor, I am sitting."

His Honor, obviously quite peeved, said, "Mr. Desmond Dirwinkle, I am tired of you wrangling... whether you're sitting or standing. It has got to stop... and I mean right now. One more violation of courtroom decorum and I will sight you for contempt *in extremis*. I'm sure that you'll find all those institutional turkey dinners provided so generously by the county each Thanksgiving to be quite tasty... for you'll have the opportunity to enjoy a number of them."

The diminutive Desmond Dirwinkle said even more sheepishly, "Yes your Honor". He froze fearing that since there was little difference between standing and sitting in the eyes of the court from a physical stand point but quite a bit from a procedural stand point, he'd take the action, or in this case the inaction, that would attract the least attention and he remained seated.

Mr. Delton P. Meriwether was sworn in after the court room calmed down... the uproar caused by the quite unexpected move. The legal counsel for Raymond Raske began his examination.

" Mr. Delton P. Meriwether, what is your profession?"

"I am a manager of a technical writing department?"

"Where are you employed?"

"I am employed by KTI... that is Kronos Technologies International."

The Honorable Judge gaveled down the murmuring courtroom audience and ended his gaveling with a sober, "Continue... damn it!"

"Does Mr. Raymond Raske work for you?"

"Yes."

"How have you listed Raymond Raske on his corporate benefits profile... that benefits profile being for the corporation Kronos Technolo-

267

gies International?"

With these words, you could hear a pin drop in the courtroom. His Honor instinctively gaveled down the silence and said "Mr. Meriwether, answer the damn question!"

Meriwether looked at the judge with great fear and trepidation in his eyes and said in a barely audible voice, "I listed Raymond, his wife Eloise, a family dependent, and..." A bewildered look spread across the face of the witness and he stopped speaking.

The lead council for Mr. Raymond Raske and the *Protect Every Animal That's Alive -- Forever United* bore in on the witness, "Did you list any other names? Give us the name and only the name... the name Mr. Meriwether, the name... I demand the name and I demand it now!"

The flustered witness mumbled "Precious... his daughter Precious."

The courtroom audience moved forward in its collective seats.

"Speak up, Mr. Meriwether! Did you say 'his daughter Precious'! Did you list Precious as the dependent daughter for Mr. Raymond Raske?"

"Yes, but..."

The courtroom audience broke into applause which the good Judge allowed to continue for several minutes before gaveling for silence.

"There are no *buts*, Mr. Meriwether. Just answer the question. Given that daughter Precious is listed as Raymond Raske's dependent daughter, would she have been eligible for company benefits such as medical care."

"Yes, but..."

"That's all Mr. Meriwether. You may step down. It must be noted at this time, your Honor, that Mr. Raymond Raske's beloved Precious is considered a person by that renown international corporation Kronos Technologies International... a person with full dependent benefits, including medical benefits!"

At this point, Mr. Raske's esteemed lead counsel paused and slowly turned to face Raymond Raske. The entire courtroom held its collective breath. The lead counsel then said with the great gravitas worthy of the moment, "And this person, Mr. Raymond Raske's dear family member... this Precious... this beloved pot-bellied pig... is imbued with personhood by one of the world's great international corporations."

The courtroom burst into applause clapping loudly and quite enthusiastically. The honorable Judge looked down at the confused and bewildered witness and said, "Step down."

Desmond Dirwinkle reflexively... and apparently... jumped to his feet and yelled, "We reserve the right to cross ex..." His Honor stared down at the diminutive Dirwinkle who went silent as the Judge's stare reignited Dirwinkle's fear of all those tasty institutional Turkey dinners so generously provided by the county each Thanksgiving. The Judge hammered his gavel on the bench and said rather shakily, "We will adjourn for the day and reconvene on Monday at 10:00 AM."

On Monday morning at 9:00 AM sharp a black limousine drove up to the court house steps from the side of the courthouse that offered an unobstructed view of the unfolding events. 117 camera crews jumped into action. This time all four of the Precious Porcine Pretties jumped out of the black limousine... the fourth Pretty having recovered from her menstrual cramps and was now apparently unencumbered in any other obvious way. In spite of the chill in the morning air, the unencumberedness of all four Pretties was complete save for the tiny purple sash flung over each goose-bumped shoulder.

269

Oxbow Lake The 2nd

The Precious Porcine Pretties introduced a new dance routine that included three splits, two somersaults, and several carefully coordinated pirouettes that took the Pretties to the top step of the courthouse. Once at the top of the steps, the four Precious Porcine Pretties chanted in four-part harmony, "She's a person just like us... make it legal... no more fuss!" many times. Huzzahs in many languages went up from the crowd of international news anchors crammed into the courthouse square as the four Precious Porcine Pretties executed a perfectly choreographed exit to the black limousine... an exit which included a daring somersault and hand-stand down the courthouse steps.

In the courtroom at a little after 10:27, Family Court Judge Anderson Vander Meer stumbled to the bench and plopped down in his chair with a thud. He put his right hand to his head, rubbed his forehead and slammed his gavel down on the bench with his left... his left hand oblivious as to the actions of his right. Thus the noise surprised him and he reacted by dropping his gravel onto the floor. He mumbled, "Court in session" and leaned back in his chair in obvious discomfort.

Desmond Dirwinkle, apparently jumping to his feet, said "Your honor, we'd like to recall Mr. Delton P. Meriwether for cross-examination." Estes Philips Williamson the 3rd, Esquire (perhaps it was actually the 4th) jumped to his feet quite obviously, but before he could speak, the honorable yet slightly incapacitated Judge waved his left hand while covering his eyes with his right, and mumbled, "Let's get on with it, recall the damn witness." Both attorneys sat down and Mr. Delton P. Meriwether entered the court room and sat in the witness box. His Honor mumbled, "You're still under oath so don't lie." Meriwether sheepishly shook his head yes.

Desmond Dirwinkle, now obviously standing, as he had walked toward the witness box, said, "On the morning of March 7 did you have any telephonic communications with Mr. Raymond Raske?"

The witness, one of the few people in the courtroom who looked shakier than his Honor, mumbled, "Yes. It was quite early and I was...".

Dirwinkle interrupted him, "What was the nature of that communication?"

"He asked for a favor... a ride to work."

"Where was he calling from?"

"A telephone booth?"

A shocked look spread across Dirwinkle's face as he allowed the words "telephone booth" echo throughout the courtroom, for beneath that diminutive personage was the heart of well disguised rhetorical tiger.

The well disguised rhetorical tiger then said "And where was this phone booth?"

"Across the street from Lincoln School."

"Did he request any additional assistance?"

"Yes."

"What was the nature of this additional request?"

"Items of clothing... pants, a shirt... and a tube of antiseptic cream."

At this point our diminutive yet well disguised rhetorical tiger exercised his rhetorical tigerness, "Hmmmm! Antiseptic cream? What did you do next?"

"I drove home, picked up the requested items and then drove to the phone booth across from Lincoln School."

"Did that include a tube of antiseptic cream?"

"Yes. It was Walgreens' store brand. Store brands tend to be less..."

"No need for a further explanation of this mysterious tube of antiseptic cream. What did you do next?"

As the questioning seemed to be quite mundane, Meriwether relaxed and became more talkative and less defensive. "I drove to the phone booth. It was still dark but the phone booth was easy to spot as the light was on."

"And what did you see?"

"Mr. Raske... dressed in shorts... briefs with a colorful floral pattern... and a tee shirt."

"Only in his underwear?"

"Yes... and the shorts had this colorful floral design. I think it was tulips... and I brought a pair of socks and sandals just in case he needed them... and good thing I did... as it turns out he did."

"And what was the first thing Mr. Raske did when you approached him?"

"He asked for the antiseptic cream I think. At least it's the first thing he grabbed when he opened the door to the phone booth."

"And then?"

"He took the tube of antiseptic cream, turned around facing away, pulled open his shorts... the one's with this colorful floral design... tulips... and apparently rubbed some of the antiseptic cream on his groinal area. And then he got dressed in the clothes I brought... including the socks and sandals... and I drove him to work."

Another flurried mummer arose from the audience which the good Judge gaveled to silence.

The diminutive legal rhetorical strategist continued, "When you arrived to work, did Mr. Raske explain why he was all but naked in a phone booth asking for a tube of antiseptic cream?"

"Yes... kinda. He said his wife had locked him out."

"Did he explain why he was dressed only in his underwear at that time and in need of antiseptic cream for his groinal area?"

"No sir."

"That is all."

The words "groinal area" having peaked the Judge's interest, he asked the lead legal counsel for Mr. Raske, "Would you like to cross?" and was quite disappointed when the rather confused counsel shook his head no.

Looking larger than his diminutive personage would seem to warrant, Dirwinkle then yelled quite enthusiastically, "The defense would like to call Eloise Raske."

After the courtroom buzz abated and the Judge's head-splitting gavel hammering ceased, the Judge, with his now peaked interest, overruled the confused objections from Raymond Raske's legal team and had Eloise Raske called to the stand and sworn in.

Dirwinkle asked, "Are you the wife of Raymond Raske?"

"Yes... at least for now. We're separated and I'm going to divorce the perverted bastard!"

The legal counsel for Raymond Raske jumped to his feet but before he could scream his objections, the honorable Judge cautioned Eloise Raske to avoid negative characterizations of her husband, "Please keep to the facts without the negative characterizations."

Eloise Raske shot back, "It is a fact. He's a god damn pervert and there's no way he's going to get his perverted fingers or any other parts of his perverted body on poor Precious!"

The legal counsel for Raymond Raske jumped to his feet and this time got to yell, "Protest... negative..."

Before he could finish his protestations, the Judge, having had his interest in the testimony further peaked by the accusations of perversion, said rather excitedly, "I'll allow the testimony for now... Dimwinkle... Dirwinkle... but be careful"... his caution directed at the lawyer and not the witness whom he wanted to hear more from regarding her potentially salacious and titillating charges of perversion.

The diminutive Dirwinkle continued, "In previous testimony, it was stated that you locked your estranged husband out of your joint residence at 105 Lonely Pine Grove in the very early morning of March 7. Is this true."

"Yes... it's god damn true!"

"Could you explain why?"

"Yes! He's a god damn pervert! That's why!"

"Please describe the events that early morning that led you to lock your estranged husband out of your joint residence."

The entire legal team for Raymond Raske sat at its table stunned and paralyzed by the unexpected testimony of Eloise Raske and offered no objections... given the potentially salacious nature of the testimony and the Judge's obvious interest in this testimony, it probably didn't matter since the honorable Judge would probably have overruled their objections.

The diminutive Dirwinkle continued, "Please take us through the events that led up to your locking out your now estranged husband."

Eloise Raske rode her high horse at full gallop into her emotional testimony, "I saw my strange husband creeping out the back door from our bedroom window. He woke me when he got up but I pretended to be asleep. I knew he was up to something pretty creepy. He slipped into those shorts with that colorful floral design again... the one's with the tulips. I've had my suspicions for a long time. He'd done it before... each time wearing those boxer shorts with the colorful floral design... the tulips. He used to wear them when we were... you know... preparing to be intimate... kind of a warm up... which we haven't in a very long time."

"And what did you see when he creeped out the back door?"

The PEATA-FU legal team voiced full-throated objections, "The word 'creeped' is biased phraseology... prejudicing jury perception. Move to strike!"

The judge, wanting to hear of Raymond Raske's perversion, yelled. "Strike the damn word 'creeped' and proceed!"

Eloise Raske continued, "He creeped... err, slithered... out to the stand of virgin pine that we own in the back of the house."

"What is this stand of virgin pine that your husband 'slithered out to' as you so correctly put it?"

The PEATA-FU legal team, confused by the unexpected introduction of a stand virgin pine and having no idea where Eloise Raske's testimony was going, was stunned to silence.

Eloise became even more animated, if that's possible, "It's a stand of virgin Eastern White Pine... three acres of old growth Eastern White Pine... pinaceae pinus strobus... I have a degree in biology... and I've wanted to sell the stand for a while. We've been offered a small fortune for it... but my strange husband adamantly refuses... and we need the money."

"So you saw your estranged husband 'slither out'... as you put it... to this stand of virgin Eastern White Pine. And then what happened?"

" So I followed him out. He never saw me. He was... how should I put this... consumed with passion."

"Passion? How so?"

"Well he hugged this one pine tree and started saying words I couldn't quite make out... I think to the poor defenseless pine tree... I couldn't hear exactly what he said. Then he lowers his shorts... he was only wearing shorts... the one's with the colorful floral design... the tulips... and a tee shirt. He starts moving his hips in and out... like he's having intimate relations with that poor defenseless pine tree. I heard him moan 'my arboreal honey bunny' several times."

At this point, the courtroom burst into uncontrolled shouting. The Judge slammed his gavel down and yelled, "Clear the courtroom. Deputies, clear the courtroom."

However, Eloise Raske continued, riding high and oblivious to the shouting, "And that arboreal honey bunny of a Eastern White Pine is no longer a virgin... he's destroyed her... it's a case of arboreal rape! He's an arboreal rapist... a violent pervert!" And she punctuated her words by pointing at Raymond Raske who lowered his head, cradled his face in his hands and started to sob. Undeterred, she charged forward on her high horse, "Ruined that poor formally virgin pine forever with sexual violence! Now what's she worth? Tell me that... now what's she worth!"

Since the trial was so controversial, there was a large contingent of deputies on hand and they quickly cleared the courtroom. As the last of the courtroom audience was shoved out the courtroom door, the Judge yelled at the two lead legal counsel, "In my chambers now... both of you assholes!"

For some members of *Protect Every Animal That's Alive -- Forever United* assembled on the courthouse steps accusation became fact as word spread through this crowd that Raymond Raske now had actually "arboreally raped" a virgin pine tree... and as he did so he had the temerity to feign tenderness by whispering the self-condemning words "my arboreal honey bunny". Other members of *Protect Every Animal That's Alive -- Forever United* assembled on the same courthouse steps remained focused on what they considered the primary issue: the humanity and well-being poor Precious Raske, the beloved pot-bellied pig. Thus the *Forever United* aspect of the gathered crowd became quite frayed... and dramatically so.

On one side of the courthouse, a group of members of *Protect Every Animal That's Alive -- Forever United*... taking a more metaphorical view of the English language and citing Raymond Raske's use of the words "arboreal honey bunny" as proof... believed that the word *animal* as it appeared in the name of their organization was just that: a metaphor meaning all none-human life... which included poor "Honey Bunny", the virgin pinaceae pinus strobus or Eastern White Pine tree who had been arboreally raped by the dastardly Raymond Raske. Armed with this metaphoric interpretation of their organization's name and the demand for justice for "Honey Bunny", they started chanting "String up rapist Raske... he's interspecies trash!"

Opposite this first group of the *Protect Every Animal That's Alive -- Forever United* was a second group of equal size from this same organization... taking a somewhat more prosaic view of the use of the English language in the naming of their organization... believed that the word *animal* meant exactly that and that the humanity and well-being poor Precious Raske, the beloved pot-bellied pig, was the primary focus of their organization. Armed with this more prosaic interpretation of their organization's name and with the demand for legal recognition of the humanity of Precious Raske, they started chanting, "Personhood for Precious that's our goal... if you don't like it, you're an asshole!"

The chanting of both groups reached a fever pitch. The emotional strain was more than either group could bear and the two groups charged and met in bloody combat on the courthouse steps as an obvious ideological split had halved PEATA-FU into two large and very angry warring parties.

As a result of the bloody combat, 17 people were hospitalized. Seven from each of the splinter groups for PEATA-FU and three deputies who were inadvertently caught in the middle of the clash as they attempted to make an arrest during the pitched battle. The "dastardly individual", as Sheriff Lionel Vander Meer described the individual who had escaped capture and arrest, had inadvertently melted into the confusion caused by the two battling splinter groups before the arrest could be made. The Sheriff's office called in reinforcements and order was eventually restored.

After an unsuccessful but very intensive two week manhunt organized by Sheriff Lionel Vander Meer to capture and arrest the miscreant who had apparently committed an "unspeakable act" during the riot, a certain Mr. Killian Sullivan the 3rd appeared at the Sheriff's station and voluntarily turned himself in when he realized that he was the miscreant. Mr. Sullivan is the son of a prominent dentist in the community, Dr. Killian Sullivan the 4th.

During the pitch battle, Mr. Killian Sullivan the 3rd, a charter member of the local PEATA-FU chapter, is alleged to have committed the "unspeakable act" of an imposed molar extraction from one of the other combatants and he did so using Orthotech molar band orthodontic dental pliers which the alleged Mr. Sullivan allegedly dropped after the alleged imposed molar extraction. The alleged dental pliers were valiantly recovered from the scene of battle by one of the three deputies injured during the aforementioned street battle. The alleged imposed extracted molar was not recovered.

Sheriff Lionel Vander Meer made the alleged "unspeakable act" somewhat speakable by leveling three charges against the younger Sullivan for a vicious, yet still unspecified, savage act which he characterized as unconscionable and a threat to western civilization as we know it and thus very serious. The three charges were: 1) the illegal use of Orthotech molar band orthodontic dental pliers, 2) an imposed molar extraction and 3) the practicing of dentistry without a license. Mr. Killian Sullivan the 3rd has proclaimed his innocence from all of the charges and has vowed to prove it. The alleged victim of the alleged and as yet undescribed imposed molar extraction has not been identified. It is unclear which splinter group either Mr. Sullivan or his alleged victim supported at the time of Mr. Sullivan's alleged imposed molar extraction.

In the Judge's chambers, the two lead counsels sat across from Judge Anderson Vander Meer, who was gulping down a light brown liquid from a large water glass. He slammed the now empty water glass down and said in almost a whisper, the quiet whisper of profound anger, "What the fuck is going on? This is a god damn family court and not an episode in the Jerry Springer Show."

The two lead counsels looked quizzically at each other but said nothing. The Judge continued, "We have a man in his underwear in a phone booth in front of a school, a corporation giving benefits to a pot belly pig who its owners consider a human daughter, a man who's in love with a tree and is having intimate relations with that tree, we have riots in front of the court house with women dancing around naked and pitched battles between various groups of perverts who are incapable of keeping their perversions to themselves as any civilized individual would. I want it stopped!"

The diminutive Desmond Dirwinkle said, "But Judge, I'm only seeking to protect the rights of Eloise Raske and protect her poor Precious. It's my job to..."

At this point, the Judge yelled, "Get the hell out of my chambers!"

Both lead legal counsels got up and the Judge pointed at Mr. Estes Philips Williamson the 3rd, Esquire (perhaps it was actually the 4th) and said "Not so fast Estes, sit your ass back down." Derwinkle's ass, along with the rest of him, fled the chambers as the foul fowl taste of Turkey crept into his terrified brain. Williamson sat *his ass* back down and the rest of him followed.

The Judge pulled a bottle from the credenza behind his desk and emptied the remainder of the bottle's light brown liquid into the large water glass before him. He held the bottle up, saw it was empty and threw it into the trash can alongside his desk. He said "Fuck" to himself and drained the water glass of its light brown liquid. He then stared intently at Mr. Estes Philips Williamson the 3rd, Esquire (perhaps it was actually the 4th) and said, "I want more. You're not paying me enough. I'm only getting one bottle of Macallan M - 1824 Series Single Malt Scotch and a god damn DVD. I want 100k... and two more bottles of Macallan M - 1824 Series Single Malt Scotch."

"Maybe I can get you 100k but no way to two bottles of Macallans."

"Okay, make it 110k and one bottle of Macallans."

"If I agree to this, what do we get for that additional 110k and one bottle of Macallan's?"

"A backdoor to what you want."

"Backdoor? For 110K and a bottle of Macallans I want to walk in the front door on a red carpet."

The honorable Judge frowned. "I thought that you were smart. Look, I'm a family court judge not some big federal muckety muck asshole judge. I can get you what you want without giving the opposition what they want... which is a concrete straight forward ruling to challenge directly in federal court."

Unlike what you may have seen and heard on all the TV commercials for those expensive Betty Ford clinics, the good Judge could get his shit together, as they say, when John Barleycorn was in the Judge's wheel-house and apparently ole John was in full control now, for he banished the "sober" Judge's raging headache and inspired the Judge's legal creativity to new heights.

PEATA-FU's and Raymond Raske's lead legal counsel, both being the same for the most part, sat back in his chair as another of those Cheshire cat legal smiles spread across his face and he said, "Look, Judge, I don't want to know what you're going to do. I do have my suspicions but the less I know, the better from the standpoint of an ethical inquiry... which is almost surely to be initiated by those fascist Christian pigs on the right. If you do what I think you're going to do, I'll throw in another bottle of Macallans along with the 110k and that first bottle."

Judge Anderson Vander Meer reconvened the court before a now empty courtroom with the exception of the lawyers and their clients... all of whom were standing. He said, "Please remain standing. I am prepared to render a decision." He looked down upon both of the legal teams, one of those teams consisting of a singular member, and their two quite frightened and apprehensive clients. The honorable Judge paused for the rhetorical effect and then said:

"This is Family Court and as a Family Court Judge, I have a great deal of discretion in these proceedings. I have decided there is no need for further testimony. I am prepared to rule in this case. As always, my primary consideration is the health, safety and well being of the dependents in the family. Thus, *contradictio in terminus*, I have decided to split the baby in spite of the wisdom of Solomon. The wise King did not have to deal with the legal complications of 57 sexual identities... and now, quite possibly 58. I've heard enough to render what I think is a fair and judicious decision."

At this point, the good Judge again paused and then, with Solomon-like gravitas, he rendered his decision:

"Mr. Raymond Raske may have visitation rights. Such visits are in the best interests of Precious. He may visit with Precious once a month for 15 minutes but his visits must be supervised by a duly qualified professional from the Protect Every Animal That's Alive -- Forever United."

Both legal teams, one being quite singular and the other being not so to the extreme, jumped into the air in joy and yelled the expletives of victory. Raymond Raske and Eloise Raske collapsed into their chairs sobbing the sobs of despair.

As news of the decision spread through crowd before the courthouse, the sounds of a reignited internecine battle filtered into the courtroom.

THIS PAGE INTENTIONALLY LEFT MOSTLY BLANK

(SOMETIMES CONFIRMATION CAUSES CONFUSION. THE ABOVE
STATEMENT MAY BE AN EXAMPLE)

IRRELEVANT NOTE FROM THE AUTHOR:

ONE MAN'S IDEAL PLATONIC FORM IS ANOTHER MAN'S
ARISTOTELIAN WATERLOO... PHILOSOPHOCALLY SPEAKING IN
BOTH AN IMMATERIAL AND MATERIAL SORT OF WAY!

The Twisted Tale of Killian Sullivan the 3rd's Alleged Platonic Imposed Molar Extraction

Killian Sullivan the 3rd sat in the county holding tank facing three charges: the illegal use of Orthotech molar band orthodontic dental pliers, attempted and successful imposed molar extraction and the practicing of dentistry without a license. After an intense and unsuccessful two week manhunt to capture him, Sullivan had voluntarily turned himself in when he realized that he was "the miscreant" who was the object of the manhunt. He was the only individual arrested as a result of the bloody riot of the two splinter PEATA-FU warring parties. His case was considered so important that he was dragged in handcuffs and leg irons before Sheriff Lionel Vander Meer himself for interrogation.

Sheriff Vander Meer (*holding up a pair of 'dental pliers'*): Are these Orthotech molar band orthodontic dental pliers yours?"

Killian Sullivan the 3rd: Yes and No.

Sheriff Vander Meer: How is it possible that these dental pliers are and aren't yours at the same time?

Killian Sullivan the 3rd: It's not at the same time. It's a time sequencing thing that involves changing Platonic ideal forms. In this case there are two particular representations of these physical pliers... only one is a physical representation of the ideal form for Orthotech molar band orthodontic dental pliers. The other is a physical representation of ordinary pliers... admittedly odd looking pliers but still ordinary pliers. The first physical representation... the physical representation of the ideal form of Orthotech molar band orthodon-

284

tic dental pliers... was owned by my father Dr. Killian Sullivan the 4th.

Sheriff Vander Meer: Platonic particular representations... time sequencing at the same time? Sounds like a time sequencing representation of a misrepresentation. You're Killian Sullivan the 3rd, right?

Killian Sullivan the 3rd: Right.

Sheriff Vander Meer: How can that be? Your father's the 4th. How can you be the 3rd?

Killian Sullivan the 3rd: Again, it's a matter of Platonic ideal forms, time sequencing and physical representations family-wise. My father, Dr. Killian Sullivan the 4th, was very proud of his father, Dr. Killian Sullivan the 3rd, who had a doctorate in philosophy and taught at the New Paltz Normal School. My father tried to follow in his father's footsteps but could only minor in philosophy... eventually becoming a dentist... greatly disappointing both himself and his father... so he named me after his father Dr. Killian Sullivan the 3rd... as he wanted me to be, in Platonic terms, another, later and precise particular physical representation of his sainted father to make up for his own philosophic failures and to cancel the eventual fate that his sainted father... my sainted grandfather... later suffered.

Sheriff Vander Meer: Let me get this straight... so your actually Dr. Killian Sullivan the 3rd the 2nd?

Killian Sullivan the 3rd: Yes... and I'm proud to say that I've majored in philosophy at a prestigious community college in upstate New York and am close to fulfilling my father's dream of my becoming a precise particular Platonic physical representation of my sainted grandfather. I'm only 18 credits from my degree.

Sheriff Vander Meer (*in increasing frustration*): Lets establish the custodial history for these pliers before we go any farther. Did your grandfather... that other Platonic particular representation of himself as you term it... ever own these dental pliers?

Killian Sullivan the 3rd: No. Not to my knowledge as he was most likely dead by then. He taught philosophy at the normal school in New Paltz like I said. He was fired for cross-dressing during a campus demonstration in support of women's rights since the school taught primarily women preparing them to be school teachers... unlike the other schools in the state university system which taught primarily men and were four year schools. The philosophy department, backed by the administration, charged my grandfather with violating his particular representation of the ideal form for a philosophy teacher by dressing as a woman and thus impersonating one. He was removed from his position because of that very particular violation of his representation of himself and his obvious misrepresentation of women physically speaking. He argued in vain that he still maintained the essence of his particular representation of the ideal form of a professor of philosophy as represented by himself even when cross-dressing... but to no avail. His removal from his physical representation of himself destroyed him. He later passed away in Sweden many years later of complications after the world's first and quite unsuccessful sexual reassignment surgery as he attempted to negate at least one of those academic charges against him. Even though I'm "Dr. Killian Sullivan the 3rd" on my birth certificate, I've dropped the "Dr." in my every day representation of myself until I get my degree from that prestigious community college in upstate New York.

Sheriff Vander Meer: Are either you or your father cross-dressers?

Killian Sullivan the 3rd: Not to my knowledge.

Sheriff Vander Meer (*again holding up the 'dental pliers'*): Since your grandfather never owned these pliers whatever their representation, did your father, Dr. Killian Sullivan the 3rd, ever own these pliers as Orthotech molar band orthodontic dental pliers?

Killian Sullivan the 3rd: Not exactly those... he owned a representation of them for a time but he held an official philosophic decommissioning ceremony on July 4th of last year... so he did own them in a previous representation as Orthotech molar band orthodontic dental pliers... which they no longer are... in fact they are no longer dental pliers at all... they've been philosophically decommissioned and now are just plain pliers from a physical representation standpoint.

Sheriff Vander Meer (*showing signs of great agitation and confusion*): But you now own them... right. You own this representation of Orthotech molar band orthodontic dental pliers (*at this point Sheriff Vander Meer waved the 'dental pliers' wildly above his head*).

 Killian Sullivan the 3rd: No I do not own them as Orthotech molar band orthodontic dental pliers... I own them all right but after their decommissioning as just plain pliers. They are no longer dental pliers... and that's philosophically official!

Sheriff Vander Meer: Let's get down to brass tacks! (*at this point the Sheriff even more frantically waved the dental or possibly non-dental pliers above his head as his frustration became even more acute*) So you deny using these pliers... formerly known as Orthotech molar band orthodontic dental pliers... to perform an imposed molar extraction on a member of an opposition splinter group of PEATA-FU that you hated while posing as a dentist... and because you hated a particular member of that splinter group because he was a member of the splinter group that you hated. (*the Sheriff attempting to prove that not only had Doctor Killian Sullivan the 3rd the 2nd attempted and successfully completed an imposed molar extraction using a pair of Orthotech molar band orthodontic dental pliers and in so doing was practicing dentistry without a license... and that he did so with hate in his heart and thus had committed a hate crime doubling or possibly tripling his punishment when he was convicted of all the crimes he was accused of committing)*

Killian Sullivan the 3rd (*remaining calm and viewing his interrogation from a rather philosophic view point*): I didn't hate the individual you claim I hated. His name is Magic Mike Mosely... he works at KTI... he's a technical writer or a programmer out there. I don't hate him. He's a good friend. We get along great even though I think he's a closet Aristotelian.

Sheriff Vander Meer (*sensing a weakness in Killian's claim of non-hatred of one Magic Mike Mosley*): So it's hate once removed but it's still hate... hate by philosophic association! I'm detecting Hannibal Lector type criminal behavior here.

 Killian Sullivan the 3rd: Why would I hate him? I was doing him a favor. He had this loose molar he wanted removed. It was loose and it bothered him... wiggling around all the time. He asked me to remove it... which I did.

Sheriff Vander Meer: So you admit you pulled this Magic Mike Mosely molar... right! And with quite possibly Orthotech molar band orthodontic dental pliers. You were performing dentistry without a license even if you didn't hate this closet Aristotelian... this Magic Mike Mosely. Where's this extracted molar now. It's material evidence and must be turned over to the Sheriff's department immediately if not sooner!

Killian Sullivan the 3rd: I can't. I don't have material possession of the material molar in question. I don't even have the immaterial possession of the material molar in question. Someone else has the material possession of this material molar and quite possibly the immaterial possession of this material molar as well.

Sheriff Vander Meer: Who, damn it! Who? Be truthful and don't add perjury to your long list of heinous crimes!

Killian Sullivan the 3rd: I guess you'd have to say the tooth fairy.

Sheriff Vander Meer: That's an anti-homophobic remark... more evidence of a hate crime! You're implying and characterizing this Magic Mike Mosley as a homosexual when he's actually a victim of your imposed molar extraction.

Killian Sullivan the 3rd: No I'm not. I mean the real tooth fairy. The fairy that sneaks into your bedroom at night and takes removed or lost teeth from under pillows and replaces the teeth with money... usually for children.

Sheriff Vander Meer (*becoming outright belligerent*): Where's this tooth fairy?

 Killian Sullivan the 3rd: Wilkes-Barre Pennsylvania... where Magic Mike's niece lives?

Sheriff Vander Meer (*with a look of pure hatred tinged with a bit of fear*): So this tooth fairy is associated with this Magic Mike Mosley's niece. What's her name and why did this Magic Mike character send his imposed extracted molar to her.

 Killian Sullivan the 3rd: It's Madeleine. I think they call her Maddy. I don't remember her last name. As to why... as I understand it... Maddy hadn't lost any teeth yet but had expressed serious doubts about the existence of the tooth fairy and that fairy's exchange of a tooth for money... usually a dollar... so Magic Mike, who had that loose molar, volunteered to send her the material molar in question to test the concept of a tooth fairy... to determine if this platonic ideal form had a real physical representation. And it did. Maddy woke up and found her uncle's tooth... the tooth of my alleged imposed molar extraction... allegedly imposed without dentist's license... that tooth was gone and a dollar coin in its place... proving beyond a doubt there was a physical manifestation of the Platonic ideal form of a tooth fairy... at least in Wilkes Barre, Pennsylvania.

Sheriff Vander Meer (*with the look of a mouse who had belled the cat*): A-ha! This Maddy misrepresented that tooth as her own to the tooth fairy... and that's fraud. And when you sent your imposed extracted molar to this Maddy, you participated in a conspiracy to commit fraud. We'll add conspiracy to commit fraud to your long list of heinous crimes. This conspiracy raises your heinous acts to high crimes and misdemeanors... you're in for it buddy... it's a special counsel for you! When the special counsel is done with you, you'll be broke and face the needle for having committed crimes that make Hannibal Lector looked like a male girl scout!

Killian Sullivan the 3rd (*now quite angry himself, yelled*): I demand to see my lawyer!

Sheriff Vander Meer: Who's your lawyer?

Killian Sullivan the 3rd: The Honorable William Perch.

At this point in the interrogation, Sheriff Lionel Vander Meer sat silently at his desk staring down at the floor. His face turned a whiter shade of pale as they say and he waved his hand toward the door to his office indicating that the interrogation was over. As Mr. Doctor Killian Sullivan the 3rd the 2nd shuffled to the door and his hand and leg restraints clanked away, the good Sheriff mumbled "... and I did it only once and I was drunk... and that prick Perch has the video".

Later that week, the Orthotech molar band orthodontic dental pliers in whatever Platonic physical representation you choose to believe became a non-physical representation of your chosen representation as they mysteriously disappeared from the Sheriff's evidence locker. Then witness accounts were misfiled in the Sheriff's office and could not be found. Then three deputies were transferred to the mayor's office as the mayor's personal security detail... positions that doubled their salaries. And with no physical evidence, no witness accounts, no deputies available to testify, the DA dropped all charges and cancelled his request for a special counsel. Mr. Doctor Killian Sullivan the 3rd the 2nd was released in whatever recognizance he chose and the case disappeared from the face of the Earth.

THIS PAGE INTENTIONALLY LEFT MOSTLY BLANK

(IF THIS PAGE DID NOT EXIST, WOULD A STATEMENT TO THIS
EFFECT BE NECESSARY?)

IRRELEVANT NOTE FROM THE AUTHOR:

BEWARE: THE MASSAGING FINGERS OF CAPITALISM'S INVISIBLE
HAND CAN BE USED FOR ECONOMIC AND ETHICAL SELF-ABUSE!

Envirobortion: an immodest proposal to save the environment and enhance human nutrition

by Robert Marinelli (?)

Editor's Note: a bit of an introduction to clarify the seemingly un-clarifiable. On one of my favorite blogs, *The New Tampa Guide to Sane Automobile Repair...* which incidentally has nothing to do with automobile repair, sane or otherwise... I read the following article whose author was listed as one Dr. Joseph Mangeleasy. I was struck by Dr. Mangeleasy's creative approach to solving at least six and more likely seven rather serious social problems with one self-funding program. I thought this proposal to be a work of pure genius.

After a bit of literary detective work as a part of my normal copyright research, I discovered that the purported author of the article, Dr. Joseph Mangeleasy, was apparently someone named Robert Marinelli, who had created the purported author for reasons that are not entirely clear to me.

I am somewhat disturbed by this discovery since I thought I had created a fictional Robert Marinelli in my own fiction, some of which appears in this tome. I am left with the unanswerable question of who created who... or is it "whom"?

For creative and unconventional commentary on today's politics and society, I highly recommend this blog.

Check it out at: *https://guidetosaneautorepair.wordpress.com/*

-- Oxbow Lake the 2nd

Envirobortion: an immodest proposal to save the environment and enhance human nutrition

An immodest proposal that also preserves and extends a woman's right to choose, is self-regulating, market-driven and self-financing while improving medical research and the environment while voluntarily reducing potentially inferior populations... all accomplished incrementally

By Dr. Joseph Mangeleasy, PhD, NSAES, Lifetime Member of Mensa International from early childhood (excluding years 1943 through 1945 inclusive) and the seven-time recipient of the very prestigious All Ivy Defender of the Faith Award

Another Editor's note: Dr. Joseph Mangeleasy's most recent biography of Margaret Sanger, 'Planned Parenthood's Prophetess of Perfection', will be available at the next full moon.

-- Kramer Killread Esquire, Editor-in-Chief
New Tampa Guide to Sane Automobile Repair
(https://guidetosaneautorepair.wordpress.com/)

September 1, 2015, Berlin, Rensselaer County, New York – Feel like this year's July 4th celebration was a little hotter than last year's? Probably true for most of you, as this July was the planet's warmest month on record. The average temperature was 61.86 degrees Fahrenheit, besting the mark of the previous July records set in 1998 and 2010 by a full one-seventh of a degree according to the National Oceanic and Atmospheric Administration. While one-seventh of a degree doesn't sound like much, it is, for as NOAA notes, the previous records were broken by a 20th of a degree or less. One-seventh of a degree is a very large jump. There is a hot time on the old planet tonight and it is getting hotter all the time!

As Californians fry, their forests burn and the drought on the west coast continues unabated, new research proves beyond a denier's doubt that the increasing temperatures are caused by the burning of fossil fuels and the other activities of Mother Earth's human populations as these rapidly growing populations attempt to provide themselves with electricity and other forms of energy for transportation, cell phones, tablets, clothing, shelter and other necessities such as food... while California's forests burn to ash. And not just in California, as forest fires burn uncontrolled in Oregon, Washington, Idaho and Montana. And the wild fires of our west are just one indication of what is to come. First you will be consumed by the heat or die of thirst and then, if you survive, you risk drowning as the polar ice melts and the oceans rise to create ocean front property in Arizona, pretty much doing away with most of California and much of the east coast. Bye-bye Manhattan, so long Florida... sacrificed to the needs of ever growing human populations as man-made climate change rages on!

"How fast are Mother Earth's ravenous human populations growing?" you ask. There are 7 billion now and that number will grow to over 9 billion by 2050. There is a lot of unprotected hanky-panky going on in the boudoirs of the under classes of Mother Earth's industrialized nations in spite of the easy availability of birth control... and in the poverty stricken of Mother Earth's third world, unprotected hanky-panky is even more rampant!

Here in America, no matter how many edible cucumbers are sacrificed in sex education classes, unprotected sex marches on or should

I say thrusts forward in our poorer neighborhoods. Given our experiences with the under classes here in America, there is little hope that making birth control readily available to third world human populations will reduce the birth rate of these populations. What is the result of all this unprotected hanky-panky... aside from aids and other sexually transmitted disease? Offspring, tons and tons of human offspring!

Do you not tire paying for all those "free" breakfast, lunch and dinner programs at your public schools... programs required by all those surplus human offspring. And there are all those "free" food stamp programs... and all those "free" healthcare programs.. and "free" cell phones and lots other "free" stuff... paid for by you and me, for there is no such thing as a free lunch unless, of course, you are a member of the hanky-panky poor and their inadvertent offspring... as their ever increasing needs destroy Mother Earth!

Those least capable of caring for the results of their unprotected hanky-panky continue to breed like rabbits. Want to get frightened? Check out Worldometer's population counter at http://www.worldometers.info/world-population/.

And over a billion of our present world-wide human populations are chronically malnourished and starving. Do you not tire of having "Dances with the Stars" or some other of your favorite programs interrupted by the burning image of a poor African child, bare-foot and almost naked, with a huge distended belly, standing in an open sewer and staring at you with those large very sad eyes, a tear running down her right cheek as she holds out her left hand pleading for a tiny morsel to eat? ... all captured on your new high-def flat screen 60-inch TV! Breaks your heart! And there is some fat blond bimbo standing off to the right of the poor starving urchin saying something like, "For 25 cents a week you can feed and clothe this poor child and give her a future."

Why the hell doesn't that fat blond bimbo skip a meal. She could feed a whole village for a week and lose a pound or two of ugly belly fat in the bargain. And what happens when you donate that 25 cents a week, a mere dollar a month? The urchin grows up and has a bunch more offspring and where there was one poor urchin standing in an open sewer, there are now ten! And now the open sewer is ten times larger. Somehow, without food, these urchins produce enough sewerage to greatly expand that open sewer. Some solution. The more you feed them, the larger this population grows. And with your heart close to breaking you continue to feed them and inadvertently expand that open sewer yet again.

The result: these billions multiply and place even greater stress on our precious environment causing even more global warming driving even more man-made climate change and you continue to feed them enabling even more unprotected hanky-panky causing more offspring causing more global warming causing more man-made climate change in a never ending cycle of environmental destruction. As economist Jeffrey Sachs, columnist for *Scientific American* and Earth Institute Director points out, "Agriculture is the main driver of most ecological problems on the planet. We are literally eating away the other species on the planet."

To expand food production, humans deforest the environment and destroy Earth's bio-diversity. Humans fertilize the fields with nitrous oxide which, in turn, pollutes the water. Their ever-increasing cattle herds produce methane by the ton and account for one third of all global greenhouse gas emissions from human activity.

Sound far-fetched? One cow releases a total of 70 to 120 kg of methane utilizing both ends to efficiently produce this prodigious output. The destructive effect of this methane on the environment is 23

297

times greater than that of the greenhouse gas carbon dioxide. World-wide there are 1.5 billion cows and bulls who burp and fart out the equivalent of two billion tons of CO2 a year, one third of global greenhouse gas emissions from all human activity... bovine revenge on a truly gastronomically Herculean scale!

What is today's solution to this bovine methane madness? You are told to give up your medium-rare rib-eye and become a vegetarian so that you can continue to feed those starving billions enabling them to continue to breed like rabbits and produce ever more starving billions.

And what other environmental policies are put in place? Reduce your use of fossil fuels, drive a very expensive electric car with a top speed of 25 miles per hour for a maximum of 30 minutes before recharging the batteries, turn off your lights, stop watching your 60-inch HD flat screen TV after already giving up your rib-eye for a bowl of rabbit food... an appropriate delicacy given that much of the population is breeding like rabbits.

How successful are all these environmental policies? Not very. Whatever success they have is countered by your humanity... your understandable inability to stand the sight of starving children and thus your humane and compassionate need to feed them. In fact not only does your compassionate feeding of Earth's starving billions negate whatever environmental progress those policies may accomplish, that compassionate feeding actually makes things worse, for feeding those breeding billions enables them to continue to breed and add even more billions of starving and malnourished to their numbers placing even more stress on Mother Earth. The destruction of our environment continues apace with the needs of our ever increasing human populations. Eventually Mother Earth will run out of even rabbit food. Soylent green anyone?

What to do about this conundrum... this Gordian knot of consuming human compassion and entangling environmental policies that fuel global warming by enabling human populations to continue to grow and to continue their inexorable destruction of Mother Earth? Truth is, Mother Earth's human populations are now committing the slow motion compassionate suicide of the species as they destroy their very source of sustenance, for they are eating their seed corn.

We must slice through this suicidal compassion and these ineffective environmental policies. With an Alexandrian slash of reason's mighty sword, we must cut this Gordian knot once and for all and formulate a nuanced solution to save Mother Earth by first attacking the problem at its source... the human uterus. That is where the problem originates and that is where the solution must begin!

The obvious and most efficient solution is some form of required sterilization combined with medical procedures, such as mandatory abortions, to control any excess population that sterilization failed to prevent under the supervision of a benevolent government. National governments, perhaps under United Nations leadership and auspices, could regulate the sterilizations of inferior populations and require abortions and other medical procedures where necessary.

However, with the unfortunate history of National Socialist Germany casting a long shadow over the future with its heavy-handed eugenics programs, mandatory abortions and sterilizations eventually evolving into a 'final solution', it is foolhardy and ultimately self-destructive to expect today's populations, particularly the elite populations of the United States and Europe, to even tolerate policies to reduce surplus breeding implemented through direct actions by governments even though they sympathize with those policies' goals. Just will not happen!

To overcome this reluctance on the part of the elites to use direct force, governments must establish a softer, indirect strategy to attack the problem and attack it at its aforementioned source: the human uterus. They must establish a strategy that encourages women to have abortions voluntarily. Such a strategy has the added advantage of eliminating the visual objects that cause self-destructive compassion. If the program established to implement such a strategy is successful, there is no need for any other programs. To reduce the financial burden of such a program and eliminate the need for direct funding by the government and the onerous concomitant tax increases, the program must also be self-funding.

How is this to be done? What program can governments adopt to encourage women to voluntarily participate? Governments should take a page from the economic theories of capitalism's sacred, gas belching cow, Adam Smith his very own self, and use his "invisible hand" to set in motion the market forces necessary to encourage women to participate in the program. In other words, governments must unleash the forces of the marketplace and use the fingers of the market's "invisible hand" to gently guide women to seek abortions voluntarily. Such a plan requires no governmental force: Women will choose to participate willingly.

How would such a program work? Easy, make the abortions free! Not only make the abortions free, but pay women to have them and pay them in such a way that there is an incentive to continue participation when necessary. There is no need to force sterilizations and abortions. There is no need for more expensive but failing birth control programs. There is no need for messy judicial proceedings that can have historical repercussions.

Many of you reading this, particularly my dedicated Progressive fellow travelers, are shocked by the use of capitalism to accomplish one of our most important and cherished goals. Remember, we have never denied that the forces of the capitalism's marketplace exist. Rather we have maintained that these forces are immoral because they create the income inequality we so detest. This proposal uses the invisible hand of government to direct the invisible hand of capitalism's marketplace to accomplish the goal of reducing the world's populations and thus reducing the destruction of Mother Earth by the munching millions upon millions. I call these abortions **Envirobortions**.

How do governments make the **Envirobortion Program** self-funding and even more invisible? They use private non-profit organizations such as Planned Parenthood to perform the **envirobortions** and allow them to manage the program. To cover costs, these organizations will harvest high-quality fetal tissue for medical research and sell the tissue to pharmaceutical corporations for research.

Pharmaceutical corporations are willing to pay and pay dearly for this basic research material as they compete to discover the next cure for some disease like Alzheimer's or some incurable genetic condition, for these cures are worth millions of dollars. Planned Parenthood has already established what can be considered a successful pilot for such a self-funding program and they already sell fetal tissue to pharmaceutical corporations.

The competition for the fetal tissue will create a market place that will cause the price for this tissue to rise enabling the non-profit organization to cover even more of the cost of the "free" envirobortions.

And the harvest is not over. There is even more money to be made to further cover the costs of the program. The non-profit organizations can then sell the remaining fetal tissue to food processing corporations. These corporations are already adept at using protein, such as that extracted from soy beans, to create substitutes for meat products in general and beef products in particular. And they already use turkey to produce substitute beef products such as "turkey pastrami," which can be purchased at any supermarket today. It would be relatively easy for them to create substitute beef products from the harvested protein.

Initially, the availability of fetal protein will be limited and thus in short supply. These food processing corporations would compete for the limited supply of this protein in order to create protein rich, high-priced delicacies. In turn, these delicacies could be marketed to compete with other meat delicacies such as Kobe beef. Kobe beef sells for at least $100.00 a pound and can sell for as much as $350 a pound.

The "invisible hand" of the unprincipled free market would direct food processing corporations to create beef substitute delicacies to compete in this marketplace and they would be encouraged to do so by the price advantage they would enjoy since the protein they are using is much cheaper than Kobe beef and other expensive beef delicacies. I have great confidence in these enterprising corporations to develop the high quality beef substitute products and the marketing strategies necessary to compete in this market. To get the program rolling, the government would offer these corporations generous tax credits.

As the **Envirobortion Program** expands and the supply of fetal protein increases, the government can set up a grading program similar to that of the USDA in order to protect the established high-priced delicacy market and expand into the less expensive markets. Thus, the highest quality protein would be labeled SUPER PRIME. The next grade would be PRIME, then CHOICE and then SELECT, the last grade. Fetal protein that does not qualify for human consumption would be used for pet food.

302

Now that the **Envirobortion Program** has expanded and the supply of fetal protein greatly increased, the same food processing corporations would develop and market less expensive beef-substitute products to compete in the much larger beef market for standard cuts of beef which will over time reduce the demand for beef. As the market for beef shrinks, the cattle herds will also shrink. As a result, there will be fewer cows to defile the environment with their double-barreled unnatural gaseous assault on our precious Mother Earth.

To maximize the quality and the weight of fetal tissue, the non-profit, following government regulation, would pay women according to the weight of the fetus. To avoid complications during an **envirobortion**, government regulation would require **envirobortions** no later than 39 weeks to avoid medical complications. Since the fetus averages a good 6.9 lbs at 39 weeks, many women, if not most, will choose 39 weeks for the procedure. After the first **envirobortion**, the non-profits would give bonuses for additional **envirobortions** to encourage continued participation in the program and insure a steady supply of the product.

How would this program reduce the potentially inferior populations who require public assistance... those who breed most and are least capable of caring for the results of that breeding activity because of their culture and the resulting poverty? The answer is quite simple: Because these breeders are in need of money, they will voluntarily participate in the **Envirobortion Program**. The chances of them changing their behavior and reducing or eliminating unplanned breeding is quite small but it does not really matter. Most will continue to hanky-panky to their vibrating uterus's delight and continue to participate in the **Envirobortion Program** for the money... a win-win of sorts in a strange kind of way.

Planned Parenthood has already provided what can be considered a feasibility study by placing 79% of its abortion clinics within walking distance of poor neighborhoods, most of which are African-American or Hispanic. That is where the market is for their abortion services.

In 2011 (the last year for which statistics are available), the Center for Disease Control found that 78% of all abortions performed in New York City were performed on African-Americans and Hispanics. There were 76,251 abortions performed. (Note: that is 526,131.9 pounds of wasted protein with a market value of more than $26 million at half today's price of Kobe beef.) Abortions of African-Americans accounted for 35,188 (242,797.2 pounds of protein, over $12 million in market value) or 46.1% of the total. Abortions of Hispanics accounted for 23,959 (165,317.1 pounds of protein or over $8 million in market value) or 31.4%. Without any laws or market incentives, the African-American and Hispanic communities voluntarily aborted 59,146 fetuses or the previously mentioned 78% of the total number of abortions performed... that is 408,107.4 pounds of wasted protein and over $20 million in today's market value. And most if not all of those having these abortions had to actually pay for them!

Here is the socio-economic nail in the coffin of the compassionate, tender hearted opposition to this program: 69% of all those having abortions are economically disadvantaged, meaning most of them are probably on some form of public assistance, meaning welfare. I publically thank Planned Parenthood for their foresight and service to America and the world, for they have proven beyond all doubt that the **Envirobortion Program** will work and work well.

The **Envirobortion Program** does not require government enforcement, for participation is voluntary. There is no heavy-handed government enforcement as in National Socialist Germany. There are no official government squads rounding up people and forcing them to abort their fetuses. There are no racial, ethnic, cultural or religious cleansing laws. There are no judicial proceedings.

Participation in the program is completely voluntary. It is self-funding and market-driven and thus "invisible" as the "invisible hand" of a benevolent government directs the "invisible hand" of the market place to save Mother Earth. It extends a woman's right to choose and makes that choice profitable. The populations least capable of caring for unplanned and probably unwanted offspring are the populations most likely to volunteer to participate as Planned Parenthood has proven.

The result of participation in the program is a slow but steady decline in Mother Earth's human populations which reduce the stress on the environment, first in the United States and Europe and eventually in the entire world as the United Nations expands the program internationally. As the world's population decreases, the need for electricity and other forms of energy for transportation, cell phones, tablets, clothing, shelter and other necessities such as food will decrease and as the need decreases, pollution and man-created destruction of the environment will be reduced and eventually eliminated.

There will be a growing and eventually significant increase in environmentally safe protein as a food source resulting in a decrease in environmentally destructive methane from cattle as the need for beef is reduced. Cattle herds will still exist but in much smaller numbers, so there will still be a supply of such delicacies as rib-eye steaks for those who can afford it. And science will have the best fetal tissue for the medical research that will lead to the elimination of such terrible diseases as Alzheimer's and perhaps even lead to the development of growable replacement human parts.

This description of the **Envirobortion Program** is quite general and needs much fleshing out. However, I firmly believe that it is the answer to today's environmental conundrum. It is a multi-faceted program that will work and work well within the cultural, economic and legal limitations of our age and it will slow-boil the forces of environmental destruction until they are lobster red and quite dead... a process that gives the human populations time to adjust. Implement the **Envirobortion Program** and the sky will be the limit... a clear, bright, pollution free sky!

THIS PAGE INTENTIONALLY LEFT MOSTLY BLANK

(IF THIS PAGE WERE UNINTENTIONALLY LEFT BLANK, WOULD A
STATEMENT TO THIS EFFECT BE NECESSARY?)

IRRELEVANT NOTE FROM THE AUTHOR:

SOMETIMES GETTING TO AND OBSERVING A CONFLICT'S BOTTOM
CAN BE A QUITE TITILLATING... DEPENDING, OF COURSE, ON THE
DEFINITION OF THE WORD "BOTTOM" AND THE QUALITY OF THAT
"BOTTOM"!

The Great Nose-Hair National Crisis

by Robert Marinelli (?)

Yet another bit of an introduction: The following collection of newspaper articles and blog entries first appeared in the previously mentioned *New Tampa Guide to Sane Automobile Repair* (https://guidetosaneautorepair.wordpress.com/). Like the previous article, *Envirobortion: an immodest proposal to save the environment and enhance human nutrition*, a certain Robert Marinelli may be responsible for what follows... a Robert Marinelli who appears to share a name with a certain character I created and who may in fact disagree with himself politically if he is the author of the previously mentioned article. Then again, he may not.

This Robert Marinelli, whoever he may be, fears a growing national crisis which has become known as The Great Nose-Hair Imbroglio... and as he warns us, "This threatening national crisis is being ignored by the Republicans who control both the House and the Senate and now have the Presidency after Donald Trump stole that office from Hillary Clinton as a result of his well documented collusion with Vladimir Putin and the Russian government."

I do not agree or disagree with this particular Marinelli's contentions herein evidenced... particularly given the potential for my getting driven from the local McDonalds by a bunch of foam-at-the-mouthers during one of my extravagant power lunches with family and friends. However, every dog has its day and this is apparently such a day for this Mr. Marinelli.

The imbroglio of which this dog-day Marinelli writes gained national attention with the tragic deaths of two individuals. First was the death of the renown owner of Tinklesworth Pharmaceuticals,

Dr. Philip "Pee Man" Tinklesworth, Esquire, who is believed to have drowned when the Italian cruise ship, the Costa Concordia, ran aground and sank off the coast of Isola del Giglio, Tuscany, Italy. Second was the death of William "Bucky Buckaroo" Turnstile, who died in an automobile accident in New Tampa, Florida. Both deaths are attributed to the mysterious, unprecedented and insidious growth of the nose hair of both these individuals.

This Marinelli contends that the growth of nose hair has become a national crisis and that the Democrat Party has attempted to martial the forces of the United States federal government to deal with this national and existential crisis while the obstructionist Republican Party has done all it can to cripple this effort with their ridiculous contention that the cost of this effort could add to the national debt.

The Imbroglio is complicated by law suits and counter law suits within and without the Tinklesworth family as members of that family wage war over who is to inherit the Tinklesworth fortune and who is financially responsible for the tragic automobile crash that killed the aforementioned William "Bucky Buckaroo" Turnstile.

-- Oxbow Lake the 2nd

147th Nose-hair Growth Fatality Reported on Interstate I-75

73 year-old Driver Killed After Being Trapped by Girl Friend's Nose-hair During Inadvertent Embrace

National crisis looms

A P-P Unbiased Wire Service -- Robert Marinelli

New Tampa, Florida – On what is believed to be Tuesday last, William "Bucky Buckaroo" Turnstile became the 147th victim in a long list of fatalities on the highways of America as a result of the unprecedented growth of nose-hair in the population of America raising fears of local, state and federal officials that America was facing a crisis of epic, epidemic and existential proportions.

In an exclusive interview with Mrs. Thomasine Tinklesworth, 23, Mr. William "Bucky Buckaroo" Turnstile's girl friend, I learned the intimate details of this tragedy. In the interest of truth, justice and the American way, I feel obligated to also report that Mrs. Tinklesworth and I had a short and very temporary relationship on the cruise ship Costa Concordia last year. The relationship lasted for a mere and very unsatisfying 7 minutes and was interrupted by the grounding and sinking of that cruise ship in Italian waters. And I am obligated to point out that this unsatisfactory relationship had absolutely nothing to do with the eventual grounding and sinking of that cruise ship! Furthermore, my relationship with Mrs. Tinklesworth did not involve unnatural acts in the normal understanding of those words as was initially reported by the online news service Medium Matters and later picked up by the New York Times and reported verbatim (verification not required because of the integrity of Medium Matters) on their sports page since Mrs. Tinklesworth had been the 2010 junior national champion of Extreme Bikini Curling.

At the time of this very temporary and unsatisfying relationship, Mrs. Tinklesworth's husband, the late Dr. Philip "Pee Man" Tinklesworth, Esquire, was at his appointment with the Costa Concordia Tonsorial Parlor in hopes of dealing with what is believed to be the insidious and unnatural growth of his nose hair.

Unfortunately, in yet another example of the devastating effects of unnatural nose hair growth, Mr. Philip "Pee Man" Tinklesworth died during that tragic grounding and eventual sinking of the Costa Concordia. There are certain unproven indications that his nose hair became entangled with the safety catch of his life jacket preventing him from securing said life jacket about his person. Dr. Philip "Pee Man" Tinklesworth, Esquire, is believed to be the first person to die as a result of nose hair growth on the high seas causing the Federal Maritime Commission (FMC) to launch a $250 million investigation into the incident.

Representative Nancy Pelosi, Democratic House Minority Leader, in a press conference after the reporting of Mr. William "Bucky Buckaroo" Turnstile's tragic death in an automobile crash as a result of the nose hair epidemic, stated, "The Republican Party's transfat... errr... trans-gress... errr... trans-fer... errr... in... errr... transgence-i-gence intransigence, as evidenced by House Speaker Paul Ryan's outrageous proposals to limit the growth in the funding for such important federal agencies as the Federal Maritime Commission, is yet another example of how the Republican Party is at war with the women of America and is attempting to make the women of America second class citizens and deny them access to birth control and reproductive choice."

Obituaries for Dr. Philip "Pee Man" Tinklesworth, Esquire, and Mr. William "Bucky Buckaroo" Turnstile

Below are the obituaries for Dr. Philip "Pee Man" Tinklesworth, Esquire, and Mr. William "Bucky Buckaroo" Turnstile published by the independent A P-P Unbiased Wire Service. Dr. Tinklesworth is thought to be the first American to die at sea as a result of the nose-hair epidemic threatening to destroy Western Civilization in general and American Civilization in particular. Mr. Turnstile is the 147th victim of the nose-hair epidemic to die in a traffic accident.

The now deceased Dr. Tinklesworth was the husband of his recently widowed bride, Thomasine Tinklesworth, who claims Dr. Tinklesworth's estate and ownership of Tinklesworth Pharmaceuticals, estimated to be worth $1.7 billion.

In a related story, Mrs. Tinklesworth has initiated an almost wrongful death suit against the estate of Mr. William "Bucky Buckaroo" Turnstile, the aforementioned 147th automobile fatality as a result of the dreaded nose-hair epidemic.

Mrs. Tinklesworth characterizes her treatment at the hands of both the Tinklesworth and Turnstile estates as "no bucking way to treat the women of America!" For more details, see the obituaries for Dr. Philip "Pee Man" Tinklesworth, Esquire, and Mr. William "Bucky Buckaroo" Turnstile below.

-- Robert Marinelli

Obituary for Dr. Philip "Pee Man" Tinklesworth, Esquire

Inventor of the "On the Go-Go Urine Purifier" is first American to die at sea as a result of the Nose-Hair Epidemic

A P-P Unbiased Wire Service

New Tampa, Florida -- Dr. Philip "Pee Man" Tinklesworth, Esquire, 78, sole owner of Tinklesworth Pharmaceuticals, and major contributor to former President Barack Obama's presidential campaign, died tragically when the cruise ship the Costa Concordia ran aground and sunk in Italian waters.

Dr. Tinklesworth is believed to be the first American to die at sea as a result the nose-hair epidemic that is threatening Western Civilization in general and American Civilization in particular. The Obama administration used the power of the federal government through executive orders to do everything humanly possible to fight this insidious epidemic in spite of Congressional Republican intransigence. The present President, Donald Trump (illegally elected through the traitorous support of Vladimir Putin) has unconstitutionally cancelled President Obama's important executive orders in this matter.

Representative Nancy Pelosi, Democrat House Minority Leader, in a press conference after Tinklesworth's inquest, stated, "The Republican trans-fat... errr... trans-gress... errr... trans-fer... errr... in... errr... trans-gence-i-gence, as evidenced by Republican Speaker of the House Paul Ryan's outrageous proposal to reduce Nasal-Hair Czar J. Smedley Snodgrass's funding request to dangerously low levels, is yet another example of how the Republican Party is attempting to make all the women of America second class citizens and deny them access to birth control and reproductive choice."

Oxbow Lake The 2nd

Dr. Tinklesworth invented the wildly popular *On the Go-Go Urine Purifier* (the OGGUP), which produces "purified" urine and blood samples masking the presence of drugs in both urine and blood tests. The OGGUP, a small tablet that an individual places under his or her tongue 10 minutes before providing a urine or blood sample for testing, has the side-effect of producing a chemically undetectable high known on the street as "pee drinkers paradise" (the PDP high) after a consumer of the OGGUP tablet drinks a small amount of his or her own urine, termed 'pissing up' on the street.

The OGGUP also has a high concentration of Vitamin K and can be used as a dietary supplement. It has been approved by the Obama era Czar still in charge of the FDA and is thus sold over-the-counter as a very popular dietary supplement.

Obituary for Mr. William "Bucky Buckaroo" Turnstile

73 year-old who led the effort to bring transgender rest rooms to New Tampa mourned by community

A P-P Unbiased Wire Service

New Tampa, Florida -- Mr. William "Bucky Buckaroo" Turnstile, 73, the 147th victim of the nose hair epidemic, passed on to his eternal reward Tuesday last after his automobile crashed through the railing of the second temporary bridge overpass on I-75 above the eponymously named Turnstile Interchange on Bruce B. Downs. His vehicle, a battery powered Humvee weighing 140 tons, landed on the experimental transgendered public rest room facility that was built at the Turnstile Interchange through his lobbying efforts that got the $18 million dollar shovel-ready project included in the former Obama administration's economic stimulus package.

Mr. Turnstile was apparently in the romantic embraces of his companion of 4 days and 5 nights, the widow Mrs. Thomasine Tinklesworth, 23, when the tragedy occurred. Mrs. Tinklesworth was unhurt in the accident.

Ron Gettelfinger, President of the United Automobile Workers Union (UAW) and chairman of the special investigative committee appointed by former Secretary of Transportation Ray LaHood, reported that there are certain indications that the accident occurred because Mr. Turnstile's nose hair got entangled with Mrs. Tinklesworth's nose hair. Apparently when Mrs. Tinklesworth pulled back in an attempt to free herself from the grasp of Mr. Turnstile's nose hair, she inadvertently forced Mr. Turnstile's nasal passages to close causing Mr. Turnstile to have difficulty breathing. As Mr. Turnstile opened his mouth to breathe through that orifice, Mrs. Tinklesworth, fearing that Mr. Turnstile was about to scream, placed her hand over his mouth resulting in his passing out.

According to testimony before the hastily formed UAW Special Investigative Committee On the Nose Hair Growth Epidemic, Mrs. Tinklesworth stated that she suffers from a rather acute hearing problem and that loud noises cause her to suffer incontinence which is why she placed her hand over Mr. Turnstile's mouth since she did not want to embarrassingly wet her valuable panties. The UAW's report concluded that the cause of the accident was Congressional Republicans' support of soon-to-be former President Donald Trump's anti-union policies.

 Exactly what Mr. William "Bucky Buckaroo" Turnstile's eternal reward will be is being contested by Mrs. Thomasine Tinklesworth. At a press conference arranged by Representative Debbie Wasserman Schultz, former Chairwoman of the Democrat National Committee, Mrs. Tinklesworth, who may have recently inherited the Tinklesworth fortune, stated that Mr. William "Bucky Buckaroo" Turnstile will have to spend a considerable amount of time in purgatory as a result of his destruction of America's first fully functional transgender public rest room. She re-iterated that some things are unforgivable and one must pay for the unforgivable and that if the payment is large enough, the unforgivable becomes forgivable. Mrs. Tinklesworth is planning to initiate an almost wrongful death suit against Mr. William "Bucky Buckaroo" Turnstile's estate.

In support of Mrs. Tinklesworth, Representative Debbie Wasserman Schultz, former Chairwoman of the Democrat National Committee, stated, "The Republican Party's intransigence, as evidenced by House Speaker Ryan's outrageous proposals to limit the growth in the funding for such important federal agencies as the Federal Maritime Commission, is yet another example of how the Republican

Party is at war with the women of America and is attempting to make the women of America second class citizens and deny them access to birth control and reproductive choice."

The transgendered community will hold a candlelight vigil at the site of the crushed first fully functional transgendered public rest room at 9:00 PM next Friday. In lieu of flowers, Mrs. Tinklesworth has requested that large amounts of money be donated to the Mrs. Thomasine Tinklesworth Defense Fund at DefendAmericanWomenfromtheRepublicansWaronThem.com. Credit card donations will be accepted and are encouraged. Mrs. Tinklesworth has also requested that all who donate to the fund also include their social security number when submitting their credit card donation.

Thomasine Tinklesworth submits "new will" panties claiming inheritance of $1.7 billion Tinklesworth pharmaceutical fortune

The following article is yet another example of how difficult it is to achieve informational sanity because of the Evangelicals who pollute our politics and society with their self righteousness. Read the article carefully and ask yourself the following question: "Would I be able to wear panties inscribed with the words 'No Rear Entry' embroidered across the rear of those panties if Evangelicals controlled our society?"

-- Robert Marinelli

Widow Thomasine Tinklesworth Turns Her "New Will" Panties Over to Court

Piggy, Woody and Regina Tinklesworth contest new panty will, claiming it's an illegally soiled effort to steal their rightful inheritance

McCrotchety Unbiased Wire Service

In a stunning move in the hotly contested battle over the $1.7 billion estate of Dr. Philip "Pee Man" Tinklesworth, his young widow, Thomasine Tinklesworth, has submitted a pair of her panties which she claims contain a new will written just below the embroidered pink "No Rear Entry" inscription which appears across the top of the rear of the panties that she claims are hers.

According to court records, the following text is written in indelible red ink across the panties rear panel:

318

"I will give you everything I own if I can do anything I want to that delicious booty of yours."

The panties were signed "Your own Tinkypoo" and dated "January 13, 2014," the day of Dr. Tinklesworth's tragic maritime nasal-hair drowning when the cruise ship the Costa Concordia sank in Italian waters.

A handwriting expert hired by the widow Thomasine Tinklesworth's legal team testified that the handwriting, although very shaky, was definitely that of Dr. Tinklesworth. In corroborating testimony, the widow Tinklesworth stated that the handwriting was shaky because she was wearing the panties at the time Dr. Tinklesworth wrote the new will on them and that her husband was filled with love-fueled carnal desire at the time of the writing making the handwriting even shakier.

At the request of the legal team for the Tinklesworth adult children and their beloved German shepherd Regina, the widow Tinklesworth was required to stand before the jury and bare her panty covered buttocks so that the jury could judge the difficulty of writing a will on her panties while she was wearing them. Two facts were obvious as a result of the evidentiary display: 1) the tear-shape of the widow Tinklesworth's more than ample buttocks would make writing on her panties while she wore them quite difficult, and 2) there would be plenty of space for the writing of an even longer will while the panties in question were being worn should the individual writing on said panties have so desired.

The six male members of the jury asked to see the displayed evidence seven more times in an obvious attempt to get a clear picture of the full impact that the shape of the widow's more than ample buttocks would have on the writing of the will on her panties while she wore them.

319

Oxbow Lake The 2nd

When the Tinklesworth adult children and their beloved German Sheppard Regina Tinklesworth contested the claim that their father wrote a new will on the widow Tinklesworth's panties, the widow Tinklesworth's legal team countered by contesting the legal status of Regina Tinklesworth in an attempt to get her removed from the lawsuit and thus cause severe psychological damage to Piggy, Woody and Regina Tinklesworth.

In an emergency ruling, a three judge panel of the ninth circuit court of appeals bestowed upon Regina the legal status of "individual with rights," thus giving the German shepherd the full rights and protections of the Constitution as a citizen of the United States of America. Furthermore, the ruling declared "Since Regina Tinklesworth is a citizen of the United States, she is, under the circumstances of her adoption, the imputed daughter of Dr. Tinklesworth and thus has the legal right to join in the countersuit with Piggy and Woody Tinklesworth as their sibling."

After the appeals court's Judge J. Smedley Snodgrass wrote the ruling of the three-judge panel to himself on Face book, he adjourned proceedings until 3 PM tomorrow as the presiding judge.

Tinklesworth Children Cleared of Incestuous Bestial Polygamy by Ninth Circuit Three Judge Panel

German shepherd Miss Regina Tinklesworth ordered returned to Miss Piggy Tinklesworth and Mr. Woody Tinklesworth, the adult children of recently deceased Dr. Philip "Pee Man" Tinklesworth, and the three citizens of the United States can now resume their constitutionally guaranteed polyonimous polyspecies polysexual intra-family throuple marriage

Three Judge panel declares Defense of Marriage Act very unconstitutional, invalidates onerous companion Utah statute and returns former state of Utah to status of territory under the control of the Democratic National Committee

McCrotchety Unbiased Wire Service

The Democratic National Committee, under the leadership New York's former Attorney General, Eric Schneiderman, won a hard fought and constitutionally significant victory yesterday when a three judge panel from the United States Court of Appeals for the Ninth Circuit struck down the federal government's Defense of Marriage Act again. In so doing, the three judge panel also struck down Utah's companion legislation, worded exactly like the federal statue. It is the first time in U.S. history that the Justice Department represented both sides of a case before the federal bench as career attorneys at the Justice Department, led by former New York Attorney General Eric Schneiderman, argued against those attorneys in the Justice Department appointed by the illegally elected President Trump.

Appeals Court Judge J. Smedley Snodgrass, who is also Very Under-Secretary of the U.S. Department of Transportation and Nasal Hair Czar appointed by the legally elected former President Obama, wrote in a unanimous opinion: "The widely discredited Defense of Marriage Act is an affront to Western Civilization by confining the wonderful institution of marriage to one woman and one man. Individuals have the civil right to marry whomever or whatever they wish whenever they wish as often as they wish. Besides, since the federal government never submitted a cogent brief in defense of the Defense of Marriage Act and since New York State's former Attorney General Eric Schneiderman presented a brilliant argument in defense of the Tinklesworth children's civil right to form a loving violence free marriage with their beloved German shepherd Regina Tinklesworth and with each other, the Ninth Circuit Court of Appeals has no choice but to declare the Defense of Marriage Act even more unconstitutional and orders the immediate return of the individual known as Miss Regina Tinklesworth to Miss Piggy Tinklesworth and Mr. Woody Tinklesworth *post haste*.

The court also orders the State of Utah returned to the status of federal territory as a result of their passing of the very unconstitutional Utah Defense of Marriage Act. That state is an affront to Western Civilization and has proven itself incapable of governing in accordance with the principles of democracy as defined by our Constitution as interpreted by the Ninth Circuit Court of Appeals and is now under the guardianship of the Democratic National Committee."

After the decision, close friend of the Tinklesworth children, Ted Danson, the famous actor and maritime environmentalist, read the following statement, "We are heartened by the very fine decision of the Ninth Circuit. We thank former New York Attorney General Eric Schneiderman for his incredible defense of the civil rights of Regina and Piggy and Woody, who anxiously await with open and loving arms for the return of their beloved Regina to resume their loving polyonimous polyspecies polysexual intra-family throuple marriage. The state of Utah... make that the territory of Utah... got what it deserved! The Tinklesworths are now free to contest the will submitted by that gold digger Thomasine Tinklesworth in which she fraudulently lays claim to the $1.7 billion Tinklesworth pharmaceutical fortune as a result of the unfortunate death of their beloved father, Dr. Philip 'Pee Man' Tinklesworth."

Government Concerned about Growing Number of Nose-hair Road Fatalities

Joint Congressional Committee to Take Action in Spite of Republican Intransigence

A P-P Unbiased Wire Service

"Nasal hair is becoming a major threat to the safety of America's transportation systems amongst other deleterious effects on all middle class Americans whose very existence is being threatened by Republican support for the top 1% of Americans who don't pay their fair share!" So stated Judge J. Smedley Snodgrass, Very Under-Secretary of the U.S. Department of Transportation and Nasal Hair Czar, in testimony before the very prestigious and important joint Congressional Committee on *Public Olfactory Occupational Health* (the POOH).

Judge J. Smedley Snodgrass, elaborating on this threat to the economic health of the United States, stated unequivocally that nasal hair growth in the United States has reached unprecedented and dangerously high rates and has become a major threat to the transportation systems of the United States. This threat is affecting every middle class American's ability to drive and smell and is a direct result of Republican congressional intransigence, which is the result of Republican negativity in the do-nothing Congress and the Republican Party's unprecedented support of the top 1% of Americans, who don't pay their fair share.

Judge J. Smedley Snodgrass cited the Agricultural Department's $500 million study that was a major part of the Obama administration's economic stimulus package as absolute proof and requested a $1.34 trillion appropriation to develop a plan to combat this major threat to America's middle class.

Senator Elizabeth Warren of Massachusetts supported Judge J. Smedley Snodgrass's request, stating, "Czar Judge J. Smedley Snodgrass is a man of great integrity as he proved by refusing many years ago to participate for a third time in the waitress sandwich activity which two late senators initiated after a late night conference to determine what could be done to support the American middle class women whose very existence is being threatened by the Republican Party as a result of their unprecedented support of the top 1% of Americans, who don't pay their fair share.

"My only concern is that $1.34 trillion will not be enough of an investment in America's future. To insure that the plan developed is of the highest quality, I am requesting that all work be done by the United Automobile Workers of America and that at least $1.34 trillion be transferred immediately to that august organization, whose support of the American middle class is unprecedented, unlike the Republican Party, who support of the top 1% who don't pay their fair share and who are destroying America's middle class."

Republican Paul Ryan, Speaker of the House, stated "Perhaps we could reduce the appropriation to $1.2999 trillion to reduce the potential addition to the deficit" in yet another example of the Republican Party's efforts to destroy the American middle class and support the top 1%, who don't pay their fair share.

On the POOH, 27 Democrats and three Republicans, lead by Senator John McCain, voted in support of the plan proposed by Judge J. Smedley Snodgrass, Very Under-Secretary of the U.S. Department of Transportation and Nasal Hair Czar. Democratic Senator Dick Durban cast a symbolic vote against the proposal on the grounds that $1.34 trillion was nowhere near enough to fund so important an effort to save the American middle class from the Republican Party who is destroying the American middle class by supporting the top

1%, who don't pay their fair share. 29 Republicans on the committee abstained.

The committee voted 30 to 1 with 29 abstentions in support of Senator Elizabeth Warren's request that an undisclosed appropriation be transferred to the appropriate organization to develop the plan.

Representative Nancy Pelosi, Democratic House Minority Leader, in a press conference after the hearing, stated, "The Republican trans-fat... errr... trans-gress... errr... trans-fer... errr... in... errr... trans-gence-i-gence as evidenced by Republican Speaker of the House Paul Ryan's outrageous proposal to reduce the funding Nasal Hair Czar Smedley Snodgrass requested to dangerously low levels, is yet another example of how the Republican Party is attempting to make all the women of America second class citizens and deny them access to birth control and reproductive choice."

Nose-hair Lab Test Results Cloud Cause of Turnstile Nose-hair Fatality

Independent Lab report apparently clears nose-hair of responsibility

American Way criticizes right-wing lab report

A P-P Unbiased Wire Service

The cause of the automobile accident in which William "Bucky Buckaroo" Turnstile was killed has been clouded by a controversial lab report. Mr. Turnstile, believed to be America's 147th Nose-hair growth highway fatality, is thought to have died when his 140 ton electric custom Humvee ran off a temporary bridge on I-75 and crashed onto the eponymously named Turnstile Interchange in New Tampa, Florida, during an inadvertent embrace from his companion the widow Mrs. Thomasine Tinklesworth. Mr. Turnstile is believed to have passed out during the embrace when his nose hair became entangled with that of Mrs. Thomasine Tinklesworth causing him to lose control of his battery operated 140-ton Humvee.

Independent Lab, a self-proclaimed independent lab, whose independence is being contested by the independent *American Way Foundation for an Equal and Just America*, issued a report that claims that the nose-hair responsible for William "Bucky Buckaroo" Turnstile's death was in fact not nose hair at all.

Dr. William Trickle, Independent Lab manager, said, upon releasing the controversial report, "We are pretty sure that the nose hair we tested was or wasn't two things.

"First it was not hair from a nose. Although we are unsure of where on the body the hair found mingled in Mr. Turnstile's nose hair came from, it was definitely not from a nose. The tested hair was short and curly and did not possess the characteristics common to nose hair.

"Second, where ever on the body that faux nose hair was originally located, DNA testing proves all but conclusively that that location was on the body of the widow Mrs. Thomasine Tinklesworth.

"We also did extensive testing on Mr. Turnstile's position at the time of death, and we're pretty sure he wasn't in a seated position. While still driving, he appears to have been bent at the waist and in a semi-prone position lying face down towards the passenger's front seat calling into question the belief that Mr. William "Bucky Buckaroo" Turnstile and the widow Thomasine Tinklesworth were in an embrace involving nose-to-nose contact. While one nose was in some form of bodily contact, a second nose was not according to the evidence we've analyzed."

American Way Foundation for an Equal and Just America issued the following blistering criticism of the report: "The Independent Lab is a tool of the extremist right wing of the Republican Party and their 'report' is an outrageous attempt to undermine the magnificent efforts of the federal government to protect Americans from their nose hair and preserve the integrity of their faces. Contrary to what the right wing Independent Lab has concluded, the nose-hair growth epidemic may have spread to other parts of the body, making the epidemic even worse than originally thought and requiring even more funding from the federal government. It behooves us to protect the integrity of the entire American body and not just the nose."

Senator Elizabeth Warren of Massachusetts, who is considered the go-to Senator for all laws dealing with native American issues, including those below the Native American waist, has proposed the *Integrity of the American Body Below the Waist Act* (the IABBWA) with a $2 trillion budget to expand the nose-hair growth activities of the federal government to most areas of the body including those below the American waist. Presently, the legislation does not deal with the area from the chin to the waist, but a separate joint Congressional Committee will hold hearings to develop legislation to deal with the integrity of this area of the American body. Presently there are no plans to develop legislation to insure the integrity of the contents of the American skull.

Senator Warren stated that since the IABBWA deals with waist, she recommends that the $2 trillion be allocated to the International Brotherhood of Waste Hauling Teamsters and be administered by Teamster's President Jimmy Hoffa Jr.

Wisconsin Republican Paul Ryan, Speaker of the House, stated, "Perhaps we could reduce the appropriation to $1.9999 trillion to reduce the potential addition to the deficit" in yet another example of the Republican Party's efforts to destroy the American middle class and support the wealthy 1%, who don't pay their fair share.

Democratic Minority Leader Nancy Pelosi stated in a press conference after the hearing, "The Republican trans-fat... errr... transgress... errr... trans-fer... errr... in... errr... trans-gence-i-gence intransigence, as evidenced by Representative Ryan's outrageous proposal to reduce the funding for the *IBBW...W..W...W something* to dangerously low levels, is yet another example of how the Republican Party is attempting to make all the women of America second class citizens and deny them access to birth control and reproductive choice."

Congressional Republicans Cut Funding to Fight Dire Impending Existential National Safety and Health Crisis

Congressional Republicans ignore existential nose hair threat and cut funds to dangerously low levels

Rooters Unbiased Wire Service

Rarely does this great nation face existential threats such as the attack on Pearl Harbor and the illegal election of Donald Trump. However, we are facing such a threat today. A safety and health crisis is lurking and about to pounce on America, a crisis that will destroy the American middle class.

And what is the response of the Speaker of the House Paul Ryan and Senate Majority Leader Mitch McConnell? To starve the effort to defeat this existential threat by cutting the funding necessary to defeat it! We speak of the nose hair national crisis. At least 148 Americans have already succumbed to this dreadful threat to our existence while President Trump, that modern day Nero, fiddles away in the splendor of one of his hotels, accompanying his fiddling with his droning song of fictitious threats from North Korea and terrorism, trade imbalances and immigration while this existential crisis deepens and the country is about to metaphorically burn in a conflagration of nose hair.

In the recent budget reconciliation bill, Republican Speaker of the House Paul Ryan reduced the initial funding to defeat this existential threat from \$3.4 billion to \$3.3999 billion.

As a sop to America's middle class and American women, both of these political hacks have allowed the funding to continue to flow to that outstanding patriot, Judge J. Smedley Snodgrass, Very Under-

Secretary of the U.S. Department of Transportation and Nasal Hair Czar, even though he no longer holds those positions in the federal government, and to the United Automobile Workers of America, including the additional $2 trillion allocated to the International Brotherhood of Waste Hauling.

Federal funds to combat existential nose hair threat cut unconstitutionally by illegally elected President Donald Trump

According to a Recently Uncovered Second Trump Dossier Move Made at Vladimir Putin's Demand

Rooters Unbiased Wire Service

Rooters Unbiased Wire Service has learned that another disastrous cut in funding to address the existential nose hair threat was proposed at the demand of the illegally elected President Donald Trump who won the Presidency through his traitorous collusion with Russia's Vladimir Putin. Why did the illegally elected President make this outrageous demand in spite of the existential threat to the United States and the dire consequences to America's middle class and America's women? Because it was really Vladimir Putin who demanded it, that's why!

Unidentified sources in the Justice Department, the State Department, the FBI and the CIA have confirmed that there is a second Trump Dossier which documents the demand made by Vladimir Putin for Trump to take such action.

Special Prosecutor Robert Mueller is believed to have found the second dossier behind his office toilet during his usual early morning use of that facility and he had it leaked to the New York Times who published it and thus officially informed the Justice Department, the State Department, the FBI and the CIA of its existence and contents using existing accepted procedure to make such evidence available to the appropriate government agencies.

As proof of the authenticity of the second dossier, unidentified Justice Department, State Department, FBI and CIA sources say that this second dossier has yellow stains and that these yellow stains have been analyzed and are apparently urine stains. The CIA through careful DNA analysis, is believed to have determined that the urine causing these stains is that of four prostitutes living in Moscow and of Vladimir Putin himself. Leaked information, confirmed by additional leaks from Special Prosecutor Robert Mueller's team, also indicates that a sixth stain is still undergoing tests but is believed to be caused by the urine of the illegally elected President Trump who won the Presidency through his traitorous collusion with Russia's Vladimir Putin.

In a joint statement released today, Democrat House Minority Leader Nancy Pelosi and Democrat Senate Minority Leader Chuck Schumer stated with great clarity and truthfulness that, and we quote, "this cut in funding threatens the very existence of the United States and is yet another example of the Republican Party's attempt to make all the women of America into second class citizens and to deny them access to birth control and reproductive choice while destroying the American middleclass by supporting the top 1% who don't pay their fair share!" Never truer words were ever spoken! Could an ashamed Abraham Lincoln or a proud FDR have put it any better?

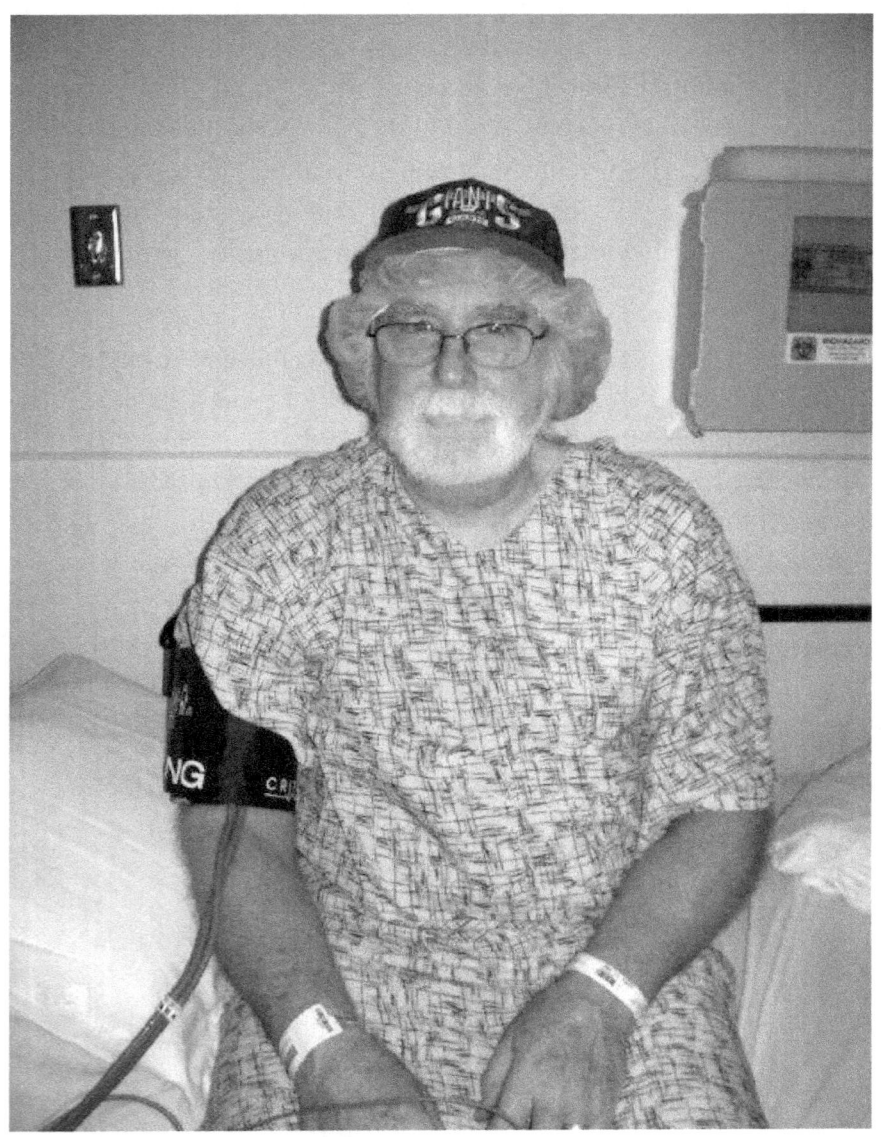

Who is Oxbow Lake, how in heaven's name did he get this way and what is his fate?

To paraphrase the profound words of a very famous and creative anonymous person, "He am who he be to be am, period!"... the "he" being me, Oxbow Lake the 2nd. This, however, may not be enough information for those of you who cannot read widely between these lines of Spartan words. Thus I, Oxbow Lake the 2nd his very self, have some more words to satisfy the more myopic amongst you... words about who I am, how I got this way and what my fate may be. Cogent words to this effect follow.

I believe that I have done a lot in my life. Unfortunately I cannot remember much of it, indicating that most of what I have done is not very memorable or possibly that my memory's gone bad on me, both being very likely. Obviously those of my deeds which may be memorable, I am unable to write about since I cannot remember them. I do remember having a mother and father, three brothers and a sister and playing in the fenced-in grounds around the walls of Sint Sink prison where my father had the unofficial title of Captain of the Death House and where he apparently enjoyed his work a great deal. He found the execution of Julius and Ethel Rosenberg an exhilarating experience. He celebrated his joy and exhilaration every evening by drinking copious amounts of Piels beer and smoking packs of Camels cigarettes. My mother was nice but never left the house for some reason. That pretty much sums up my childhood.

I did go to high school at a place that nick-named itself the Sint Sink Indians, but to eliminate the possibility of insulting a tribe of Indians that no longer existed and all of whose tribal members had been deceased for a very long time, some board of education removed the "Indians" part of the nick-name. I'm not sure what the former

335

Sint Sink Indians call themselves today (the Sint Sink Zeros?), but at least they're not offending those long dead Sint Sink Indians in those happy hunting grounds in the sky. Go Zeros!

I've been married several times and am presently married and have a bunch of kids and step-kids and three to four grand-kids... maybe it's five by now. During much of this time I worked at KTI in the Hudson Valley and never really fit in there but did manage to make a lot on money writing things that I believe may have destroyed my memory. I did go to college at Albany State or SUNY at Albany or the University at Albany (I can't remember which) and I believe that I did graduate with a major in English literature. I think that I taught in high school for a year at some place on the Hudson River named after Henry Hudson's boat before having my memory destroyed at KTI.

I got laid off by KTI and took a course in writing at Columbia University taught by the now deceased novelist Raymond Kennedy who wrote one of my favorite novels, *Ride a Cockhorse*. KTI apparently felt bad about forcing me into what became an early retirement and paid for the course.

The Adventures of the Posse of Little Horses was my first novel. It's pretty long (97,000 words, give or take a word or three). It was published by ShipWreckPublications and is now available online from both Barnes & Noble and Amazon in paperback ($13.95) and in Kindle and Nook ebook editions ($4.99). It is funny as hell and makes fun of lots of people who deserve it!

I originally called it a "hardboiled detective novel" of sorts for reasons I do not remember. Perhaps "softboiled detective novel" would be better. Anyhow, I now call it "humorous crime fiction" at the strong urging of ShipWreckPublications who have agreed to publish all my novels provided I allow all funds to be processed through off-shore bank accounts. It's actually more of a "humorous satiric novel," but I don't dare broach this with my publishers, who are quite adamant about just about everything. When I talk to the publishing mogul who founded and runs ShipWreckPublications, Mr. Robert A. Ward the 3rd, I feel like I'm in a *Godfather* rerun, but an author's got to do what an author's got to do.

The novel was inspired by at least two novels and a series of hardboiled detective stories. The two novels are humorous, wonderful and distinctly hardboiled in their fashion, but surely not hardboiled detective stories: Raymond Kennedy's aforementioned *Ride a Cockhorse* and John Kennedy Toole's *A Confederacy of Dunces*. The detective hardboiling of this mulligan stew, at least what there is of it, came from reading Steve Hamilton's hardboiled detective novels... all of which have really neat titles. I thought that I was writing hardboiled detective stories like Mr. Hamilton, but his inspiration appears to have been more ephemeral upon reflection. When he reads my claim that he inspired me, he'll probably ask me to remove his name, but it will be too late! Ha, ha!

I originally gave my first *opus erectus* the title *The Universal Posse*. I was never quite satisfied with this title and slowly but surely it became a kind of not-working working title. However, I could not think of a better one. Kennedy, Toole and even Hamilton had come up with such wonderful titles making mine seem rather pale and prosaic in comparison.

Then rather serendipitously, someone copied me on an email with the following tag line: "*When a true genius appears, you can know him by this sign: that all the dunces are in a confederacy against him.* -- Jonathan Swift." Ironically, the author of the email is a lifetime member of the confederacy posing as a true genius. One has to be suspicious of individuals who even hint that they are true geniuses, for they are more than likely undercover agents for the dreaded and ubiquitous confederacy.

Under penalty of hubris, I feel obligated at this point to interject that I do not consider myself a genius, true or otherwise, and do believe that I am not a member of the much dreaded confederacy. However, in all humility during the writing of this essay, I leave these matters for others to decide... at least for now.

Anyway, the quote from Swift made it quite clear where Toole got the title for his novel. This was news to me. I suspect that my rather forgetful mind had known this at one time but forgot to inform the rest me, for as that great *Irish-American Indian* troubadour Jimmie Dale Gilmore sings "my mind has a mind of its own" and my mind, in particular, often operates as an independent entity. On its own initiative, having been inspired by that Swiftian barb, my mind marched forth, bad memory and all, to seek out a better and more appropriate title for me.

This inspiration took my mind to perspiration (thank you, Mr. Thomas Alva Edison) and off went my soon-to-be perspiring mind in search of this better title. On the internet, my mind found a site of famous quotes. It went to the site's compendium of famous quotes by Jonathan Swift, who as it turns out, said a shitload of memorable things. Undaunted by volume, my mind plowed through them, apparently thinking that if Swift were good enough for Toole, surely he was good enough for the rest of me. But according to my mind, no combination of the words that could be strung together to form a better title for my novel ever passed through the Reverend Swift's lips, modestly or otherwise... at least as far as my mind could determine from that Irish malcontent's blasts of irreverence as documented on this website.

My mind thought that perhaps it should investigate the quotes of

Oscar Wilde, for like Swift, he too was Irish and said a whole bunch of pithy criticisms of mankind's follies. (What is it with the Irish, anyway? They've surrounded me: Kennedy, Toole, Swift, Wilde and Gilmore. Even Hamilton, I suspect, has a touch of Irish blood. They all are so clever, pithy and… malcontent, each in his own way. My mind always thought that the Irish deserved each other, even when they're alone, and here I was intellectually encircled by a mob of them.)

Anyway, my mind ditched the Oscar Wilde gambit for me on the grounds that the frilly Mr. Wilde was much too literary and far too clever by three-quarters for someone such as the rest of me. Then the name Mark Twain popped into my rather independent mind. At first my mind was a bit suspicious of someone who had to use an alias to become famous, but then concluded that this need for ano-nymity was evidence of the severity and social unacceptablity of his quotes and so off my mind went, stomping through the fertile ground of the quotes of Mark Twain, AKA Samuel Clemens. After reading many of his barbs, my mind concluded that Mr. Twain or Mr. Clemens, take your pick, must have been of Irish descent, and if his biography claimed otherwise, there was surely an undiscovered Irishman somewhere in his family's wood pile, as they say.

Then my mind came across these words of Mark Twain: "Against the assault of laughter nothing can stand." My mind, now drenched with contemplative sweat, jumped (metaphorically speaking) high into the air and yelled at the rest of me, "You silly bastard, make your title out of those words". Try as I might, I could not, and so in desperation I re-titled my first novel T*he Adventures of the Posse of Little Horses* after a kind of tequila shot glass.

Why and how did I adopt the pen name of Oxbow Lake... if it is in fact a pen name? Oh, you didn't know? Surely you didn't think I'd use my real name... which may appear to be a pen name if it is in fact a pen name. If you want to know why this is possible... using a possible pen name... read a couple of my novels. I could have used the name Ward A Bobb the 3rd, which I think is actually an alias, and may in fact be a "reverse" pen name, but this name was all too common and more prosaic than even the non-working working title for my first novel, even when adorned with an undisclosed middle name and a 3rd at the end. For example, I often get calls from someone in Oklahoma looking for a long lost relative who uses the alias Ward A. Bobb the 3rd, which I don't believe to be me. To overcome this anonymity through commonality while still preserving some anonymity at the same time, I decided to adopt what may be my pen name. The big question was and probably still is: which one?

I enlisted my mind again even after considering the job it had done finding a more intriguing title for me. After all, what choice did I have? My mind thought it might be useful to search around the term *mark twain* since it was Mark Twain's words that had inspired my first novel's inscription in a back-handed sort of way. After fumbling about the internet searching for Mississippi river boat terms and some safe water words I could use, my mind stumbled upon the rather mysterious and undefined term *oxbox*.

My mind knew not what the term meant and decided to google said term. Fortunately, it misspelled or mistyped the term, incorrectly entering the term oxbow, which, as serendipity would again have it, is the first word of a term used on rivers throughout the world, including and particularly the Mississippi. The full term is oxbow lake. It sounded familiar and intriguing in a distant echo kinda way.

An oxbow lake is a small lake located in a former meander loop of a river. It is generally formed as a river cuts through a meander neck to shorten its course, blocks off the old channel, and then migrates away leaving a lake behind, an oxbow lake. Eventually, oxbow lakes silt up to form marshes and finally meander scars. There's a bunch of them in various stages of oxbowness decorating the lower Mississippi.

Could there be a better pen name for the likes of such as me, particularly when writing in the shadow of the likes of a Mark Twain, et al and for a publisher named ShipWreckPublications? I think not! So here I am: what I believe to be the newly minted Oxbow Lake, a writer with an off-shore banking account to which I have no access, more or less left behind to eventually silt up literarily speaking to become a meander scar, but it is my beautiful scar.

Note: as a legal precaution, I am believed to have added the "2nd" to the end of my apparent pen name in case there is already a "1st" skulking about... which it turns out, there is!

At the rather insistent and enthusiastic inspiration of ShipWreck-Publications' VP of Critics Coercion and Revenge, I seem to have written a second novel, *Spanking Yesterday*, which has been available since 2013 although not many seemed to have noticed in spite of its brilliance. (At the time of its publication it was nominated for the prestigious but now defunct literary award the *Costa Concordia Award for Fictional Excellence*... which it finally won, after a bit of a literary kerfuffle, again apparently unnoticed.

Turns out the novel appears to be very autobiographical and follows the tragic career of one Ward A. Bobb... apparently the 3rd... at Kronos Technologies International or KTI where I believe I actually worked. The characters in the novel are friends of mine, many of them now former friends, and others I worked with when I labored at that emotionally unbalanced corporation before being rather unceremoniously "laid off" after returning from what my vicious critics at KTI have exaggeratedly termed an insane asylum... his... my...

341

stay in that institution caused by my being forced to work in an insane corporate environment where the abnormal was considered normal in the abnormal sense of that word.

On the back cover of *Spanking Yesterday*, or maybe it was his or my other novel Mr. Kramer Killread implies that I wrote this particular novel with the help of the real Ward Bobb. Mr. Killread is full of brown, foul smelling balderdash! Mr. Killread, a very appropriate name for this man, is probably basing this assumption on two things.

First, there's the rather suspicious statement on the back cover: "Oxbow Lake the 2nd is a pen name used by Ward Bobb the 2nd, which is an alias. Oxbow claims that neither of them have been institutionalized although one of them may have worked at IBM for a considerable length of time."

Need I quote more. The proof is in the corporate pudding for I worked at KTI and not the fictional IBM! Someone is playing with the facts and creating an alternate reality here.

Second, there's those two letters that appear rather mysteriously in the introduction to *Spanking Yesterday*... the first a ridiculous letter from the publisher, Robert A. Ward the 3rd, questioning the authorship of *Spanking Yesterday*... the second scurrilous letter from a supposed Ward Bobb the 3rd claiming that they, this mysterious fantasy author named Ward Bobb the 3rd, wrote the novel. Actually the name Ward Bobb the 3rd is a reverse pen name that I use to protect my anonymity. I have no idea who actually wrote the letter claiming authorship or partial authorship of my novel.

Using this scurrilous second letter by this mysterious Ward Bobb the 2nd... in a move instigated by Robert A. Ward the 3rd, the Godfather-like and self proclaimed Publishing Mogul, ShipWreckPublications LLC has added to the cover of *Spanking Yesterday* after my name as author the following: "(with Ward Bobb the 3rd?)".

Although the phantom Ward Bobb the 3rd claims in his scurrilous letter that "I am not concerned about being compensated", he adds rather ominously "... at least for now". And then the even more ominous "While I am not a litigious man, I assure you that I can become so."

I believe that this entire additional-author imbroglio is an attempt by that publishing Mafioso, Robert A. Ward the 3rd, to steal royalties that belong to me. I thought he'd eventually halve them between me and this phantom author, Ward Bobb the 3nd. However, not satisfied with stealing half of my royalties, ShipWreckPublications LLC appended to my name as author on the cover to this, my third tome, *Sint Sink Tales & Other Disturbing Frictions*, the following: "(*et allii?*)"! That's Latin for "and others" I suspect.

At first I thought that the question mark indicated the possibility that there were no additional authors, but now I realized that it's true meaning is that there is the possibility that there is more than one, probably many more authors to be recognized and paid... a possibility I am sure that ShipWreckPublications high-powered legal staff will realize... cutting my royalties even more.

Dear reader, as you laugh and ponder your way through this, my brilliant third tome *Sint Sink Tales & Other Disturbing Frictions*, contemplate the financial fate of your poor unremunerated author. I am already in the hole for the several thousands of dollars I had to pay to bribe the printer to surreptitiously add this plea to the end of this latest tome of mine. (Fortunately Robert A. Ward the 3rd, in true Mafioso tradition, is a man of action and not contemplation, particularly the contemplation inspired by reading, and so this plea will go undetected for some time.)

Oxbow Lake The 2nd

My fate is in your hands, my faithful readers! I beg... I plea... for the sake of America's eternal literature, that one of you out there start a *gofundme* account to keep this poor unrecognized but brilliant writer from starving at the black hands of that literary Mafioso Godfather Robert A Ward the 3rd... and that all of you donate to this *gofundme* rescue!

Oxbow Lake the 2nd
April 1, 2019
New Tampa, Florida

TO LET OXBOW KNOW HOW MUCH YOU ENJOYED

HIS WONDERFUL LITEREARY FRICTION,

EMAIL HIM AT be498ar@earthlink.net

A Posse of Little Horses Teaser for
Oxbow Lake's 1st Novel

Take a gander at the front and back covers of *The Adventures of the Posse of Little Horses* to whet your appetite, if those unsolicited praises didn't do the job, and if you're still not convinced, there's a wonderful excerpt awaiting you at <u>www.shipwreckpublications.</u> <u>com</u> for your perusal.

HUMOROUS CRIME FICTION   U.S. $13.95

Why read this stupid novel? Because its funny and dirty . . . in the literary sense of both words. If you are titillated by someone else's ox getting gored, this is the book for you! It'll make your funny bone twitch at someone else's expense . . . provided you have a funny bone to twitch.
-- Kramer Killread, The New Tampa Guide to Sane Automobile Repair

Blackmail . . . Sex . . . Drugs . . . Tequila . . . and throw in a bunch of murders . . . Does it get any better?

Why would a Mexican drug cartel blackmail Jamie Steinkraus's father-in-law? Could it be to get possession of the mountain chalet Jamie gave to his young bride? Can detective Big Louie Fazzano solve the mystery?

Will Jamie and his Posse of Little Horses elude the cartel's hit men as they flee west on Route 66? Will their supply of Brand XXX tequila last long enough to get them to California?

Oxbow Lake the 2nd is a pen name used by **Ward Bobb the 3rd**, which is an alias. Oxbow claims that neither of them have been intentionally institutionalized although one of them may have worked at IBM for a considerable length of time.
The Adventures of the Posse of Little Horses, winner of the Costa Concordia, is Oxbow's first novel and his best to date.

What can modern psychiatry do to cure Jamie's young wife of her obsession to give herself to black men whom she believes are Zulu warriors?

Cover illustration by Karen Mathis
Author photograph by Lisa Lazzaro

Visit www.ShipWreckPublications.com

ISBN 978-0-9839766-0-8
51395

9 780983 976608

Unsolicited Praise for Oxbow Lake's *The Adventures of the Posse of Little Horses*

"I re-ckon Oxbow Lake is a pen name. Is that damned idiot Ward A Bobb the 3rd ashamed of his work?"
- Sam Clemens (channeled through Bob Dylan)

"If I were alive, I'd have written it myself, only differently and better!"
- Mark Twain (You Dead Tube)

"The Adventures of the Posse of Little Horses does not make me regret committing suicide."
- John Kennedy Toole (Giggle Beyond Internet Site)

"The bastard plagiarized my Ride a Cockhorse after I died so I know that at least part of it is good."
- Raymond Kennedy (scratched on a bar near Columbia)

"Worst punctuated novel I've ever read. The man's obsessed with ellipses... he's out of his freakin'... elliptical mind!"
- Lisa Lazzero (freelance professional punctuator)

"It has some damn short sentences which is damn good. Too bad they don't make any damn cents."
- Ernest Hemingway (channeled through Groucho Marx)

"He's my intellectual mini-me. Mr. Oxbow Lake the 2nd knows how to really torture a thought."
- Marquis De Sade (channeled through VP Joe Biden)

"To get this novel published, Oxbow will need at least two sets of knee pads."
- Senator John "Bluto" Blutarsky (Animal House séance)

"I find Oxbow Lake's novel to be vulgar and despicable, and I have only read the first page."
- Charles Dickens (channeled through Hugh Hefner

A *Spanking Yesterday* Teaser for Oxbow Lake's 2nd Novel

Take yet another gander... this time at the front and back covers of *Spanking Yesterday* to whet your appetite. If those unsolicited praises didn't do the job, and if you're still not convinced, there's a wonderful excerpt awaiting you at www.shipwreckpublications. com for your perusal.

HUMOROUS CRIME FICTION   U.S.A $13.95

Well ol' Oxbow Lake has banged out another must read novel! He's done for insanity, corporate culture, and American life what Linda Lovelace did for the... However, it won't take a deep reading of this great novel to appreciate Oxbow's hilarious satiric view of humanity.
-- Kramer Killread, The New Tampa Guide to Sane Automobile Repair

An insanely funny semi-tragic masterpiece of science friction (yes, friction) by the unrecognized comic genius Oxbow Lake... perhaps with the help of the real Ward Bobb... if he exists.

Spanking Yesterday is a novel written as a journal by the fictional and schizophrenic Ward Bobb who is institutionalized. Ward's obsessed with H. G. Wells' *The Time Machine*, which he views not as science fiction, but as revelation and prophecy. As part of his treatment, he must write a journal of his life, particularly his life at Kronos Technologies International (KTI) where he managed a technical writing department and where, in spite of... or perhaps because of... his mental illness, he fit right in. Amongst his odd yet corporately semi-acceptable actions, he sells stock to fellow employees... his Tribe of Pubs Creeps... in a departmental library of pornographic books and pictures and then uses pictures from the library to control the behavior of the programmers with whom he works.

Ward becomes convinced that the KTI corporation is controlled by Wells' cannibal Morlocks who are establishing a beachhead and threaten human kind. When he reviews his journal entries and comments on them, as his psychiatrist has recommended, he finds that someone else is writing disparaging remarks in his journal. It all becomes too real and he is convinced that he must spank yesterday and take action!

Cover illustration by Karen Mathis
Photograph by Lisa Lazzaro

If you don't laugh at our books,
you're probably dead . . .
or should be!

Visit www.ShipWreckPublications.com

ISBN 978-0-9839766-1-5
51395
9 780983 976615

Unsolicited Praise for Oxbow Lake's
Spanking Yesterday

"Regardless of Mr. Lake's many requests, I refuse to make this novel required reading for my computer science courses at this university. However, I may buy a remaindered copy for myself when they're available provided the discount is substantial, of course."
-- Dr. Roger Grice, Professor, Something to do with Computer Science

"My place in literary immortality remains unthreatened by this source. It's too late."
-- Mark Twain (You Dead Tube)

"Is Spanking Yesterday a novel? Who wrote the damn thing? I find it all quite confusing, but then again, I'm dead. Hopefully those who are alive will be less confused, but I have my eternal doubts."
-- John Kennedy Toole (Giggle Beyond Internet Site)

"It appears that not only can't you keep a good man down, you can't keep a plagiarizing bastard down either."
-- Raymond Kennedy (scratched on a bar near Columbia)

"Well I can now say that Mr. Oxbow Lake's first novel is the second worst punctuated novel I've ever reviewed. The author or authors of this tome are even more obsessed with ellipses and remain out of their freakin'… elliptical minds!"
-- Lisa Lazzero (alias Lisa Lazzaro) Senior Freelance Punctuator

"It can be safely said that Dave Barry is now the second funniest writer alive (and quite possibly the third), and that Carl (stuttering a's) Hiaasen has dropped out of the top 10,000 behind an ethnic German graffiti scribbler named Sanas the Fakir from Jaipur, India, who spray paints jokes on bathroom walls about snake charmers who get bitten between their legs by their cobras!"

-- Kramer Killread, Editor (The New Tampa Guide to Sane Automobile Repair)

"The dirty parts are real good!"

-- Super Amazing Steve Nash (Poet of Ill Repute)

"Oxbow needed at least two sets of knee pads to get his first novel published. I hope for his sake that he kept or replaced them."

-- Senator John "Bluto" Blutarsky (Animal House séance)

"I find Oxbow Lake's second novel to be as vulgar and despicable as the first, and I haven't even bothered to read the first page this time."

-- Charles Dickens (channeled through Hugh Hefner)

How to Order Oxbow Lake's Other Books

• To purchase the paperback ($19.95), order online at www.amazon.com or www.barnesandnoble.com

• To purchase the Kindle and Nook eBooks ($4.99), order online at the Amazon or Barnes & Noble sites respectively and, we hope, respectfully

For quick links to make online purchases, go to *www.shipwreck-publications.com* and while there, check out our site... before we get shut down by the politically correct fascists who still ban and burn books and shut down sites they don't like.

Our site contains lots of interesting stuff about the actions of our rogue publishing house and while there, read some free short stories by Oxbow Lake his very own self and excerpts as well from all of his published books.